D0464727

DARK PARTS OF THE UNIVERSE

Also by Samuel Miller

A Lite Too Bright

Redemption Prep

DARK PARTS OF THE UNIVERSE

SAMUEL MILLER

KATHERINE TEGEN BOOKS
An Imprint of HarperCollins Publishers

Documents in Part 7 are either directly sourced or heavily
inspired by firsthand accounts of actual events.

"The Abandoning of 'Old Town'" (pp 383–384) is used with permission of the
St. Louis Post-Dispatch, altered only for detail and to remove disturbing language.

"Devils of the Hills" (pp 393–394) uses direct quotes from residents of Pierce
City, Missouri, obtained through the State Historical Society of Missouri.

Katherine Tegen Books is an imprint of HarperCollins Publishers.

Dark Parts of the Universe
Copyright © 2024 by Samuel Miller
All rights reserved. Printed in the United States of America.
No part of this book may be used or reproduced in any manner whatsoever without
written permission except in the case of brief quotations embodied in critical
articles and reviews. For information address HarperCollins Children's Books,
a division of HarperCollins Publishers, 195 Broadway, New York, NY 10007.

Library of Congress Control Number: 2023942523
ISBN 978-0-06-316048-4

Typography by David Curtis
24 25 26 27 28 LBC 5 4 3 2 1
First Edition

to south dakota & its teachers

DARK PARTS OF THE UNIVERSE

PROLOGUE

WHERE I COME from, people believe in God.

Not the new, hippie God they talk about in the cities, some metaphor for forgiveness or something like that—the real God. The angry one. The God that sends plagues and kills children.

The God that enforces His order on the universe.

Even people who didn't believe could feel it, an energy that settled all debts and punished all debtors. It was a simple fact of life. In Calico Springs, you got what was coming to you, whether you liked it or not.

For a lot of people, this could be a depressing notion. It meant the tragedy of their lives was something they earned. All the failures, foreclosures, and funerals—they were part of a cosmic plan, decided by an all-knowing God.

You could forgive people for giving up.

But I never spent one second worrying about that.

Me and God, we had an arrangement. I was being saved for a special purpose. I knew that, because when I was five years old, I died.

You wanna know what it's like to die?

Easy, is what it is. Everything about it, simple as letting go. All your worldly weary, disappearing into darkness. All I woulda had to do is let go of the rope, and I'd have been another stone in the cemetery, a story my parents told with decreasing frequency.

It was five full minutes, my heart stopped beating. That's what Dad said. The exact amount of time it took to drive from the house to the hospital.

But I didn't let go. I fought and kicked and screamed like hell. I yanked that rope until I felt what was on the other side, then pulled some more.

It was two days after that, I was passed out. Both alive and dead. Lying in a bed at St. Agnes.

In that time, everybody in town came by. All hours of the day and night, they crowded into the hospital room and prayed over me. Teachers and the folks from church, not just our church but every church, the mayor and the developers, the cops on duty and every firefighter at the station—all joining hands, praying for my survival.

And then, quick as a miracle, I woke up.

It was just Mom in the room with me. She'd fallen asleep with her head on my chest. The first thing I saw when I came back to life was her tiny cross, poking up through the blankets.

He gave you back to us. That's what she told me. *God kept you here for a reason.*

Ever since that day, it became a fact they constantly reminded me of, my heroic origin story. I was special. I was chosen. I was here for a reason.

William Eckles, Miracle Boy.

That was ten years ago.

Ten years, I'd been waiting for that reason.

I never doubted. I prayed every night. I knew the day was gonna come when my purpose here would be realized.

And then, one day, I heard about the Game.

PART ONE

THE GAME

CHAPTER 1

GROWING UP, I thought Calico Springs was the only place on Earth.

As far as I was concerned, human beings crawled out of the muck at the Ripley County Bridge and only built civilization as far as the overpass to Highway 19. I knew other places existed, but why bother with shit that doesn't affect you? Our world was only two miles wide; we could touch every corner in an afternoon.

Me and Bones used to ride end-to-end, knocking on random doors, trying to memorize who lived in every house. Dad called us town historians. 15 Poplar, where Miss Wilson said a prayer that made her kids disappear. 22 Willow, the creepy old house they tried to turn into a FunZone until they realized it was haunted. And, of course, Old Town, the remains of what used to be the city center, still sitting by the river in all its burnt-out, decrepit glory.

I slow-coasted past it on my bike, letting the downhill slope carry me to the river.

It was almost night, and all around me cicadas screamed and razor-thin blades of grass reached out of the ditch, perfectly still in the simmering heat. Southern Missouri summers are perpetually sticky. You just get used to it. You use bug repellent, then you become it. And there were a lot of bugs, a shit ton of them, swarming like an army of the dead, marching up from the water.

My life to this point had been defined by two enormous forces—God and the Current River.

May was its highest month, after northern snow melted and gathered steam as it rushed hundreds of miles downstream. In late fall, when the water was low, you could camp all the way down in the Basin. But days like today, when you got this close, you had to watch your step to make sure you weren't already underwater.

Half of Calico Springs still lived within a mile of the water, and we'd have drowned every year, if not for the sheer strength of our resolve to live there. We built barricades, massive operations that had to constantly be repaired and reformed. We bought trucks with elevated lift gates that could handle high water and built houses on stilts for when the Basin flooded out. It was a war that had raged for centuries, the river vs. the town. Unstoppable force, immoveable object. Dad always said it was because for people here, the only thing worse than living in Calico Springs was living anywhere else.

I dropped my bike and wiped the cracked screen of my phone. It showed a map, mostly cold and colorless, except for a bright blue dot in the center, blinking like a beacon. I compared it to where I was standing—the dot was fifty feet ahead, clinging to the side of the only road that crossed the map's central feature. It was on the bridge.

There were only four steel bridges left in Missouri, and if you asked anybody in Calico, they'd tell you this one still wasn't finished. Massive as it was, long as it had lasted, it had the feeling of being unstable, like at any minute, a screw could come loose and send the whole thing the way of the *Titanic*. The steel beams were all different colors, the result of a hundred years of disjointed construction. We all knew the "No Pedestrians" sign was there for liability reasons—there was plenty of room on the shoulder to walk, so long as you kept your head up.

I followed the blue dot out to the center of the bridge and stopped when the marker for my location lined up with it. I was in the exact middle. I could tell because directly below me was the central truss. I spent a few minutes waiting, but best I could tell, there wasn't anything to discover, other than the sun, fading as it set over the river.

I was about to give up when I noticed the small concrete island below me, a construction platform where the truss met the water. I checked my phone. Technically, the platform was on the blue dot too, but there was no way to get to it unless you had a . . .

I froze as I looked back to the shore.

Below the bridge on the Calico side, tied off as if it was left on purpose, there was a small rowboat waiting for me.

* * *

I first heard about the Game at work.

I only got the job in the first place 'cause Bones started base-ball back in February, which meant I suddenly had a shitload of free time, and I'd outgrown all my old hobbies. I didn't wanna get a job in town, not that anybody would hire a fifteen-year-old anyway, but there was a bait and tackle shack on the other side of the river called Short Bill's that paid cash, so I started working two days a week when Short Bill went to his firefighter classes.

It was a Tuesday afternoon, and Rory Braun and Tyler Arrington were stocking up for a night ride. Rory and Tyler were the worst kind of townie—three years post-graduation, working for their dads, acting like the town was theirs to inherit. Along with a couple other recent Calico graduates, they called themselves Dirtbags and wore it as an aesthetic, all baggie jeans and white tanks, which was especially ironic considering Tyler's dad was one of the only rich people in Calico Springs.

When I came back in from the dock, Tyler had his phone in my coworker Abe's face.

"Swear to God. It can get you *anything* you want. All you gotta do is type it."

Abe was Bill's son, only a couple years older than me, but he went to school across the river in Lawton. He talked to everybody like they were friends, which I had only recently learned was an act. Abe was Black, like most everybody in Lawton, and he told me some of the white folks from Calico Springs, Rory and Tyler included, were always saying crazy shit to him, talking to him like he was stupid. He tolerated it because it was his dad's shop and he had to, but he told me on multiple occasions he had a personal policy of never crossing the river. One time, when I invited him to a fire department barbecue, he told me, "Don't take this the wrong way, Willie—but I'd rather set myself on fire."

"It does what now?" Abe asked them.

"Couple nights ago," Tyler said, "we told this thing we wanted to get laid, and it took us to a party in Summit where we didn't know a single soul . . . and both of us pulled."

"Wow," Abe said. "You guys definitely wouldn't have any reason to lie about that—"

"Swear to God. You don't gotta believe us, it fucking happened."

"And that's not all, either," Rory added.

I drifted inside a couple steps, making myself invisible behind the register.

"Last night, we were out at my grandma's cabin. We told it we wanted a dog . . ."

Tyler kicked at something below him in the aisle. I craned my neck and there, nipping at his feet, was a beautiful, dirt-brown mutt. A pit mix, I figured, by the size of her paws. She couldn't have been more than a month old.

"McShay said they were born three days ago. And this Game brought us straight there."

My heart started to pump as I stared at the little thing, still

11

getting her sea legs against his sneaker. She did look like a miracle, a second too slow for the world. I'd heard stories like it before, of prayers asked and answered, but I'd never heard of somebody finding it in an app—

"Hey, Blackbeard."

When I looked up, Tyler had turned his attention to me. "Don't go getting any ideas, all right? I don't think this could find you a new eye." He brought his bait up to the counter, raising a finger to flick my eye patch. "Where'd you buy these things, anyway? They got an eye patch bin at Walmart?"

I shrugged. I'd been one-eyed since I lost my right at age five. We couldn't afford a prosthetic then, so most days I wore an eye patch, and there were only a couple jokes people could make about it. At this point I'd heard them all so many times even the comebacks were stale. "Your mom knitted it for me," I told him. "Her technique's getting sloppy."

Tyler didn't even flinch, just shook his head and laughed. "You're a wild dude, miracle boy."

This was how things went for me in Calico Springs. Everybody knew my story. They'd all been there when it happened; they could see it every time they looked at my face. As a result, they treated me different. Fragile, I guess. I'd insulted Mrs. Arrington straight to Tyler's face, and he didn't even take me seriously enough to get pissed about it.

As he set his phone down on the counter, I snuck a look and saw the logo for the first time—

MANIFEST ATLAS

"Losers," Abe mumbled once they were out of the store.

"Imagine how much free time you gotta have to make some shit up like that, with the dog and everything . . ."

I ignored him. I was already downloading it from the App Store. When Manifest Atlas opened, the screen dissolved into a perfect black sky, stars hurtling forward, flowing and blurring, dissolving into a river of text that read—

PREPARE TO CHANGE YOUR DESTINY

"God damn, Willie," Abe said, glancing over my shoulder. "You paid eight bucks for that?"

I tapped through the prompts, agreeing to the Terms and Conditions and Rules of Use, landing on a blank screen with a small blue box in the center. The graphics were old-school, robotic, and pixelated, with just three words at the top. A question:

WHAT'S YOUR INTENTION?

A lot of people say they believe in God, but not a lot of them actually live it. Most only believe when it works the way they're used to, like good things happening or sports teams losing. But if you really believe, you realize God's will is everywhere, hidden in everything.

God talks to us in funny ways, Mom said. But He's always talking.

And if He'd delivered a miracle to Calico Springs, I sure as hell had to make sure Rory Braun and Tyler Arrington weren't the ones to receive it.

I didn't have to think, I knew my first intention. Ask for a miracle. I typed—

A SIGN

* * *

I climbed down to the water carefully, double-checking every time I set my foot down to make sure the mud wouldn't collapse below me. The boat was an old dinghy, with a chipped-up oar laid across the middle like it was just asking to be borrowed. There was an inch of stale water inside.

"I'll bring it back," I said out loud to nobody, shaking the knot off the channel marker it was tied to, and kicked out into the water.

Immediately, the current whipped me downstream. I paddled hard, angling toward the platform. Our side of the river was part-swamp, so over the years, I got good at being on the water. In fact, the only people I knew who could pilot a boat better than me were Dad and then Bones, in that order.

When I got to the central truss, I steered into a break in the concrete and let the current hold the boat in place. I steadied my balance against the truss, kept hold of the rope as I pulled myself onto the platform.

It was a hell of a lot bigger up close. The steel was deep maroon, chipping silver at the joints, with a few long plates holding it together. I had to shuffle to see the whole thing, checking up and down for signs of life. The Calico side was untouched. I couldn't imagine anyone had been out here in ages.

I kept my steps small, my body clinging to the steel, even as the rope yanked and pulled in my hand. I got around to the other side of the platform and froze.

It was the first thing I saw, taking up the entirety of the plate. I chanced grabbing the steel with my rope hand so I could confirm on my phone, to be sure I was seeing it right.

This was it. The blinking blue dot. The target I was given. A sign.

I stared at it, my heart in my throat.

It was simple graffiti, written at eye level. The message was clear and obvious, an answer for those who seek it.

In bright red spray paint, someone had written—

MORE WILL FOLLOW

CHAPTER 2

EVERY TIME BONES made a bet, he made it with his chest.

He could do that, I think, because he genuinely believed every strain of bullshit that came out of his mouth. There's no risk betting when you know you're right, which meant he'd always bet the house and never accept defeat.

I was young when I learned I could use that to my advantage.

"Bullshit," he called when I told him about Manifest Atlas. "Tyler and Rory are fucking with you, and you bought it."

"Except I saw the dog," I told him. "How do you explain that?"

"A coincidence. And not even a crazy one. McShays have, like, a thousand dogs. I bet a new one's having babies every day."

"What about my message?"

"Imagine finding a spot in Calico that wasn't covered in spray paint—"

"Then bet me," I said. "If you're so sure it doesn't work, then back it up. Bet me."

Like a game show host, I gestured to the garage in front of us, afternoon light and sawdust giving our dad's old shit a golden glow.

Ever since Mom kicked Dad out of the house, they'd been at war over the boxes in the garage. Mom said he had to get them out, so she could park her car during storms. Dad said he didn't wanna move it all out just to move it back in again when she changed her mind. Mom told him she was gonna sell it, and Dad called her bluff, so she hung a few signs around the neighborhood and deputized me and Bones, even said we could keep the money, so long as we got rid of it.

Bones's eyes stopped in the middle of the room, landing on Dad's old recliner.

"I want the chair."

"Fine," I agreed. "But if I win . . . I get your room."

I watched his face drop. "You've thought about this," he said. I shrugged and he studied me, hard, looking for breaks before finally, like a good little fish, he took the bait.

"Deal," he said. "If this thing works . . . you can have my room when I leave."

He'd just come from baseball practice, and infield dirt still spotted his face and hair. Pound-for-pound, Bones and I had the same genes, but he had them better. He got all the parts of Dad that people brought up in public—the watery blue eyes, the sticky blond hair that clumped and fell and swooped in the right places, skin that would tan in the summer—and I got stuck with our mother's round nose and murky brown eyes, skin so pale I was almost see-through, even in July. It was as clear a sign from God as you could ask for that he was born to be a front man, and I was born to sing backup.

That's how it had been our entire lives, but I didn't mind the arrangement. A lot of people found it poetic to say their brother was their best friend—but me and Bones actually were. We spent all our time together. Growing up, it was every summer day on our bikes, walking to and from school. When I got to high school, the other upperclassmen left their siblings to the fishes, but Bones did the opposite. He invited me everywhere, dropped me off and picked me up at work, brought me along on every trip. He let me hang out with his friends, so much that they'd become my friends. I hadn't hung out with anybody my own age in years. I went to prom as an eighth grader. In my grade, I was a fucking legend.

But that'd all be over at the end of the summer. Bones was headed to Westminster in Fort Woodman, two hours away, on a baseball scholarship. We always knew God gave Bones an unholy anger, but sometime around sixth grade, he figured out how to channel it into a fastball and became the best pitcher anybody in Calico Springs could ever remember. This spring, a coach from Westy's baseball team came to watch him pitch, and they offered him a full ride by the third inning.

We didn't talk about it, though. Bones didn't like bringing it up or looking past the summer at all—almost like sometimes he forgot it was happening. That was just fine with me; I hated talking about it, too. It wasn't just Bones—our entire friend group was leaving me behind. It'd be just me and Mom in the house. I didn't have my license yet, so she'd have to drive me everywhere. I'd have to make all new friends. I'd be on my own for the first time ever. I was content to live in the summer like it was never gonna end.

Me and Bones set up two long tables across the bottom of the driveway and arranged the items in order of value, best as we could figure it out. It started with old magazines and post-ers, CDs of bands we'd never heard of, shoes and old jackets, and finally, an ancient stereo system.

As we worked, I found myself watching Bones, not animated like usual, strangely focused on the task at hand. He kept check-ing his phone, even though I knew he wasn't texting anyone, and glancing at the street around us.

"You good?" I asked at one point. He shook off the question.

When we finally finished, we set up two folding chairs and opened a box of cash with twenty dollars in fives that Mom had given us to make change. As we sat waiting, he finally turned to me with a serious look on his face.

"I got some news," he said.

I had to squint into the sun to look back at him. "Yeah?"

"I've been thinking hard about it . . ." he started slowly. "For the last couple months, really, but especially these last few weeks. I decided . . . I'm gonna stay in Calico next year."

A smile rippled outward across his face, so wide I thought he was fucking with me, but he wasn't laughing.

"You're serious?" I asked.

"Dead serious. It doesn't make sense, starting over, going to some random school nobody's ever heard of. If I stay here, I can build my empire."

He threw his hand out, so I took it and dapped him, which became a hug. I felt my heart start to race, my chest flooding with relief. I wouldn't have to start over, either. I wasn't out on my own.

"Are you gonna stay at the house?" I asked.

"Not for long. Soon as I've got the cash, I'll get my own place, probably something by the developments. And you can come stay, party, anytime you want."

It didn't take hardly any imagination to picture it. . . . We'd daydreamed it before. We used to bike past the golf course houses, when the golf course was still open, picking out which ones would be ours. "What about Westminster?" I asked.

Bones's face twisted up. "What about it?"

"Uh, I mean, you're not going, then?"

"Fuck Westminster!" Bones spat. "What's the point? Play for a team nobody cares about? Nobody goes to their games, Willie. They're smaller than here. I'm not wasting the time and money—"

"But you got a scholarship—"

"You still gotta pay for shit, Willie! Food, books, housing . . . If I stay here, I can make money. Trust me. I got a plan. I'm gonna take this town over."

I dapped him again, my head spinning. Excited as I was, it still felt a little rotten. It had only been a couple weeks ago they'd announced his scholarship at the Seniors Night game, and we'd gone out to dinner afterward to celebrate. That night, the scholarship was the thing we were all excited about.

But Bones didn't have a shred of doubt, as he looked out across our street, our town, our world. "This is where I belong, Willie," he said. "I'll get my own place, my own truck . . ." He turned back to smile at me. "And you and me will keep tearing up these streets."

When she got home from her shift at Dairy Queen, our neighbor Rodney came to help us with the sale. She was still wearing her bright red polo, which had become a sort of uniform for the hot girls at our high school. Donald, the creepy manager, was known for only hiring blond-haired high school girls, which Rodney hated, but as she often reminded us, a job's a job.

"How come your dad has so many *Playboy*s?" she asked, thumbing through a stack. "Doesn't he know about the internet?"

"Someone told him they're gonna be valuable," I explained. "Like Beanie Babies."

It took her less than a minute to look it up. "You can get this one on eBay for forty cents."

Rodney was a genius, one of those rare kids in Calico who actually had a plan, and for reasons Bones sometimes wondered aloud about, she had been our best friend for ten years.

Rodney's family moved in when she was in second grade, same grade as Bones, the year I started school. Both of her parents were pastors, the serious kind, so at her house, she had all kinds of rules. She figured out pretty quick it wasn't like that at our house. She started spending every summer day with us, watching movies with our dad that would make her parents cry. That became every day of middle school, and every day of high school when Bones started driving. When Rodney got a job, me and Bones started hanging out at Dairy Queen. When Bones made varsity, me and Rodney went to watch his practices. For ten years, we'd traveled as a pack.

She was going to Mizzou in the fall, one of the two Calico kids who got in every year, but on an honors program. She was even going up early for a computer camp. It was a big deal, even if she didn't act like it. So I was surprised she didn't have much of a reaction when Bones told her about his change of heart.

"Oh," she said. "Build an empire of what?"

Bones looked taken aback that he had to explain. "There's money everywhere," he said casually. "Trust me, I got a plan."

"Sure." Rodney zeroed in. "What's the plan?"

Bones flicked his eyes between us, like he was trying to decide if he could trust us, before finally whispering a single word. "Land."

He dropped it like it was a bomb, like the idea alone merited an explosion, but neither of us said a word, so he explained. "Real estate. Cheap as shit right now, but the more they build, the more it goes up. It's the perfect time. I'll get a job at the developments for the up-front cash, start with one property, then flip that into a couple more, develop those—next thing you know, I own half of Calico Springs."

Rodney took it in. I waited for her to poke a hole, tell him he had it all wrong about the marginal value of real estate something or other, but she didn't. She just smiled weakly.

"That's awesome. Congrats."

Joe Kelly was less impressed when he came by. "Construction?" he asked. "That's your master plan?"

"It's real fucking money," Bones said. "People are getting rich out there."

"My dad told me I could get a job at the developments in half a second. He said I could walk into management, no questions asked."

"You should do it, then," Bones said. "Better than blowing all your parents' money being the worst player on the Lake Area Tech baseball team."

"Except I'll have the one thing you don't," Joe said. "To not have to spend all day surrounded by sweaty dudes."

He didn't show it to anyone else, but I saw my brother's shoulders deflate. He cared what Joe Kelly thought.

Joe Kelly was a rare kind of creature in Calico Springs, a shark in a swimming pool, too big for its environment but too smart to kill everything around it on instinct. So instead, he just swam around with his teeth clenched, enjoying life at the top of the food chain.

The Kellys were a family of sharks. His dad was the mayor, his grandpa before that. He was also a pitcher on the baseball team, which meant he and Bones had spent their lives at each other's throats. Even though Bones was the better pitcher—there wasn't a day it wasn't true—Joe Kelly was the golden boy in Calico Springs, so he was the captain. It was only in the last couple months he'd started coming over, since Dad moved out and Mom stopped giving a shit about what we did in the garage, which made it an easy place for Joe Kelly to drink.

"Seriously," Joe Kelly added. "I could talk to my dad for you, if you need the job."

"I'm good," Bones said. "I'll get it myself. Now can we please, for the love of Jesus, stop talking about next year? For like . . . three months? I'm telling you—there's no way what you're gonna do is better than what we're already doing. In case you forgot—we're three days away from the summer of our lives. The river, the fair, the bonfire . . ."

He winked at me. There was a town ordinance against fires taller than two feet, but one night every summer, for the last six summers, Dad agreed to stand guard and tell the cops to fuck off so we could throw a party. This year, Bones was planning on burning the city to the ground.

"You can go to school for the rest of your lives. For the rest of the summer, please—no more college talk."

The sale got started, and folks from all over town started showing up to poke their heads in, check out the record collection, see if there was anything worthwhile.

Half the people seemed to only be there to talk to Bones about the playoff game. Calico was hosting the regional championship against Summit the next night, with a trip to state on the line. Calico never made state in anything, but this year, people were talking like we had a shot at winning the whole thing, thanks to Bones's right arm. I overheard multiple people, grown men, asking him how his arm felt, telling him how excited they were for the game, about their plans to travel to the state tournament in Springfield.

Bones was a legend in Calico Springs. Based on that alone, I realized, his plan was a smart one. He was a made man. If he wanted to build an empire, he could do it. If he wanted to buy half the town, they'd sell it, then buy it back after. He could probably be the mayor if he wanted. Bones was strategic like that, always one step ahead of the rest of the world.

As things were starting to wind down, I saw a man I recognized but couldn't place poking through Dad's old shoes. It was rare. Most of the time I knew people's names straightaway. He was tall, with a thin frame and a sharp, angular face. He wore a cowboy hat and a baby blue sweater. Even he had to know how intense of a combination it was. He looked distracted as he cycled through the shoes.

"Can I help you with anything?" I asked.

His eyes lit up when he saw me. "Willie Eckles," he said, his voice excited. "I know you. I prayed for you. Me and my wife— ex-wife—we were in the hospital room."

I nodded. "You did a good job."

He reached across the table to shake my hand. "Winston Lewis," he said. The name clicked into place, something political. There'd been an election a few months back and Winston had his name on yard signs all over town. "I'm looking for your mom. Is she around?"

I glanced back to the house. Mom didn't have visitors very often, especially not since Dad moved out. Especially not men in baby blue sweaters.

He seemed to understand, because he quickly clarified, "She signed up for a committee at church. I'm just dropping by to follow up. Might as well buy some shoes while I'm here."

He stepped a little closer, and I got a better look at him. Ever since I was a kid, I'd had an accidental habit of watching people a second too long, noticing things they didn't want noticed. Winston's eyes had thick black bags underneath, dark like they'd been there for a while. I knew what it meant—I'd seen it on Dad a hundred times. This guy was drinking. To the point he wasn't sleeping.

I jerked my head back toward the house. "She's inside," I said, and he smiled to thank me as he passed around the table.

As it turned out, Dad didn't actually have that much valuable stuff. There were a couple bids on the baseball card collection, some disagreement over a table, and a run on shoes after we dropped the price, but most people said it was a bust and didn't spend anything. When we were down to our last few customers, we'd netted sixty-eight dollars.

Joe Kelly and I started bringing the unsold boxes back to the garage, stacking them on the workbench. He let one go with a thud, knocking over a toolbox, and as he went to pick it up, I heard him behind me.

"Holy shit . . . check out this antique!"

I turned and felt my heart stop. In his hand was a small, side-loading, wood-handled Glock 42 semiautomatic.

My body reacted before my brain did. I felt my tongue get heavy, like it had doubled in size to take up most of my mouth. I tried to tell him to put it down, but nothing came out.

"Thing's gotta be from the seventies," Joe Kelly said, carelessly turning it in his hands. "One of those ones they used to play Russian roulette with."

Rodney saw my face and looked to Joe.

"Put it away," she told him, but it just made Joe more amused.

"Probably doesn't even fire anymore," he said, raising the gun to shoulder level, pointing it at the back wall, then swinging it around toward me. I panicked as I felt the barrel in my direction, stumbling backward, tripping over an empty box and collapsing to the floor. I hit the ground with a thud, my ass hard against the concrete. I tried to hold my face steady, but tears stung at my eyes.

"Oh my God, Willie," Joe laughed. "It's just a fucking gun—AHH!"

Outta nowhere, Bones flew at him.

He was on him like a blur, faster than Joe could react. He swung violently for Joe's arm, grabbing and twisting it into submission, ripping the gun free. "What the fuck?!" Joe yelped, but Bones didn't stop. He checked Joe forward to the ground, his arm still spun up behind him, a pure show of how much stronger he was.

"You psycho! We've got a game tomorrow. You coulda broke my arm!"

Bones didn't even look at him. He marched past him to the bench and replaced the 42 in the toolbox, tucking it away. When he turned back, it wasn't to Joe, it was to me.

I nodded and took a few breaths to get back to normal.

"It wasn't even loaded!" Joe Kelly shouted. "Someone wanna tell me what the fuck that was all about?"

Our dad bought the 42 on the day Bones was born.

As he told it, he'd drive around Calico Springs with the gun on the dash and his newborn son in the front seat, showing him off and telling people he needed the gun because "now he had something worth protecting." It wasn't until I was older, and adults started being honest with me, that I learned, as is always the case, the story was much better than the reality. Turns out the 42 was more often used to settle arguments at bars and play cowboy when he was drinking alone in the garage, which makes sense, because the most vivid image I have of Dad to this day is him passed out cold in the recliner, gun resting on his chest, barrel end up.

One night, when Bones was seven and I was five, we stayed up late, getting it in our heads that we might make decent cowboys, too, if we could just get our hands on the proper weaponry.

Turns out we were wrong. Bones was a terrible shot, even worse then, when he needed four fingers to pull the trigger. He was aiming for the chair.

You ever hear of that old Christmas movie, "You'll shoot your eye out"? Sounds stupid, right? How could you shoot out just your eye? Wouldn't you think it'd hit something else, like your brain?

Turns out, it's incredibly rare, less than half of one percent. So rare that it falls under the scientific definition of a miracle. God, working. When Dad put me and Mom in the back seat of the car, my face was covered in blood and my heart had stopped. For five minutes, I was dead.

And Bones sat next to me the whole drive, thinking he'd killed me.

Ever since that day, Bones had made it his mission to never, ever let me take shit from anybody. I was eight the first time he beat the shit outta somebody over my eye, some kid named Salem who called me a pirate at Rodney's birthday party. He'd been suspended twice for fights at school. One time he got banned from a Little League tournament in Summit after some dumb coach tried to argue it wasn't safe for me to play. It cost our team a championship, but Dad bought us ice cream on the way home.

Some people thought it was cute, or honorable. Some people thought it was weird and possessive. But I always saw it as exactly what it was—love born from guilt, the residual kind that never gets admitted and never goes away.

"You sure you're all right?" Bones asked me after everyone else had gone home. "Joe's a dickhead. Everybody knows it."

"It wasn't even that serious," I assured him.

Once the boxes were packed, we sat on the roof of the garage, just the two of us, listening to the pulsing creak of the insects, the heat of the day wearing off quickly into night. Bones kept a supply of rocks in the storm drain, all about the weight of a baseball, that he could chuck into the O'Neils' yard across the street.

"Not too late," I said. "Whatever you want, we can go out and find it. Settle this bet."

Bones settled his shoulders and chucked a rock at the biggest tree, effortlessly drilling the bark. "Maybe some other night," he said. "I gotta get some sleep. Game tomorrow."

"I'm glad you're staying," I told him. "I didn't know what the hell I was gonna do when you left, anyway."

Bones snorted, smiling without his teeth. "Yeah . . ." He drew it out, extending his hand to my shoulder. "I'm glad, too."

He meant it as he said it, but I watched him a second too long, and the smile on his face disappeared, leaving a hollowed-out look in its place. There was something he wasn't telling me, but I knew better than to ask.

CHAPTER 3

THE NIGHT OF the baseball game, I went out to test Manifest Atlas again.

I knew I'd have the streets to myself. Everybody in Calico Springs went to the games, even people who didn't like baseball. It was a town event, an opportunity to crack a few at Prentice Park and the cops couldn't say shit 'cause they were usually there, too. Except me. Bones had a thing about me being there when he was pitching. "It feels like you're judging me, staring at me like that," he'd told me once, so the next game after, I tried hard to smile at him the whole way through, but we both decided that was worse. Even though he never said it out loud, I knew he preferred if I didn't go to the games, and he just recapped them to me at Dairy Queen after.

I biked over an hour before to help Mom load boxes of candy and popcorn into the concession stand. She'd been helping more since Dad moved out, trying harder to be a part of Bones's life, or at least to look like it to everybody else. She had on a white-and-blue tee with the Calico Night Rider in the center, and had even painted a little "#15" on her cheek for Bones.

Mom said she liked to go early so she could talk to all her friends, but she usually spent most of the game in the concession stand or tucked back in the bleachers. I knew the real reason was that if she went early enough, she wouldn't have to run into Dad.

Dad was always coming late or leaving early and absolutely unashamed of lying about it. All through high school, he'd been notoriously unreliable, making a habit of stopping by to show his face, then landing on his bar stool at Leo's by the third inning. When he did show, he'd hover around the first few rows with the other dads, where they could talk shit to the ump and trash to the dads on the other side. There was already a small group of them gathered—I saw Joe's dad, Bill Kelly, in a bright red quarter zip, alongside a tall, broad-shouldered man, John Arrington.

There was no way Dad would miss tonight, I figured. Tonight was Bones's moment.

"Ladies and gentleman, welcome to the regional championship. Tonight's game decides a place in the Missouri Class B State Tournament!"

Even with a half hour to go, the stands were already almost full. The whole place was buzzing with nervous energy, except for Bones. He was playing long toss in right field, smiling and laughing like it was nothing. It was an act, I knew it, but Summit didn't.

The teams headed back for the dugout, and I said goodbye to

Mom. As I grabbed my bike from the rack, I felt a tiny drop of rain against my shoulder. There was still sun fighting through a battalion of dark gray clouds. I pulled away from the stadium, slow at first, pumping back and forth, starting to swerve through the empty streets.

Behind me, I could hear the echo of the public address system ringing out—

"Simmons, Hartman, and Smith, and coming to the mound for your Night Riders . . . Matthew . . . Bones . . . Eckles. . . ."

Ever since Bones told me about his decision to stay, I'd had a feeling I couldn't shake. It was good news, I knew that, and my life would be better having him around, I definitely knew that, too. But in a way I couldn't explain, it felt like something was lost. I loved Calico Springs. But lately, I was starting to see what it could do to a person. Maybe Bones was right to stay here, maybe he had a plan, but I didn't. And in my stomach, I was stuck on the idea that if I didn't start swimming soon, I'd drown.

I stopped and opened the game.

WHAT'S YOUR INTENTION? it asked.
SEE MY FUTURE

The target was a few miles north, blinking on the side of a narrow, mostly transparent line on the map, probably a hiking trail or goat path. I knew I wouldn't be able to follow it; that deep in the Basin, the roads got rewritten every summer when the river came up, so whatever path it was clinging to was likely long gone.

I biked until the road ran out and dropped my bike in the ditch. I took a few steps toward the trees, but froze before I got there, my foot hovering in the air.

Below me, there was a mess of tangled barbed wire, patted down into the grass. I was close enough to the river that the land should belong to no one, the way the river belonged to no one, but the barbed wire suggested otherwise. The nearest house was over two miles up the road and belonged to the only rich person I knew—John Arrington.

I checked both ways and stepped over the wire, into the Basin.

Here's some small-town history, the kind that always sounds more like myth: John Arrington was a descendent of a royal bloodline in Calico Springs. The Arringtons were the first to open a mill in 1830, and the last to close it down. I'd passed his house on the way in, all three stories of it, but his backyard spread amorphously into the Basin behind it, covering most of the river's edge on the north side of town, a sort of redneck *Lion King* situation—it was just assumed everything the river touched was his.

Bones liked rich people, especially the ones he knew, because he saw himself as a rich-person-in-training. Rodney always argued that would never be the case, precisely because of what people like the Arringtons had done to Calico Springs.

Calico was broke, along with everyone in it. Its history was one of bitter disappointment, businesses that promised the world then left before the sun came up. First it was the mills, then it was the railroads, then it was the Stanfield Brick Factory, which closed in 2008 with promises to reopen "when the economy turned around." In every instance, spread across centuries now, there were glimmers of hope, maybe a decade of prosperity, then the same result, the rising and falling of the tide. The businesses left, the jobs left, the money left, and the people of Calico stayed.

Not that it mattered to me. I was too young to remember a time when anybody had shit.

I checked my phone. I was a few hundred yards off the target, which meant it was hidden somewhere in the trees ahead. I picked up speed.

There was something about the intermittent darkness, the unpredictability of the ground below me, that put me on edge. I wasn't breaking any rules, at least none that I knew of, but it still felt like I was sneaking onto something, like I didn't belong.

I had to feel my way forward to walk. Everyone always assumed having one eye meant I couldn't see for shit, but it wasn't really like that. I saw different. I couldn't see wide, but I could turn my head. Sometimes I got surprised by how close things were, but if I had the time to let my eye adjust, I could use the size of things to figure it out, like those computers that can guess a sentence from just a few words. But all that got worse in the dark, as colors drowned together, making everything look like it was on the same plane. Like I was walking into a painting.

Ahead of me, I could see moonlight streaming through a gap in the trees. I nearly ran at it and froze as I hit the tree line. A sudden wind shook my spine and I steadied myself against a tree, my fingers disappearing into thick, patterned breaks in the bark.

"What the hell . . . ?"

It was a clearing, wide-open, unnaturally so. In the center, there were stumps of various sizes; it looked like it was done up for some kind of ritual.

I compared it to my phone. I was within a hundred yards. This was something.

I poked around the clearing. There was trash thrown about, a rope, some artillery, empty beer cans that were starting to lose their color, but nothing that said anything about my future. Around the outside of the circle, there were more trees with slash marks chiseled into the bark. I made wider circles, checking my location against the nearby trees, but the farther I got from the clearing, the fewer signs there were of anything to discover. The sky rumbled overhead, and a light rain started to drip against the tree cover.

I stopped, listening for the river, but all I could hear was the cicadas, now screaming at me to get out. I felt the air turn colder, the wind curling its fingers on the back of my neck. I looked up into the rain, and when my head came back down, I saw something in the distance.

It was a building, old, small, and decaying, but holding its own against the wind and rain. A barn. Warm yellow light spilled out. It felt like a secret, the way it was tucked outta view, like it had lived a hundred years in the Basin and no one had noticed.

A raindrop hit my eye, and when I opened it again, the light was gone, and the barn with it. I blinked a few times, but still nothing, just darkness where the barn had been.

I stared at the break in the trees, remembering the barbed wire. How could someone build a barn this close to the water? Was somebody living out here?

I walked at where I thought it had been. Maybe it was the Game, showing me a vision of my future, but I'd never even been to a farm.

I moved a little faster, my feet sinking into the mud, working harder to pull out of it, until—

The ground under my foot disappeared. I fell forward, hard, and braced myself for the ground, but it never came.

My stomach dropped out of my body as I fell. I caught something with my right arm, but I couldn't hold it, falling until finally I hit solid ground with a smack, face-first.

I thought I was dead. It'd be poetic, at least. Laid to rest in the river.

As I became aware again of the blood and tendons moving in my body, I reopened my eye to see any trace of light was gone. I must have passed out.

As I sat up, I realized it wasn't the light that was gone, there was still a burnt-orange glow, it was just farther away. I could see it in the sky above me; it was around me that was dark . . . walls of dirt. I was in a hole, a deep one, dug with purpose, at least six feet into the earth. . . .

I scrambled to my feet.

I was lying in a grave.

"HELP!" I started screaming. "HELP ME!"

I clawed at the sides to pull myself out, but when I tried to grab for the walls above me, dirt came off in chunks. Water pooled at the bottom, making it difficult to even lift my shoes from the muck. "Help!" I screamed to no one. "Please, somebody, help me!"

I remembered a YouTube video about people who ran up walls with counterforce, so I threw my back against the dirt, sinking in and throwing my feet at the opposite wall. I pushed as hard as I could, but the wall under my foot gave. I went crashing down into the base, water splashing around me.

"HELP ME!" I screamed again, then stopped. I thought I heard something, someone, moving through the forest.

"Hello?" I asked, quieter. Silence, until . . .

A dog started to howl.

My stomach dropped as I remembered the barbed wire I'd stepped over. The reality of the moment slammed into me. I was trespassing. This was somebody's property, and I'd found their grave. I could be killed, and in Missouri, it would be my fault.

"Shit!" I tried again, churning my feet faster to get better leverage. I pushed like hell against the soil, the dog getting closer, his bark on high alert. Finally, I got far enough up to grab a root, and pulled myself up into the mud, onto the earth, alive.

The Basin was quiet. I lay still and let the rain fall on me as I caught my breath. I was alive. The devil hadn't got me yet.

I listened close, taking in all the sounds. The soft impact of raindrops on leaves. The brushing of branches in the wind. The rush of the river. The frequencies started to garble into a neutral static, until another noise cut through, low at first, but growing in clarity as it got closer—a voice, calling for the dog. Somebody was out here with me.

I sat up, inching away. My best move was to cower, hide, and hope Old Yeller didn't sell me out. I took measured breaths, crawling toward a hollow in a nearby tree. Inch by inch, I reached back. . . .

My hand slipped into the earth. I yelped. There were two more graves behind me.

Only a few hundred feet away, the dog exploded.

I scrambled to my feet and took off. Without looking back, I crashed through the forest. The dog followed, his bark desperate and angry. I thought I heard someone calling for me as well, but it was difficult to tell over the sound of my own wet gasps for air.

I kept my eyes forward, trying not to think about tripping. The road materialized and I threw myself back into the ditch, collapsing next to my bike.

It was quiet. I couldn't hear anything behind me. The dog,

the voices, it had all disappeared. Almost like it couldn't pass to the outside of the Basin.

I went to check the time on my phone, but the Game was still open. The map had been replaced by a text box.

THANKS FOR PLAYING.

No score, no acknowledgment of the target, just a confirmation that the Game was over. In the chase, I'd forgotten why I was out there in the first place. I was playing the Game. And it worked.

Of course it did. There was no way that could be an accident, the target was too perfect. I'd found exactly what the Game sent me out to find.

I'd asked to see my future, and it put me in a grave.

The Game was telling me I was going to die.

I found an awning at Cotton Park to hide under and texted Bones. The game would be almost over by now, and biking back in the rain would be hell, so I huddled in the corner, hidden, and watched the road. There were no cars in or out of the Basin. If someone had been in there with me, they were still there.

I opened the app a few times, watching the starry sky dissolve into text, but closed it before it asked for my intention, trying to fully circle in my head the power it had just shown me.

My future was death. My destiny was a grave. There was no other way to interpret it. I didn't know why the grave was there in the first place, but it didn't matter. The Game knew it was there. It brought me straight to it, on my command, as simple as answering a question.

Twenty minutes later, Bones's truck came tearing down the road, ramped over the curb, and pulled straight up to where I was sitting. Bones hopped out, and his face fell when he saw me.

"Willie, what the hell?"

"I'm fine," I told him. "Just got stuck out here."

He threw my bike in the back of the truck and grabbed me a towel. He was still wearing his jersey, the Night Riders logo sagging from the soaked cotton. The heaters in the cab were on full blast as I climbed in.

"It works," I told him as soon as the doors were closed. "Manifest Atlas. I tried it tonight, and it fucking works."

He didn't say anything, but his eyebrows creased in confusion.

"The Game," I said. "I asked it to show me my future, and it took me into the Basin. I saw this barn, so I figured that was what it was taking me to, but when I tried to walk toward it . . . I fell in a grave. Then somebody tried to chase me out, away from it."

I waited for his shock, or excitement, or concern, but it never came. Bones didn't say anything, not understanding what it all meant.

"That's my future," I said quietly. "It's telling me I'm gonna die."

Bones pursed his lips and continued to ignore me as he drove, taking the sharp turns of the Basin with confidence.

"Wow," he finally said. "That's crazy."

"Yeah." I nodded, then realized: "Oh shit. How was the game?"

He shook his head.

"Are we going to state?"

He shook it again, his lips pressed tight together. "Nope. We're not."

"Really? What happened? I thought you said Summit sucked—"

"I did. They do," Bones choked. "But the fucking ump wouldn't give me a break. He was calling the smallest zone I've ever seen, and then it started raining but they wouldn't call the game. Everybody in the stands knew we couldn't keep playing, but they'd got a couple runs on me, so they were racing to finish the game and the ump just let them. So we lost."

I watched him, his lip twitching. I didn't press, but Mom filled in the details for me later that night. Bones had started great, but after giving up back-to-back walks in the third inning, he got in his own head and lost control. He walked four more batters, threw a couple meatballs just to get something across the plate, and by the time the bloodshed was over, he'd given up six runs, and Calico's season—Bones's career—was over.

I watched him driving, intently focused on the road ahead.

"You've still got the club season," I said, but he rolled his eyes.

"No one gives a shit about club season, Willie. That's just to fuck around before everybody goes to college."

"Well . . . if you wanna play again, you could always take the scholarship—"

"I get that you're trying to make me feel better," Bones said flatly. "But please, shut the fuck up."

We were quiet for a while as we drove. I watched out the window as the billboards flew by. Most of the ones on the way into Calico Springs had gone political, about babies dying from abortion or Democrats rioting in cities. Pam Smith's Auto Sales had a billboard clarifying that in her store, they stood for the flag. I was surprised somebody had asked.

"Maybe you could ask Manifest Atlas for a trip to state. What I've seen, it'd find a way. Maybe get Summit disqualified or something."

Bones glanced over at me again, but still didn't say anything. As the gravel turned to pavement and we passed the sign for the Calico Springs city limits, he rapped his fingers against the steering wheel a few times.

"You couldn't build a barn that low," he mumbled.

"What?"

"You said you saw a barn in the Basin? You couldn't build it that low; the river would level it. Remember when Dad said they tried to pour a foundation and it wouldn't stick?"

"I'm just telling you what I saw."

"Maybe it was a shack or a lean-to for some tools—"

"It was a full-size barn."

Bones sucked his teeth. "And why would somebody chase you out? The Basin's public."

"Maybe they thought I was gonna steal something—"

"You're two miles from any house. Who are you gonna steal from?"

"Whoever owns that barn!"

"Okay," Bones said quietly. "Okay."

"I'm not making it up," I told him seriously. "I'll prove it again, for the bet—"

"Oh," Bones said. "That's what this is about. I forgot. The bet."

"I just told you, I'll prove it again."

Bones rolled his eyes, and I gave up. It was pointless trying to convince him. There would never be anyone Bones would believe over himself. He started humming, which he did whenever he wanted to change the subject, so I started humming, too, slightly louder, a discordant melody.

CHAPTER 4

THE NEXT DAY at school was one of the last of the year, and teachers knew there was nothing they could do to stop the momentum building toward summer, so they filled the obligatory hours with old DVDs they could pass off as educational.

I had study hall with my history teacher, Mr. Burns. He was former military, patriotic in a real American flag kind of way, one of those teachers who loved what he taught so much, he took it too serious. His room was covered with American memorabilia, American flags on everything down to his coffee cup. He also had a strict no-phones policy, even in study hall, but I could see he was completely absorbed in the fantasy baseball lineup on his computer.

Looking off in another direction, I pulled out my phone beneath my desk, and with as little attention as possible, I navigated to the App Store.

There it was, the cryptic logo, looking cheap and digital, ill-fitting in the box on the screen. There were four reviews, none with text. The Game hadn't been rated, which meant there was a content warning at the top, and its description was one line:

PREPARE TO CHANGE YOUR DESTINY

I clicked the Details tab and scrolled.

There were four lines—Creator, Developer, Designer, and Customer Support.

All four were blank.

The only text, in fact, was the copyright at the bottom.

© *CHANGE YOUR DESTINY MARKETING LLC*

I stared at it for a long moment, trying to understand why someone wouldn't take credit for their work. If I'd invented an app, especially one with this kind of power, I'd tell everybody and their sister. So the only explanation was the opposite. They didn't take credit on purpose. They didn't want anybody to know.

After lunch, they herded us into the old gym for an assembly.

"Oh, no, Willie," Ms. Calloway shouted at me as I climbed the bleachers. "Freshmen are down here."

"I'm sorry, Ms. Calloway," I said without stopping. "They told me to sit up here, for my eye and all."

"Right," she said, as if it made any sense at all, and I joined Bones and Rodney in the back row.

When Principal Cameron stepped to the mic, he looked uncomfortable. "We were supposed to have the full city council today." He looked around. "But looks like we'll have to get started a couple short. They're here to give you all some exciting information about the upcoming merger with Lawton."

From the back, a few students booed.

Lawton was an even smaller town on the other side of the river. It was less than ten miles away, but it might as well have been a million. The schools were rivals, the churches were rivals, even the grocery stores took swipes at each other with their coupons. Every now and then, you'd hear a story about somebody's son dating a Lawton girl, and people would shake their heads and laugh and wonder about how that was gonna go for him.

For as long as I could remember, people had known Lawton was failing, but now, evidently, it had gotten so small and so broke, it didn't make sense as its own town anymore, so they were going to push us together. Which meant everything was getting pushed together, including the high schools. It came outta nowhere a few months ago, after they did a city council election and the next day, half the council announced the plan, and that they were gonna vote for it, which evidently was all it took. They published an article, scheduled a vote, and come July, we'd officially become—

"The Calico Springs–Lawton Municipal Area!"

"Horrible fucking name," Bones muttered.

People were pissed about the Calico Springs–Lawton Municipal Area. Some had even made yard signs that said "Protect Calico" or "Calico Strong," but the way everybody was talking, it was a done deal. The paperwork was underway with the government, and the teachers had spent the last couple days expanding their classrooms. Now, the city council was in front of us, telling us how exciting it would be to have new class-mates, and how at least we didn't have to drive all the way out to their shitty schools.

"By consolidating after-school activities, we'll be able to offer more options to students," a councilwoman named Linda said. She was friends with Mom. I remembered her most from when she freaked out on the ref of one of our youth soccer games. "New clubs, new teams. Activities we've never had before—a debate team . . ."

Bones shook his head. This was his big problem with the merger, consolidation. Back in early spring, he'd been afraid they were gonna merge sports early and some pitcher from Lawton would come in and take his spot. "That's what consoli-dating is," he explained to me harshly one day. "They're gonna have to give half the spots to them, even if they suck."

We'd heard from most of the council when the back door to the gym swung open, and I saw Principal Cameron sigh with relief.

"Ah, good," he said. "Students, here to talk about the eco-nomic benefits of the town merger, please welcome the builder behind the new developments, and city council member, John Arrington."

Arrington looked every ounce a businessman, a red flan-nel button-up tucked into nice jeans, real straight to the point, no bullshit. One summer, Arrington coached me and Bones in Little League, and he always talked to us like we were his fifth-grade employees.

Arrington took the mic and walked to the center of the court, away from where the rest of the council was watching. "I know we've all made up our minds," he said, gesturing to them. "And I know we're all excited about debate teams. But if you'll allow me, for just a moment, to play devil's advocate. . . ."

The other speakers shifted uncomfortably.

"There are towns that have done this all over Missouri, this consolidation process. And I'll tell you this, there's data on it . . . the people in those communities do not like it. You ask them two years, five years after, they'll tell you, things did not get better."

You could hear people shuffling, some whispers as he spoke. Principal Cameron looked confused and tried to get his attention, but Arrington was on a roll.

"I mean, what really changes? We all still live in the same houses, right? They wanna come to our restaurants, they can come now! No, the only thing that actually changes is policy. Make no mistake, this isn't about unity. It's not about bringing everyone together. They want our tax dollars. *Your* tax dollars."

"John, this is absurd—" Linda stood up, trying to interject, but Arrington didn't even acknowledge her, he just kept making his point straight to the students.

"Talk to your parents tonight. Ask them, how does this affect us? Our family? Remember, the city council's still gotta vote—that's what this time is for—and they work for you. Not the other way around.

"You know what the most valuable currency in a small town

is? Not money. Money's nice, but it only gets you so far when everybody knows everybody. Only thing you can really take to the bank is trust. Community. Knowing your neighbor, counting on your neighbor. We've been building Calico Springs for a hundred years. Do you wanna give that away?"

He looked intensely at the crowd of kids in front of him, like he was really asking each of us the question. Some kids were nodding. When he got to the back, his eyes hovered, and he asked it more pointedly. I stared back, my stomach dropping.

"What happens if that goes away?" he asked.

"Willie," Bones whispered. "I think he's looking at you."

I was on edge the rest of the day.

It wasn't just Arrington. The feeling from the night before lingered, like I didn't belong, I'd crossed into somewhere I wasn't supposed to be, and it was only a matter of time before I got in trouble for it. Which made my heart skip when the intercom box screamed, and Miss Joy's voice squawked out:

"William Eckles. Please come to the principal's office immediately."

There were a few obligatory "oohs." Even Mr. Burns looked confused. "What'd you do, Willie?"

I'd only been to Principal Cameron's office a few times, over a few minor issues. For the most part, I thought he liked me, or at least he tolerated me, which is better than you could say for most of the real country kids at the school.

When I got to the door, I heard men laughing inside. Miss

Joy nodded to me, and I pulled the door back to reveal Principal Cameron sitting at his desk and John Arrington leaned against the bookshelf behind him.

My heart hiccuped back into my throat.

"Willie," Principal Cameron said. "You know John Arrington?"

"Yes, sir," I said. "Good to see you, Mr. Arrington."

"Howdy, Willie." He nodded to the chair in front of Cameron's desk, and I sat. This close, I could see his face was sun-beaten and tough, a fat under-lip that had permanently re-formed to hold tobacco. "You good?" he asked.

"I am," I said.

"How's your eye doing?" he asked, as if it was obligatory.

"Same, I guess."

Principal Cameron looked uncomfortable as he nodded to Arrington. "Sounds like Mr. Arrington had some property stolen from his land last night, and he thought you might be able to help."

I glanced between them. "I don't see how."

"I've got property down in the Basin," Arrington said. "We had some trespassers last night. Not a big deal but looks like some stuff was taken."

I caught myself blinking unnaturally and adjusted my patch to play it off. "I wouldn't know anything about that," I said. "I wasn't in the Basin last night. Just doing some fishing at Cow Pond, north of town."

Arrington laughed. "They still got fish in that pond?"

I shook my head. "If they do, they didn't wanna come home with me."

"You were out pretty late, then?"

"Nope, about 8:50," I told him. "I checked the clock when my brother picked me up. I was trying to make it home for the new *Criminal Minds.*"

This was one of Bones's core principles when it came to lying. If you're going to add details—and you should add details—it helps to explain why they're pertinent.

Arrington shifted his weight. "I'm surprised I didn't see you at the baseball game," he said. "Biggest game of your brother's career, and you decided you'd rather fish?"

I felt my insides tighten at the mention of Bones, but I let it come and go without a reaction. "Sounds like I didn't miss much."

Principal Cameron looked to Arrington to see if he was satisfied, but Arrington was staring at me. It felt like there was some question he was trying to ask, but it was the kind that couldn't be asked with words. Instead, he was trying to pull it from below my skin.

"Come on, Willie," he said quietly. "What we're talking about is serious business."

"Willie's a good kid," Principal Cameron interjected. "I've never had a single problem, and you know how many of these kids I have problems with—"

"I agree." Arrington didn't look away from me. "You're too smart for this kind of nonsense, and I know you don't come by trouble on your own. You can save yourself a lot of hell if you just tell me what you were doing out there last night."

I could feel the sweat forming on my hands, but I stared coolly back. "Out where? Cow Pond?"

After a long, hard moment, Arrington nodded. "Okay. Well, you hear anybody talking about being down by the Basin, let me know, all right?"

"Yes, sir."

"And spread the word—no going out tonight. There's gonna be a town curfew."

I froze, halfway up. "Why'd we have a curfew?"

Arrington raised his hands, as if it was obvious. "'Cause there's robberies in the area."

I nodded and kept my head down the whole way out of the room.

CHAPTER 5

BONES WAS GASSED up the whole way home from school about the assembly.

"They're trying to steal the town!" He accentuated his point by waving a Popsicle around. "I knew it smelled funky, but this is goddamn rotten—"

"Do you even pay taxes?" Rodney rolled her eyes. "You know, it might actually help things around here. More money, more stuff, more activities—"

"Easy for you to say," Bones told her. "You won't even be here."

It hadn't been rare for Bones and Rodney to go at it in the last few months, especially over meaningless shit. I knew the exact moment it started, too—six months ago, when they inexplicably decided to start dating, and then broke up two months later and went right back to being friends without saying anything about it. They'd never said who broke up with who, which made it clear to me that Rodney had broken up with Bones. I called those "the dark months."

Since the dark months, they hadn't stopped being friends—everything about the way we hung out was the same—but lately, it was like they'd forgotten why.

When we got back to the garage, Joe Kelly and his new girlfriend, Sarai, were already waiting for us, sitting with their legs crossed on the couch. "Oh great," I heard Bones mutter as he put the car in park and shut up quick about the merger.

"Hey, Bones," Sarai called to him as he got out of the car. "Crazy assembly today, huh?"

Joe Kelly went through girlfriends quick. We all knew it, 'cause it usually got talked about a lot. I knew most of them, and usually, they were all pretty much the same—but Sarai was different. She had dark brown skin and black hair pulled back so tight on the sides of her head it looked almost painful, with curls in the back. She dressed sort of like one of the boys on *Stranger Things*; every day a different bright-colored T-shirt from an event she hadn't been to—today it was parakeet green and said "Lawton Day of Service."

The main difference, though, was that Sarai liked to pick fights. Usually, Joe's girlfriends were quiet, afraid to wade too far into the conversation, which made me feel a certain kinship with them. Sarai wasn't afraid of anything. She'd been on the debate team at Lawton. She said arguing was her favorite sport. And when she played, she usually won.

"You know Arrington has no actual skin in the game, right?" she said to Bones. "He's probably never even been to Lawton, let alone to the school. He doesn't have any idea how bad we need it."

"He probably pays more tax than you," Bones said, afraid to look her dead in the eye. "He might have a little skin in the game. . . ."

"Which makes him a greedy piece of shit!" she said. "Personally, I think we should do what's best for everybody, not just for John Arrington. And besides, it doesn't matter, anyway. It's already voted. John Arrington can't change shit—it's happening."

Behind her, Joe Kelly ignored the conversation and settled into our dad's recliner. It wasn't a secret his dad hated the merger and only started supporting it after people brought up getting a new mayor along with it. Every time Sarai mentioned it, I noticed Joe bowing out, saying less than normal. Arguing with Sarai about it was a lost cause—we all knew the real reason she cared so much, and it didn't have anything to do with taxes.

Sarai had only moved to Calico Springs two years ago, when her mom got remarried to a white guy and moved their family across the river . . . which meant she'd left all her lifelong friends behind. She talked about them constantly, so much they'd started to take on an imaginary quality—they were good at the stuff her friends here weren't, they were capable and fun and freethinking in a way people in Calico would never be. "If you love 'em so much, how come we never see 'em?" Bones asked her once.

"'Cause they hate it here!" she told him. "And I don't have a car to go back there; I might as well be in Egypt."

That was how Sarai talked about her new home. She talked shit on everything—the racist teachers, the shitty new houses, the parks that didn't have enough picnic areas. I could always tell Joe Kelly took it personal, like it was actually him she was talking about. So instead, whenever it came up, he steered us away.

Today, he steered toward me. "What'd they call you to the office for, huh, Willie?"

It was the first time anyone had looked at me in ten minutes. "Oh," I said. "Arrington wanted to talk to me."

Bones sat up. "About what?"

"He thought I stole some shit from the Basin last night."

"Well . . ." He waited. "What did you steal?"

"Nothing. There wasn't anything to steal. It's the Basin. I don't think that's what it was actually about. I think he wanted to talk to me because he knows I saw his graves."

It was one of those moments I could feel the wind in the room change. It got Rodney's face out of her laptop—she'd been fixated on it since we arrived. Joe Kelly rarely spent longer than a half second looking at me, but now he was staring.

"Graves?" he asked quietly.

I nodded.

"You saw graves in the Basin? Multiple graves?"

I nodded.

"What were you doing there?"

Bones's face puckered.

"I was playing a game," I explained. "A phone game. You tell it what you want, it brings you to a target. And it took me to the Basin, and as I was walking . . . I fell in a grave."

For dramatic effect, I left a little eerie silence at the end.

"What'd you say you wanted?" Rodney asked.

"To see my future."

"Holy shit," Sarai said softly, a little bit of pity. "You're gonna die."

It was silent for a long moment before Joe Kelly leaned into the middle of the circle.

"Bullshit."

He threw his hands up and looked at Bones. "I'm sorry, Bones, but I call bullshit. That didn't actually happen. Your brother is making that up—"

"I don't care if you believe me or not, it happened," I said urgently, my chest getting hot.

"'It happened,'" Joe Kelly parroted, all nasally and gross. He looked around, realizing no one else was laughing. "I'm sorry, but it was probably a hole—"

"It wasn't a hole!" I shouted, my face flushing red.

He lurched back, like I was attacking him. "Wow, okay, spoken like someone who's definitely not lying. . . ."

He sat up, glancing around the circle, and finally looking back at me, like he was an adult and I was a kid. "I'm just saying, Willie. Sometimes you take shit too serious."

I glared back. He was talking about the day before, how I reacted to the gun. I wanted to tell him he was the asshole in that situation, but I knew it would just prove his point, so I sat back. I didn't know what else to say, so I stared at him.

He smiled back pityingly. "You look like you're gonna cry."

"I don't know, man," Bones said with a shrug. "I heard Rory and Tyler used it to find a dog."

We both looked to him in disbelief.

"No," Joe Kelly said, shaking his head quickly. "Rory and Tyler are full of shit, too."

Bones shrugged. "Maybe. Or maybe it actually works."

It made Joe laugh. "Okay, I'll bet you a thousand dollars it doesn't work."

Bones nodded to me. "How about twenty?" Bones said. "We test it tonight."

I kept my face steady, not to give anything away, but my chest flooded with relief. Bones, as usual, seeing the light at just the right moment. Saving the day.

"There's a curfew tonight," Joe pointed out.

"Even more fun! A curfew in Calico Springs? What's the worst that happens, we run into Deputy Schnack?"

Sarai looked genuinely intrigued. Rodney did, too.

Joe Kelly was looking between Bones and me, I think trying to decide if we were hustling him. "So we try this app one time," he said. "And if it doesn't find whatever I choose, you'll give me twenty bucks—"

"You can't be the one to choose it!" I cut him off. "You're biased. It has to be somebody impartial."

Sarai raised her hand immediately. "I'll do it."

"Except it has to be something you really want," I urged her. "Something you actually could find."

Joe Kelly rolled his eyes.

But Sarai took the assignment seriously. I handed her my phone and she stared at the question. "What's my intention? Something . . . specific. But not too easy or obvious. Something . . . interesting. What is my intention?"

A thought struck her, and she smiled wickedly. "I've got it." She looked directly at me. "Something bloody."

At dinner that night, Mom told us she'd signed up for a new committee at church and was gonna spend Thursday nights there for the foreseeable future. "It's for the merger. To help figure out how to combine the two towns' laws."

I remembered the man from the garage sale. "That's what that guy was here for?"

She nodded. "Winston Lewis. Yeah, he's working on it for the city, from the Calico side. His wife's from Lawton."

It was a rare novelty, a cross-river family, so rare that it connected dots in my head. "That's Sarai's stepdad?"

She nodded. Bones looked uninterested.

Mom used the silence to turn the focus to me. "I ran into Mr. Burns at the grocery store. He said you got called to the office to talk to John Arrington?"

I explained the misunderstanding with the fishing, and the truck, and the *Criminal Minds* episode. Bones listened quietly, nodding into his wedge fries as I spoke.

"I thought you said you were gonna go play that game last night?" she asked pointedly.

"Yeah, I was."

"But you told Arrington you were fishing?"

I shrugged. "I did both."

Mom didn't say anything for a minute, but I could see she was thinking about it surprisingly hard. She put her fork down. "I have to know where you are," she said firmly, like we were in trouble. "I know you boys are adults, and I promise I won't get in your way. But I want your locations, from your phones—"

Bones had heard enough. "Why do you even care so much?" he snapped.

She looked between us. "I don't want either of you getting in trouble."

Bones rolled his eyes. "You were never this paranoid when Dad lived here."

It made Mom recoil and pull her hand back from mine. Her body kinda froze. "I just want you to be safe," she said, and withdrew the line of questioning.

It was a harsh thing to say, but in his defense, Bones wasn't wrong. After Dad moved out, Mom had started watching us much more closely. She talked to our teachers behind our backs, asked us where we'd been every time we came home, even called other parents sometimes to make sure we were where we said we were. She told us she didn't care what we did in the garage, so long as we stayed at the house, which Bones assumed was her way of keeping up the surveillance state.

"It's because she's afraid we're conspiring to go live with Dad," Bones told me once. "She doesn't wanna lose custody."

We'd made a pact to tell her as little as possible about our comings and goings, so she wouldn't get worried or ask too many questions, and Bones was right, it was easier this way.

But I knew he was reading her wrong. I'd never once heard Mom talk about us living with Dad. I don't think Dad even wanted that. She had a different fear, one Bones never had a view of, 'cause he hadn't seen what I'd seen.

I'd always been a horrible sleeper. I'd wake up at the slightest noise, and once I was up, there was no prayer of ever getting back down. Which meant every time Dad's truck came scream-ing into the driveway at five a.m., it shook me outta bed. On more nights than I could count, I'd laid there half-asleep and listened to Dad tell lie after drunken lie, about where he'd been or who he'd been with. I'd hear Mom cry, call him an asshole, beg him just to tell her what he was doing, she didn't even care if he stopped doing it. "I don't have to know everything," she'd beg him. "Just tell me a little." But he didn't. It sounded like Dad liked lying to her, testing what he could get away with. They'd go round after round at the table, only for her to sweep every-thing under the rug by breakfast. Bones hadn't seen any of that, and when I tried to tell him about it, he said it was normal. He still couldn't figure why she'd kicked him out.

But I knew. Mom wasn't afraid of us choosing Dad. She was afraid of us becoming him.

I found Bones playing Xbox in the garage after dinner. I sat behind him for a minute, calling out zombies in the warehouse he was clearing out. When he hit his first respawn, I told him,

"I don't think we should ask for something bloody."

He ignored me, clicking through a few menu options, so I kept going.

"I've already seen how dangerous this thing can get. I don't think we wanna mess with the universe like this. I mean . . . what if I'm the something bloody—"

"Willie." He paused the game and sat up, looking at me seriously. "I mean this sincerely, and with complete respect . . . shut the fuck up."

"What?"

"We're not gonna find something bloody. We're not gonna find anything."

I recoiled, confused. "But . . . you said it to Joe today, the Game works—"

"I just didn't want him to embarrass you, so I backed you up."

He turned back to the screen, like it was obvious. I felt like I'd been punched in the stomach. "You don't actually think it works?"

"Of course I don't!" he said. "It sounds insane. You can't just wish for something and then get it, all 'cause you've got an app. Everybody would do that. There wouldn't be anything left to wish for."

"Well, maybe it only works certain times or for certain people."

"The game on your phone randomly decides when it wants to alter the course of the universe, just because you asked it to?"

"That's how God works—"

"That is not how God works," he snapped back at me. "If that's how God worked, we'd have a bigger house. Dad would be here. I'd be . . ."

He slowed to a stop. We were quiet for a long minute.

"I'm sorry, Willie. But you have to learn when to draw the line. Say goofy shit like that to me, make a ridiculous bet about it with me, whatever, it's fine. But if you say shit like that to guys like Joe Kelly? They'll eat you alive. You want friends, don't you?"

I glared at him.

"Do you? 'Cause if not, you can say whatever you want. You could just be one of those weirdos, spend your whole life working at Pizza Hut, telling people about aliens, if you want."

"I want friends," I mumbled.

"Okay. Then ease up on the crazy shit."

I let it get quiet as my stomach wrung itself out.

"I don't mean to hurt your feelings," he added. "I'm just not always gonna be here to defend you, you know?"

"Oh, you're not?" I asked. "Why? Where are you going?"

Bones's face dropped. He stared at the screen, the game still running, with fire in his eyes; opened his mouth to speak, but whatever bullet he was loading, he left it in the chamber. Instead, he clicked off the console and went to his room, and I didn't see him again until midnight.

CHAPTER 6

RODNEY SHOWED UP first, taking the mission seriously—black hoodie, black gloves, even a black ski mask. She'd been sneaking out to our house for so long, it was effortless at this point. We were pretty sure her parents knew and had just given up on her soul. A few minutes later, Joe Kelly's truck lights pulled into Trinity Lutheran a few blocks down, and Sarai and Joe made their way to us in the dark, armed with a water bottle of whatever liquor Joe's parents had in excess—tonight, gin. We passed it around, taking pulls until the clock said 12:30.

I handed my phone to Sarai, but she was already holding Joe's. "I downloaded it," he said. "Just had to make sure it was legit."

She punched out the intention, letter by letter, before emphatically pressing the Go button. The screen spun for longer than usual, neon-blue dots bubbling under the surface of the map but never quite emerging, as the Game tested all the infinite possibilities. I could feel my stomach squirming as I watched.

"Here," Sarai said, handing him back the phone. "I'm not gonna know what it is, anyway."

I snuck a glance at Bones as the screen whirled. He looked bored, barely taking it seriously enough to even play the part.

"Okay, we got one," Joe Kelly said, pinching the screen to zoom. "Looks like the spot is on the river, on a sharp-ass bend. . . ."

He fell silent. That got Bones's attention.

"Jesus." Joe Kelly looked up. "It's at the mill."

"In the middle of the night?" Rodney asked.

"Yeah, that doesn't count. It's gonna be locked up, anyway."

"You can get in through the back," I argued.

"But the water's up," Joe Kelly pointed out.

"Why does that matter?" Sarai asked.

"The back of the mill is the river," Rodney explained. "So when the water's too high, it blocks the back entrance."

"It's not that high. Besides, this was his idea," I said, pointing to Joe Kelly. "He can bitch out if he wants."

Joe Kelly raised an eyebrow and looked to Bones, who still hadn't said much.

"Bet's a bet," Bones said. "Let's find something bloody."

The Calico Mill was the biggest in the area, some said in all of Missouri. Even though we were three generations removed from its use, the town still talked about it like it was holy ground, the source of all good things and a beacon of hope for good things that may come again. It was built on the sharpest bend in the river, which channeled the downward water flow into hundreds of tons of pressure, slamming against the rock face. This made it perfect for milling, and kept it safe when the water rose, but created an impossibly violent current. As the warnings went, the current below was so fast and the pull was so strong that once you hit water, you were gone, and there was nothing anyone could do but scream for help. When it was built in the mid-1800s, it took ten years and forty men, and by the time it was completed, the river had swallowed eight of them. According to local legend, you could still hear the cries of the men who drowned, calling for God as they were swept away.

The five of us sat in two rows, shoulder to shoulder, in Joe Kelly's truck. I'd never been in his truck before—it still smelled like fresh plastic. Evidently, people had taken the curfew seriously, 'cause the roads were empty, so we drove with our lights off.

"How does Arrington have the power to just shut the town down?" Rodney asked.

"Money," Joe said.

We made it through the neighborhood streets without seeing another car, but as soon as we turned onto Highway 19, a pair of headlights lit up the windshield.

"Shit—" Joe yanked onto the shoulder and killed the engine. We all held our breath as the lights approached and an old Toyota Camry cruised innocently by.

No one spoke for the next two miles, until we pulled onto the narrow Mill Road that led up to the river's edge. We got as close as we could, a half mile from the mill, parking behind a huge willow tree. "No flashlights 'til we're away from the road," Joe Kelly said. "I don't want anybody seeing us out here."

We walked the first half in darkness. The closer we got, the more the river roared, threatening us from below. "You guys see that?" Joe Kelly asked at one point, fumbling for his flashlight. He scanned the area in front of us, only finding an empty thicket—

"Ah!"

Bones leapt at him, and Joe Kelly recoiled, which finally got Bones to crack a smile. "It's okay, buddy," he said. "If this is too much for you, you can wait in the car."

Joe Kelly shook it off and kept walking. The air was getting thicker, and occasionally we'd hear a car roll by on the highway behind us, enough to send us into a crouch. The edges of the mill had started to form when we were interrupted again.

"Wait." It was Rodney this time. Everybody stopped. "Do you guys see that? The lights?"

She was pointing through the trees, into what looked like a far-off, moonlit path. I could see a reflection, curved light against a patch of pure darkness.

"What lights?" Bones asked.

Rodney stared at it. "It looks like a mirror, or . . . a window, maybe? Another car?"

We waited breathlessly for another sign—the sound of an engine, the flicker of an interior light—but none came. We kept moving.

The mill grew as we approached it, magnificent and decrepit.

The wood paneling down the face of the building was stripped to discolored parts, and rusted metal tanks hovered above, threatening to topple over into the debris surrounding us. The iron doors on the front were chained up like an asylum, but on the far side, a set of wooden stairs disappeared down the edge of the cliff, into the water below.

We were silently assessing the risk when I heard the faint echoes of someone laughing.

I wasn't the only one. The whole group's eyes darted around. Bones and Joe Kelly swung their flashlights wildly.

"Well," Sarai said, ricochet light revealing she was smiling. "At least someone's having a good time."

"That's not laughing," Joe Kelly said. "It's screaming."

I looked out to the river, feeling its chill as I remembered why we were here. We were going to find something bloody.

"Fuck this," Bones said, quick and final. "The river's too high. I don't wanna see anybody try those stairs. This is pointless."

"So I win?" Joe Kelly said. "Just like that?"

"I don't care," Bones said. "Let's just get out of here."

He turned to walk back, and Joe Kelly and Rodney took a few steps after him.

But I stood where I was, staring down the steps. They were slanted and chipped, built into the rock god knows how long ago. But they'd survived a hundred rainy seasons already—

And the Game had sent us straight here.

Bones noticed I wasn't moving. "C'mon, Willie. We gotta get back. Now."

Sarai hadn't followed, either; she was watching me from even closer to the steps.

I felt a flare in my chest as I looked at him. I realized a power I'd never had before. I didn't need his permission.

"Gimme ten minutes," I said. "I just wanna check it out—"

"Willie, don't be an idiot," he said.

"I've done this a million times—"

"Not when the water's this high, you haven't," he said. "You're not going."

"I mean, it's just my imagination, right? If the Game doesn't work, there's nothing dangerous in there—"

"Willie," Bones said for the third time, pleading now. "You win. The Game is real, I don't care, just don't be a fucking moron. You can't go in there alone—"

"I'll go."

Sarai had been observing the standoff from the head of the group, and she stepped forward now. Bones ignored her, still staring me down.

"Then he won't be going alone," she reasoned.

Bones's eyes flickered to Joe Kelly. "It's really not a good idea," Joe Kelly warned her. "It's one of those parts of the river where if you fall in, you die. The current's too fast, we couldn't catch you."

But Sarai didn't seem bothered. She looked to me. "You've done it before, right?"

I smiled to Bones, aware there was nothing he could do, and shrugged. "I just wanna see what's in there."

It took him a minute, but eventually, Bones made a show of

handing me his flashlight. "Fine. Guess I'll just have to explain to Mom that you died 'cause you're a fucking idiot."

I took it from him, and without looking back, I started off after Sarai toward the mill.

The path leading to the mill was jagged, dotted with debris from the old building and beer cans from parties that had never properly ended. I felt more sure of myself with every step. I was alive with adrenaline.

The instant we reached the top of the wooden stairs, that confidence disappeared. I looked down. It was too dark to see the surging water below, but I could hear it, slapping up against the rock, a hundred feet straight down into pitch-black death. Sarai had paused, her eyes rolled backward into her head, and mumbled something unintelligible—a prayer, I realized—so I decided to do the same.

Dear God. This would be a shitty way to die. Amen.

Sarai extended her foot toward the top step, but before she got there, a rustling noise froze us both.

It came from below the ridge, not more than ten feet under us. There was something beneath the stairs. She held a finger to her lips and started to lean over. I followed suit, and as soon as my head was hovering over the ledge—a dozen white birds crashed past us, frantically escaping into the sky.

We both stumbled backward as they flew, watching until they became white specks and were finally swallowed by the blackness of the sky.

"I've never seen doves in Missouri before," Sarai said.

"Me neither."

Sarai took one more deep breath and started down the stairs. She walked quickly, like she was trying to get it over with. I was much slower behind her, sensitive to everything from the softness of the wood to the mist against my socks.

I distracted myself by making conversation. "How long did you live in Lawton?" I asked.

"Since I was born," she said.

"I haven't seen you much."

"Yeah, well. In case you haven't noticed, we don't like y'all very much."

It caught me off guard. I'd never actually thought about how Lawton people felt about us. I assumed they liked us, seeing as how everybody always talked about them wanting to combine towns.

"Why don't you just hang out over there, then?" I asked. "If that's where all your friends are?"

Sarai got quiet, navigating the stairs without looking back.

"Sarai?"

"I'm trying to figure out why you would ask me that," she said.

"Oh." I choked. "I guess, I've been here for my whole life, and I've never met anyone who wanted to spend more time in Calico Springs."

Her shoulders relaxed, and I caught a glimpse of what looked like a smile in the refracted light. "Y'all must be growing on me." She shrugged. "Plus, I don't have a car."

We reached the bottom of the stairs, and Sarai waited for me, analyzing the long, narrow wooden platform that ran along the entire back of the building. "How do we get in?"

I pointed to a broken window on the far side, three feet off the ground. "That's how Bones and I always do it."

She nodded, staring at it, before jerking her head toward the rock face above us. "Is he always like that?"

It took me a minute to realize she was talking about Bones. "Like what?" I asked.

"You know. Telling you exactly what to do, how to do it. . . ."

I snorted. "No, he's fine."

She wasn't being funny. "You know you don't always have to listen to him, right?"

"I know that."

"Except you always do." She started to inch her way down the deck. "I've known you for two months, and I already know you care way too much about what he thinks. Why?"

"It's not like that."

"Okay," she said. "Then what's it like?"

My insides got hot, trying to answer. It felt easy, as obvious as waking up, but when I put it into words, all I said was, "He's my brother."

"Did he save you from a burning building or something—"

"He just looks after me," I said. "A lot of people try to give me shit, 'cause of my eye or 'cause I'm small . . . but Bones doesn't let anybody say shit. Which is good, 'cause this town can suck if you're different." She wasn't getting it, so I gritted my teeth and added, "You wouldn't understand."

She raised an eyebrow at me. "You wanna bet?"

It caught me off guard again, but she was right.

We reached the window, and Sarai studied the broken frame delicately, her fingers feeling for weaknesses in the wood. Once she found two solid places to put her hands, she grasped the frame and slowly, awkwardly lifted herself through and into the mill.

As soon as I landed behind her, it was as if the sound of the world was sucked back into a wormhole. The thick walls kept the river noise out, which made the building feel like it was outside of time.

Above us hung a complex web of ancient machinery, metal wheels of all different sizes, huge barrel cylinders on rusted tracks, and a piping system connecting it all. On the far end of the room, there was a main waterwheel, twice my height and lurking in the corner with the grandeur of an ancient monster. Through the years, it was clear the river had infiltrated the building, slashing and spraying through the shattered glass windows, and now it felt like the entire place had a steady drip.

Sarai was a few feet ahead of me, examining the underside of the central flume that fed water into the main wheel. "It looks like there's something here," she said, and lobbed a small piece of wood toward it.

It echoed as it skipped across the floor behind me, and I watched it disappear into the darkness in the corner. The lurking feeling returned, but I tried to ignore it, not wanting to appear afraid in front of her. No matter where I pointed my flashlight, the room remained empty.

"Do you believe it actually works?" I asked her. "The Game?"

She thought about it for a second. "I don't know what I believe," she said. "But if it does work . . . I'm glad we found it."

As if her words had summoned the spirit of the river, a wave crashed against the side of the building, sending its vapor into the room.

"It's rising," I said.

"Oh, relax, rivers don't rise that fast."

Despite her nonchalance, I noticed her checking the window every few seconds. I circled the room as well, but I knew I wasn't looking for anything. My eyes were following her.

"God, this place smells like shit. Which I think is actually kind of incredible," she mused as she walked under the wheel. "This was once the most impressive thing in the entire area. There were probably kids who couldn't imagine their lives without this mill. And now?" She shoved the massive wheel to demonstrate its brokenness. It creaked and swayed above her, and she cackled at it. "I guess that's how history goes," she said, turning back. "Generations turn, empires fall, wheels break. . . ."

Without warning, the ghosts of the mill came back with a vengeance.

Whatever was holding the wheel behind her in place snapped with a loud crack, and it began to spin. For a single moment, the machinery of the mill kicked into gear, and the standing water that had built in the central flume went rushing forward, spilling over the sides and dousing us both. A loose piece snapped off and hit the ground behind me with a powerful thud. The room shook. I rushed for cover, but it was over before I could get there. The wheel caught, the old wood of the building swayed, and the droplets on the floor settled.

We both stood slowly, face-to-face beneath the central flume. "Are you okay?" I asked. She stepped into the light, staring directly at me, her face twisted in terror.

"Whoa. Sarai?"

It was as though she'd become someone completely different, possessed by an unfamiliar spirit. I hadn't seen her even flinch yet, and now her whole body was shaking. She took two steps toward me, and her mouth hung open, but she was silent.

"Sarai, what happened? Are you hurt?"

I took another step closer and noticed that the water covering her had small droplets of color in it, orange and red. I reached for her shoulders to steady her and noticed the water on me had the same hue.

Sarai wasn't looking at me, she was looking behind me, her arm shaking as she extended it toward the floor. A few feet behind where I'd been standing, the flume was still depositing the last of its water onto a pile on the ground. A pile that hadn't been there before.

I approached it slowly. The thud hadn't come from falling machinery, it was this lump, flushed out of the central flume; a mess of dark cloth with pale accents, soaked in bright red.

Something bloody, she'd said.

Sarai clutched my hand as we both stared down in silence. Cracked, broken, crumpled, and forgotten; something bloody. It was a body.

PART TWO
THE BODY

CHAPTER 7

"I DON'T THINK we're entirely understanding this, Willie, so I'm gonna ask crystal clear. The reason you went to the mill— the only reason—was a video game?"

"Not a video game, Your Honor. A phone game. An app."

"You don't have to call me Your Honor, Willie. Nobody's on trial. You can just call me Officer Lyle."

"Yes, sir, Officer Lyle."

"And this phone game . . . It told you to go exactly to that spot at midnight?"

"Technically, the midnight part was our choice."

"Our choice?" Deputy Schnack asked. "You all made that decision? Not just . . . I don't know . . . your brother?"

"If I remember correctly, the decision was made mutually."

Officer Lyle smiled. "You're doin' fine, Willie. Nobody's in trouble here, trust me. We got bigger fish to fry than a couple kids out after curfew."

I nodded. There were bigger fish to fry. Body-sized fish.

I'd never been in this part of the police station before. Only the front part, when Mom took me after somebody stole my bike, and the jail on a fifth-grade field trip. Officer Lyle sat across the table from me, asking the questions and jotting notes in his little notebook. He was tall and narrow, mostly friendly, but his skin sucked into the contours of his face and created little pockets of shadow.

Behind him, Deputy Schnack hovered against the back wall, hiding in the darkness, quietly chewing on his mustache. At least that's what it looked like from where I was sitting.

"Did anyone tell you to play this game tonight?" Lyle asked.

"Technically, it was a bet."

"Between who?"

"My brother and Joe Kelly."

"Huh." Deputy Schnack stepped forward and clicked his tongue.

Schnack used to go to our church, back when we were still going every Sunday. He was the kinda guy to wear his police uniform during the service and stand in the first row of the balcony, looking out over everybody. It scared the shit outta people, seeing that badge, and I think he liked it that way. He wanted everybody to know he was police.

"It's important we know everything about what happened tonight, Willie," Schnack said, pulling a chair to sit with us at the table. "Anything that might be important."

I tried to hold my face steady, but I must have squirmed, cause Officer Lyle sat up almost immediately. "What is it?"

I waffled. On one hand, I knew almost certainly anything

I told them would make its way back to John Arrington. He'd know I'd lied about being in the Basin.

But that was nothing compared to what I'd just seen. There were bigger fish to fry.

I cleared my throat. "The other night, I was in the Basin . . . and the Game brought me to some graves."

Neither of them moved. Their eyes flickered between one another, but Officer Lyle didn't write anything down.

"I've tried this game three times now," I told them. "And it's worked every time."

"Got it," Schnack said slowly, stroking his mustache. "I see."

"People are gonna keep using it," I added.

We sat there a few seconds longer, both their faces blank, but they didn't ask any follow-up questions. Lyle stood, offered to get me another Sprite from the vending machine, and then they left. With the door cracked behind them, I could hear them whispering down the hall.

It sounded like they were laughing.

After ten minutes, I was free to go, and Officer Lyle walked me to the front door. "You can wait in the station 'til your mom gets here, but I think your friends are outside."

I could see Bones, Rodney, and Joe Kelly waiting on the front steps, each with a pop of their own in hand. The police were holding on to Joe Kelly's truck for the night, so they were all waiting to get picked up, talking over each other, eyes wide and excited. It was the first time any of us had ever been witnesses to anything.

Officer Lyle put a comforting hand on my shoulder. "Be careful out there, all right? If you're gonna keep playing with this thing, just . . . mind where it's sending you, okay?"

Something struck me, and I looked back past him, to the dark hallway of the station. "Where's Sarai?" I asked.

"Who?"

"The girl who found the body with me."

"Oh yeah," Lyle said, like it just struck him as well. "Lawton girl. She's still answering questions."

Neither of us moved. Something in the way he said it felt funny in my stomach, like he wasn't remembering her name on purpose. Like there was some reason she was just a Lawton girl and not Sarai. He didn't look bothered by it, though. He patted my shoulder for what had to have been the hundredth time, and I watched him walk back down the hallway and disappear, the clack of his shoes against the linoleum ringing the whole way down.

"Willie! Holy shit!" Bones leapt toward me as soon as I walked out. "Are you okay?"

"I got you a Sprite," Rodney offered, and I took it, trying not to look shook. "You were in there for a long time."

"Christ, fuck." Bones was keyed up and serious. "Did they try to stick it on you?"

"Stick it on me?"

"Think about it," Joe Kelly said. "Random kid goes to an abandoned mill in the middle of the night. All of a sudden, a dead body appears? That's pretty fucking suspicious."

"It didn't appear. . . ." I tried to say, but Bones was heated.

"I told you not to go in there!" he yelled. "I said it was a stupid idea, and now we gotta get a fucking lawyer so you don't get a murder charge—"

"You don't have to get a lawyer," Rodney said, straight to me.

"Yes, we do!" Bones raged. "That's how it fucking works. You get a lawyer who negotiates with the judge or one hundred percent they'll try and stick it on your broke ass—"

"Excuse me!"

A voice from across the street interrupted him, which was good, because most times when Bones got on a roll coming up with worst-case scenarios, he wouldn't stop until the world was in ashes. A brown-haired man, in brown pants and a brown jacket, jogged toward us—or rather, toward me.

"Are you William Eckles?"

Bones stepped in between us. "Depends who's asking."

Sweat flopped off the man's hair. "My name is Mitchell Ballis, and I write for the *Springfield Journal*."

"You're from Springfield?" Rodney asked. "That's two hours away. How'd you get here so quick?"

I realized I didn't know what time it was. Probably two a.m., maybe four.

"I was on the scanner tonight—I came as soon as I heard." He looked at me. "You're the one who discovered the body, right? That's what the deputy told me."

I looked to Bones. He nodded.

"Yes, sir," I said. "Me and Sarai."

"Were you able to identify it?"

"Yes," I said, and the whole circle leaned in, eyeballs first. I cleared my throat. "It was definitely a body."

"Oh, Jesus," Bones muttered.

"I'm sorry." Mitchell Ballis looked amused. "I mean, could you tell who it was? The deceased?"

"Oh, no, sorry. Just a bloody lump."

"White guy, Black guy?"

"White guy, I think, but it was dark, and we got the hell outta there."

He scribbled in the little notebook in front of him. Bones watched him.

"Why are you so interested?" Bones asked. "Is this gonna be in the paper?"

Mitchell Ballis nodded.

"Well, we were there, too. You could ask us some questions."

"You didn't even see the body!" I objected. "Besides, I was the one who wanted to play the Game in the first place."

Mitchell Ballis stopped writing. "The Game?"

We all froze for a half second. "It's a stupid phone thing," Bones said.

"Is that how you discovered the body?" Mitchell Ballis asked me. "A game on your phone?"

I could feel Bones glaring, so I kept my mouth shut. Thankfully, before he could ask anything else, a pair of headlights washed over Mitchell Ballis's glasses, and a wide silver car pulled down Main, right up to where we stood. Joe Kelly's dad, Bill Kelly, pulled himself out and slammed the door.

He was quiet as he walked over to us, and we were, too. There's some people you just don't speak in front of. Even in his pajamas, he looked like the mayor.

"Who's this?" Bill Kelly asked immediately.

"Mitchell Ballis, sir. I write for the *Springfield Journal*—"

"Holy hell. You're a reporter. And you're here doing what? Harassing children?"

"Just asked them a few questions, nothing uncomfortable—"

"Well, nice to meet you, Mitchell Ballis. I'm Bill Kelly. I'm the mayor here. And in Calico Springs, when someone goes through something traumatizing, we don't badger them about the details. We take care of them. We ask them if they're okay."

He looked back at the circle, maybe realizing that he hadn't asked any of us if we were okay yet.

"You can report on what the police officers tell you, because those are adults. But these are kids. Anything they say is off the record."

"I've already spoken with them, on the record—"

"You need me to get some officers out here to explain to you how privacy law works in Missouri?"

Mitchell Ballis gritted his teeth. "Understood. Nice to meet you, Mayor Kelly."

"You have a safe drive home now." Bill forced a smile and watched Mitchel Ballis walk all the way back across the street to his Buick and slam the door, before turning to put his arm around Joe. "You kids have had a long night. Rodney, Bones, Willie, y'all need a ride?"

"I'll go with the boys—" Rodney started to say.

"We're not going that way," Bones cut her off. It caught me off guard, but before I could ask, Bill volunteered. "We'll drop you off, it's no problem. Come on, Joe."

Joe didn't move. His eyes were fixed on the station, down the hallway. "Sarai's still in there," he said to his dad. "Can we wait for her to get done?"

Bill Kelly followed his gaze. "I've gotta be up for work in a couple hours, buddy. Who knows how long this'll take?"

"She went in same as us, she'll be done any minute."

"Her dad's probably already on his way. Sorry," he corrected himself, his tone sticky and condescending. "Her stepdad."

Joe didn't look convinced, but he didn't fight it. He'd told us a few times his dad had been weird about Sarai coming over to their house, and how he'd subtly talk trash on her family.

They said their goodbyes, and we watched them pull off, leaving just me and Bones in front of the station. The bars were closed for the night, so the only sounds were the distant pops of car engines on the highway. The only people out would be wandering around the twenty-four-hour Casey's, yakked out of their minds and looking for a G or a torch to light it with.

"What do you mean we're not going that way?" I asked. "Where's Mom?"

He spit into the bushes near us. "You shouldn't tell people about the Game," he said. "Not reporters, not police, not anybody."

"Why not?"

He looked at me like it was obvious. "'Cause it sounds like

you're making it up. And the only reason to make it up is if you've got something to hide."

"But lying about the Game is hiding something."

"Not in this case." He shook his head. "Lying's the only sane thing to do."

"But . . . aren't you scared?"

The question caught him off guard. He shook his head. "Scared of what?"

I lowered my voice. "We asked for something bloody—"

"So you told the fucking cops."

"I asked to see my future! That's three times now. This isn't a coincidence, it's fucking working."

"God dammit, Willie." He spit in the bush again. "You probably made yourself look guilty in there. Probably made all of us look guilty."

I shook it off, stiffened my lip, and ignored him, but in my head, I remembered how Schnack stared at me, like there was some part of my story that wasn't adding up.

"When's Mom gonna be here?" I asked again.

"I didn't call her."

"Why not?"

Bones snorted. "Sure, and give her another reason to be all paranoid about us?"

"Okay, well, can we at least wait for Sarai before we walk back? I don't trust those cops in there with her."

That stopped Bones completely. He looked at me sideways. "The fuck does that mean?"

"I don't know," I said. "I got a bad feeling. They couldn't even keep her name straight."

Bones took a second to think about that before shaking it off. "We're not her babysitters, Willie," he said. "And we're not walking, either."

As he said it, I heard an engine kick to life down the street and roar toward us, the sound rattling the stale storefronts on Main. Not thirty seconds later, Baby Blue came flying down the street, driving like the only car on the road.

"Hey, Dad!" Bones shouted as soon as he cut the engine.

Dad popped out of the truck full of energy, took two strong steps toward us, and grabbed me by the shoulders. His hair was freshly buzzed, down to the skin, and he was wearing an old flannel shirt, one of three or four he kept in steady rotation.

"Boys," he said, a smile hidden just below the intense stare. "I'm gonna get you the fuck outta here."

"We're already out, Dad," Bones laughed.

"No sons of my mine are gonna be thrown in this potshot, piece a' shit jail," he said, and marched toward the door to the station.

"Dad, we're fine," I said. "They told us we could go—"

He put his shoulder into the door and started shouting as soon as he was inside. "What right do you have to detain my sons? On what grounds? What crime has been committed?!"

Bones and I were both cracked up now, watching from the doorway as he slapped the desk at the front a few times.

"Hey there, Markie," Officer Lyle said, shaking his head.

"Take me. For God's sake, Lyle, just let my boys be free! I'm sure they didn't mean to kill nobody. And if they did, I'm sure they had a good reason."

"Your boys are fine," he said. "But you keep up with this shit, you might not be."

"You know something, Officer." Dad leaned his body on the front desk, full ham. "While you sit behind that desk . . . these boys are the real heroes."

"Go home, Markie. Before I start asking if you're all right to drive that truck."

Dad swiped a cigarette from behind Officer Lyle's ear, spun back to us, and winked.

"Come on, boys." He smiled. "I know a way better police station down the block."

CHAPTER 8

SOMETIMES WHEN DAD made a joke, it stopped being a joke pretty quick after.

"Fucking losers," he kept saying, as he flew along the overgrown asphalt on the east side of town. "You know they hauled my ass all the way down there once, just 'cause of a party in my own yard? My yard!" He swerved hard left. "You can't be disorderly in your own domain."

Bones was nodding along to the gospel, and I was in the jump seat, trying not to puke.

Dad had replaced the 42 on the dash with a new gun, a nicer and smaller one with some flames on the handle. It sat in the same spot, visible through the windshield for all to see, bumping with the suspension. Bones noticed it, too.

"Holy shit, Dad!" He grabbed it. "Look at this piece!"

"Hey," Dad barked. "Put that back up there. And quit saying *shit*. You're a kid."

Even from behind, I felt Bones bristle at it. Dad had a way of doing that, standing as close as he could to Bones to make him look small by comparison. Bones hated it every time, but still, he did as he was told.

Dad drove with little regard for the road. He'd spent his entire life in Calico, so he was used to streets like this, so empty you'd have to go way outta your way to hit something. He tapped the steering wheel with a manic rhythm. "So . . ." He adjusted the mirror to see me in the back seat. "Bones said you saw a body at the old mill?"

"Yeah," I told him. "It was up in the waterwheel."

He let out a low whistle. "Jesus. Nobody told you boys about the curfew or what?"

"Police said they weren't upset about the curfew, they got bigger fish to fry."

"Sure, that's what they tell you now. . . . You couldn't see who it was?"

I shook my head.

"Cops tell you anything?"

I shook my head again.

His eyes flickered up to the mirror. "What about the Lawton girl?"

I flinched. There it was again. I sat up. "You mean Sarai?"

"Sure," Dad said. "She know anything about it?"

I shook my head. "How would she know anything about it?"

"You never know." Dad shrugged. "Probably just some fucking drifter. God knows how long it's been up in there. Still . . ." He looked at me square. "It's not good to be getting wrapped up in shit like this, Willie. Lucky for you, your old man gets drunk with half the force, otherwise you might be in some real shit."

"Told you," Bones muttered.

Dad turned on him slow in the front seat. "And how come you didn't see it? Where were you?"

"I didn't go in the mill."

"Why not?"

"'Cause it was stupid. The water was up, you could barely get in."

He snorted. "But you let Willie go?"

I felt Bones's body tense. He lowered his voice. "I tried to stop him, but he just ran off—"

"And you let him? No part of you thought it might be dangerous for Willie to go down into the mill like that, with just some random girl from Lawton—"

"I told him a hundred times, I'm not gonna fucking tackle him—"

"You're supposed to look after him!" Dad near shouted. It had stopped being a joke. "And quit saying fuck. You're a kid."

Bones was steaming; I could hear it in how he was breathing. "I'm not a kid," he said defiantly, under his breath. "Willie's not, either."

Dad sat up in the driver's seat, gripping the wheel tight. "That's right. I forgot. You're an adult now. Except you don't have a job. You ain't paying rent, you ain't going to college, you can't look after your little brother—so what exactly are you good for? Huh?"

That shut Bones up completely. He just sat there in the

passenger seat, his head hanging as low as it could hang.

In Dad's eyes, Bones had committed a cardinal sin, maybe the most unforgivable—he'd failed to protect the family. In his book, there was only one way to really show somebody you loved them—you protected them. You stood up for them. You didn't let them take shit.

Even if they didn't need it.

Neither of them saw, not that they would have cared anyway, but in the back, I was steaming, too. My entire life, Dad had looked at me like I was hopeless, like losing my eye made me half a person. He talked about me in front of me like I needed constant surveillance and couldn't make decisions for myself. He loved to remind Bones that it was his lifelong job to look after me, on account of it was his fault I'd lost my eye, ignoring the fact that he was the one who left the gun out in the first place, where a seven-year-old could find it.

"I was fine on my own," I said, leaning toward the front seat. "I didn't need looking after."

But they both ignored me.

I sat up as Dad passed out of town to the south. There were a couple Airstreams along the road, squatters who moved in every spring when the snow melted, but mostly it was just trees and cows. After a mile, the roads all became gravel, a network of half-developed veins cutting through the hills, all sharp turns and dead ends.

I kept expecting Dad to pull in to one of the trailers, but

when he finally turned, it was onto a paved road, with a lit-tle stone sign that read "The Estates." I'd never been up here before, only heard about it—I usually figured these houses were reserved for just the real rich folks.

Bones and I stuck our faces to the glass, marveling as we pulled into a driveway. "This is your house?" he asked.

"All two thousand square feet." Dad smirked in the front seat.

It was massive, at least twice the size of our house, and brand-new. Dad pulled into a big garage that smelled like plas-ter and jumped out before us. "I'm not the only one who's missed you, you know," he said. He flung the door to the house open, and Libby, our basset hound, came bounding toward us.

"LIBBY!"

Libby followed us in, nipping at our heels. It felt even bigger on the inside. The living room was two stories tall, with brand-new furniture sitting around in plastic wrap. "Technically it's a rental. I haven't even had the time to move in," Dad explained as he tore the plastic off a couch for us to sit on. "Been working so damn much, I'm basically full-time at the developments now. You wouldn't believe how much money some of these contractor guys make."

I watched Bones take it in, marveling at the size and the smell of everything. Dad came back from the kitchen with a few cans of Miller Lite and handed one to Bones, then paused, looking at me.

"How old are you now?"

"Fifteen," I said.

"You probably think beer tastes like piss."

"No way. I like it."

"You like piss?" Dad said and roared with laughter as he handed me the can. I cracked it and took a baby sip. It was sticky and warm.

He sat down opposite us in a new, squeaky leather recliner. "Great game the other night, by the way," he said to Bones, tipping his beer. "Like I always told you, pummel 'em with the heat right away. They'll never recover."

Bones's lip twitched. We both looked at him sideways. Dad was prone to bad jokes, but this was particularly cruel.

"What?" he asked, like he had no idea what he'd said.

"Nothing." Bones shook his head.

"You didn't see me? Shit, I was on that ump's ass for you the entire first inning—"

"Yeah, no, I saw you."

Dad took a long, contemplative sip of his beer, then sighed and stared at us. "What about your mom, then?" he asked. "How's she doing?"

It was only a matter of time before he asked. I knew all this— picking us up, the big house, the new furniture—it was a show for us to report back to Mom. Dad knew how she was doing; that's not what he was asking. He wanted to know how we felt about the new arrangement. He was fishing for an answer, a confirmation that life wasn't going on without him.

"Not great," Bones said, giving it to him. "She doesn't do

anything, really. Just goes to church, comes home, watches TV."

Dad nodded, satisfied. "I been keeping up on my *Criminal Minds*. I can get it on my phone now."

"I don't even know why she kicked you out in the first place," Bones said. "She's just pissed all the time."

But Dad smiled. "No need for that. She'll come around when she comes around. No sense tryna tell a smart woman what to do, she always knows better." He ran his hand over his scalp. "Maybe when my hair grows back in. Or maybe by my birthday. Tradition's tradition. I ain't letting this little hiccup get in the way of my birthday barbecue. Maybe you all come out here, we do it in this backyard. . . ."

I fell back into the couch, my body shutting down but my brain still on fire. I half listened as Dad and Bones started talking construction and politics. A couple beers later, he was nodding off, so Bones and I found a quilted blanket, put our heads on opposite sides of the couch, and lay down in silence. Every time either of us tried to shift our body, the new leather squeaked, so we both lay there, frozen.

Before too long, Bones was snoring in harmony with Dad, and I was alone, sucking in the recycled air. I closed my eyes, begging them to stay closed.

I've never been able to sleep places that aren't my bed. I stay up all night, checking the doors and windows, waiting for something terrible to happen. It's the kind of thing you hear from people who spent years in combat, or got kidnapped, or some otherwise horrifying event. For me, I'm back at the hospital. I'm trapped in my body, unable to move, covered in blood, stuck in the darkness, watching life slip away from me.

Sometime later, it could have been an hour, it could have been three, I started to feel a soft shaking. I clutched the edge of the couch, felt its legs shuffle against the hardwood below me. I looked up; the giant light fixture overhead was starting to shake and squeak; the front door rattled against the frame.

I checked the other two. Dad was still out cold on the recliner, Bones too, so I stayed frozen, looking out the tall window behind my head.

It wasn't just the house . . . the whole ground was moving. Down the road that led to the river, trees were trying to flee their roots. I'd felt this before, once, when I was eight. During a thunderstorm, the river had gotten too high, and it pushed up over the levees. Me and Bones, Mom and Dad, clung to each other in the upstairs bathroom, watching the water rock the foundation of our house.

I stared at the opening in the trees, where I knew the flood was coming.

When it came, the wave was slow, intentional, swelling as it moved toward us. I lay paralyzed in place, nothing to do but let it wash over me. As it inched closer, it started to flush with color, murky, sticky . . . red. It wasn't water. It was blood, flooding the streets of Calico Springs.

The wave crashed onto the road and shot outward in all directions, sending debris everywhere. A chunky, discarded mess rushed toward us and struck the bottom of the house, a mess of hair and bones—it was a body, just like the one in the Calico Mill. Not just one, dozens. The wave of blood continued to roll down the street, leaving a graveyard in its wake. As I looked across the wreckage, I saw that each body was marked, glowing soft blue, blinking, a target marker—

And with one heavy gasp, it was all gone.

The house was silent.

Bones shifted slightly, the soft cry of the couch reminding me I was awake. I took a few more deep breaths. Out the window, an innocent wind pushed tree branches back and forth. No blood, no bodies.

It was a dream. Not like a regular dream, though; I could still feel every detail of it. I was still living in its logic, the same exact view out the window.

Because it was more than a dream, I realized. It was a vision, a confirmation of what I already knew. Something terrible was coming for Calico Springs. And it was coming from the Game.

I couldn't go back to sleep, so instead, I lay with my eye open, staring at the window, waiting for the sun.

MANIFEST ATLAS is a hypothesis and a revolution in brain science. It leads users in the direction of their intentions, using the power of their own mind.

Can human consciousness influence the outcome of events in the physical universe? Can human beings manifest their intentions?

QUANTUM PHYSICS tells us that physical matter, when viewed at the smallest possible level, is not made up of atoms but of waves. Nothing about our reality is defined. Everything is changeable.

MIND-MATTER INTERACTION studies have demonstrated time and again that humans have the ability to influence the future by directing the power of their consciousness toward a given outcome.

MANIFEST ATLAS is a tool to concentrate and direct the power of human consciousness.

The only limit to **MANIFEST ATLAS** is the mind of the user.

CHAPTER 9

WHEN MOM PICKED us up in the morning, she didn't yell. Her face was puffy, like she'd been crying, but she didn't say anything. She hugged us as we walked out of the house, nodded to Dad, and drove us home. She had breakfast waiting, Hy-Vee donuts and bacon, and sat at the kitchen table, watching us eat, careful not to say anything that sounded like she was mad. It was like we'd broken her.

"We're all going to the river after school," Bones said, testing the waters. "Last day tradition. All the seniors swim out to the sand bar, take a big picture . . ."

Mom nodded quietly. "That's fine."

He took a few more bites. "We didn't realize the curfew was such a big deal last night. And the cops said it didn't matter, we weren't gonna get in trouble, anyway—"

"It's okay," she said again. "I'm just happy you're okay."

We ate in silence. Mom was playing with a napkin on the table, folding it over and back. Her brain was like that, always organizing, setting something straight. It was kinda eerie, actually, how quiet she was being. When she finally did say something, it was to me.

"So you were playing a game, it told you to go to the mill, and the body was just . . . there?"

I nodded.

"How did it know?" she asked.

"It didn't," Bones said, his mouth full. "It's a coincidence."

Mom looked to me. I thought about what Bones had said the night before, about telling people about the Game, and shrugged.

"I mean . . . it's an incredible coincidence, right?" she asked. "It took you directly—"

"It's not magic," Bones interjected.

"Not magic. I mean . . . are you sure somebody didn't know there was a body there? And then, I don't know . . . tell the game?"

Her phone started buzzing on the table.

SARAH CHURCH

"Your girlfriend's calling," Bones pointed out.

Sarah was one of Mom's friends from the church, a lady from Lawton who drove over for every service, Bible study, and choir. Lately, Mom had been staying after, hanging out with Sarah— she'd even come to the house a few times. She was short, Black, Mom's age, but seemed older because she was always offering people candy. It was the first time I saw her spend time with somebody other than Dad, ever, really. She picked up the phone and disappeared into the living room.

"She's pissed, dude," Bones said, as soon as she was gone.

"She just said we could go to the river," I pointed out.

"It's an act. Trust me, she's giving us the silent treatment. This is DEFCON five."

I didn't say anything and started packing my backpack. Mom could be emotional. I'd seen her go quiet on Dad like this a few times, but this didn't feel like that. She wasn't avoiding us, and she didn't look angry. She just wasn't talking. If anything, she looked scared.

When she came back into the kitchen, she'd painted on a smile and went straight to grab both our hands. "Let's pray, before you go."

Bones's eyes flashed toward me. I couldn't remember the last time we'd prayed as a family, apart from meals, and even that we'd been skipping most of the time.

Mom took both our hands and bowed her head, so we did the same.

"Dear God," she said, nearly squeezing the blood outta my fingers. "I ask that you watch over my sons and keep them safe. Empower them to make good decisions. We know we can't stop bad things from happening, Lord, but we ask that when they do, you give us the power to protect one another. And we ask as always that you deliver us from evil. For thine is the kingdom, and the power, and the glory. Amen."

The lunchroom on the last day was a rare kind of high. The doors were open, fresh air blowing through, and they were pumping classic rock hits through the speakers. Even teachers were getting in on the fun, playing cards and taking selfies with the students.

Me, Bones, and Rodney were huddled at a table by the dishwasher.

"Other than the cryptic-ass website, there's nothing about the company who made the Game online. No website, no LinkedIn, nothing. But that doesn't mean we're the only ones playing. . . ."

Rodney had already gone even deeper into the internet than me. I watched over her shoulder as she clicked through what looked like a hundred tabs open on her laptop and landed on a blacked-out website with a neon-green border.

"SECRET ATLAS," it read at the top.

"There are forums, where other players post their experiences. I made a profile to snoop around—"

"Hot Rod?" I read over her shoulder.

She shrugged. "I thought people might respond more if it sounded like a boy."

She started scrolling, posts and names and profiles flying past faster than I could keep up with. "There's some really, really crazy shit on here. Dozens of posts, mostly people swearing the Game worked for them or describing crazy experiences . . ."

Words flashed past as she scrolled—*creepy, lost, inexplicable, dead.* My head spun as I imagined each of them a story like ours. The Game wasn't just spreading, it had already spread.

"Do they know anything about it?" I asked.

"There's debate on the individual stories, but nobody can

figure out how it works. Literally, there are computer programmers on here who are trying to reverse engineer the build of the app and getting nothing. I was actually thinking it might make a good project for my program at Mizzou."

Bones groaned loudly. He'd been sitting quietly across the table for the entire conversation. "Do we have to work on college research projects now?" he asked. "It's our last day of high school, ever. We should be drinking it in."

He gestured to the rest of the room, to all the other tables that looked like parties, the smiling, beet-red faces and TikTok dances.

"Do you think they know yet?" Rodney asked. "About the body?"

"No." Bones shook his head. "When they know, we'll know. Trust me."

The police had asked each of us not to talk about it until they made an official statement, as it was still an open investigation. Mom told us they wouldn't say anything until they'd identified the body, but we knew it was only a matter of time. This was Calico Springs, everybody had a cousin or an aunt at City Hall, and everybody loved a dead body.

Joe Kelly's tray was nearly empty as he approached our table, a single slice of pizza and a carton of white milk. Neither had been touched. "Where's Sarai?" he asked.

Rodney and I shook our heads, and his face imploded.

"Really? No one's heard from her?"

"We have trig after lunch," Rodney offered. "I can check in—"

"I've been to her locker like five times," he said. "She's not at school. And she's not responding to texts, either."

I felt my stomach turn over, the sickly feeling from the night before coming back. Immediately, in my head, I saw the long hallway of the police station, disappearing into darkness, the last place I'd seen Sarai.

"I'm sure it's fine," Rodney said, clearly unsure. "After the night she had, I wouldn't wanna come to school, either."

"She probably just ditched the last day," Bones added. "Once you've got enough days, they can't hold you back for attendance, she knows that."

The table got quiet. I could see they were turning over the same thought I was. There was no reason for the cops to keep her overnight . . . unless they thought she had something to do with it.

Joe Kelly hadn't moved, staring blankly at his tray. "You don't think she blames herself, does she?" he asked. "I mean, it'd be stupid, but . . ."

"Blames herself for what?" Rodney asked.

Joe cleared his throat. "She was the one who asked for 'something bloody'—"

"Is it true?" Our table rocked as a junior boy, Matt Kerry, threw his hands down on it and looked wildly between us. "You don't gotta tell everybody, but my brother's a cop." He lowered his voice. "Y'all found a body in the mill?"

Joe Kelly looked around the circle before turning back to Matt. "Don't know what you're talking about, buddy."

Matt looked past him to Bones. "Aw, come on, Bones, you can tell me. . . ."

"We don't know shit, Matt," Joe said again and shooed him away, but it didn't help. Right away, I started to feel eyes on us, the gravity of the room sucked in our direction. Every time I saw Matt, he was at a different table. The word was getting out.

Joe Kelly noticed it, too. "We have to protect her," he said, huddling us together. "People are gonna find out about the body . . . but we don't tell anybody about the Game. Especially, especially—we don't tell them that she asked for it."

By the time we got to the river after school, all of Calico High knew about the body in the mill.

It was all anybody was talking about, and as a result, the whole mood was sideways. Everybody looked like they were partying, there were beer cans and bathing suits, but the conversations were hushed and damp. Even the weather agreed—it was unusually cold and gray, occasional wind punishing anybody who dared to get wet. Some people were trying to ignore it, pushing on with the summer, but others stood around, looking disturbed and whispering rumors.

Nobody was more pissed about it than Bones. I watched him stalk around, trying and failing to get people excited about the impending summer. Finally, he went straight for the Bluetooth speaker, killing the sound and jumping on a log. "Hey, hey." He waved around at everyone. "I just wanna get this outta the way. Yes, we found a body last night, at the Calico Mill."

Everybody turned. He had the party's full attention.

"Yes, it fell from the waterwheel, and, yes, it was an extremely difficult experience for all of us. I personally know that I will never be the same. I'd just ask that you respect our privacy and not ask a shit ton of questions, to me, or Joe Kelly, or Rodney, or my little brother, Willie. Just take it easy on us, all right, and, uh . . ." He raised a can of Natty Light. "Let's try to celebrate?"

A few people cheered, he kicked the music back on, and the crowd descended on us. People I hadn't talked to in years, girls I would have sworn didn't know my name, suddenly swirling, trying to get a question in between everybody else.

What did it look like? Are you okay? Was it a murder? What were you doing?

I looked over at Bones, who was milking the shit out of it. At the moment, he was talking to Samantha Lyle, a senior from the volleyball team in jorts and a one-piece swimsuit. Sam Lyle had famously dated Tyler Arrington when she was a freshman, which made her an honorary Dirtbag, and she still went to their parties.

"What did it look like?" she was asking him. "Could you see the face?"

"It was fucking terrifying," he said, lying his ass off. "In person, dead bodies are just so much more alive, you know?"

I listened for a while as he told her the story, invented details so casually tossed in with the real ones that it didn't make sense to keep track anymore. I couldn't believe how quickly he'd flipped. Yesterday he was begging me to keep this whole thing a secret, and today he was turning it into a major motion picture. Anything for the story, I suppose.

I slipped away down the beach to try to find Rodney, but didn't see her anywhere. I made three laps before I finally wandered back to the truck and saw Joe Kelly and Rodney huddled near his car.

"What?" I asked as I approached.

"Her phone's off." Rodney grimaced. "We've been trying all day. It just started going to voice mail."

Joe Kelly wasn't saying anything, just glaring back at the beach where everyone else was hanging out. I looked a little closer and saw it was Bones he was watching. "We have to keep this quiet," he repeated. "This could get really, really bad for her."

"We're gonna go drive past her house," Rodney said. "Just see if we can make sure she's home."

"I wanna come," I said. "Just let me go tell Bones."

Rodney looked to Joe, who didn't argue, so she nodded.

When I found Bones, he was still completely zeroed in on Sam Lyle. They'd moved on from the dead body, and he was telling her a story about some party at a baseball tournament last year. As I approached, I saw him take his phone from his pocket, eyes up the whole time, and ignore a call without looking away from her once.

"Bones," I said, and he glanced at me, shaking his head so slightly that unless you were looking for it, you wouldn't notice.

"Gimme a minute, Willie."

I rocked back on my heels and waited. Behind me, I heard another phone ringing, loud iPhone chimes. I turned, looking for the source of it, and saw that over in the parking lot, Rodney's phone was to her ear, too.

Bones's phone buzzed again.

CALL FROM: MOM

Again, he ignored it. All up and down the beach now, phones were ringing, faces were twisting in confusion. I heard someone shouting but couldn't make it out. Something was happening.

I took out my own phone and dialed Mom. She answered on the first ring.

"What's going on?" I asked.

She was crying on the other end.

"I'm sorry," she choked. "I just, uh. The police just put out a statement. The body you found . . ."

She heaved, and the signal dropped. Cell service sucked at the beach; I was only getting her voice in fits and starts. I spun as I tried to listen, landing on Joe Kelly. He had his phone to his ear; his face was pure white.

". . . to the head . . . did it himself . . . and I just wanted to tell you and Bones I love you."

"Who was it?" I asked urgently. "You cut out."

"It was Winston," she choked. She took another huge breath. I could hear her putting on a brave face. "It was Winston Lewis. Your friend's stepdad."

Posted on: May 12

STATEMENT FROM THE

CALICO SPRINGS POLICE DEPARTMENT

CALICO SPRINGS, MO—At 1:23 a.m. on Friday, May 12, Calico Springs PD responded to a call from the Calico Mill regarding unidentified human remains. There, they recovered the body of WINSTON LEWIS from the Calico Mill, declared dead at the scene.

Cause of death has been determined as a gunshot to the head. Calico Springs is investigating the circumstances of his death, but at this time, no foul play is suspected.

The family confirms his memorial will be held on MAY 17 at GRACE BAPTIST CHURCH.

do NOT play manifest atlas

> **CaliJane402: DO NOT PLAY MANIFEST ATLAS.**
THERE IS A MALEVOLENT FORCE, BE IT HUMAN OR
OTHERWISE, BUT IT HAS A PURPOSE FOR THIS GAME.

this is dead ass true, and before any of you come for me, I
dont care if you believe me bc i just need this to get out there.

I am deleting the game. I am begging all of you to do the
same.

as many of you know, I started playing manifest atlas with
Steven about a year ago. I know he was super active on here but
I dont think he ever told you about why we started playing in the
first place.

Long before we found this forum, long before
@whataboutsteven as you know him. we had our own reasons.
Not to be tmi but steven and I liked to be risky about our business
if you know what i mean. so manifest atlas was perfect. we would
use it to find places where it felt crazy to hook up and do it. Parks,
hiking trails, alleys. no lie we had sex in like four parking garages.

Fast forward six months, we broke up. the details dont matter
but it was super heart breaking and neither of us really wanted it
but thats life. so yeah. everything sucked without him. that's life.

little by little i tried to put it back together. i moved in with my
sister, I blocked him on all my socials, i went back to school. he
did the same, or so i thought.

a few weeks ago, I showed my sister MA. she's younger

than me, and she liked it mostly bc she just moved here, so it was cool for us to get out and explore. one time, the game brought us to this hiking trail. I know it's mid, esp compared to what some of the people on here have experienced. but it was exciting to us.

I kept playing. i know its corny but i started to feel like myself again. one night, i even felt comfortable enough to ask the game for what I really wanted. LOVE.

the game brought us to this strip mall in my town. I know you guys don't know Kinsberg, but if you know someone from here, they know what i'm talking about. there's this random strip mall that's way off in the middle of nowhere, and nobody even really knows why they built it in the first place bc it's so remote, and the only store that is still open is a dollar general, and even that store closes early.

so me and my sister pull up, and we see there's a bunch of cars in the back. RIGHT where the blue dot was. We drove a little closer and we could see there was people like hanging around. I'm not new, I know kinsberg can get messy so we didn't go over there. So we just sorta watched.

And then, not five minutes later, a cop pulls up on us. He turned his lights on right behind me.

WE FREAK OUT, we get out of the car, but the cop doesn't stop. he speeds over to where the other cars are. we were not trying to stay for that shit so we pulled off.

the next morning, I check twitter. THERE WAS A SHOOTING. AT THAT STRIP MALL. SOMEBODY GOT SHOT.

THE GAME TRIED TO BRING ME TO AN ACTIVE. FUCKING. SHOOTING.

I showed it to my sister. We were so freaked out. It felt like fucked up, like it was on purpose.

but that could have been a coincidence. INSANE but maybe a game error or something.

It wasn't until the next day when I realized that the game is actually truly evil. Either whoever made it is playing the real world like its the fucking Sims—

—or its something much much much fucking worse.

the victim was steven.

he was the one who got shot. i asked for LOVE and the game brought me right back to him—then took him away.

> **Tiger45:** . . . .

> **Callientina:** 🧢 🧢 🧢

> **YourDad:** are you single then?

> **KatieBug12:** yours is not the only story. do NOT play this game.

> **HotRod:** Where is Kinsberg?

> **CaliJane402:** missouri

> **HotRod:** DM me?

CHAPTER 10

WHEN SOMEBODY DIES, they're everybody's friend.

I couldn't believe how many people had something to say about Winston's death. Half the churches, restaurants, and banks in town changed their signs out front to offer tribute. Facebook was flooded with messages of condolences, every minor memory of Winston Lewis—town hero, local savior. Even Joe Kelly said he'd walked in on his dad, who'd hated Winston when he was alive, saying a prayer for his family and his soul.

Mom took it harder than almost anybody. She couldn't even talk about it, other than to remind us over and over how she'd just seen him, he'd just been at the house. Instead of making dinner, she sent us to Cherry Street for grilled cheese, but when we brought it back, she didn't touch her sandwich. It sat there on the arm of the couch while she scrolled Facebook and cried.

"I didn't realize she cared that much," Bones said as we ate alone in the garage. "I doubt she'd cry like that if I died."

Dad had called both me and Bones, too, to make sure we

were okay. He didn't seem nearly as bothered. "It happens around here," he told me, matter-of-fact. "People get to feeling their life's a tragedy, and they do something stupid they can't take back."

Bones thought the same way, even going so far as to complain about how hammy people were being online about it. How people died all the time and nobody made this big a deal.

It was midnight when we finally heard from Sarai. Joe Kelly had driven by her house twice, both times reporting there was a police car in the driveway. She finally texted to let him know she was safe and with her family. She hadn't been responding because she was pissed we'd all left her behind at the station. She said they'd told her she could go outside with her friends, and we were all gone. Joe Kelly called Bones to let us know, and it took him two minutes to go from panicking about her well-being to complaining about her unrealistic expectations.

I knew people who had died before. A couple teachers, friends' brothers, but never like this, never a suicide. This was different, even Bones knew that. Winston was different. He was involved, he had a job and friends and shit to live for. It made it all so hard to believe.

And some people didn't.

There were other posts on Facebook, ones with hundreds of comments, so much activity that the algorithm put them on everybody's feeds. *"THEY SAY NO FOUL PLAY. . . ."* a woman named Suanne from Lawton wrote, attaching a screenshot of the police's statement all circled and underlined. *"BUT THEY*

WON'T SAY IT WAS SUICIDE???? *This is how they do it folks. Plausible deniability."* Another was more blunt and brought up Sarai's mom. *"He got Killed for marrying a Black woman from Lawton. Period."*

Both posts were flooded with comments from both sides of the river, telling them to shut the hell up, saying it wouldn't help with the healing, and besides, there was no proof of anything, anyway.

But I knew something they didn't.

I hardly slept that night, turning it over in my head.

The body in the mill hadn't been there for ages, like Dad had suggested. Winston Lewis had been alive and well only three days ago. Which meant whatever happened, happened in the seventy-two hours between the garage sale and the mill. Something in the universe had changed. That change had caused Winston's body to be there when Sarai and I went looking for it.

Maybe the Game was more powerful than I thought. Maybe it wasn't just capable of finding things in the universe—but changing the way things happened.

Which would mean the Game didn't just find Winston Lewis. It might have killed him.

"You think he got murdered by an evil app?" Abe asked.

"I didn't say exactly that—"

"Yeah, I've seen this movie before. I hate to ruin it for you, but it sucked."

It was just me and Abe at the shop the next morning,

surprisingly quiet for the first day of summer, so he was helping me put the rental kayaks in the water, in case things turned around.

"Do you wanna know the ending? They delete the app. Problem goes away."

"I didn't say the app was evil," I explained, never sure if he was really listening. "I said it works. It can create things in the universe. Good things, evil things, doesn't matter."

"Huh." Abe nodded. "Like a genie."

Abe was only a couple years older than me, a senior at Lawton, but he lived more like an adult than any kid I'd ever met. He had his own car, he basically ran his dad's business, he even had an older girlfriend who owned a house, but I'd never met her because she never came to visit him at the store.

"So you're saying Sarai sets this intention . . . and all of a sudden, her stepdad turns his truck around, drives out to the mill, and shoots himself?"

"Maybe not exactly like that," I said.

"Then exactly like how?"

He waited for me to answer.

"Okay." I sat back against a pole, thinking. "Like this. Let's say he was supposed to go to a meeting at City Hall. But when he gets there, turns out the meeting got delayed, so he figures 'That's fine, I'll go to Leo's to wait for a little bit,' and he gets a little drunk.

"Now he has to drive back, but they're doing that construction on Poplar, so he has to take the long way, and he realizes—he's been wanting to take a picture of the mill for the library's photo contest. So he drives out to the mill. On the way out, he realizes he's got his gun with him. Usually he keeps his gun locked up in a gun safe at his house, but they've got mold at his house, so he had to take it to get it cleaned. He gets to the mill and gets nervous, but hey—he's got his gun, right?—so he brings it out with him.

"Then he's walking down to go get his picture, and all of a sudden, a bunch of birds fly up! He gets freaked out, accidentally fires . . . and that's it."

Abe thought about it for a surprisingly long time, working quietly as he did.

"So . . . in your mind . . . the Game can control the City Hall schedule, the mold in his house . . . and the flight of the birds on the river?"

I winced. It didn't sound as compelling when he repeated it.

"Naw, man," he said eventually, tying off the last boat. "It's not an evil game. But it's not his fault, either. If anything killed him . . . it's the curse."

He gave the knot a final yank with extra violence and started back toward the shop, so I followed him.

"The curse?" He ignored me, so I kept following. "What curse?"

He looked amused. "My bad, I thought this was common knowledge. You ever notice how Calico Springs has a history of crazy deaths?"

I shrugged. I knew our life expectancy was lower than the

state average, they told us that in health class, thanks to the pill mills. "You mean the ODs?" I asked.

"Not the ODs," Abe said. "Insane deaths. Unexpected ones— fishing accident, drowning, murder." He paused. "Suicide. Way more than other towns."

"Bones told me about the lady who jumped off the bridge—"

"Which one? Three people have jumped off that bridge since the store has been here. You ever google 'Calico Springs homicide'?"

I shook my head.

"Save your innocence." We got inside the shop and he stopped at the counter to look at me pityingly. "I take no joy in telling you this, but it's not a coincidence . . . it's a punishment."

"For what?" I asked.

He smirked. "Seriously, no one's ever told you about this before? It's your own town's history." Abe looked to the door, still not a customer in sight, and leaned against the counter. "Well, first of all, you know Calico Springs used to be all Black, right?"

I squinted at him. "No it didn't."

"Yes, sir. That's why it exists in the first place. A hundred fifty years ago, it was settled by a bunch of freed slaves, moving north along the river after slavery ended. They found this little bend, built a mill, and called it Calico Springs. Like, the material?"

He raised an eyebrow at me, but I didn't say anything.

"Then a hundred years ago, a group of white people showed

up and claimed the town was theirs. They built a bunch more mills, started trying to take the town over. Finally, one night, they got a mob together and ran them out—ran *us* out—across the river."

My stomach churned. It wasn't any story of Calico Springs I'd ever heard, and I'd heard most of them. "My dad's family's been here five generations," I corrected him. "That's way more than a hundred years. We have a Civil War monument. That's more than a hundred years old—"

"And what side of that war were they on, huh?" Abe smirked at me. "I'm surprised nobody at your school ever told you this. That's why the towns are separated. 'Cause y'all stole the land."

My chest burned hotter as he pointed at me, like suddenly this was my fault.

"Anyway, as the story goes, on the night they were running the Black people outta town, there wasn't a single cloud in the sky, until—bam. Outta nowhere, there's a crack of thunder, and it starts *dumping* water. So much water, flooded the river, and destroyed downtown Calico. And of course, you know what that was, right?"

I clenched my teeth.

"It was God putting a curse on the land under Calico Springs . . . that no life there would ever prosper."

He let the last few words linger, then smiled, satisfied, waiting for my reaction. It was a scary story, except for one fact—

"I live in Calico Springs," I told him. "And God saved me."

Abe stopped in his tracks to laugh out loud.

"I'm serious," I said. "You just made all that up. God wouldn't do that. He doesn't have any reason to punish Calico Springs."

"You're sure about that?" Abe said, shook his head, and kept on his way out back again. "Call it what you want. But that's why your game's all fucked up. You're playing on cursed land."

He said it with a smirk, which made me realize the whole thing might be a joke.

Still, the rest of my shift, I felt my eyes drifting back to the bridge, to the river. People talked about Calico Springs like there was something wrong with it, some invisible force we were all at war with. You don't get out, that's what they said. You get along. Maybe there was a reason for that. Maybe there was something we'd done to piss off God, and we were still paying the price.

CHAPTER 11

I'D ONLY BEEN home for an hour that afternoon when there was a knock at the door. Bones was still at practice and Mom was on the phone, so I answered, expecting another one of our neighbors had gotten tricked into selling energy drinks, but instead, Sarai was waiting, a bandana tied around her head and her forehead covered in sweat.

"You're alive," I said.

She took a small bow.

"Bones isn't here. I can text him—"

She shook her head. "I came to talk to you, actually."

I suddenly became aware of every sweat gland in my body. She looked over my shoulder to where Mom was hovering in the doorway to the kitchen, watching us.

"Hi, Mrs. Eckles, I'm Sarai—" she started to say, but it was all the invitation Mom needed. She nearly ran at her, wrapping her in a huge hug. "I'm so sorry," she sobbed into Sarai's shoulder. As the hug lingered, it started to feel like Sarai was the one consoling her. "He was such a good man," Mom said.

"You know, he was just here. . . ."

When the marathon hug ended, Sarai smiled at her, then looked to me. "Maybe we can talk out back?"

Even though she was a junior, Sarai was only a year older than me, on account of she had skipped kindergarten. I was intimidated as I followed her around the side of the house. Aside from Rodney, I didn't really talk to girls. There was a girl in my grade, Cara, who asked me to be her boyfriend online in fifth grade and still sometimes texted me about homework. Then there was Rodney's friend Caroline, who I sometimes got paired up with on group outings. We'd gone to the prom together with everyone, but she usually spent most of the time looking for chances to talk to other people. Hanging out with Sarai alone, a girl who wanted to talk to me, was a new ball game.

"Where have you been?" I asked.

"My house. The police wouldn't let us leave for two days, so they could give us updates."

"I thought you got arrested," I told her.

Sarai smirked, stretching out as she sat on the picnic table in our backyard. Dad had taken it after it was retired from Cotton Park and painted it Calico red and white, but after ten years, it had sunned-out to a pink pastel in the midday sun.

"They wanted to," she said. "Who's that one cop, with the mustache?"

"Deputy Schnack."

Her lip twitched. "Yeah. Him."

It was intense, I realized, how put together she was. She was living through the saddest thing I'd ever heard of in real life. I wondered if she'd talked to anyone outside her family for two days, or even more insanely, why she'd chosen me to start.

"What can I do for you?" I asked, taking a seat on the bench.

She readjusted, staring forward for a long minute. "My whole family's staying with us. My mom's sisters, their kids, Winston's brother and sister, their kids . . . They're all at his house. . . ." She flinched as she corrected herself. "Our house. It's so weird. I'd never met half of them before, and now it's like . . . what are we supposed to say? 'Sorry'? 'It's not our fault'? Nobody knew what to say, so nobody really said anything.

"Everybody was being real nice to each other. Trying to be normal. But then there's just this cop sitting outside. They had a car in our driveway for the whole day—three straight shifts. Every time they'd switch, the new cop would come in, say hi, my aunts would offer him coffee . . . and then while they were making it, I overheard them just casually . . . asking him questions."

I flinched. "Questions?"

Sarai nodded slowly. "They were all trying to play it cool, like they didn't wanna say too much or imply anything, especially in front of my mom . . . but it was like they knew something wasn't adding up. *Where'd the gun come from? Where was he that night?*—"

"Why'd he drive all the way out to the mill?" I suggested, before thinking better of it.

Sarai's jaw froze for a second, but it melted quickly. "Yeah, like that. It was kinda like they didn't wanna say there was even a chance he didn't kill himself . . . but they also didn't believe he actually did."

My throat suddenly felt dry as I realized the weight of what she was telling me. If he didn't do it himself, that meant someone—or something—else had.

"What did the police say?" I asked.

"They kept giving us the same line—*No reason to think it's foul play, gonna investigate anyway.* Hours went by, same thing . . . no matter how many questions we asked, it was just, *We'll look into it, we'll see, trust me, we'll figure all of it out. . . .*

"And then last night, outta nowhere, they just left. The car in the driveway just pulled off. My aunt Bella was the only one who saw it, and she ran out onto the lawn in her bare feet to stop him, but when she got there, he just cracked the window and said, *We investigated. No reason to think it's foul play.* Like a fucking prerecorded message."

The edge of her mouth twitched again, her anger vivid and under control. "Except my room is in the front of the house, next to the driveway. So if I opened my window, I could hear their radio the whole time. . . . They weren't doing shit. They were fucking around, I could hear them laughing."

Sarai took a deep breath, set her eyes on the horizon, where it cut between the houses on the other side of our yard. "Now everybody at the house is just sitting there. They don't wanna go home, but they don't know where else to go, what else to do."

"What's your mom think?" I asked.

Sarai's lips pressed tighter, like whatever she had to say, she didn't wanna say it. She shook her head and ignored the question.

"They're all planning the service, going on like it's nothing. I can tell they all want answers, but no one can do anything about it . . . except for me."

Sarai took her eyes from the horizon and looked down at me for the first time. I sat up, my heart pounding in my chest.

"'Cause I have something they don't," she continued. "I have a lead."

"I told the police about the graves," I said quickly. "They already know . . ."

"Did you feel like they took you seriously?" she asked.

I remembered vividly hearing Lyle and Schnack talking in the hallway outside my questioning room. They didn't bother writing it down. They were probably laughing about it now.

"No." I shook my head. "They didn't."

"Well, it seems to me," she said, "like if you were gonna kill somebody . . . you'd probably wanna dig a grave."

She hopped down off the picnic table and stood over me, nodding to her van at the front. "You think you could find them again?"

Sarai drove her mom's blue Ford Aerostar minivan. It looked weathered from road trips and fast-food stops, and had a booster seat in the back, for her little sister, she said.

"My mom and Winston got pregnant after a couple dates. That's why they got married so fast. She's three now. Elsa."

"How's she doing?" I asked.

Sarai shrugged. "My aunt keeps saying she doesn't understand it, but it's because they didn't actually explain it to her yet. They told her he was golfing for the first couple hours. Now they've tried to tell her he's gone for good, but she keeps arguing with them about it. She thinks he's still golfing."

I winced, imagining what it would be like to explain death to a child. "Did you like him?" I asked.

It made Sarai laugh. "My dead stepdad?"

"Is that not cool to ask?"

"No." She shook her head. "You're just the first person to ask it. No, not at first. I figured he was like everybody over here. Full of shit, talked too loud, vaguely racist all the time. And his house is so big and ugly . . ."

"But I guess he grew on me." Her face tightened. "He loved my mom, a lot. He was obsessed with her. That was the whole reason he ran for city council and did all the merger stuff in the first place. Just to impress my mom. It was kinda disgusting, sometimes. Simp."

She had talked herself into a smile, but as soon as the thought ended, the smile disappeared.

"You know a lotta people said he was biased about the merger," I told her.

"Of course he was," Sarai said. "Everybody's biased, about everything. He was just biased toward my mom. Toward *us*."

I shrugged. "How's your mom doing?"

Sarai ignored the question.

We drove for a while in silence, both of Sarai's hands on the wheel, her neck craned forward like a grandma.

As horrible as the circumstances, as bad as I felt for Sarai, and for her little sister, I could feel something alive in my chest. Since I'd started playing the Game, I'd felt like nobody was taking it seriously. Nobody was taking me seriously. Even when it led us to a dead body, it still felt like everybody wanted it to just go away. But Sarai didn't.

The houses thinned as we got closer to the Basin. The farther you got from town, the more remote the properties got. There were families out here we rarely ever saw around town, real country families with huge hordes of kids who kept mostly to themselves. They didn't play sports, a few families didn't even go to school, but you'd always see them when you drove by, out on their front lawns, playing just like any other kids. A girl on an old trampoline noted the unfamiliar vehicle as we drove by. She stopped jumping to stare at us.

"Do you ever notice how people watch each other in Calico Springs?" Sarai asked.

"I think it's like any other town," I said.

She shook her head. "It's not like that in Lawton. People really watch each other here. Like everybody's afraid somebody else is watching them. It's creepy."

I twitched at it a bit. I didn't much like the implication. "Dad told me the reason people even move to Calico Springs is 'cause they don't like being fucked with," I told her. "Not by the government, not by their neighbors, nobody. Code of the Hills."

She snorted. "What's that, some kinda hillbilly fight club?"

"I guess. It means you don't tell on what other people are doing, no matter who's asking. So people can really be themselves."

Sarai frowned at the road. "Some people shouldn't be allowed to really be themselves."

I sat back into the passenger seat, taking it as a joke at first. It was completely upside down from how I saw the world. As far as I was concerned, to each their own kingdom, their own rules, their own life.

But as I watched the properties fly by, I realized Sarai was onto something serious. Maybe some folks shouldn't be themselves. Maybe some folks needed watching.

We parked her van as close to the river as the road would allow. In the late afternoon light, the Basin looked harmless. The wall of trees that divided it from the outside world was less defined; there were no lurking pockets of darkness, just hot, muggy air and the buzz of insects. I clocked a patch of newly matted grass in the ditch, the spot where I'd laid my bike.

We quickly found the barbed wire, still swallowed by the mud below us. I followed it for a ways, but it seemed to only run for about twenty yards before it ran out into a harmless tangle. It looked more like trash than a barrier to anything.

As we walked, she laid out her full theory. "So they make

a plan to bury him, somewhere where the ground is soft and easy." She kicked at the ground and the mud below her shoe gave with no resistance. "They come out to bury him, just like their plan, but instead . . ."

"They run into me," I said, and shuddered at the idea I'd been alone in the Basin with a murderer.

Sarai nodded. "They change their plans. They have to think on the fly, so they drive a couple miles north and dump him in the mill. Make it look like some dramatic suicide."

We walked quietly for a moment, my stomach knotting itself up.

"There were three," I said quietly.

"What?"

"Graves. There were three graves."

We tracked inward for another five to ten minutes, studying each clearing we passed. I described it to her, but nothing we came across looked quite right, all too circular to be nothing, but too lopsided to be the one I'd seen. We made wide, concentric circles around the target, allowing us to cover more terrain, stopping only when we felt the ground getting too wet, too close to the water.

The system was imprecise. I was trying to use the bends in the river to triangulate where I'd been, but the river was everywhere, water coming in and out all over our feet.

"I have an idea," Sarai said and took her phone from her pocket, already open to the Game. Over her shoulder, I watched her set the Game's radius to two miles, the length of the Basin, and type her intention—

GRAVES

We both watched as the map materialized. The blue dot was a quarter mile in, north of where we were standing. "Is that it?" she asked.

I nodded, half-confident.

As we cut our way north, I noticed immediately the proliferation of tupelos, the drooping trees with V-shaped cross branches I'd seen the night before. As we approached the target, I turned to one, and when I blinked, an image of the barn flashed between the branches. I ran to it, followed it for ten yards . . . but there was nothing on the other side.

"The branches?" Sarai asked.

I nodded.

She stared at the tree for a moment, then turned. "What about those?" She pointed to identical tupelos, with identical branches.

As I made my way to them, I noticed another set, then another, and another. The V branches were everywhere, and none of them offered a clear view forward, even in the light.

"So it could be any of these?" she asked.

I shook it off and rechecked the target on my phone.

I got quiet as we got farther north. We'd passed the blue dot and circled back around, when I started to question the details of my own story—had I really been this far in? This far north? Was I sure it was a grave? Had I actually seen three of them? Were they really that deep?

Sarai could sense it, and she stopped speaking after a while, too. I don't know if she was even looking for the graves. Every time I glanced at her, it was like those videos of people sleepwalking into dangerous situations. Her head bobbed as she glided around the thousand-year-old swamp.

Twenty minutes later, we found ourselves back at the same clearing for the hundredth time. "Those were the first branches you pointed out," Sarai said. "We've been here before."

"Maybe someone filled the graves already," I suggested, only realizing after I said it how insane it sounded. "Like they knew I'd be back."

"Maybe," she said quietly. I could see the hope she had when she came to the house fading.

I scanned my surroundings more urgently. There was nothing there. We stood for another long, awkward moment, waiting for something to happen, but nothing did.

It was like none of it had ever happened.

Sarai found a stump in a nearby clearing and sat. I stayed where I was, watching her, not saying anything. It felt like a century before she started talking.

"That first night," she said quietly. "The mustache cop, he asked me all these questions—Did someone tell you to go to the mill? Did someone tell you to turn that wheel? Like I knew it was gonna be there. Like I was in on it. He was so harsh. . . . It was like he already decided I knew. . . .

"Then, the next day, when he came to our house . . . he sat me down in the living room and asked me again, in front of my mom and my whole family—"

"Why?"

"'Cause he thought I was lying." She wiped her face with the bottom of her shirt. "He thought I was lying, and I'd tell the truth if my mom was there. I told him the same thing, the truth, and I think even he believed me 'cause he backed off but . . . but my mom didn't."

She took a deep, unsteady breath, her chest shaking as the weight of the last two days poured out.

"That night, she came into my room . . . and asked me if there was any reason I would lie to the cops. I tried to explain—I didn't know anything, the Game was random, but—she didn't believe me. The only thing she could figure to ask me was, Why?" Sarai's voice caught in her throat. "Why would I want something bloody?"

I kicked at the ground, begging it for any sign of something that proved I wasn't a complete liar. There was nothing I could do, no assurance I could give. I'd given her hope, and now I'd taken it away.

When I looked back to Sarai, she was staring at the ground.

"What?" I asked.

She reached down slowly, and when she came up, she was holding an old beer bottle.

"It's fucking nothing," she said, and with the full force of her body, she stood and hurled the bottle at a tree across the clearing. The glass shattered, and I ducked.

"Wait." I tried to stop her.

"What? You think someone's gonna see us?" She found another bottle and smashed it, again, letting its pieces fall to the mud. "The Code of the fucking Hills, right? Nobody bothers anybody, and the police don't do shit, and everybody moves on—and nobody gives a shit that my baby sister's real, actual dad is dead!"

She stopped suddenly, the words ringing through the river valley.

"I saw those," I said quietly. "Those beer bottles. I saw them the other night. This was the clearing. If those graves were here, they're not anymore. Someone filled them in."

Sarai didn't look at me. She stared past . . . at the tree where the bottles had smashed. I followed as she walked toward it and raised her hand.

Her fingers began to move against the tree next to her, tracing breaks in the bark. I remembered them from the night in the Basin, feeling them when I touched the tree, but in the light, I could see what she did. . . . They weren't random. They were patterned, a design.

I looked at my phone. We were standing directly on top of the blue dot. This was the target.

"What the fuck . . ." I whispered.

The cuts were sharp and intentional, a series of lines, short but deep, the kind that would require incredible force. Eight cuts around the outside made up a circle, and inside it, a simple drawing of a bird, its wings outstretched, diving straight into the earth.

"Does that mean anything to you?" I asked. "A bird?"

Sarai shook her head. "It's not just a bird. It's more specific . . . like those birds at the mill."

I saw it as she did, lead hitting my stomach.

"It's a dove."

Teenagers in a Small Town Discover Dead Body with the Help of "Paranormal" App

by Mitchell Ballis

CALICO SPRINGS, MO—Five teenagers from Calico Springs stumbled upon human remains after going to a location prompted by an app-based adventure game known as Manifest Atlas.

The remains were the body of Winston Lewis (54), a long-time resident and city councillor in Calico Springs. His remains were found in the waterwheel of an abandoned mill—out of use since 1948. He is survived by his wife, Linda Lewis, his stepdaughter, Sarai (16), and daughter, Elsa (3).

The police released a statement confirming the victim died of a gunshot wound to the head. While the statement claims they have no reason to suspect foul play, and a source within the department confirmed the wound is consistent with a self-inflicted gunshot, police have yet to officially declare the death a suicide. A source inside the department also tells the Journal *the gun used belonged to the victim, and his truck was discovered at the scene.*

The real mystery, however, is that his remains were discovered.

Manifest Atlas is described by users online as a mix between a "digital Ouija board" and a "GPS-driven adventure game." The game asks users to enter an intention and returns coordinates to explore, claiming the act allows users to "change their destiny." The website claims to "lead users in the direction of their intentions, using the power of their own mind." We attempted to reach out to the creators of Manifest Atlas for comment, but no contact information is available online, through the app, or on the App Store.

The Calico Mill has been out of use since 1948 and rarely, if ever, sees visitors. Access is prohibited, and the mill is frequently monitored by Calico Springs police.

"That body could have sat there for months," said Jonathan Burns, a teacher at Calico High. "No one goes in that mill. Ever."

However, police confirmed Winston Lewis died on Wednesday evening, around 8:15 p.m. Barely twenty-four hours before his body was discovered.

The teenagers did not speak with the Journal. However, a close friend revealed the group's intention for the search that brought them to the body. When prompted by the game, they asked to manifest "something bloody."

While it should be noted that there is no evidence, scientific or otherwise, to suggest that an app-based phone game would be capable of producing a dead body, the Journal will have more on this story as it develops.

CHAPTER 12

WHEN I WOKE up the next morning, Mom had two copies of the *Springfield Journal* on the kitchen table.

It was on the front page, a photo of Winston Lewis from his most recent City Hall meeting, smiling at a camera with some constituents, next to a photo of the Calico Mill in the ugly daylight, looking plain and not at all scary.

"This is insane," Mom said. "People have been calling our house all morning. I don't even know how they got the number. Evidently it's all over Facebook. Look!" She pointed to the window. "There's a news van outside. He came to the door an hour ago. I told him he'd have to wait to talk to you."

Bones peeled out of his room in a cutoff tank, his hair still lopsided from sleep. "Did you just say there's a news van?" He yelped when he saw the headline on the kitchen table.

I watched out the hallway window as a man with a thick beard ate a donut, sitting in the back of a truck labeled "KBS-7 News." He was staring at our house. When we made eye contact, I ducked away.

Bones gave commentary as he read. "Jesus, he's got a lotta detail in here. . . . And a rat in the police? Wait, how'd he figure out about . . . ?" He got to the end. I watched him read the second to last paragraph. Something bloody. His eyes slowed down, and he glanced over at me.

"You didn't talk to him, did you?"

"Who?" I looked over his shoulder at the article. "Michael Ballis?"

Bones glanced back to the page and nodded, satisfied that I'd gotten his name wrong. I buried my head in my phone.

It wasn't a lie. I hadn't talked to Mitchell Ballis. Technically, it was a DM.

After Sarai dropped me off, I couldn't stop thinking about the idea that her family could have all these questions, and instead of ever getting answers, people would just stop paying attention. It seemed extra tragic, the idea that you could watch something fade into oblivion without even being able to make a single noise about it.

But I realized I had a power I'd never considered. It was Bones who told me about it, really. He'd told me how stories like this—sensationalized accounts of video games and dead bodies—could attract unwanted attention. But Sarai said she wanted attention. So I figured it was the least I could do.

Bones had made his way to the window and was staring at the news van as the man on the back set up his camera and started recording the house. "This is gonna be a shitstorm," he said, shaking his head. "This just became the whole fucking summer. . . ."

* * *

"Absolutely, one hundred percent, big fat fuck no to all this—"

The girl whose face was floating in front of Mitchell Ballis's article had three different nose rings. "I told y'all, Missouri is fucking messy—"

Rodney held her phone out, scrolling the Manifest Atlas tag on TikTok. She swiped up to a video of someone's driveway, where four teenagers stood in a circle, holding hands, their phone between them on the ground. Slowly, they each started shaking, more and more violent, until they were all four flailing uncontrollably. The camera zoomed in on the phone, open to the Game, landing on their intention as the music exploded in time—

HOLY SPIRIT, ACTIVATE

"Happy Christ," Bones watched over our shoulders. "Did these people all make videos this morning?"

"Some of them," Rodney said, bouncing between phone and laptop. "It's one of the top posts on Reddit, too."

On the other side of the garage, Sarai was quietly reading the article for a second time. Her face had barely flinched, but she didn't look upset.

Joe Kelly, on the other hand, was enraged. "Who told him?" he asked, throwing accusing eyes to every person around the room. "We explicitly said, no one tells what our intention was. How the hell did he find out?"

I kept my head down.

"Do you have any idea how insane this is about to be? People are gonna go crazy with conspiracy theories, thinking Sarai is some devil death-summoner or something—"

She raised an eyebrow behind him.

"—and thinking her stepdad got killed by an app. The last thing Calico Springs needs right now is a bunch of attention, making it seem like we're this evil little town . . ."

I could hear his dad's voice as he said it. I imagined it had been a rough morning at the Kelly household.

"And think about her fucking family," he kept on. "They need space to chill and heal, instead of making her stepdad's death some huge news story."

The words hung heavy in the air. I braced myself, waiting for Joe Kelly to focus his rage in my direction, but instead, Sarai set the newspaper down on the table between us.

"I don't wanna chill," she said.

Joe glanced back at her. "I just mean, respecting your privacy," he said quietly. "Not having everybody talking about your stepdad at the grocery store—"

"I want them talking about him at the grocery store. At least then people are talking about him. If this is what it takes, then great. All I care about"—she turned from Joe to the rest of us—"is figuring out what happened."

Joe Kelly looked like he'd been punched in the stomach.

"What happened?" he asked. "You think something happened to him? Like . . . not . . . he didn't . . . do it himself?"

He was trying to be careful with the way he asked the question, but Sarai was cavalier in her response.

"Yes," she said. "I think he was murdered."

I felt the entire room freeze, all three of them stunned into silence. I knew the weight of what they were trying to process, I could see every instinct they had pushing it back. Rodney was the first to start nodding, to ask if Sarai was okay. Bones had turned around, avoiding eye contact with her. Joe Kelly looked like he was in physical pain.

"Who?" he asked quietly, more like an accusation. "Who do you think killed him?"

"Do you know how many people were pissed that he married my mom?" Sarai said. "It coulda been anybody. John Arrington? The mustache cop? As far as I'm concerned, anybody in Calico Springs could have done it."

As she said the names, Joe Kelly's face twisted further. He wasn't even trying to hide his disbelief anymore, he was just swallowing it, looking at her like he knew a just kidding was coming.

"No, they couldn't have."

It was Bones. He was looking at the table in front of the couch, where Sarai had dropped the newspaper.

"What do you mean?" she asked.

"Look." He pointed to the bottom of the page, below Ballis's article, where they'd published the official statement from the police. "It says he died Wednesday night."

"So?" Sarai asked.

"So . . . Wednesday was the baseball game."

Sarai shifted in her seat, the information letting the air out of her theory.

Joe Kelly nodded in quiet agreement. He was right. Everyone

she'd just named, everyone in Calico Springs, had been at the game.

"Except me," I said.

Bones nodded. "Right."

I swallowed. "And whoever was with me in the Basin."

The group got quiet. It felt like we'd reached a gulf, unable to see each other all the way across it. Joe Kelly was having an impossible time processing, clearly trying not to look upset, but it was obvious Sarai wasn't going to back down. Bones just looked pissed off by the whole thing. I saw a way forward and sat up.

"What about the Game?" I asked.

"What about it?" Bones asked.

"It's the one thing we know for sure," I said. "I mean, we don't know what happened to Winston. The police don't know and aren't gonna help. The one thing we know, as a fact, is that the Game brought us to that body in twenty-four hours. Not only that, it found the graves. . . ."

He tried to hide it, but Joe Kelly rolled his eyes.

Sarai agreed with me. "He's right. It had to be more than a coincidence. Plus, there's all those stories online—"

"Then what?" Joe asked. "What is it? Magic? I read those stories, by the way. They're bogus. Some people saw some weird shit when they were creeping around late at night? Of course they did! It brought me to my ex-boyfriend's house? No, you brought you to your ex-boyfriend's house, and you blamed it on the Game. I'm sorry." He turned to me specifically. "But it's not some fucking conspiracy. Those people are just bored."

Sarai sat up behind him, fire in her eyes. "Do I look bored to you?" she asked.

Joe Kelly shook his head, backing off immediately. "That's not what I meant—"

"You're missing the most important part." It was Rodney now, rereading the newspaper article between us. "Somebody made this thing."

"So?"

"So what if they did it on purpose? What if they have something to do with it?"

Even Bones agreed with her, his lips curling in a curious smile.

"This is the most exciting thing to happen to Calico Springs since I've been alive," I said. "And we're right in the middle of it."

"So what do we do?" Joe Kelly asked innocently.

Sarai smiled, her answer prepackaged, like she'd been thinking about it. "We do what the police won't," she said. "We play the Game."

WHAT THE FUCK IS THIS?

Teenagers in a Small Town Discover Dead Body with the Help of "Paranormal" App

by Mitchell Ballis

> **Tiger45:** the game led them straight to the body. someone pls explain to me how that's not completely fxxked

> **tunatuna:** this is fake. right? right?

> **Tiger45:** wrong

> **FramesJanco:** brb booking my ticket to calico springs

> **Tiger45:** no actually

> **SaraWattso:** wait i wanna go

> **EddyLiteBeam:** Its exactly what i Was talking about. if u find a vortex with a weak energy barrier, this game will rip right thru

> **Tiger45:** I said this same thing. this is dark science.

> **username55:** meaning what exactly?

> **FramesJanco:** meaning we're about to see all kinds of evil shit coming from calico springs

> **EddyLiteBeam:** energy barriers divide us from the spirit world. this game forces mass consciousness to direct its energy toward upsetting the energy barrier

> **Tiger45:** No shit, this is like a 2 hour drive for me.

> **tunatuna:** There's no hotels, where are we supposed to stay?

> **JohnbaJuis:** you're serious about this?

> **SaraWattso:** I saw a couple Airbnbs

> **Tiger45:** is anyone else actually going?

> **tunatuna:** yes

> **hyphentown8:** Yep!

> **SaraWattso:** I leave tomorrow

> **username55:** Affirmative.

> **FramesJanco:** looks like it.

> **EddyLiteBeam:** fuck it, why not.

> **rarebear:** seriously yes

> **Mikeeeel:** yes

> **JohnbaJuis:** see u there!

PART THREE
THE OUTSIDERS

CHAPTER 13

I GOT UP early the next morning, before anybody else in the house.

I went on Mom's laptop and found a detailed map of Calico Springs, one with all the streets and city buildings labeled. I blew it up huge and printed it across four sheets of paper— it took me almost five tries to get it right—then taped them together on the wall of the garage, full lines of tape on every side so it wouldn't budge. I took the pack of thin markers from the elementary craft box we kept in the supply closet and drew four small blue dots—one on the bridge, two on the Basin, and one on the mill.

Bones found me in the garage as I was finishing. "What's that for?" he asked.

"Tracking results."

"You think we're gonna forget?"

I stepped back from the map and admired my handiwork. It looked professional, like one of those maps in the control room in a spy movie. "The Game isn't always obvious about its answers," I told him. "It doesn't always give you what you ask for or how you expect to get it. So it might take us a minute before we see it, like God."

"Like God how?"

"Funny way of talking," I said. "Always talking."

Bones was quiet, studying the map as he chewed his morning Pop-Tart. He didn't look upset about it, just curious.

When he spoke, it was to the map, not to me. "You know his truck was out at the mill, right?" he asked. "Winston Lewis?"

"Sure, I saw."

"Rodney saw it that night. In the woods, you remember—"

"I remember."

He took another big bite, thought a little harder. "Did he look all right to you? When he was here for the garage sale?"

I pictured Winston Lewis in our driveway, and the first thing that came back to me, the most vivid detail, were the dark circles under his eyes. Bones had seen it, too. That, coupled with the wobble in his walk, told me at the time, he'd been drinking. Now I wondered if it was something worse.

"He looked a little rough, I guess. Why?"

Bones was quiet for another long while. I could tell he was really thinking, being strategic. "Can you imagine if we heard Dad killed himself?" he asked.

Tragic as it was, the idea of it made both of us bust up laughing.

"No chance," I said. "Nobody'd buy it."

"We'd all assume he got drunk and popped himself, end of story." He stopped laughing quick. "You know," he added.

"When someone goes through something real traumatic, their brain makes up reasons for them to not believe it. You know that, right?"

His eyes were still on the map. We weren't talking about Dad anymore. We were talking about Sarai.

"I know," I told him.

"Okay," he said. "Just wanna make sure we're not jumping to any conclusions." And he shot me a warning glance before disappearing back into the house.

If it was up to me, nobody would ever leave the casket open at a funeral.

There was nothing more inhuman than a corpse, the way they did the face up with all the powdery makeup, pumped it full of chemicals to keep the chest from caving in, and made it smell like Lysol and rat poison. I understand people need to say their goodbyes, but it's not like the soul's still in the body, anyway. Might as well say your goodbyes to the Lord, and let your memories be of the living.

In the case of Winston Lewis, they couldn't display his face on account of bone damage, so they decided it would be less creepy to close the casket at the neck. It backfired completely, having his body, stiff in its suit, floating on its own, decapitated by wood paneling. Mom only glanced in for a second, then she shuffled us away, clearly disturbed.

The funeral service was being held in the cemetery behind Grace Baptist, the biggest cemetery in Calico Springs, right in the heart of town. It was a scorching day, almost a clean hundred, and the wool of my sweater felt like a necklace of bugs. The whole of both Calico Springs and Lawton had come out to pay respects, for the most part separating themselves on either side of a center aisle. With heads bowed, I counted almost two hundred people.

"Jesus Christ," Bones mumbled, pulling at the neckline of his identical sweater. "There's too many fucking people here."

"I guess he had a lot of friends," I said.

"Those aren't friends, those are spectators."

Dramatic as it was, it didn't feel far off. It wasn't like a normal day at church, with people mingling around before the service, talking about the heat. The whole thing was tense, nobody talking to anybody. Sarai and her family stood in the front, heads high over the open casket. A group from Lawton surrounded them, hands on backs and shoulders for support. Everyone else spread out across the yard, standing among the tombstones.

I scanned the crowd wider. Behind us, there were a few people I didn't recognize. Young people in tight jeans and floppy hats, dressed like it was just a day at the park. For a second, I thought they might be spirits, up from their eternal homes to pay respects . . . until one bumped into me.

It was a boy, not much older than me, with thick blond hair and a Mizzou T-shirt, trying to slide past. I saw Mom side-eye his T-shirt. He stopped, and for a second it looked like he was about to say something, but Mom leaned over first.

"This is a funeral. Show some respect."

He nodded, and Bones glared at him, so he shuffled away. I watched him go, feeling like we'd been invaded.

"Welcome, everyone. Would you please pray with me. . . ."

Father Leonard had made his way to the pulpit at the front. I liked Father Leonard. The old pastor, Father Jones, talked all creepy and slow, especially when he was talking to the kids, and always smelled like actual shit. Father Leonard was younger, he had energy, and even swore sometimes when he was really trying to make a point.

"Lord, today we beg your forgiveness. Forgiveness for your son Winston Lewis. We pray that you make known his virtues and make clean his sins. . . ."

I felt Mom shift next to me. We all knew which sin he was talking about.

When Father Leonard finished his prayer, he nodded to everyone and took an awkward step back. He glanced at the family. "Unfortunately, I'm unable to perform last rites today. . . ."

My stomach turned. There was only one thing you could do on Earth to guarantee you'd never make it into the kingdom of heaven—and that thing was suicide. It was the only unforgivable sin, because after it, there was nothing left to forgive. Even Father Leonard wouldn't pray for your safe passage to heaven—they knew it wasn't in the cards. For his sake, for the sake of his soul and his family's peace, I said a short prayer that Sarai was right and Winston hadn't actually killed himself.

It was quiet on the lawn for a long minute when a man stood in the front, on the Lawton side. He was Black, short, and wide, but surprisingly agile as he moved up to the body. When he turned, I saw he had the preacher collar on and recognized him as the pastor from Lawton Methodist.

"Hey y'all," he said. "I'm Ronald Baker. The family has asked me to be here today to help lay Winston to rest."

Bones let out an audible groan, which made Mom cut her eyes at him.

"If they do two pastors at my funeral," he whispered to me, "then bring me back to life and kill me again."

Pastor Baker stood for a minute with his palms up, hovering over the casket, before looking across the congregation. "Would you pray with me?"

I felt people looking around for one another, reluctant as they bowed their heads. Lawton Methodist had a reputation for doing shit that the other pastors in town preached against, like celebrating Jewish holidays or putting up a nativity scene every Christmas with all Black characters. To them, it wasn't real church. I heard Mom call them "Diet Christ." And if Father Leonard wouldn't perform last rites on Winston's body, then it meant Pastor Baker doing so was in open rebellion.

He put his hands on the casket and bowed his head. "Almighty God. We know your love is righteous and all-knowing. We know it sees our true hearts and reveals them. . . . We know Winston Lewis is already forgiven. We know he's earned his place at your table."

I opened my eye to sneak a peek at the rest of the crowd. A few faces were turning—asking God's forgiveness was one thing, assuming it was another.

Almost like he could feel them, Pastor Baker pushed harder. "We know all things are possible through the teaching of your son, Jesus Christ, performer of miracles, pardoner of the unpardonable. Bring Winston to his eternal peace. More than that, Lord God . . ."

I looked up to the front and saw that Pastor Baker had opened his eyes, too, and was speaking directly to the bowed heads around him. "We ask that you forgive us. We know we're proud and full of folly. We know that we let our mortal disagreements stand in the way of eternal salvation, a salvation that can't be reached here on Earth. We ask that you make us brave enough to confess our sins and strong enough to heal."

I lowered my head just in time to avoid his gaze. It wasn't subtle—he was talking directly to our side of the aisle.

After the ceremony, we moved to a big tent with air conditioners where they'd set out the crackers and coffee. Mom and her friend Sarah put up a poster board with information on the merger and started handing out stickers that said "Unity." She put one on both me and Bones and told us to let everybody who asked know where to get them.

"I didn't know your mom was into politics like that," Rodney pointed out when we joined her at a table in the corner.

"She's just bored," Bones said, stripping the sticker once he was out of her view. "And trying to stick it to our dad."

Sarai was at the front of the room, standing at the end of a table crowded with photos of Winston. The line to offer condolences stretched more than halfway around the tent, and she was businesslike at the front of it, greeting everybody with solemn nods and handshakes.

Next to her stood a woman who had to be her mom. She was shorter than Sarai, her skin was darker, and her style was sharper, half her face covered by a large black sun hat. They were talking to different people, but in her arms, three-year-old Elsa was trying to jump from her mom's arms to her sister's. I watched them for a few moments. They didn't interact once, even with Elsa going back and forth between them. The longer I watched, the colder it felt. I wondered if Mrs. Lewis still blamed Sarai for that night.

"Who were all those people at the back of the cemetery?" Rodney asked.

"Tourists," Bones said.

"Tourists of what?"

"I don't know, but Dad said the Motel 6 is all booked up tonight."

I scanned the tent. It didn't look like any of the strangers had made it through to the reception. On the opposite end, Rory and Tyler were huddled with the other Dirtbags, as formal as I'd ever seen them in black button-ups and jeans. John Arrington and some of the richer men from the development wore black suits. As I watched, I saw the group of them circle up and put arms around each other. It took me a second to realize—they were praying.

Funerals brought out the best of small towns. All around the tent, high-school teachers and friends' parents and folks from Lawton were mourning over tiny plates of food, laughing in spite of the occasion. There was a food table, already stacked high with casseroles for the family. There was a table of police officers, and at the center, the mustache cop, in full uniform, was doing a magic trick for a group of kids.

I tried to imagine one of them was a murderer, like Sarai said.

That was my problem. . . . I'd felt it since she first said it could be anybody—I knew the anybody she was talking about. They'd served me food at church, coached my baseball teams, driven me to tournaments, helped redo the siding of our house for my mom, and gone hunting with my dad. They'd crowded into the hospital room when I was five and prayed over my body until I woke up.

The idea that one of them could be a murderer meant either I'd been blind about them all these years . . . or it meant the devil could get to anybody.

I didn't notice as Rory and Tyler approached our table.

"Look at this," Tyler said, pulling himself a seat before any of us could say anything about it. "Town celebrities. *Springfield Journal*; that's big time."

He used his beer to greet Bones and Rodney before landing on me. "Hey there, miracle boy," he said. "Did you tell 'em where you first heard about this noteworthy game of yours?"

Tyler was probably twice my size, almost a carbon copy of his dad but with a worse beard and less self-control. He always looked a little bit unstable but in a smiley way. Like he'd kick your ass without even knowing what he was doing.

"I told them," I said. "Seems we're better at it, though."

Tyler smirked and turned his attention to Bones. "I just wanted to come over here and say . . . you got fucking hosed the other night."

It took us all a minute to realize he was talking about the baseball game.

"Such a shitty way to go out. That guy had it fucking out for you. I'm surprised you didn't break his jaw."

"Absolute bullshit," Rory added.

"Thanks," Bones said. It sounded genuine.

"I said since you were a freshman, best athlete I've ever seen in Calico Springs, any sport. Remember my senior year when you broke that kid's wrist?"

They all laughed, Bones seeming to enjoy the mythologizing, even if it was Tyler Arrington. I could see him getting more comfortable between them . . . they were both looking at him like he was golden.

"We're gonna have some parties this summer," Tyler said. "First one next Friday. At my grandma's old cabin. She's dead now, so. We can do whatever we want to the place."

It sounded awful. I tried to imagine something I'd want to do less with a Friday night than watch the Dirtbags slam Coors

Lights and destroy an old woman's home filming unimpressive stunt videos—

"Sounds good," Bones said. "We'll be there."

I sat up. Rodney was surprised, too, and we crossed glances looking at him.

"She'll come, too?" Rory pointed at Rodney.

"Sure," Bones answered for her, and Rodney's eyebrows tightened even further.

"Maybe," she said, fake-polite.

Tyler took down Bones's phone number and stood up. It was the nicest I'd ever seen them, and Bones seemed genuinely pleased. Before they turned to go, Tyler leaned back in. "Oh. You gotta tell me how you actually found that body."

Bones snorted but Tyler didn't flinch. He was serious.

"You read the article," Bones said. "The Game sent us—"

"Come on," Tyler groaned. "We can keep a secret. How'd you know it was there?"

He stared at Bones, and I watched Bones process it, ultimately landing on a joke. "Right," he said, playing along. "I mean . . . I've got my sources."

Tyler's smile widened. "Fine," he said. "Be that way."

I studied Tyler for a break in his manner, but there was nothing. He wasn't lying. He really thought we knew the body was there.

"How's the dog?" I asked him.

Tyler froze, confused. "What dog?" He looked to Rory. Nothing.

"The one you found," I said. "At McShay's farm? Using the Game?"

Rory slapped him on the shoulder. "Remember!" he said. "We said we found Jezza—"

"Oh my God!" Tyler shook his head. "No, dude. I've had Jezza for months. We just like fucking with that kid at the bait shop."

"He thought you were serious!" Rory nearly shouted.

"Christ." Tyler's voice dripped with pity, and they exchanged a look, laughing at their own bullshit like it was an instant classic. I felt my face flush, and Bones glared at me from across the table, I told you so etched in his eyebrows.

I was on my third run through the snack table when Bill Kelly approached me.

I ignored him at first, assuming there was somebody more important nearby, but he circled, stopping in front of me.

"Willie," he said, and smiled into my face, with big shark teeth.

"Hey, Mr. Kelly," I said. "Beautiful service."

"Beautiful service," he echoed. "My wife and I just wanted to see how you were doing. Joe told me that night was . . . traumatic for you."

I couldn't remember saying anything like it to Joe, but I nodded, anyway. "I appreciate that, I'm doing all right."

He put his hand on my shoulder. "I've always been so fond of you and your brother. After all that you've been through." He looked straight at my eye patch. "To persevere like you have . . .

I want you to know, our family is always here for you if you need anything."

We stood awkwardly for a moment, his hand heavy, pressing me down where I stood.

"I did wanna ask," he added, "would you do me a quick favor?"

"Sure, I guess."

He nodded behind me. "Could you just go over and ask your mom to close up her little station?"

I looked over. In the corner, Mom was having a spirited conversation with a few folks from Lawton, starting to resemble a crowd.

"I wouldn't be asking," Bill continued, "if it hadn't made some of the folks with the church uncomfortable. I'm sure you know, funeral's not really a place for politics—"

"What's going on?" Joe Kelly cut between a few tables, stepping in quickly to join our conversation. "Did Willie do something?"

"Oh no." Bill looked at me. "I was just asking him to have his mom pack up over there, at the request of the church."

I looked between them. "I don't know how things are done in your house, Mr. Kelly," I said. "But I don't tell my mother what to do."

He laughed. "Trust me, I get it. But it's better you talk to her than me. Don't wanna make it seem any bigger than it is."

Joe looked at me expectantly.

They were both a few inches taller than me, so I had to tilt my head back to look between them. I didn't understand how a poster board about the merger constituted politics, but more than that, I was surprised I had to say it again. "I'm afraid you're gonna have to tell her yourself, Mr. Kelly."

His gaze tightened. He wasn't the kind of guy who was used to hearing no, especially from high schoolers. He looked like he might say something vile, but before he had the chance, Joe jumped in.

"I'll do it."

Bill's face relaxed. "That'd be great, son," he said, and glanced at me with disdain. "Good to see you, Willie."

As he walked off, Joe gave me a small shrug, like we were in on it together. He waited until his dad was out of earshot. "It's not a big deal," he whispered.

"Why's he even care?" I asked.

"I don't know," Joe said with a small grimace. "But it's easier if you just do what he says."

He marched over to where Mom was now standing. The table was too far away to hear, so I watched the scene play out in silence. Joe approached, they hugged. He put on a face, she laughed. He laughed. As he talked, her face went confused, then cold. She looked past him to his dad at the table. Joe Kelly whispered one more thing . . . and Mom reached over, snapping the poster board down onto the table with a loud crack.

CHAPTER 14

THE NIGHT OF the funeral was the first time we all got together to try the Game.

Sarai came with Joe Kelly in his truck, and it looked like they must have talked because she was laughing as she hopped down from the passenger seat. Rodney brought her laptop, and Bones stayed on his phone to keep himself from looking too interested. I waited until I had everyone's attention, then laid out a plan.

"Our first order of business should be figuring out what the Game knows," I said. "'Cause it knows something. We use simple intentions to get it to reveal things to us, in its own way."

"How do we do that?" Sarai asked.

"We experiment," I said. "Set intentions for general things and let the Game choose how it reveals the information to us. We can get more specific—"

"Why don't we just set it to catch a killer?" Bones picked his head up from his phone.

Sarai looked to me, but Bones pressed on before I could say anything. "I'm serious! If we're gonna experiment, we might as well try the most interesting thing, right? And if it works . . ."

He glanced to me. "Like, actually works . . . then we'll have our answer."

I could feel him testing me—this was his way of proving right away the Game didn't work.

"We should be more broad," I said. "It's not gonna give us all the answers like that. We should do something open to interpretation—"

"Why not?" he asked, now talking directly to me. "Why not ask it for exactly what we're looking for?"

I shifted. "Because we might get it?"

Sarai was watching from between us. She gave it a second of thought and sided with him. "With any luck," she said, and typed the intention—

CATCH A KILLER

We piled into Joe's truck. The sun was just starting to set over the bridge as we pulled up and parked in the first building with a lot, once a saloon-style bar named Smiley's, its guts now spilled out across the concrete lot. We walked down toward where the target blinked by the water, and as we crested the hill, the sharp, charred edges of hollowed-out buildings started to emerge, welcoming us to Old Town.

Behind me, Bones started whistling a familiar melody.

When Calico Springs was first built, there were a dozen mills on the river, so it followed that the town center would be on the bridge. After two hundred years of being punished by flooding, it had migrated up the hill, but the remains of what used to be Calico Springs still stood along the road, flooded to the studs and being sucked back into nature by climbing weeds and water damage.

We kept it, though, because it was one of Calico Springs most notable contributions to American culture—it was the basis of an indoor roller coaster at Old West World in Branson called Fire in the Mill.

We used to go once a summer when we were kids, and we'd always end up riding Fire in the Mill over and over until we left. You started in an indoor cave, fake crickets and false branches to simulate the Calico swamp. In the first room, you rolled past a saloon, what Smiley's used to be, full of animatronic people drinking and partying. A man with a guitar on the front sang a folksy refrain—

The river, the river's a beautiful sight,
But beware when the river swamp turns to the night.

As the coaster cranked around a corner, you were plunged back into darkness.

Artificial stars twinkled overhead, mirrors making the ceiling look impossibly deep . . . distracting you from the masked faces peeking out of the blackness around you.

You turned again, this time passing through a chute into the mill, and the coaster crept to a stop. All was quiet for ten seconds, before an ancient, prerecorded voice shouted, "Fire in the mill!" The whole room lit up orange with artificial flames.

The masked men leapt out around you, laying their torches to the machinery. The coaster shot forward away from them and false beams in the ceiling collapsed overhead. The first time I rode it, I started crying at that spot.

The final room was the part of the story people in Calico Springs loved to tell. The animatronic characters came back, the same ones from the bar, and made an assembly line to get water from the river to put out the fire. Sixty-seven citizen firefighters, they said, the entire crowd from Smiley's, rescued everyone in the mill. The coaster hit its max velocity, water splashed around you, and before you knew it, you were back in the gift shop. The name of the coaster had become a rallying cry—

"Fire in the mill!" Bones shouted as we walked down to it, and we all echoed, our voices carrying through the river valley.

Now Old Town was abandoned. By day, it was a spot for teens and townies from both sides of the river, mostly the ones who smoked pot. By night, it cleared out and the drugs got harder. Everybody knew if you were looking to get yacked in a spot where cops would leave you alone, Old Town was the place to do it.

We kicked our way through it, mostly trash now. There was hardly any brick left standing that wasn't tagged with graffiti—it had become a proxy war between towns, played out in spray paint. I could tell we were all being quiet as we crept through except for Bones, who seemed to be making as much noise as he could.

I felt my attention shift to Sarai at the head of the group. She was unamused, glaring at the old buildings with real disdain. She hadn't said anything since we got out of the truck, I realized, and she'd kept real distance between herself and the group. I followed her eyes and immediately, I noticed something.

"Look." I pointed to one of the largest structures, a wall on its own. "There's a pattern in the graffiti."

I traced a line with my finger in the air, a perfectly drawn pink horizontal, unconnected to any other art. Sarai and Rodney joined me, watching as I kept my finger moving, the pink lines extending onto other buildings, hidden inside the graffiti, a coded message, visible only if you really took the time to look at it. I felt my heart start to race—

"They're survey markings," Joe Kelly said.

I didn't turn around.

"They do them for construction," he explained. "When you survey a spot, you mark the property corners. Looks like they're doing it for the foundations around here."

"About time they knock it down," Bones said.

"Maybe that's got something to do with it," I suggested. "It's not showing us a murderer . . . it's showing us their motive. Construction . . . zoning . . . the developments . . ."

I looked to Sarai for help but she wasn't paying attention, instead staring over my head at the tree line. We'd wandered too far from the road to see it, the river too loud to hear it, but we could still feel the spill of headlights, shimmering against the branches behind us.

Sarai's neck stretched as she waited a second longer, but the lights didn't pass. The car had stopped.

All it took was a few silent glances and we all understood the situation. Joe Kelly and Bones moved to the front, creeping back toward the road. The headlights got brighter, cutting between the broken structures. Bones crested the hill first, pausing for a second to look at the car on the other side of the road.

As we watched him, the lights went out. No one moved.

Joe Kelly joined him on the shoulder, and together they walked straight for the driver's window. As I stared at the car, its shape got clearer—it was boxy—a blue beater; I recognized it from the shop.

Joe Kelly knocked hard on the window. "What are you doing in there, creep?" He banged again and the door opened into their chests.

"It's cool, it's cool, it's cool—"

Sarai saw him before I did.

"Abe?"

"Didn't you hear me say it's cool?" Abe pushed his way out of the driver's seat. "Don't gotta bang on the window like that. This thing's fragile."

As Joe and Bones stumbled back, Sarai pushed her way through and jumped into him with a hug. "Oh my God," she shouted. "I'm so happy you're not a murderer. Why'd you have to sit in the car all creepy?"

"I wasn't sitting creepy, I was just sitting—"

"This is Abe," she said, introducing him. "He's one of my best friends from Lawton."

"Yeah, I know him," Joe Kelly said, offering his hand, even if

I could see he was still on edge.

"We thought you were here to kill us," Sarai explained. "It's a long story."

"What are you doing here?" Bones asked.

I'd been hovering on the edge of the circle, but as I leaned in, Abe threw his arm around me immediately. "Oh man, this is embarrassing," he said. "This is embarrassing. . . ."

He turned his phone between us and the Game screen blinked: *THANKS FOR PLAYING*

"I told you!" I said. "I told you it was worth trying out—"

"Yeah, except it doesn't work," he said. "Unless one of you has a thousand dollars cash you wanna give me, then this thing is busted."

"The Game brought you here?" Joe Kelly asked. "This exact spot?"

Abe glanced down to his phone. The blue dot was gone, which made him less sure, but he still said, "I think it was this spot. Why? What'd y'all ask for?"

I hadn't noticed the five of us naturally forming a semicircle around him. As Sarai answered, I realized we had him surrounded. "To catch a killer."

Abe's eyebrows raised, flying to a joke. "Well." He looked past us, back toward Calico Springs, then glanced at me. "It shouldn't be too hard finding one of those around here."

THE COMPANY IS FAKE.

> **HotRod:** I found the business license for CHANGE YOUR DESTINY MARKETING LLC. it's all fake.

It says their primary business purpose is marketing but they have no clients.

They have no web presence whatsoever, no other references online other than paperwork. there's no contact.

The name listed is literally Dick Hurts

> **Tiger45:** Physical address?

> **HotRod:** a warehouse in St. Louis that sells car parts. It's a fake company.

> **Tiger45:** jesus

> **HotRod:** Whoever made this thing is actively working to make sure no one finds out.

> **HotRod:** can someone do building ownership check? Land records or something?

> **tunatuna:** would be at city hall. most land records are in person only

> **FootballMary:** calling all st louis????

CHAPTER 15

I STARTED TO think about the Game all the time.

In the mornings I'd play by myself, setting little intentions, like *SOMETHING HOLY* or *A SURPRISE*; things I could always find. On my own, I'd started putting together a list of places that the Game sent me related to Winston Lewis, just to see if there was some answer in the things that mattered the most to him. Lying in bed some nights, I'd see the cold, gray map of Calico Springs in my head, covered with blue dots. I kept it quiet around Bones, mostly 'cause I knew he didn't care like I did, but Rodney was a different story. It turned out Rodney cared more than I did.

As HotRod, she'd been spending hours on the websites, responding to posts about crazy experiences and positing theories with the other computer science geeks. She kept us updated on what the forums were saying, talking about them like it was a place we'd all been.

For her, it wasn't even really about Sarai's stepdad, she told me. It was the Game itself that presented something of a computer programming mystery—if you could figure out how it worked, you could figure out what it was really for and why it was created.

"So many people in the forums work in computer science, design—people who do exactly what I wanna do," she explained to me one day in the garage. "And they really give a shit about what I have to say. I'm somebody on there."

"You're somebody here, too," I told her, but she shrugged it off, like it wasn't true, or at least she didn't believe it.

One afternoon, when Joe Kelly and Sarai were having lunch at his family's house, Rodney came to the garage to enlist our help.

"The company's a fake," she told us. "I found their business filing online. They used a fake name and a random address. So whoever made this thing went to extreme lengths to make sure they weren't found out."

That got Bones's attention. "Okay . . ." he said, really thinking.

"The other thing," she added, "is that all the really crazy stories are local. It's all in Missouri—mostly southern Missouri, even. There's a few in St. Louis but a lot of it is around here."

"What does that mean?" I asked.

"That tells me someone's controlling it. That they have access to some backend, and they're using it. That's what most people online think, too."

I saw Bones turn it over in his head. Rodney was watching, too. "Wow," he said slowly. "That . . . makes sense."

She smiled, victorious. "Right? So if they can control it, then they probably see every intention that comes in. . . ."

"So what do you wanna do?" I asked.

"I wanna ask the Game to find the Creator."

Our first few targets yielded nothing—duffers, as Bones called them. The first was at the County Fairgrounds, empty and seemingly abandoned. We searched it high and low before deciding to try again. The second was just outside the school, the most popular corner for pickups; a place we'd all been a hundred times.

Our third target was floating in the woods, somewhere inside the trailer park behind Casey's, so we parked behind the gas station and started to walk, when Rodney suddenly announced—

"Shoot. I have to go home after this."

"It's only eight," Bones protested. "You got two hours."

"I know, but my phone's about to die, and if my parents text me and I don't text back immediately, they won't let me leave the house for a week."

"Why didn't you charge your phone? You know we don't have an Android charger."

"I did! I swear it was fully charged. . . ."

We walked in silence for a while, Rodney's head in her phone.

"It's always tracking your location," she said. "Manifest Atlas. Did you know that?"

I shrugged. I wasn't really a Terms and Conditions kind of person. "I mean, it has to put the little dot where I am on the map—"

"No." Rodney stopped me. "I mean, all the time. It's got your location even when the app isn't open. That's why my battery is getting destroyed. . . ."

I chewed on it. "Why would the Game need to know where you are all the time . . . ?"

Before I could get to the end of the thought, I was interrupted by shouting erupting in front of us; two male voices, the words indistinguishable but the tone clear as day. They were pissed.

Bones leapt in front, an instinct for incoming threats, and charged past a few trailers to a house on the end. As we got past the last one, we heard the clearest shout yet—

"Give it back, you fucker!"

The space behind the trailer opened into a huge yard, the grass patchy and scattered with metallic scraps and appliances. In the center of it, two men were at each other's throats. I recognized one, Bobby, a townie as old as the town itself, so familiar that I'd heard Dad refer to this area as Bobby's Trailer Park. He was shirtless, holding an iPhone and waving it around above his head. Ten feet away, cowering back from him, was the blond boy from the funeral.

"He has my phone!" the blond boy shouted. "He stole my phone!"

Bones and I leapt into action, going straight at Bobby. I could tell he was yacked from the glazed look in his eyes. Bones could, too, so he spoke direct, asking, "Is that your phone, Bobby? Is that your phone?"

Behind us, Rodney corralled the terrified blond kid away.

"Fucking kids!" Bobby shouted. "Sneaking in my yard!"

"Bobby!" Bones had his arms wide, so if Bobby swung at him, he'd be able to contain it. "Bobby, it's all good. It's just us."

That gave Bobby a moment of pause. He took a breath, and in one smooth motion, Bones swiped the phone back.

"Hey!" Bobby snapped. "That's mine!"

"No, it's not," Bones said, clear and simple. "Go inside, Bobby. We'll get him out of here."

The blond boy was cowering behind Rodney, watching the whole thing with wide eyes. Bobby leaned over to look at him. "I'll kill you," he said almost conversationally and marched back toward his porch.

"Oh my God," the blond boy said as Bones returned his phone. "That was incredible. You're like a zookeeper."

"Yeah, he's a person, actually," Bones spat back. "And what the fuck are you doing in his yard?"

"There's no fence," he pointed out. "I was in those woods and I didn't realize I was in his yard until . . . I'm Connor, by the way."

We guided him back to the street. He was wearing the same Mizzou T-shirt he'd worn to the funeral, a roaring tiger on the front, and one of those backpacks that fed you water like a baby. He was smiling now, just like he had been at the funeral, but I could see he was disoriented.

"Where are you from?" Rodney asked. "'Cause it's clearly not here."

"Yeah, people keep telling me that."

He didn't seem bothered by it. He ran his hand through a mop of thick blond hair, looking Rodney in the eye, practiced and attentive, the kind of obvious charm that made Bones roll his eyes.

"I saw you," I told him. "At the funeral."

He nodded. "Sorry if that was creepy. I recognized you from the article and I wanted to say hi, but I didn't want to be rude. Funerals, you know?"

Bones was walking in front of us, for the most part ignoring Connor, but that got him to turn around. "Why would you come to a stranger's funeral?" he asked. "Why are you here?"

Connor looked between us, his fullest smile on display. "Isn't it obvious? I'm here to play the Game."

The sun was going down, so we agreed to drive Connor back to his Airbnb, a small house near the old golf course that I recognized as the house that this old woman, Mrs. Johnson, had died in.

"Yikes," Connor said when Bones turned the truck engine over. "Sounds like the starter. I could probably hook you up with a new one."

"It's fine," Bones said. "That's what it's supposed to sound like."

Connor joined me in the back seat, and Rodney sat back against the passenger side door to look at us. "Who were those other people at the funeral?" she asked him. "Are they your friends, or . . ."

"Yes and no," he explained. "There's a community of us online. We've been following Manifest Atlas since it started showing up in the forums. I study app design in school."

Rodney's eyes flashed back toward him. "I'm going to school for computer engineering next year," she said, nodding to his T-shirt. "At Mizzou."

His face erupted in a smile. "Well, hello, new classmate. I'm second year design."

Bones's grip on the steering wheel tightened. "Shouldn't you be at school, then? You know, doing college shit?" he asked. "Seeing as, you know, you're in college."

"Great question," Connor said earnestly, cutting through the obvious sarcasm. "Kind of a long answer."

"Oh, good," Bones mumbled.

"I'm not sure if you know what a technologist is. . . ." Silence gave him his answer. "Right. Well, it's somebody who believes technology is the answer to all the world's problems. Part of that is knowing that those solutions will happen in ways we can't even understand now. Like, if you tried to explain the internet to someone in the Civil War. We don't know what we don't know . . . yet. And a huge part of that is quantum mechanics."

His cadence was bouncy and hypothetical, like a golden retriever who knew too much about physics. "Quantum mechanics basically comes down to the idea that nothing in our world is determined, so any future outcome can be changed. By what? We don't know. Like a change in the weather. Who knows where weather comes from? Or why you're turning left here. . . ."

I couldn't tell if he was distracted or if it was spite, but Bones jerked the wheel back and went straight through the intersection instead.

"See!" Connor said. "Infinite factors, infinite outcomes."

I shook my head. It didn't make any sense to me, but maybe it wasn't supposed to.

"Most technologists believe human consciousness will one day be able to alter physical reality on a quantum level. Maybe sooner than we think. So when I heard about Manifest Atlas, I thought, 'Oh, cool, someone's trying to crib basic quantum theory, make a little game out of it.' That's fun but . . . pointless. You know? Because we're still generations off from actually making this kind of technology work, right? But I kept an open mind. The only reason I got into computer science in the first place is because I think computers are capable of incredible things. Exponential, infinite things. Things we can only dream of right now."

I looked at Rodney—she was nodding along. It was almost exactly what she'd been saying about the Game from the start. This was her religion, I realized. I'd just never heard anybody read the scripture.

"So I read all these crazy stories people were posting, and at first, I figured it was a joke . . . then I started to read some stories that I couldn't explain . . . and then I heard about you guys finding that body."

He shuddered, as if reckoning with the reality of it, or at least trying to look like he was. "I couldn't explain it . . . but it validated everything people have been saying online about the Game for months. That it could move the world to its will. That it worked. And something like that . . . I mean, I don't have to tell you what that would do to the world. I had to test it myself . . . and I figured, if you're gonna truly test it, you gotta make sure all the variables are accounted for. So I couldn't just go playing it in Columbia. At this point, it's verifiable fact. Manifest Atlas works best in Calico Springs."

He looked around at us, sort of like we were special, and sort of like we were subjects. "That's why a bunch of us decided to drop whatever else we were doing and come here. To play the Game."

"What forums?" Rodney asked.

"All of them," Connor said. "App Magic, Keepers of the Code, the best one for this specifically is called Secret Atlas—"

"I know Secret Atlas," Rodney said. "I post on Secret Atlas. I thought people were kidding about actually coming here. . . ."

Connor's eyes narrowed on her. "Rodney," he said, turning her name over and over. "Rodney . . . Rod. You're HotRod."

Rodney's face lit up.

Connor pointed to his shirt. "I'm Tiger45."

"Holy shit!" Rodney shouted. "Holy shit, you're Tiger45! All those people at the funeral—"

"That's us!" Connor leaned forward to hug her, but the seat got in the way, so he awkwardly took her hand and squeezed it. "I can't believe it. You live here?"

Rodney beamed in the front seat, and Bones watched with a

careful eye, like he could tell he was being played, he just didn't know how yet.

"Yeah, I don't know," he said. "If it was me, I would definitely stay in Columbia, rather than spend my summer in some random small town where nobody knows me."

Connor shrugged with a smile. "I don't know. If someone told you there was an app that was unlocking secrets of the universe . . . you wouldn't wanna see that for yourself?"

"That guy was a tool," Bones announced the next day in the garage.

Rodney was busy on her laptop, and I was inputting the previous night's target on our map, so neither of us responded.

"Imagine being in college," he continued, "and deciding you're gonna bail just so you can go fuck around in some small town on an app, hanging out with high schoolers—"

"I think it's cool," I said without looking back.

"Of course you do. But it just sounds like bullshit. Unlock the secrets of the universe? I swear, this shit is turning everybody crazy."

"Yep." Rodney looked up with a smile, not at Bones but at me. "And you're sitting in your garage with two of them."

Bones looked back and forth between us. I could feel him realizing he was on the outside of the argument; not just this one but every argument we'd had in the last few weeks. I knew he blamed me for it, like he felt I was taking his friend on purpose and not realizing the truth that I could see plainly: he was pushing her away.

He didn't say that, though. He must have decided it wasn't worth it and instead got up to get himself a pop from the fridge, mumbling as he walked away.

"I'm the only sane person left in this town."

FACEBOOK POST

Dale Powers
Lawton, MO

College acceptance letter, received!!!
My intention for the last year had been to GO TO COLLEGE.
I've been working my a** off in class, applying everywhere
in 100 miles, but nothing. So I decided to ask the Game.
It brought me to the post office. It seemed like a bust. I
asked the lady at the front if they knew anything about me
going to college, or had any mail, or anything. Nothing.
Then today, my mailman comes, and guess what? A letter
from Central Missouri State. I got a f**king SCHOLARSHIP.
If that isn't proof, I don't know what is.

FACEBOOK POST

Robert Burns
Calico Springs, MO

I found a MILITARY BUNKER that is clearly a preparation for WAR!!!

The Game brought me into the Basin. My intention was ARTIFACTS. And I found what is most certainly a bunker, left over from the bushwhacker days of guerrilla warfare in Calico Springs.

Look at the positioning of this wooden slab. It is set up to receive gunfire. If you check its positioning, it is angled toward the Bridge Crossing, which has always been the central route into Calico Springs. More than that, it is FIRMLY SECURED in the ground. As you can see.

> **COMMENT (1)**
> **Ruth Lewis**
> **Calico Springs, MO**
>
> That's a grocery store pallet

FACEBOOK POST

Joshua Morena
Calico Springs, MO

The Game Found Yoda!!!!!!!!
He was wandering out on the Johnson's farm. Who the hell knows how he got there, but we found him!!!!
Or rather—THE GAME FOUND HIM.
Seriously. We were looking for a lost dog. And that's right where it led us. Thank you to everyone who helped us hang signs, but God's will is stronger.
I do not know how it works, but it works. Believe in the Game.

CHAPTER 16

IT TOOK ONLY a week for the better part of the Calico Springs–Lawton Municipal Area to begin changing its destiny.

The article inspired a wave of downloads from all kinds of people, all different ages, around town. Somebody made a Facebook group for people to post their experiences, and it got almost a hundred members in the first three days. Mr. Burns was a frequent poster. He spent a whole day on local historical archaeological finds. There were the outsiders, their confusion as obvious as their clothes, popping up in the most average parts of town. Rodney swore she saw a couple of cops with their heads in their phones.

And the more people played, the more we collided.

It felt like at least once a night, we'd run into someone. Usually interactions were friendly, casual nods and courtesy fist bumps. Most people we saw didn't take the Game too seriously, just something to do or an excuse to trespass. Others did it just to fuck with strangers. We'd heard stories about a Josh Robins and his shithead sophomore friends lurking around the forest, running up on other players just to scare them.

Most people assumed it was a coincidence. "It's a small town," they'd say. "There's only so many places." But as it kept happening, the explanation started to fall short. We'd be a mile from town, off the beaten path, and a Toyota Camry would go crashing past us, some bearded man driving. Whenever we compared targets, they were identical.

But still, the Game started to feel more like a social event than anything. If we ever found a big enough group in the parking lot of some restaurant, we'd end our night there. As club season started up, Joe Kelly and Bones didn't play quite as much, so when we did, we took it less seriously.

It had the opposite effect on Sarai.

For her, the Game had only gotten more urgent, even if she liked to pretend it hadn't. Some days when we met up to play, she'd walk into the garage, already sweating from hours spent in the sun. If anybody asked, she'd lie, but I saw her filling in results on the map. Every night when we decided to quit, she'd argue for one more intention. I started to wonder if playing the Game, even by herself, was maybe just better than spending time at home. Every time I saw her, she always had a look in her eye like something was chasing her.

Then one night, we found out, something was.

I was sitting in the garage with Bones on a Monday night when Joe Kelly texted us in a group with Rodney—

God dammit

Has anyone heard from Sarai?

I heard Bones groan as he read it. "Jesus," he said. "Not again."

Even though the sun had gone down, it was still sweltering hot, so Bones and I had our shirts off in the garage. He'd taken Dad's recliner, and we were watching a video on his phone of two men in the jungle building an underground swimming pool. It was incredible how in sync they were as they moved, how simple they made everything seem. A few times, Bones remarked that he and I could probably pull something like that off in the backyard if we could just get our shit together, and there was some bamboo for us to use.

Without warning, the garage door shook violently, and both our heads shot up.

"What the fuck was that?" I asked.

We waited one, two, three seconds, and the garage door rattled again, louder this time, and didn't stop until Bones shouted, "Okay, okay!" back at it. Hesitantly, he clicked the opener, only letting the door up a few feet before stopping it.

Sarai ducked underneath, sweating like hell. She went straight for the workbench, where we hid the leftover booze. She took a big swig of gin before collapsing on the couch.

"Someone's following me," she said.

"What do you mean following you?" Bones asked. "You were out there by yourself?"

She answered with another pull from the bottle.

"You shouldn't be out by yourself—" Bones lectured again.

"Joe had baseball—"

"Yeah, me too. Four hours ago."

She steadied her breathing, and I sat down across from her on the couch. "What happened?"

"I was coming back from Cotton Park and I saw this car slow way down at the end of the street—and as soon as it saw me, it turned its headlights off. So I turned around, went back through the park to come down Willow instead, and I'd gone maybe a hundred feet when I heard it pull up behind me again, still with its headlights off. So I ran across the street where there's that little alley loop, and when I got back around to Willow—"

"The car was gone?" I asked.

"Gone. So I pretty much ran here and didn't stop."

"Did they follow you?"

"I don't know. I just ran."

Without hesitating, Bones went to the workbench and retrieved the 42, then ducked under the open garage door, disappearing into the darkness of the street.

Sarai sat next to me on the couch, staring at where his feet had just been. "This isn't the first time," she whispered. "Someone was following me the other night, too, but I thought I was being crazy so I didn't say anything."

"Who?" I asked.

She shook her head. She was breathing slowly, listening. A dog was barking several streets down, but there was no car noise. After a few seconds, Bones came back in.

"Nothing," he said, returning the gun to its hiding place. "But you really shouldn't be out there alone, not after that."

Sarai nodded, her eyes still glazed and distant. "Do you mind driving me home?"

Bones rolled his eyes. "We're sort of in the middle of something—"

"I'll do it," I said. I hopped up from the couch, a second too quick, and busted my knee against the table. I kept smiling, pretending it wasn't that bad, but a few cans fell off the other side and hit the ground.

"God dammit, Willie," Bones muttered. "I'll do it."

"Seriously, I can—"

"No, that's stupid," Bones said. "You might get stopped, and then you'd both be in a ton of shit."

"But there's less cops at night."

"I'll do it," Bones said definitively.

"I'll come . . ." I suggested, but Bones ignored me, and Sarai followed him out the side door.

On her break the next day, Bones told Rodney about Sarai's visit.

"She shouldn't go out on her own at night. It's idiot behavior."

Rodney nodded absent-mindedly, her face in her phone.

Bones noticed, sneaking an upside-down glance to see who she was texting. "Still," he said, "I can't imagine anybody in Calico Springs is following people around. . . ."

Rodney looked up. "You think she made it up?"

"I didn't say that." Bones corrected himself quickly. "I'm saying, maybe she saw someone park their car and she thought they were following her so she took off, when actually . . . it was just somebody parking their car."

Rodney thought about it. "I also don't think it's crazy to imagine somebody in Calico Springs would follow a young Black girl around at night."

Bones rolled his eyes.

"You may not wanna hear this," Rodney continued, "but there are a lot of fucking weirdos in the world."

"Yeah," I added. "Remember that guy in Alaska who went to people's work and pretended to be a customer and then kidnapped them and tortured them in his garage?"

"Willie, that was *Criminal Minds*."

"Yeah, but it was based on a true story."

Bones picked at the leftover fries Rodney had brought out for us. "It's a pattern," he said. "Usually, when somebody thinks everybody's out to get them . . . it has more to do with them."

Rodney spooned her ice cream casually. "Sarai's young, she's wandering around late at night, she's Black—"

Bones recoiled. "See, you keep trying to make it a race thing."

"She's not making it a race thing," I said. "She just said she's Black—"

"Holy fuck, Willie." He turned to Rodney. "Willie's only defending you because he loves Sarai and won't shut up about her."

"When did I ever say that?"

"You didn't have to. You almost knocked over the table trying to drive her home last night."

"The table was just closer than it usually is!"

Rodney laughed, which made Bones smile, and I felt my face get hot so I buried it in my arms on the table.

"I'm just saying, maybe we should be careful about validating some of her . . . impulses, you know?"

Rodney shrugged, and I clenched my teeth.

CHAPTER 17

I DIDN'T MENTION Rory and Tyler's party in the days leading up, hoping Bones would forget about it, but it was the first
thing he said when he woke up that morning.

"We're leaving at seven. Don't accidentally end up in Egypt
or something, okay?"

"Are you sure they're gonna be okay with me coming?" I
asked.

"You'll be with me," he said. "Just don't say too much. Don't
give them any reason to think you're gonna be trouble."

He showered and got dressed an hour early, putting on a
new shirt Mom had bought him at the outlets that he said made
him look like a "California dickhead," but I guess that was the
look he was going for. At seven, Joe Kelly and Sarai pulled up,
but there was still no sign of Rodney. It wasn't until twenty
minutes later that she finally showed, not from next door, but
from the passenger seat of a green Subaru hatchback.

"Who the hell's that?" Bones asked, and before Rodney could
answer, blond Connor was hanging his head out the driver's
side.

"What's up, boys!"

Bones froze. His eyes flashed between Connor and Rodney, taking a cartoonish amount of time to put the obvious information together. Connor stayed in the car, head out the window, directly in front of our driveway.

Rodney was still wearing her bright red DQ polo. "Is that what you're wearing to the party?" Bones asked her as she walked to the garage.

"Actually," she said, "I don't think I'm gonna go."

Bones's face collapsed. "What? Rod, we told them you'd come!"

"I don't think they're gonna miss me."

Bones stared at her for a moment. No one else in the garage said anything.

"Rodney." He was pleading now. "We've been best friends for twelve years, we've got basically two months left 'til it's over, and now you wanna ditch us for some random golden retriever boy you just met?"

I looked out to the Subaru where Connor was bopping along to the song in an ad for a car dealership.

Rodney bit her lip but didn't speak, so Bones looked to the rest of the group for support. "Am I wrong? Is that not exactly what's happening here?"

Joe Kelly shrugged. Sarai turned her face away like she hadn't heard him. We all knew better than to get involved. It would only strengthen his resolve.

Finally, he came back around to Rodney. "Am I wrong?"

She tightened her lips. "I guess I wasn't aware our friendship was over in two months."

"Basically! You'll go to computer camp, then college, and we'll never see each other again!"

"That's not true," she protested. "I'll still see you every time I'm back in town."

"Maybe." Bones dropped his voice to a volume where I could hear the hurt in it. "Maybe I'll be too busy making money by then. And you'll have to fucking . . . schedule an appointment."

It was quiet for a long moment. Even though Connor still looked oblivious in his front seat, I noticed his window was down, so there was no way he hadn't heard the entire conversation. I almost admired it; how relentlessly optimistic it was of him to just sit there.

"Rodney, please," Bones said with a kind of urgency I'd rarely ever heard in his voice. "It's our last summer."

Slowly, painfully, she gave in. "Okay," she said finally. "Okay, you're right. But I told Connor we could hang out, so he's gotta come, okay?"

Bones shrugged.

"Do you wanna ride with us in his Subaru—"

"Absolutely fuck no," Bones said, and he marched out to the truck.

Tyler's grandma's cabin was south of town, overlooking the river, right at the turnoff to the new developments. It was safe from the water on a ridge, sticking quietly out of the woods and barely visible from the road. Tyler and Rory were sitting on the porch, two beers each, watching as guests arrived.

"Bones," one of them called as soon as he jumped out. "You made it!" His tone dropped as he saw the rest of us pile out of the two trucks. "And you brought a fucking army. . . ."

I watched Tyler's eyes scan across us, sticking on Connor, then Sarai, then landing on me.

"Sorry, Bones," he said right away. "We're not babysitting tonight."

It took him a minute to realize he was talking about me. "Babysitting? What do you mean? Willie's basically in college at this point."

"He's a sophomore," Tyler said, surprising both of us.

"He's a senior in dog years. Trust me, Willie parties all the time."

"Yeah, come on, Willie." Rodney grabbed my arm and walked straight toward the door, gambling that they wouldn't lay hands on her.

She was wrong. Tyler leapt up from his chair, and instead of getting in our way, went straight for her hand, wrenching it from my arm and keeping ahold of her shoulder. "Are you fuck-ing deaf?" he spat in my direction. "Or just blind?"

Immediately, Bones stepped between us. "Say it again."

"Easy," Rory laughed. "No need to get all hostile. We just can't have any issues with Tyler's parents. If they see somebody that young, they'll know there's minors and shut the whole thing down. Sorry, Willie."

Bones exhaled and took a few steps back, wincing as he

looked between me and Tyler.

"It's okay," I said. "I'll take the truck. I can pick you up later."

"You can't drive on your own."

"I was gonna end up driving your drunk ass home, anyway. Don't worry about it."

Tyler smirked. "See, he's the smartest one of all of you."

Bones handed me the keys. "Nothing stupid, all right? I'll text you when these guys change their minds."

"We won't," Tyler assured me. "But we'll see you for the backyard bonfire, right?"

Back in the truck, I drove toward town, then pulled off into a turnout overlooking the river. I didn't have anywhere to be and didn't feel like going home. It was the first time Bones ever let me have the truck by myself, and it felt like a shame to waste it.

I got out and walked to the ledge. I watched the river flow. It was at its high-water mark for the year, which I knew meant the current below was violent, pulling with the force of a hundred semitrucks. From this high up, though, it looked like it was barely moving. It flowed peaceful and innocent. Hard to imagine someone being swept away in it, the way they talked about it in stories. But I guess everything looks okay from far away.

When I got back in the car, I had two missed texts. I had to do a double take to confirm I was seeing it right—they were from Sarai.

I wanna go home

Can you come back and pick me up?

* * *

"It's weird to see you driving," Sarai said, her feet tucked under her on the passenger seat. "It's like . . . a dog driving a car. It just doesn't compute."

"You know I've got your life in my hands and terrible depth perception, right?"

She smirked and looked back to her phone. "Eye on the road, pal."

She didn't seem upset after leaving the party. When I got there to pick her up, she was already seated on the curb in front, alone.

"Why'd you wanna leave?" I asked.

"I didn't wanna go in the first place. But . . . I had a feeling this was how tonight was gonna go."

I stirred a bit in my seat, suddenly nervous, like I was doing something forbidden. "This?" I asked.

"You wouldn't get in," she said. "Bones would let you have the truck. And we'd be able to expand our radius."

I glanced over at her lap, where Manifest Atlas was already open on her phone.

"I've been playing every day," she continued. "But my mom won't let me use the car, so I've been going to the same spots, over and over. I wanna try somewhere new."

"Like where?" I asked.

"Like Lawton."

The excitement in my stomach turned sour.

Sarai noticed. "What?"

"I just don't know if Bones would want me taking the truck

all the way out to Lawton."

Sarai's lips pursed. I watched the air slowly deflate as she nodded and settled back into the seat. "I understand," she said flatly.

I took a deep breath. I realized I had no obligation to what Bones did or didn't want. He hadn't extended me the same courtesy. Not tonight, or any night, really. And if he never did what I asked—then why should I be obligated to do the same?

"So we should make sure he never finds out," I said, reassuring myself with a nod.

Sarai lit up with a wicked smile. "Aye, aye, captain."

"What are we looking for?"

"We've been so literal with our intentions," she said. "Murderer. Winston. Weapon. I remember you saying the first day, you've gotta be open to interpretations. Cast a big, wide net, then make sense of the puzzle in front of you after."

"You remember what I said?"

"Of course I do."

My chest swelled. It's nice to be taken seriously.

"So let's do that. Let's ask for something you could answer in a thousand different ways and just . . . see what it gives us. How about . . ."

AN EXPLANATION

CHAPTER 18

IT WAS EASIEST to get to the bridge by staying on the minimum maintenance roads along the river, instead of going all the way back into town and coming down the main road. I drove with extra caution. The turns were sharp, and I knew anyone who lived up here probably took the corners with angst, so I inched around every one, leaning my face to the mirror to get the cleanest look.

When we got to the bridge, I slowed to a crawl, feeling every bump as the truck rattled across.

Sarai watched me from the passenger seat, amused. "Are you afraid of Black people or something?"

I shook my head. "What? No—"

"'Cause you don't have to worry. You're with me, everybody knows me, it'll be cool—"

"I'm not afraid," I protested. "Why would you ask me that?"

She smiled. "You're holding your breath."

I made a show of letting it out, low and slow. "I go to Lawton twice a week, you know."

"You go to the bait shop twice a week," she said. "You go to *one place* in Lawton. That's not even the real Lawton. When's the last time you actually went into town?"

I shrugged. "A baseball tournament? I don't know, why would I?"

She sat back, resting her case. I didn't show it, but I realized she was right. The town was right next to us—soon it would be a part of us—and it was completely alien to me.

The road on the other side curled with the river, closer to the water than any road in Calico Springs. The river looked different on this side. Calico was the high-water side; other than the Basin, there were ridges and beaches to hold back the water. On this side, the river reached right up to meet the road. The buildings looked different, too. They were smaller, older, their bases discolored by water damage like what was left of Old Town. A few were fully destroyed, just their foundations left.

Sarai guided me, narrating as we drove.

"That place used to have the best pancakes in the world. Seriously, I think they won an award for them or something. Oh, you can get to the water if you walk down that way. Me and Caroline—that's my best friend—we used to swim there almost every day, and we didn't find out 'til high school it was actually one of the most dangerous parts of the river . . ."

I could hear the excitement in her voice, but when I glanced over, I saw in the reflection in the window that her face had fallen.

"What happened?"

She shook her head. "Nothing."

I didn't think it was my place to talk, so I focused on driving, slow and steady. Every time we passed a car going the other direction, I ducked slightly in the seat, just in case it was someone who might report seeing me to my family. Sarai noticed but didn't say anything. I guess she understood.

"They forgot about me," she said finally. "My friends. They all moved on."

I could hear the pain in her voice. "I mean . . . like you said, it's a long way to drive—"

"It's not even that. I mean, it was that. But they all have cars, they could see me if they wanted to. They just moved on. They barely text me back anymore, they've all been together every day, they got new best friends, and I got . . ."

"Us," I said.

"Yeah." She snorted. "Exactly."

The truck started to rumble as cracks in the pavement below us widened into potholes. I tried to steer around them, but the whole road was a mess of unsteady concrete.

"We've got better roads," I pointed out.

She shrugged. "Welcome to the broke side of the river."

I grimaced. "I thought *we* were the broke side of the river."

That made her laugh. "You know the developers haven't built a single thing in Lawton? They haven't even hired anybody from here to work on the developments."

"Why not?" I asked. "Joe Kelly said they're hiring anybody—"

"Same reason they don't want a merger. Because it would help us. They don't wanna share anything—taxes, developments, any of it—with Lawton. They want us to die." Sarai was quiet for a minute. "You know your brother doesn't want the merger to happen, right?"

I glanced back at her. "Neither does your boyfriend."

"What's that mean?"

"Nothing." I shrugged. "It kinda seems like, you're his girlfriend, and it obviously affects you way more than it affects him. . . ."

"Yeah, I'm his girlfriend," she repeated. "But his dad is his dad. And if you're raised one way, believing one thing for your entire life, then I can see how it would be tough to change that all right at once."

"Doesn't mean you have to date him."

"No," she said, smiling again. "But it means I can forgive him and see through it to the good stuff. Like how loyal he is. And how hard he's trying." I don't know if she was convincing me or herself, but she didn't feel she'd done a good enough job, because she added, "He's not an asshole, you know. He just . . . grew up around assholes. And I personally think it's cool to watch someone . . . fix their own programming."

I thought about it, the way Joe Kelly talked to her versus the way he talked when she wasn't around. I couldn't figure out which of those was the programming and which was who he actually was. I'd never really thought about it like that, like we were something outside of who people were telling us to be.

We were all getting programmed I decided. And I'd never thought much about what—or who—was programming me.

* * *

Our target took us to the far end of Lawton, almost outside the city limits, before we made a sharp left turn away from the water. After a half mile, Sarai held up her hand to stop me and showed me the target point in the middle of a forest-green blob. "This is the easiest way to get there."

As I pulled off, our right wheel sank into the mud. Sarai surveyed the tree line in front of us.

"We're gonna have to cut through."

"We can drive around. Try the other side?"

She shook her head. "It'll be easier this way. Trust me."

Everything felt wetter and heavier as we kicked our way through the muck. It looked the same as our Basin, but intensified: hotter, louder, stickier. I noticed a few different kinds of dragonflies, the type that usually roamed the waterline. We must have crawled over a dozen fallen trees as we walked.

"Are you sure nobody's gonna get pissed we're here?" I asked her at one point.

"Why would they get pissed?"

"'Cause I don't belong here."

Sarai shook her head. "I don't know why you're so obsessed with the idea that anybody belongs anywhere."

I thought about it surprisingly hard. Maybe that was my programming, the idea that people belonged certain places and not others. Put like that made it seem like there was some reason to program me. Like there was something they wanted me to steer clear of.

We'd been walking for a quarter mile when we came upon a building from behind. It was creepy, cabin-like, its concrete foundation marked by water damage. The shingling had been redone recently, from what I could tell, and the surrounding trees were tickling it in the wind.

There was a light on inside, a faint flicker from the basement, but otherwise, it looked abandoned.

"Turn your light off," Sarai whispered.

We met the target point about fifty yards behind the building. Using her phone, we inched ourselves directly on top of it, at a wedge created by a fallen log perching against a tupelo that was starting to droop from its weight. It felt almost fortified, sitting purposefully on the edge of the muck.

"An explanation," Sarai whispered and crawled into it.

I kept my eye fixed on the building. Despite its placement, so removed from the world, there was something about it that didn't feel lost. "Do you know what that building is?" I asked. She shook her head.

Sarai turned her phone to take a photo. The camera flashed, and I noticed something on the grass below her.

"Should we check the building?" she asked.

I held my finger to my lips and crawled past her into the crevice, flipping my light on.

"What?"

I brushed my hand through the tall grass, exposing some of the mud below. "Look."

Nearly a dozen cigarette butts peeked out of the flattened grass below. I picked one up. It was still round, instead of flattened like the ones that die in gutters. The tobacco sticking out was still brown.

I felt like I could hear Sarai's heartbeat as she crouched next to me. "Someone's been here," I whispered. "This exact spot."

I took the most complete cigarette I could find and secured it in my pocket. As I stood to step out of the crevice, my phone light tilted up to the building—just in time to see a figure running straight at where we were hiding.

Sarai screamed. We both scrambled backward, tripping over branches. My head slammed against a tree, sending my phone flying. The silhouette closed quickly, its arms up, holding an unmistakable object—a baseball bat.

"Who are you?" a voice bellowed after us.

I tried to pull myself up on a nearby branch, but it ripped under my weight. "Come on," Sarai screamed from behind me, but my phone was lost below the grass line. I tried to feel for it as I shot up, but as I turned, I collided with a low branch, sharp edges of its knots scraping my face. The world went blurry as I fell.

The figure stopped abruptly, upside down.

"Hold on, you're just kids."

At this decibel, the voice was vaguely familiar.

"What are you doing here? And why are you stalking my church?"

CHAPTER 19

PASTOR BAKER DIDN'T look like a pastor in this light.

He was wearing a Mizzou sweater and flannel pajama pants, a faint reminder of hair electrified to the side of his head. He had the same stout, back-and-forth walk as I'd noticed at the funeral, but up close you could see the gray in his facial hair, the wrinkles in his face.

"Tell me who you are," he panted. "So I can call your parents."

"I'm Sarai, this is Willie. We're not trying to hurt anybody."

He stared at her, and I watched the realization dawn on his face. "My God," he said. "I'm so sorry."

She nodded. The bat fell from his shoulder.

"What are you doing out here? I almost . . ." He looked down to the bat, disgusted, and threw it back across the lawn.

"We're playing a game," she explained. "It's a phone game. It gives you locations—"

"The one from the news," he said. "It brings you to locations on private property?"

"I guess."

Pastor Baker rubbed his temple. "I'm sorry. I hope you can forgive me. I've been on edge lately. Feels like there's a lot of folks moving through these woods, not to mention the police patrols, these curfews . . ." He looked genuinely troubled. "Hard to know what to think."

"They're probably playing the Game, too," Sarai said.

He blew air between his lips, scanning the forest. "Gotta be pretty self-important to think you're being stalked," he said. I could tell he didn't all the way believe it.

Sarai looked behind him to the building. "I thought your church was the big one downtown with the chapel? This doesn't look much like a church."

"It's temporary," he said. "Our building's stuck getting renovated. Haven't been able to put the money together to finish yet."

"Do you always work in your pajamas?" I asked.

He smiled. "Don't tell anyone, but it's a temporary home, as well. Just 'til we're back on our feet. Y'all interrupted my TV time."

Pastor Baker offered me his hand, pulling me out of the woods, his eyes still darting around with caution. "Best you go home," he said. "It's getting late, and they're talking about making the curfews permanent for the summer—"

"Pastor Baker," Sarai interrupted him, her voice quiet. "Can I ask you something?"

He nodded.

"The Game . . . it's all about intentions. You set an intention, and it brings you somewhere to find what you're looking for. Places you'd never ever go on your own. And I used it—we used it—that night." He knew exactly what night she was talking about. "Any chance you can . . . explain how that happened?"

I smiled at her choice of words. An explanation.

But Pastor Baker didn't smile. He stared at her, so seriously that she took a half step back.

"Why don't you two come inside for a moment," he said, and turned without waiting for a response.

He led us to the basement, a cozy room with green carpet and a few flowery, old couches. There were thirty folding chairs set up around a makeshift pulpit and cheap plastic table, more AA meeting than church. I saw his cot in the corner, an old edition iPad next to it. It was a humble existence, but then again, so was Jesus's.

"Manifest Atlas." He chewed on the words. "I get it. Like a map, but of things you want to manifest." He took a small zip-lock bag from his pocket. "You mind?"

We both shook our heads, and he loaded a dip of tobacco in his front cheek.

"Let me ask. Have you thought much about how this Game works? The technology?"

Sarai looked to me.

"Best as I can tell," I explained cautiously. "It's God. Something like a prayer."

That got a smile out of Baker. He shook his head and spat in the bottle. "Realistically, it's a random number generator. To your point, it relies on the mind of the person playing to create an explanation. . . . But that says more about the power of the mind to create explanations than to create dead bodies."

Sarai frowned. "So . . . you're saying it doesn't work?"

"I didn't say that."

There was something chilling in the way he said it, like it demanded an apology, so I immediately said, "Sorry."

He reached behind him, taking a Bible from below a nearby chair. "Do you both believe in God?"

We nodded.

"Do you believe that He has a plan for you? A direction He intends for your life to go?"

Again, we both nodded.

"And do you trust that plan? Do you trust Him with your direction?"

"Sure," Sarai whispered, with a small shrug.

"Good." He started to thumb through the Bible. "So let me ask you . . . how do you think God feels about you taking direction from this game?"

We were both quiet for a long minute.

"God made the Game," I said. "Right?"

"Lord's got plenty of ways of speaking to you," he said, still looking for the right chapter. "He doesn't need an app. In fact, this whole book here is full of stories of people finding their own apps, finding ways to resist that path. Change it, move off it." He found what he was looking for and used his finger to draw a strong crease in the book. "You got any idea what happens to those people?"

We shook our heads.

"'The Lord will send on you curses, confusion and rebuke in everything you put your hand to. Until you are destroyed and come to sudden ruin . . . The Lord will plague you with diseases until he has destroyed you . . . The sky over your head will be bronze, the ground beneath you iron. The Lord will turn the rain of your country into dust and powder; it will come down from the skies until you are destroyed.'"

We all sat in silence for a moment.

"Sounds pretty bad," I said.

Neither of them looked at me. I realized he hadn't really been talking to me.

"Have you noticed bad things happening to you since you started to play this game?"

"Um . . ." I felt her hesitancy. "I guess I have seen . . . maybe some people following me . . . and I've been having nightmares. . . ."

Baker nodded along, like he expected all of it.

"And, uh, of course—"

"You found a dead body."

I felt a small chill, hearing him say it in the context of the sky turning to bronze.

"Was that my fault?" Sarai asked.

The creases around Baker's eyes softened. "No. No, no, no. That's not it." He set the Bible down. "God is not unreasonable.

He understands that we stray. But, for the time being, and all times . . . walk the path, Sarai. Especially around here. Walk the path, and you will be rewarded."

His eyes lingered on her for a moment, before Baker stood up and collected our empty cups. "I had a false idol phase in college," he said. "Worshipped Prince, the singer. Started thinking that maybe he was the one with the plan for me. Turns out, I was just smoking way too much pot."

When I couldn't see him in the kitchen anymore, I turned to Sarai.

"I don't think the rain is gonna turn to dust or whatever," I assured her. "I think that's just a story. . . ."

Sarai was staring at the Bible he left behind. "He's not even talking about the Game." She shook her head. "He's warning us."

"Warning us what?"

"Not to leave the path. Not to ruffle feathers. He's saying the Game is pissing people off, and God doesn't want us to do that. Fucking pastors."

I sat up. It hadn't occurred to me Pastor Baker might be speaking in code. It wasn't the first time I'd noticed it, me and Sarai speaking different languages. She heard things I didn't hear. The curses, the confusion, the dust and powder and sudden ruin—that's what he was saying happened to people who broke the rules in Calico Springs.

"People over here always say that," Sarai continued. "Just stay out of the way, just keep your head down, don't make trouble . . ."

"What do you think?" I asked.

"I say, fuck the path."

When Baker came back, he'd placed me on the map. "You're Markie's boy," he said. "I've met him many times—is he still working on that catapult thing?"

"No." I shook it off. "He gave that up years ago."

"How far did he get?"

"I'll show you. It's still just a big pile of junk in our back-yard. . . ." I went into my pocket, but there was nothing there. "Shit—I mean—shit. Sorry."

Baker smiled. "Big fucking mistake," he said, and pointed up to God in the ceiling.

"I left my phone out back. I'm just gonna . . ."

I scrambled up and out the back door. When I got outside, my eye took a moment to readjust to the sudden darkness. I couldn't even see the tree line ahead of me, so I felt my way there, back to the fallen log.

When I was pretty sure I was in the right spot, I started kicking at the grass below me. The air felt wetter than before, which made the ground feel less stable. I was in the right spot—I could tell by the cigarettes—but my phone wasn't there.

I stood up, confused, and listened to the darkness. I heard a buzzing noise, and twenty feet away, saw the light of my phone peeking through the grass.

Bones was calling me. I watched as the call went unanswered and the phone flipped back to its lock screen, peppered by noti-fications. I could just make out the text—ten missed calls, all from Bones.

"Shit," I muttered and fought my way toward it. I couldn't imagine how furious he'd be, especially if he learned where I was, who I was with, and what I was doing.

My foot caught as I tried to step over a branch, so I froze it in the air, my motion stopping—but the sound didn't. Something else was moving.

"Hello?" I asked quietly, not wanting an answer. My whole body pulsed to my heartbeat. I scanned the area around me, nothing but milky blackness. Instead of looking down at my phone, I waited, my eye angled up. For a full minute, I breathed with the forest.

The phone started to buzz, and in the halo of light it created, a pitch-black figure materialized—less than five feet away from where I was standing.

"AH!" I screamed and fell backward. I heard the sound of the thing taking off away from me, pushing dirt and branches in my direction. I could only make out pieces as it ran—huge, towering, dark. It was really there. I knew it was there—

But Bones would never believe me. I had to prove it. I swept up my phone and took off after it.

"Stop! What are you? Stop!" I crashed forward, pushing branches inches from my face as I ran.

The forest thinned, opening into a clearing, and across it, I saw the dark figure again. It had the form of a person, but its edges were amorphous, a piece of the darkness around it.

"Stop!" I shouted again. It turned to look back at me and the air left my lungs.

It wasn't human. Where the face should have been, a black hole swallowed the light around it, skinless and blank. Two eyes, painted white and misshapen, stared back at me, a white mouth gaping. Above them both, on either side of the forehead, were small but unmistakable horns.

It was the face of the devil.

I stumbled back, and my feet slid from under me, Baker's warnings about leaving the path ringing in my ears. I hit the forest floor hard and my patch went flying, exposing the soft skin over my eye to the crunch of the forest floor. Bark, dirt, and small rocks skidded along my face. I screamed.

The devil disappeared.

Rolling over, I gingerly tapped the area for damage. I felt for my eye patch, but it hurt to even open my eye. I could feel my face burning, blood leaking from my forehead. I didn't want to go back to the church looking like this—I didn't want anyone to see my socket, ever, especially Sarai—but the longer I waited, the worse the stinging in my head got. I tied a bandana from my pocket loosely around my eye and started back toward safety in darkness.

Unsure of the path, and now terrified to leave it, I had to feel my way, tree-to-tree, to get back. Every few seconds, I stopped to listen, to make sure I wasn't being followed.

"Willie?" I heard Sarai. "Willie, are you still out here?"

"I'm here," I called, ducking my face to hide my eye.

I didn't know how to explain to her what I'd just seen. The way it appeared from nowhere, the way it moved, the way it sucked light from its surroundings, the horns . . .

I found the clearing by listening for it, the echo of bugs softer where the trees weren't. My shin collided with a fallen log, and I knew it was the right one, our log.

"Oh my God, Willie." Sarai found me. "What happened?"

I turned and stared off after the devil, keeping my face away from her. "I saw something," I said. "Someone—something—was out here."

"A person?" she asked.

I nodded, then shook my head. "Yes, I don't know. I think so."

Sarai put an arm around me, pulling me into her body and clutching me to her chest. Our breathing falling into rhythm as we listened and stared out into the pitch-black forest.

"Willie," she whispered. "This is where the Game brought us, right here." She took a deep breath. "Whoever attacked you . . . they're using the Game."

I stabilized myself against the tree, but as my hand hit it, my fingers slid into something—a break in the bark, smooth and intentional. It was a carving. I felt my way down it, around it, an emblem of some sort, spreading in multiple directions, placed there to be discovered.

It was etched on purpose, fresh, rough, and hurried but intentional—the circle, the wings, the beak, diving to the earth.

It was the dove.

PART FOUR

THE CREATOR

FACEBOOK POST

Katey Ulrich
Calico Springs, MO

I HAVE FOUND EVIDENCE OF SATAN HERE IN CALICO
SPRINGS!!!!
I was playing MANIFEST ATLAS which I know most people
on here have heard of now. It sent me to the woods behind
Kal and Jen Sullivan's house, and I saw the most disturbing
image I've ever found in Calico Springs.
THE BONES OF A DEAD ANIMAL, LAID OUT IN THE WOODS,
STRUNG UP LIKE IT WAS SOME KIND OF SHRINE.
DEVIL WORSHIPPERS BEWARE. YOU ARE NOT WELCOME
HERE. I SHALL WORSHIP NO OTHER GOD BEFORE THE
LORD GOD AND WE WILL DO BATTLE.

FACEBOOK POST

Kal Sullivan
Calico Springs, MO

Leave my wife's art alone, you monsters.

I have seen too many comments about Satan worship and I will not tolerate it.

It is art. It is a celebration of the life of a deer. She has spent two years gathering the bones to make that art in our yard. Do you know how hard it is to find deer bones in Missouri? Not easy. Do I understand all of the hobbies that my wife has? I do not.

But am i happy when people come online and say her life work is just a bunch of devil worship? NO.

It's red paint. Not blood. Red paint.

FACEBOOK POST

Dale Seltzer
Calico Springs, MO

This is a final warning to all of you fuckers.

I know you're all on here, reading these, so heed this warning and heed it good. I own all the land north of Crestview, til you get to the basin.

If you keep going on my property, I WILL SHOOT YOU. I dont care how you got there. I dont care if God himself sends you there. I WILL SHOOT YOU.

My goats are very easily scared. They do not like to be disturbed. If they fall, it takes nearly an hour to get them upright again.

So beware, all of you Atlas people. Keep playing this game, you are one step away from a bullet in your FUCKING BRAIN.

CHAPTER 20

BONES COULD BARELY look at me the next day.

Rodney was supposed to be working the day shift at DQ, so we invaded our usual booth, but as soon as we got there, Bones tucked himself in the corner with his hood up and his face in his phone, and we sat in silence for almost a half hour.

Evidently, he'd called me ten times the night before because he'd been thrown out of the party.

The story, as I could figure out from him, was that people were passing around a bottle of Captain Morgan, and in trying to take his second go at it, Bones went over the edge. He puked, violently, in and around Tyler's grandma's kitchen sink. Tyler saw it and tossed him immediately. Joe Kelly tried to reason with them, but there was a strict no puke policy. Rodney and Connor sat with him on the curb for almost an hour while they waited for me, but they had to leave for Rodney to make curfew. So as the party started to filter out, everybody saw him—helpless, stranded, and covered in his own vomit.

And it was clear who Bones blamed for that.

"You are responsible for the truck, which means you need to be there when I call you!" he screamed on the way home. "If I can't get home when I need to, then what the fuck do I need you for?"

He'd been too drunk to tell him anything on the drive, and today, he woke up not talking, which sucked, because I needed to talk to him. I finally had something he'd have to take seriously, immutable proof that we were all in danger. I squirmed in my seat, the information eating at my throat until it finally got out.

"Bones, something happened last night."

"When?" He looked up, bloodshot and wild. "When you were stranding me out in the fucking boonies?"

I let it pass.

"What happened?" he asked.

"I got attacked."

He shifted in the booth.

"I was looking for my phone in the woods—and when I found it, somebody was there. And they shoved me over, and I hit my eye on a branch and ran away—"

"Where were you?"

I swallowed. "In Lawton."

Another wave of rage crested on Bones's face. "You took the truck all the way to fucking Lawton? No wonder you got attacked, they were probably trying to rob you."

My stomach twisted. "It's actually really nice over there."

"Were you by yourself?"

I kept my face straight and nodded. Sarai and I had agreed, I couldn't lie about where I'd been, at least not to Bones, but that didn't mean I had to tell him everything.

"So . . . when I asked you to be responsible with the truck, you actually decided to fuck off to Lawton—"

"I can only say sorry so many times."

"Well, say it again."

"I'm sorry."

He took a minute to decide if it satisfied him. The hood came off, and he sat up to look at me more directly. "Are you okay?"

I nodded.

"Lemme see your eye."

I turned up the patch, and he winced.

"We gotta get some antibiotics on it."

"I'm fine." I dropped it and leaned forward, trying to show him I was serious. "Bones. Something serious is going on. This is proof. Somebody—something—is using the Game to hurt people."

He thought about it, staring out the window. "It was probably just somebody fucking with you," he said quietly.

"They weren't just fucking with me! I'm serious. It was the exact spot where the Game brought me, somebody jumped out and attacked me, and they . . ."

I trailed off, which made Bones blink back toward me. "They what?"

I took a deep breath. "They looked like the devil."

"Jesus." He shook his head and threw his hood back over it.

"Bones," I repeated, but he was back into his phone.

I kept staring, lines being drawn in silence down the center of the booth. We disagreed constantly, but I'd always trusted him to take me seriously when it mattered, to be there for me when I needed help. But evidently, that protection only applied when it suited him. Evidently, he only cared about me when I did what he told me to do.

"It's a crazy story, Willie," he said, without looking at me. "But I don't think many people are gonna believe it."

I knew what he really meant was, he didn't believe it. What he really meant was, I was on my own.

I spent the rest of the day trying to understand why someone would want to control Manifest Atlas.

It made sense, plain as Sarai said it, and Rodney had been saying it all along, that someone was using the Game. To intimidate me, I figured.

The Game led me to those graves. The Game led us to Winston's body. The Game led us to the spot where the devil attacked me in the woods.

The part I couldn't square was why. If someone had murdered Winston Lewis, why would they want a bunch of teenagers to find the body? And if that same person had dug those graves, why would they want me to find them? What could possibly be the point?

The only one I landed on was the same I'd felt since the beginning—that the Game continued to work. Which meant the devil in the woods was somehow an explanation.

I was watering the plants in our backyard that evening when a Toyota Camry pulled up next to me and parked. No one got out, and the driver was hidden behind tinted glass, so I kept watering, aware of the eyes on me. After a few minutes with no movement, I pulled my phone and dialed 9-1-1, my finger hovering over the Call button, just in case. . . .

But the door finally swung open, and Deputy Schnack lifted himself out.

"Hey, Willie." He walked toward me, hands in his pockets. He wasn't wearing his uniform, instead a plain white polo with the school logo embroidered on the pocket. "Just doing a little gardening?"

"Chores," I said. "What about you?"

He smiled. "Oh, 'bout the same. Your brother home?"

I shook my head.

"You mind if I holler for a second?"

I glanced back at the kitchen window behind me. Mom was at church, so I knew the house was empty, and it felt like Schnack knew it, too. Like he'd chosen this time, scoped it out so I was alone.

"You sure I shouldn't have my mom . . ."

"Oh no." He shook his head. "Nothing like that. Just a friendly conversation."

I nodded and took my time walking back to the house to kill the hose. Deputy Schnack had been on Sarai's list of people she thought might have it out for Winston. The mustached cop, the one who tried to set her up in front of her mom.

We'd disqualified him as a suspect, same as everybody else, but I realized—I'd seen his car the night I went to the Basin. Deputy Schnack wasn't at the baseball game.

When I turned back to him, I made sure to stand at least twenty feet away, so whatever he wanted to say, he had to say it loud.

"First," he said. "I just wanted to make sure you're doing okay. What you saw . . . No kid should have to see that. Hell, most guys on the force have never had to see anything like that. Could give you nightmares."

I stared back at him. I hadn't told anybody about my nightmares. Lucky guess, I assumed, but he had this way of talking that made it seem like he already knew more than he was letting on. Like he was one step ahead of the conversation.

"I'm all right," I said quietly. "I've seen plenty of dead deer."

He chuckled. "Good, really good."

He took a couple absent-minded steps toward me, closing the gap by half. It was disorienting, seeing him in normal people clothes. It clearly felt off for him as well—the jeans fit awkwardly, a little too tight, so he had to keep doing a shuffle with his hands in his pockets to keep them from riding up.

"I was just following up on a few outstanding questions, and I was hoping you could help me get my head around that, uh . . . that game you were telling us about."

I didn't move. For however he'd sounded in the police station, it sounded like he was taking it serious now.

"You said it gives you a spot to go explore?" he asked.

"A target."

"Right. And that target, it's right there on your phone? Dot on the map?"

I nodded.

"Got it." He adjusted his jeans again. "Now . . . here's my question. Is it possible to control the Game? Put your own locations in, decide in advance?"

It was a more complicated question than he realized. Of course you could control the Game, that's what an intention was. But the means of controlling it, the ways in which your intention influenced the target, and who was giving that target—that was the part we didn't understand.

I assumed he meant literally, so I shook my head. "You'd have to be a hell of a lot smarter than me," I told him.

"Got it. . . . None of you, know how to do that?"

I shook my head again.

"All right," he said, a little disappointed. It was obvious what theory he was chasing. He didn't think the Game brought us to the mill that night on accident.

"And it was your phone, right?" Schnack asked.

"I'm sorry?"

"The target, that night you found the body? It was on your phone?"

I shifted a bit, picturing the night for the first time. The gathering in the garage, the all-black clothing, the gin bottle going person-to-person, Joe Kelly with his arms over the back of my recliner, the screen spinning, Bones lurking behind . . .

"No," I said. "It was Joe Kelly's phone."

"But you saw it, right? You saw the target was on the mill?"

I felt a hiccup in my throat. "Yeah," I said. "Yeah, I saw it."

He nodded again and turned back to his car. "All right, thanks, Willie. Go easy on the watering, gonna be a wet summer yet."

I watched him walk away, the image of that night still alive in my head. I couldn't believe I hadn't thought about it, but he was right. We didn't look at it together. We didn't crowd around the phone to see the target for ourselves. It was Joe Kelly alone who'd seen the map, and Joe who told us to go to the mill. If Joe Kelly knew something we didn't, he didn't even have to control the Game. He just had to hide the screen.

"Oh, Willie?"

Schnack stopped on his way back to the car, checking around us one more time for wandering ears. "You didn't hear it from me, but . . . you might wanna go easy playing that game."

"Why?" I asked.

"We've had a few incidents . . . mostly out-of-town folks. Just some people upset, is all. You take care."

I watched him work to crouch back down into his car, fighting the tight inseam of his jeans.

There was more to this than just the question, I realized. There was the fact that Schnack was still asking questions at all. And he was doing so in blue jeans that didn't fit, jeans that he clearly never wore . . . because unlike everywhere else in his life, he couldn't wear his uniform. Because this wasn't police business.

Deputy Schnack was operating on his own, which meant either he didn't agree with the police . . . or he knew more than the rest of them.

I FOUND AN ADDRESS.

> **TunaTuna:** FINALLY. it took forever, but we got the ownership records for the building in St. Louis and guess what? The name listed is FRANK MARTIN. And he's got an address in REDDING BLUFF MISSOURI, an hour away.

> **HotRod:** HOLY SHIT YES!! Send send send!!!

> **Tiger45:** Don't wanna burst bubbles, but you don't have to validate your business license address, they might have just put down the warehouse to be safe

> **HotRod:** Maybe maybe not, we gotta check it out either way, right????

> **Slinky:** Who's going?

> **HotRod:** OMWWWWWW!!!!

CHAPTER 21

IT WAS A few days later, Rodney made the biggest discovery yet.

Bones had picked me up from work, and when we got home, Rodney was waiting in the garage. She stood when she saw the truck approaching, beaming ear to ear. I saw Bones's face lift, smiling back, before he turned farther and saw Connor was waiting in there, too.

"Seriously, man," Connor said. "My dad sells parts. You say the word, we can swap out that converter. Sounds like there's a dead animal in there."

Bones ignored him, slamming the door with extra force.

"I got a reply," Rodney said, her face flushed. "Late last night. Someone in St Louis went to a courthouse to look at land records. . . . We found the Creator."

My heart skipped. "Are you serious? Who is it?"

"The name on the filing is Frank Martin," she said. "Probably a fake, like every other name, but the physical address has to be real . . . and it's in Redding Bluff. They live two hours away."

"We think they live in Redding Bluff," Connor tempered her. "We don't know anything for sure."

I understood why Rodney was so excited. "That must be why all the stories are local, like you said." I nodded to Connor. "The Game hasn't spread. We're like . . . the testing ground."

Rodney handed me her phone, open to a forum where someone had posted a photo of the address, handwritten on an official document in block-letter handwriting, and turned back to the map on the wall, starting to fill it in with our results from the last few weeks. "This is it," she said. "This is our answer."

17666 Poplar Court Way. I clocked the last three numbers, trying hard to make it nothing more than a coincidence.

"Testing ground . . . for what?" Bones asked.

"We're gonna go find out," Rodney announced. "Tomorrow morning, before my shift."

"I'm in," I told her. "We should decide how to approach them, especially since they're probably not going to want to tell us anything, at least not right away."

"Sarai's coming, too," Rodney said. "But Joe's gotta help his dad, so we still have two seats in the car."

She looked to Bones, so I did. He squinted toward the sun, like he was thinking hard about it.

"Shit," he said. "Me and Willie can't go."

"Why not?" I asked.

He looked at me. It was obvious. "Dad's birthday, dude. The barbecue, remember?"

My stomach dropped. "I thought he said Mom didn't wanna do it this year."

"I guess she changed her mind."

"We can go early," Rodney said. "I've gotta work at two—"

"Lunch is at noon," Bones said, matter-of-fact. He saw I disagreed and pulled out his phone. "You want me to call Dad for you, tell him you're gonna try to make it to the first family meal in three months? He'll rip your fucking head off."

I dropped my head, and Bones looked back to Rodney and Connor.

"Have a good time, okay? Take some pictures for us." He turned his lip up and walked inside.

Bones was right, there was no way Dad would let me skip. If I showed up late, it'd be even worse. I felt a few tears well up in my eyes.

"Willie," Rodney whispered. "We can leave before he wakes up. We'll have you back in time, I promise."

I glanced at the doorway to make sure Bones wasn't hovering. I'd never left the house without telling him, let alone somewhere two hours away. If he found out, it would be a category five, full-on shitstorm, the likes of which I'd never endured before.

But Bones had made it clear, I was on my own now.

At five the next morning, I grabbed the bag I'd hidden under my bed and slid my feet onto the wooden floor of my room as slowly and gently as I could. I got dressed in silence, listening for noise throughout the house, but other than the quiet tick of Mom's old grandfather clock in the living room and the birds outside the window, it was perfectly quiet.

I slipped out into the hallway and measured each step toward the back door, but as I passed Bones's room, I paused.

I never did anything without Bones. So much so, my brain had re-formed around our being inseparable. Every terrible moment I'd ever had, every time I'd screwed up or gotten myself into trouble, he'd been there to cushion it. It occurred to me, if something went wrong today, it would be mine and mine alone to deal with. For a minute, I thought about texting him, even if it meant pissing him off, just so he'd know where I was if things really went south.

But I didn't. Instead, I inched open the sliding door, just far enough that it didn't hit the part that squeaked, and ran down the porch, past the garden, and to the street, where Connor's Subaru idled three houses down.

Sarai was waiting in the back seat, packed in with the contents of Connor's dorm. Pillows, blankets, a whiteboard, a mini iron, a poster of Isaac Newton ripping a bong. She had signs of sleep, bags under her eyes, and stray hairs that were usually pulled tight, but her face was alive and excited. "Ready to catch a killer?" she asked when I crawled in.

Connor drove slowly, responsibly, commenting every few minutes on how little shoulder he had and how many semis there were. We talked excitedly the whole way up. I told them about Schnack's visit, leaving out the part about Joe Kelly, which made Sarai even more convinced the deputy was a genuine suspect.

"He's the one who ignored the Game initially," she said. "And he hates people from Lawton, my mom said it, even before this. He's always watching us. I bet he was the police car Pastor Baker was talking about, hanging out at his church. . . . It had to be him."

After an hour, Sarai nodded off to sleep, and Connor put his AirPods in to listen to meditation music, so it was just me and Rodney awake.

She turned around and wedged her face between the two front seats to look at me. "What are you gonna tell your brother?" she asked.

I sometimes forgot how well Rodney knew us. She'd been there for all of it, the years of growing together, the reliance on each other, she'd seen it firsthand. She knew what it took for me to lie to Bones, and how airtight that lie would have to be.

"Called into work," I said. "I already talked to Abe, he's gonna cover for me."

"Hide your bike?"

"Behind the bins in your backyard."

She smiled and nodded, approving the plan.

I readjusted in the back seat. "I don't know why he didn't just come with us."

She nodded, tight-lipped. "Why do you think that is?"

I shrugged. "I don't know. It's like he doesn't want anything to do with the Game, he's suddenly hanging out with Rory and

Tyler. Even when he talks about the bonfire, he talks about them, not us. Ever since he decided he was gonna stay in Calico Springs instead of college, it's like he's a whole different person. . . ."

It was subtle, but I saw her face fall slightly, a drop in her eyebrow.

"What?" I asked.

Rodney swallowed and sat up, looking out the front, like she hoped the car ride might be over.

"What?" I asked again, more urgently.

She shook her head. "Willie . . . Bones didn't decide to stay in Calico Springs. It was his only option."

"Yeah, sure, other than the scholarship. . . ."

"No," she said. "He never had a scholarship. He told everybody he did, but . . . I read the letters from Westminster. It never existed."

I recoiled at that and sat up. "What do you mean letters? They gave it to him at the game, when their coach came to watch, he offered it to him on the spot. . . ."

Rodney shook her head again. "He only started telling people that, like, a month after. He didn't even get in."

It landed like hot acid in my stomach, fighting up into my throat. Even for Bones, this was too elaborate a lie. No one could keep that up. The announcers at the baseball game, the dinner with our family, the calls to every relative, the high-school yearbook—surely Bones wouldn't have the stomach to look all of them in the face and lie like that? Selling them on a future that he knew was never going to happen?

"No fucking way," I told her, suddenly certain she was jealous. "You're not the only one who can get a scholarship, Rod. He wouldn't . . ."

She didn't say anything, just let me fail the end of my own sentence. As I remembered the day he told me, I realized, of course he would. Lying to someone's face, sticking to it despite proof of the contrary . . . it wasn't just something Bones was capable of. It was who he was.

"I'm sorry, Willie," Rodney said with real regret. "He made me swear I wouldn't tell you, but . . . I guess I figured you should know."

I sat back against my seat and watched out the window, tears stinging the corners of my eyes. I held them back and instead just glared at the passing highway signs. He'd made it about us, best friends our entire lives, tearing up the streets. But it didn't have a single fucking thing to do with me. It was him, failing, and blaming it on me.

Rodney checked Connor, oblivious in the seat next to her, and leaned in farther. "That's why we broke up," she said. "I found out, and when I brought it up, he told me he was doing it for me, so we could keep dating . . . like, he thought he was protecting me or something. But it wasn't to protect me. He was trying to control me."

We got to the address just before eight a.m., as the world was waking up.

Redding Bluff was one of those towns that used words like "paradise" to describe itself and you couldn't tell whether it was ironic. They had the best malls in southern Missouri and every fast-food restaurant under the sun. The houses all looked like screen-printed copies of one another, the same design with different trim.

I kept waiting to pass into the town center, where the malls were at, but it never came. Once we were off the interstate, it was the edges of town—suburban, quiet, rich. We looped the block three times before realizing, 17666 Poplar Court Way wasn't an office building or even a home—it was a high-end apartment complex.

"Jesus," Rodney said. "They don't even have an office, it's just a house."

"There's no unit number on the address," I pointed out.

"Shit." Connor pulled into the back of the lot. "We're not gonna know who we're looking for. Did we just drive all the way up here to . . ."

Before he could finish, Sarai was already out of the car. She slammed her door behind her, and without waiting, she took off for what looked like a leasing office in the front.

"She can't just walk in," Connor said, but she did exactly that.

I held my breath, and less than a minute later, she was on her way back across the lot. Rodney rolled down her window.

"They all have separate entrances," Sarai said. "Separate addresses."

We'd made a plan on the way up to approach the front door all together, knock, and just start asking questions. I was in charge of taking a video from my phone, keeping it hidden at my hip so we wouldn't scare off whoever answered. We'd keep asking questions, one after another, until they either let us inside or shut the door on us, in which case we'd stay at the front. Sooner or later, they'd realize we weren't going away.

Sarai led us through the complex, reading addresses aloud as she went. She was loud, bopping like she belonged. Maybe because she was that confident or so she wouldn't lose her nerve, I could never tell. Toward the back of the complex, shielded from the lot and up one flight of stairs to a small landing . . . we found 17666.

It was new and expensive, I could tell. The lock wasn't on the handle with a key but on top of it, one of those fob machines where you touched your key. Sarai stared at the door for less than a second before letting loose three authoritative knocks. I put my camera up on my hip and pressed Record.

Nothing. We waited and then tried the doorbell.

Again, nothing. I wasn't sure what I expected to hear inside—confused voices? A dog? Crying children? None of it came. The apartment seemed empty.

I watched Sarai process, leaning out to survey the floor, the patio that stuck off the back.

"I guess nobody's home," Connor observed, clearly angling like it was a good reason to give up. He was the most anxious of any of us, which didn't make sense, seeing as he had the least skin in the game, but I guess that was just his personality.

I went back down the stairs and gave the place a full survey. The unit had glass windows on the front, at the second level, a garage below it. I tried the accessible windows, but all of them were locked.

We stood in silence for a long minute.

"How long do we wait?" Rodney asked.

As we stood there awkwardly, a man made his way across the parking lot, stopping for a second to give us a curious look. He waved, so we all waved back, like we belonged.

"Let's leave a note and get outta here," Connor said, once the man was in his car. "Something about this is giving me a really bad feeling."

I watched Sarai calculating something in her head. She took a deep breath. "I'm sorry, everybody," she said. "But . . . somebody killed my stepdad. And this motherfucker knows who."

Before any of us could stop her, so quick we forgot not to scream, Sarai reached into her bag and pulled out a small hammer. "Wait!" Connor tried to shout, but it was too late. She swung the hammer down hard at the door handle.

The handle rejected the force with a loud *clank*. Connor and Rodney recoiled, but she lifted it, readying to do it again.

"It's not gonna open!" Connor shouted.

"I just need it to pop out," Sarai said.

"Okay, well, you're not gonna—NO!"

She swung it down hard again. This time, she connected, the silver plating over the handle denting, some of the inner machinery along with it. Sarai didn't wait, raising the hammer for a third time, and Connor scrambled toward her, putting his arms around her. "It's not worth it—" She struggled to get one more swing in, but he was around her, turning her from the doorway—

When there was a soft clicking noise.

"Guys!" I pointed.

Like magic, shot straight down from heaven, the door handle glowed green.

Rodney stabbed at it, catching it before the light disappeared, and the handle pushed all the way down. She held the door open by half an inch, all of us catching our breath. I looked up to the sky and said a small thank-you.

Slowly, with barely any force, Rodney pushed the door open, and I watched her face twist in profile.

Whatever we were doing, it wasn't fun anymore.

"We can't stay here," she said urgently.

"What?" I asked.

Keeping the camera running, I turned to follow her inside and walked into a wide-open, bright-white mess. The house was trashed.

Not unclean or left urgently—it was destroyed. There were papers thrown across the floor, kitchen appliances around the room, a television on its side. There was something here, and someone had turned the place over looking for it.

It didn't look like the office of a tech company or the home of a tech creator—it looked empty, like whoever lived there barely lived there.

My breaths were measured as we silently crept into the kitchen. The stove was left open, the microwave clock was blinking, the appliances were unplugged. I let the camera lead, noticing something else.

There were no photos. Nothing on the fridge, nothing on the shelves, not a single piece of identifying information. I kept moving, into the office, where paper was scattered across the desk and the floor. I turned it over—it was blank.

I started to get the same eerie, terrible feeling we were being watched. I scanned for cameras but didn't see any immediately, but that didn't mean they weren't there. I felt the creak of every floorboard, the room bending toward me with every step I took.

"Sarai," I whispered, unsure of where she was at. "I don't think we're going to find anything."

No answer. I crept down the hallway, clocking the nails on the wall where photos no longer hung.

"Sarai," I whispered again, my stomach sinking as I reached the end of the hallway, one door left, a presence looming inside—

"Hey!"

I jumped out of my skin. She was behind me, emerging from a bathroom. "I found something."

"Good," I said. "'Cause I couldn't find anything. It's like no one actually lives here. Or if someone does, I don't know anything about them."

"I know one thing." Sarai's face was electrified, her hands trembling as she held a single paper in her hand. "This was in the copier. I don't think they meant to leave it behind."

This page wasn't blank. On it was printed a map, topograph- ical and detailed, with all kinds of measurements and markings that I didn't recognize. The area, however, I recognized imme- diately; the only place in the world I really, truly knew.

It was Calico Springs.

CHAPTER 22

WHEN I GOT home, the garage door was wide open and Bones was sitting in the recliner in a polo shirt. I didn't bother asking to be dropped a few houses away, instead letting Connor pull straight to the top of our driveway. Bones stared at me the whole way down.

"You look nice," I told him.

"Where the fuck were you?"

"Work," I said.

"Funny. I went to pick up some line this morning, and you weren't there."

I shrugged. "Must not have seen me."

"You're a terrible liar," he said. "Better try harder than that when you tell Mom, 'cause if she finds out you went all the way to Redding without telling her—"

"Shh."

Bones balled up his face, all-knowing. "See? I thought you were at work."

He followed me into the house, stalking from behind. I kept

my head down past the living room, but Mom wasn't there. The whole place had been cleaned, to the point it was barely recognizable. I heard the clattering of pots and pans from the kitchen and headed straight for my room, slamming the door before Bones could follow.

I changed my shirt and by the time I hit the top button, Dad's truck was pulling into his old spot in the driveway. As soon as he opened the door, Libby bounded out the driver's side and ran straight for Mom, who collapsed to the floor, laughing as he licked her up and down. She'd put curls in her hair, which I knew took her hours, and she was wearing a silk-looking shirt with flowers all over it. I couldn't remember the last time she'd dressed up like that.

Dad walked up behind Libby, a flannel tucked into his jeans and a bouquet of grocery store flowers in his hand.

"Hey there, Willie. Bones." He hiccuped as he got to Mom. "Jenny."

"Come on in," she said, smiling at him. "Let me show you around."

Dad had gone all out. He brought his own pitcher of lemonade and two different premade salads from the store, along with a case of Miller Lite, a pack of hot dogs, and a rack of bacon to wrap them. Once he dropped the food on the back porch, he went to the back of his truck and wheeled out a brand-new grill, one of the big ones with the monster metallic hoods. He plugged it in for us and fired it up, passing out beers from a cooler he kept at his feet. Mom cracked one with him, and I watched them share a silent, satisfied toast.

Everything at our house was different when Dad was around. I'd forgotten what it was like. We talked more on the patio than we'd talked at three months' worth of dinners—everything from the merger to Trump to the county fair, the episode of *Criminal Minds* where the nerdy one's mom ended up being a psycho, the end of the school year to the start of the summer, the level of the river to the fishing Dad was doing on the Bend even though he shouldn't have. By the time we finally sat down around the table, Mom was red in the face from laughing so much.

Bones looked thrilled. He even offered to pray.

"Dear God. Make the summer last forever. Thanks for the food. Amen."

Libby curled up at my feet, knowing I was his most likely target for scraps, and we ate, smiling at each other over ketchup stains.

"How's things going with the committee?" Dad asked Mom, innocently enough. "Unity, you call it?"

She shrugged. "It's fine. Something to do—"

"They pay you for that?"

"No, but. Good work's good work."

Dad nodded. "Well, you shouldn't have to be working at all," he said, gesturing to the bounty in front of us. "I've been getting more work than even I can handle. John said he's got a couple investors from St. Louis looking to turn the developments into a resort spot. That's a lot of new builds, but . . . you know John.

Not many people he trusts."

Dad took a long sip, proud of himself. It was hard to deny how nice it was—I was on my third bacon dog and nobody had said shit.

"You should see what he's doing for the county fair next week. Putting up one of them huge stages for the band, massive sound system, and he's paying for all of it himself, just a little gift to the town. . . ."

Out of the corner of my eye, I saw Bones set his food down and sit up, like he'd been waiting for this break in the conversation. "Actually, Dad," he said, "I've been meaning to talk to you. With me staying in town, I was thinking . . . how about if I come get a job with you? Working on the developments."

Dad's chewing slowed, but he didn't say anything right away, instead stabbing at the potato salad on his plate with a fork.

"You think you could put in a good word?" Bones asked. "I mean, you said it yourself, it's more work than you can handle. I figure I'd be a shoo-in."

The smile Dad gave him was more of a grimace than anything. "Didn't you graduate a month ago?"

Bones nodded.

"And you're just thinking this now, huh?"

"Well, yeah," Bones said. "It's my last summer here, so I was just waiting 'til the summer's over—"

"Oh, good, I mean, as long as it's convenient for you."

I saw the flicker in Bones's eyes get frantic. "I just didn't want to be a bother, but I could start today if y'all need. I'll start yesterday, just . . . tell me where."

Across the table, Mom had stopped eating and was watching Dad intensely. Dad glanced to her, as if reading her eyes, then back to Bones.

"I don't know, son," he said. "I don't know if you're cut out for this kind of work."

Bones's eyes got wide, his face blank. I couldn't help but feel bad for him. Dad had spent the last three months telling us how good the job was, how much work there was to go around. Joe Kelly had acted like anybody with a pulse could get in. And now, evidently, Bones wasn't good enough.

Mom went back to eating, and I thought I saw what looked like a small smile on her face.

"Dad, come on," Bones urged. "You can't even talk to them for me—"

"Maybe in a year or two, when you've grown up a bit."

"What am I supposed to do—"

"I'm done talking about it," Dad said, and shrugged at him, like there was nothing he could do. We went back to eating in silence, and I saw his eyes flash once more to Mom before turning on me.

"What about you, Willie?" he asked. "What're you up to?"

"Oh . . ." I said. "I guess I'm mostly just playing this game, Manifest Atlas. Trying to figure out what happened to Winston Lewis."

Dad's face balled up. "What do you mean, what happened?"

"We're friends with his stepdaughter. She thinks the cops are lying."

"Mm," Dad said, amused with a bit of pity. "Well, wouldn't be the first time cops around here lied about something."

He took a few loud bites, then added. "I'm sure you know what they're saying about that game though, right?"

I sat up. "Saying what?" I asked.

"How someone's using it. Manipulating it. Trying to stir shit up around town. A chaos agent, they said." He looked to Mom. "You heard that?"

She nodded.

"Evidently, whoever runs it is using it to send kids to dangerous spots, trespassing, trying to raise some hell—shoot, they sent you boys to a dead body!"

"Who's they?" I asked.

Dad shook his head. "Who knows."

"Makes sense," Bones said.

"No, it doesn't," I argued, not even trying to hide how stupid it sounded. "A chaos agent? How would the chaos agent know to send us into that mill?"

Dad shrugged. The answer didn't matter to him.

I felt my skin get hot. "So a chaos agent just guessed Winston Lewis was gonna kill himself—"

"Enough." Dad straightened up and looked between me and Bones. "I don't like this. I'm gonna say new family rule. No playing that game 'til they get all this sorted out."

Bones glanced at me sideways.

"It's not dangerous," I told him. "I've played it a hundred times. You just have to know what you're doing—"

"I'm not letting my sons tear this town apart," he said. "Can't control everything, but we don't have to contribute to it, either. It's a rule."

Bones dragged his fork around his plate, not saying anything. Dad kept chomping, perfectly content while I glared at him from the opposite side of the table.

Suddenly, I remembered why I hadn't missed having Dad around. He wasn't just a tyrant, he was a careless one. He was a judge and jury with no principles, but once he'd decided how he felt, he never changed his mind. I'd barely seen him this summer. He only went to Bones's games when he could be bothered, and only checked in at home when there was something he wanted out of it. He hadn't said shit to me, and now, without a second thought, he was trying to ruin my summer.

"Huh," I said. "I didn't realize you got to make the rules here anymore."

The noise of eating stopped on a dime. I felt our collective hearts skip as Dad's spine straightened. Bones sat up, too, suddenly in caution mode, ready for Dad to explode.

"You're my son," he said, like he was in pain about it. "Everything I do is to protect you. Rules I make, they're to keep you safe, because you're my son. When that stops being true, then you don't have to listen anymore. Until then . . ." He settled back into his chair, and smiled at Mom, like it was a joke. "I get to make some rules."

Mom nodded. Bones started eating again, but Dad didn't look away from me. He was waiting for an apology, but I wasn't gonna give it.

"Doesn't matter," Bones said, flat and casual. "Game was getting boring, anyway."

After dinner, we had ice-cream sandwiches and sat on the back porch, listening to the symphony of bugs pick up. I watched Dad angle his chair toward Mom on the patio. I couldn't explain why, but since lunch, she'd seemed to be more open to him, like he'd done something to please her.

"It's nice, right?" He nodded to the table, where the food was starting to attract a swarm of flies. "Haven't had a lunch like this in a minute."

He looked to me and Bones for support. Neither of us said anything.

He took a long sip, never looking away from Mom. "I mean, that grill lives here now," he said with a noticeable slur. "We could be doing this every Saturday, if we wanted—"

"Thank you, really," she said, and stood up to clear the plates. Dad didn't move. He rolled his eyes at us and waited for her to come back out.

"What do you think about that, sweetheart?" he asked. "Starting a Saturday barbecue once I move back in. . . ."

"We don't need to talk about this now." Mom didn't even look at him.

"Well, maybe we should."

I felt Bones freeze next to me, neither of us watching but both listening. Even when I was young, I always recognized when my parents were talking for my benefit. It was controlled and coded, a performance, so I didn't have to know what the real conversations sounded like. But this sounded like the kitchen table conversations they had at five a.m. This was real.

"I'd like a chance to make my case," Dad said sincerely.

Mom didn't look happy, but she didn't stop him.

He stood up, all formal. "I'm a new man. I mean, look at me. Look at this. I'm here. I'm healthy. I'm making the most money I ever made in my entire life. I'm waking up, I'm going to work, I'm coming home. I'm not drinking too much, I'm not living in mess, I'm making a home . . . but it doesn't feel like home yet."

Mom's lips tightened, like she didn't want it to look like she was about to cry.

"I'm right here. It doesn't have to be like this. I know you feel it—people looking at us different, talking about us—but I'm right here. I'm not going anywhere."

Mom was still standing at the table, swaying back and forth.

"Move back in with me," he said. "We can sell this place by the end of the year—"

"I'm not ready yet," Mom said. She was smiling when she said it, still trying to pretend this was just a friendly conversation. "My sister's coming in a couple weeks, and then I'm going to see Mom in July, so maybe . . . maybe we can talk about it again, after that."

"They can stay with me when you're gone!" Dad protested.

"They can get their stuff moved in—"

"Markie." Mom stopped and looked him in the eye. She wasn't fucking around. "I really don't wanna talk about this in front of the boys."

I watched something flip in Dad. The fun, formal gentleman she'd invited over was gone. The dad who used to shout at the TV when we were sleeping, stay out 'til five a.m., and punch holes in the garage drywall when he was drunk, was back.

"You know I don't need your permission, right?" he asked. "I'm the one paying the mortgage. . . . I can sell it if I want."

I felt my lip start to quiver, my hands balling in rage. That was why Mom had changed her mind about Dad coming over. She didn't have a choice—he was still paying for the house.

"I understand," Mom said, holding her ground. "I'm just not ready."

Dad must have realized he went a step too far, because he didn't push it. He sat back down and muttered, "Of course."

It ushered in the longest silence of the night. Mom kept cleaning the table, focused on what she was doing. Dad lit up a cigarette, the first I'd seen him smoke all summer, and sat staring at the tree line, drinking with more abandon. But when the silence broke, it was Bones.

"We don't care!" he shouted. I tried to get his attention, to let him know I did care, but he was looking straight at Mom. "We want Dad back! Whatever he did, I guarantee, we don't care."

"Bones," Dad said cautiously.

"Drank too much? Drove drunk? Didn't come home when he

said he was going to? Hell, cheated on you?"

"Bones—"

"It can't be worse than this! You're fucking miserable, Mom. It's like you want to be sad all the time—"

"Matthew Eckles!" Dad raised his voice, enough to choke the words out of Bones's throat. We sat in suspended animation. "You do not talk to your mother that way."

Even though his body faced Bones, I could feel us all waiting on Mom, for her reaction to what Bones had just said.

"Not tonight," Mom snapped at Bones. She gathered the last of what was on the table and disappeared into the house. After twenty minutes, Dad gave up on waiting and followed her.

"I don't want him back here," I whispered to Bones, defiant, holding my ground. "You're eighteen, you go live with him. But I don't want him back here and neither does Mom."

Bones spat on the ground and ignored me.

A few minutes later, Dad came back out, loaded up his grill in silence, and he was gone.

CHAPTER 23

THE RIPLEY COUNTY Fair was always the second weekend in June, a celebration of the end of the high water and another year, the town victorious over the river.

It was a swirling mess of the best Calico Springs had to offer. Carnival rides, brought in on semitrucks and assembled by eighteen-year-old stoners, threatened death for children willing to brave them. Animal showings and beauty pageants gave every kid in the county a chance to be a hero for a night. We lit off fireworks and somebody's dad's band played Eagles covers until the cops decided to shut it down, which they were usually too drunk to do.

I could chart the most important summers of my life by the county fairs, we all could—first kiss when I was nine, behind the Scrambler; first fight when I was eleven, after this kid Roman said I was too pussy to throw a punch. I didn't really remember the county fair after I died, but Mom told the story all the time, how'd they brought me up onstage and played a slideshow of my time in the hospital, set to a sappy country song, before holding me up like Simba while the whole town cheered.

We agreed to meet on the fairgrounds, and right away, I could feel the vibe was sideways. Bones was still silently protesting Connor's existence, which was making Rodney resentful of Bones. Sarai and Joe Kelly were talking loudly, like they were pretending nothing was wrong, but I could see their heads in constant motion, watching for anybody who might be watching them. I'd never seen them spend time together in public, I realized. Even at the funeral, they barely interacted. Most people wore red-and-white Calico attire, but Sarai showed up in a green long-sleeve with the Lawton tiger logo from eighth-grade volleyball.

"We're gonna get a lotta compliments on that thing," Joe Kelly said, but he took her hand and held it in public, anyway.

By the time we got there, the party had already started. The lines for the games were extra long. I could see folks buying extra drinks and slamming them as fast as they could, buying out the food trucks. I could feel it—people had money this year. It wasn't just Dad, half the town was coming up off the developments, and they were spending it like it was going outta style.

They'd built out a stage, with eight loudspeakers stacked on the sides, and to kick things off, Bill Kelly ambled to the front in cowboy boots and a Calico Pride shirt.

"Not this asshole again," Joe Kelly said, a little too loud for a joke.

Bill started off by pointing out the fair's attractions, thanking the sponsors—which meant a personal hand for John

Arrington—and hyping up the raffle, four times larger than last year. I could feel the crowd getting loose, excitement in every direction.

"Calico Springs is a city of brotherhood and sisterhood," Bill Kelly boomed in his politician voice. "I see people all over the news these days, crying, saying America ain't what it used to be, saying you can't trust your neighbor anymore, we're too divided. I wish that they could see what I see, every day here in Calico Springs and in Lawton. Have a look at what I'm looking at right now."

The crowd roared. They loved it. And scanning the life in front of him, it was hard to disagree. People were happy. They were together. There were Unity shirts mixed in among the red-and-white sea. I found both my parents, smiling with their respective groups, families from both sides of the river, joined by their children or their church.

"Here, Willie." Bones snuck me a water bottle. I took a heavy sip. Gin, again, but it didn't sting my tongue like it used to. My taste buds were adjusting. I took another couple quick sips.

"Three generations ago, my wife's family went looking for paradise along this river and like so many others, she found it here. I know many of you folks from Lawton have that same history, generations and generations. I don't know about you all . . . but I'm proud of where I'm from!"

More hoops and hollers, glasses raised.

"Part of that," he said, "means I don't like being told what to do or what's good for me. That sure as hell ain't the Calico

Springs way, or the Lawton way. Which is why I've made an important decision. That's why . . ."

He paused, looking out across the crowd. I noticed Joe's whole face had tightened up, like he knew what was coming and it wasn't good.

"I've decided to reject the city council's pass-through proposal on a merger between our two towns, and instead, send it back to a popular vote."

The crowd erupted, the loudest cheer of the night. But I could see in front of me, it wasn't everyone. There were entire pockets of the crowd that looked stunned in silence.

I glanced back to Sarai—her mouth was hanging open, and behind her, Joe Kelly's fists were clenched as he glared up at the stage.

"I know some of you won't be happy with me saying that. I know there's a lot of complicated emotions wrapped up in this, but I believe our city has made a mistake by letting the process get this far. . . ."

The crowd started to sway, whispering to their neighbors, disbelief spread across their faces. I saw Pastor Baker at the front had turned his back to the stage, like he was trying to get away from it.

"We are not Alcester. We are not Hudson. We are developing. We are not in a place of desperation—"

"That's bullshit!" A voice cut through the crowd, inspiring a wave of boos after it. Others fought back by cheering louder. Bill Kelly talked over all of it.

"What we reaped is coming to us tenfold. We can build two thriving towns! Separate but equal, the way we have always been. Some of my best friends live in Lawton—"

"That's bullshit!" another voice shouted—it was Sarai, her frustration boiling over. Joe Kelly stood his ground behind her, trying not to look too affected by the fact his girlfriend had just screamed at his father in front of the entire county. Next to me, Bones noticed and glared at her, mumbling something about getting herself in trouble. She must have felt it, because she quickly stood back.

Past him, on one of the bar risers, I saw Rory and Tyler had heard it, too.

They were standing with the biggest contingency of Dirtbags I'd ever seen, all holding double-sized beer cups, the kind they probably had to buy themselves at Casey's. Tyler's facial hair had grown even more irresponsibly since then, and his eyes looked bloodshot, so I was guessing they probably were a little yacked as well.

I couldn't help myself. I counted weapons on the holsters of the men around them. Five.

And at the front of the group, John Arrington stood watching the growing discontent, a small but obvious smile on his face.

I scanned the crowd, wondering how many people were jumping to the same conclusion as me, the conclusion Sarai had drawn that first night as she sat on our picnic table—

There were five people on the city council, and the vote for the merger had passed three to two. Except now there were only four.

The reason Bill Kelly could fix the merger how he liked, was cause Winston Lewis wasn't alive to stop him.

The night started to get blurry after that.

I had a few more sips from the water bottle Joe brought, and we split the rest into individual cans of Arizona Tea. I could feel my balance fading, and people started running into me more. We weaved through the crowd together, stopping every time we saw someone we knew. Rodney and Connor faded in and out of the group, disappearing then reappearing with the Game people, all older hipster types. I think I met a person named Tuna. Even Abe had showed up, and him and his friends from Lawton tried to get me to ride the Scrambler and started calling me Scooby-Doo, which I think was meant to be endearing.

All the events had ended, and the dance floor was starting to crowd up, flooded with full-grown adults. The music on the speakers was so loud you had to shout to hear anyone. The whole night was pulsing.

I could feel the dark energy building. There were sideways glances, bubbling anger out in the open. Bill Kelly's speech had turned the whole thing unstable, like bottling something that wants to explode. And one person was having more trouble with it than anybody else.

"He did this on purpose," we overheard Sarai whispering harshly at Joe. "He waited until Winston was gone, but this is what he wanted to do the whole time. How do you not see that?"

Joe didn't say anything. It had been an hour, and no matter how many times he'd apologized, told her he agreed with her and not his dad, she kept going back at him.

She didn't notice it, but I could see Bones was fuming at Sarai, trying to keep as much distance from her as possible. Every time she said something, I'd see him mumbling to himself, like he wanted anyone watching to know he disagreed.

He was watching me, too. I kept quiet, even if I knew everything she was saying made sense.

"The crazy part is, it's everybody here. He coulda got up on that stage and said straight up, 'We murdered Winston!' and half the crowd would go nuts cheering, 'cause everybody hates Lawton so fucking much—"

"You gotta chill with that," Bones snapped, quietly enough that he could play it off, but it was clear he was serious.

Sarai didn't back off. "Chill with what?"

"Talking like that around here," Bones said.

"Talking like what?"

Bones took a deep breath, leveling himself. "You're gonna get yourself in trouble."

For a second, it looked like Sarai understood, but there was a fire in her eyes I'd never seen before. "Why?" she asked, straight to his face. "Afraid that whoever killed him might hear me?"

It was too loud.

Bones's eyes doubled in size, and Sarai noticed a second too late—behind her, Rory had turned around on the platform. He whispered something to Tyler, and they both closed on us.

Bones threw one last angry glance at Sarai, then backed away from her.

"What are y'all talking about?" Tyler asked as he approached, his eyes directly on Sarai. "Sounded interesting."

Joe Kelly stepped between them immediately. "Just drunk," he said. "We're fucking around."

Tyler was drunk, too. I could see it in the way he was swaying. "Aw, come on," he said. "I wanna hear what she's so worked up about."

Sarai had taken a few steps back and was staring at him cautiously. "It's nothing," she said, and repeated, "I'm just drunk."

"Nooooo." Tyler drew out the word, shaking his head playfully. "That's not what it was. You're mad. Why? Cause his daddy said you can't have our table scraps anymore. So sad. Too bad for your piece of shit town."

"Tyler, you're fucking embarrassing," Joe Kelly said, and tried to shove him out of the circle, but that just made Tyler shove back.

"No, no, no, I'm good," he mumbled, playacting like he didn't want a fight. A few steps from where they were talking, Bones was still on red alert, looking ready to jump in at any minute.

"You guys need it, too, huh?" Tyler cocked his head to Rory. "We were just driving around there the other day, and your town is *dirty*. Trashy, dude. I feel bad."

Sarai flinched at him, completely silent. In my head, I tried to will her to run away, but she just stood there, staring at him.

"Too bad your inbred stepdad had to go and die, huh?"

"Yeah," Sarai said through gritted teeth. "You wouldn't know anything about that, would you?"

Tyler's eyes narrowed, and his smile disappeared. He wasn't even pretending it was a joke anymore.

"Say it. You're gonna accuse somebody, fucking say it. Who?" He pointed underhand to Joe Kelly. "Your boyfriend's dad? The fucking mayor? My dad? Me? You think we don't hear that shit from your side of the river all the time? If you're gonna say it, then fucking say it!"

Across the circle behind him, I saw Abe shoving his way through the crowd. "What's going on?" he shouted, trying to push into the airspace between Tyler and Sarai. His friends got caught in the mass of people behind him, both of them shorter and smaller than him.

"Back the fuck up, kid." Tyler swayed drunkenly toward Abe. I felt the party constrict, the beat changing at the worst time, faster, pulling everyone closer to the center.

Rory noticed Bones hovering on the edge of the circle. "Cool friends, little Bone," he said. "What, nobody in Calico will hang out with you, so you had to go dumpster-diving across the river?"

"I don't really know that guy," Bones clarified, taking another step back.

"Just back away from her," Abe said, drawing up to his full height.

"Chill!" Joe Kelly said. "Everybody fucking chill out."

Tyler was smiling again. This was exactly what he'd wanted. "You are so fucking lucky I don't hit girls," he said to Sarai, and as he swayed, I clocked the tiny holster clinging to the back of his belt.

My heart started to pound in my ears. Of course he was packing. Of course he wouldn't be scared.

"It's all good," I tried to add to the voices of reason, but the music kicked up even louder, a verse exploding into a chorus. I saw Abe put a hand on Rory's chest, stopping him from moving any closer to Sarai—

Rory rounded on Abe, and Tyler crashed into both of them, rocking Abe backward—

They didn't have to say anything. Before Rory had time to react, Abe swung, landing the first punch.

That was it. The excuse they'd been looking for. Rory and Tyler both launched at him, which sent Abe's friends collapsing in on the circle as well. The screaming started.

Without thinking, I flew in their direction, aiming myself straight at the spot between Tyler and Abe. I closed my eye and braced for impact, but before I connected with anything, I felt hands on my shoulders, and I was jerked backward, wrestled to the ground.

"No," Bones shouted, holding me down, ten feet from the action. "Not your fucking fight."

From the ground, I could see Tyler and Abe tangled up, Tyler swallowing him up with longer arms and better position. Tyler caught him in the face, a *crack!* against his nose so loud that I could hear it over the speakers. Along the ground, I saw Abe's face spilling blood onto the grass.

People from around the fair were starting to notice, but the other Dirtbags had created a barrier, not allowing anyone to intervene.

Across the circle, Abe's friends had managed to corral Rory forward, into a sort of wrestler hold, and were keeping him there, not allowing him to escape. Joe Kelly was bear-hugging Sarai to his chest, keeping her out of the fight.

I looked back along the ground, through the tangle of legs, to where Tyler had gotten position on Abe, and my stomach dropped.

No one else could see it, but Tyler's hand was reaching toward his waistband.

Everything slowed down. I went to scream, but the air had left my lungs. I was the only one who could see it, the holster unclipping, Tyler's fingers wrapping around the 9mm.

"Run!" I tried again, but it was too loud. Tyler turned over Abe, his arm unraveling toward Abe's face—

In an act of pure desperation, I kicked Bones's shins, releasing his grip on my shoulder. I dove forward away from him and onto my feet, launching myself directly for Tyler, swinging at his face with the force of my entire body.

It didn't land clean, but it caught his nose, sending a spurt of blood out on a frozen rope. I stumbled backward with him, my momentum carrying me into his chest. As soon as he'd gathered himself, he threw me to the ground headfirst.

I saw Bones as I fell. He was frozen in place. He hadn't done shit.

Rory turned back to Abe, blood on both of their faces, the gun still in his hand. I hadn't disarmed him, only pissed him off more. He took another step, raised the weapon slightly. I screamed again, trying to spring at him—but a pair of hands threw me back into the ground. From over my head, I watched a blur of cloth explode into the collapsing circle, and in what felt like half a second, Tyler was yanked backward, and the gun was out of his hands.

"Knock it the fuck off!"

Rory and Abe's friends did as they were told, bringing the whole moment to a halt. I sat up. In the middle of all of it, holding Tyler by the collar, a hero standing in the way of any danger was Dad.

"He's my son," Dad shouted, playfully lassoing Tyler by his shirt. "If anybody's fighting around here, I want in."

There was uncertain laughter. Even Tyler smirked, though he never took his eyes off Abe and spat on the ground where he'd just been standing. Dad returned his gun, making sure it went back into the holster, and Tyler and Rory stomped off, back to the riser.

Dad took my hand, helping me brush the dead grass from my pants. "It's a party, buddy," he said, clasping my shoulder. "No need to turn it into a brawl. Made that mistake a few too many times."

Bones was glaring forward, clearly avoiding my eyes.

"What the fuck was that?" I spat at him, under my breath. "He was in trouble."

Bones kept ignoring me. The crowd started to separate, breaking in all different directions. The Dirtbags had returned to their bar riser; Abe's friends were holding his shirt to his face to stop the bleeding as they led him away. He stopped as he passed me. "Make sure she gets outta here okay," he said to me and no one else. I looked around, but I didn't find Sarai anywhere.

"You're welcome, by the way," Dad told Abe. Abe stared him down for a few seconds, then left without saying anything.

It left just me, Bones, and Dad in the center of the wake of the chaos, eyes still on us.

"I'm gonna make sure there's no hard feelings," Dad said. He was looking at me when he said it, then he looked to Bones. "Maybe you oughta come with me. Seeing as, you know, you didn't punch anybody." He looked at me, a little more serious. "You gotta be careful, Willie. Don't tell somebody to go to hell unless you can make it happen."

Bones looked at me for the first time since the fight. His eyes were vacant, like I was a stranger. He nodded, and they walked off, leaving me on my own.

CHAPTER 24

I WANDERED AROUND the fair twice, talking to no one, and when I saw Bones start back for the truck, I followed. He clocked me behind him but didn't slow down, so I followed in silence, twenty feet behind across the lot.

When we got to our truck, Sarai and Joe Kelly were sitting across the bed from each other, arguing loudly. Joe Kelly turned to Bones as soon as he saw him.

"Can you please tell her I'm not crazy for not trying to fight Tyler and Rory over some guy I barely know—"

"You didn't have to fight them!" Sarai shouted back. "I'm saying it sucks that you didn't try to stop them!"

"What are you talking about?!" he shouted. "I did try to stop them, I tried to defuse the situation! Did you not hear me?"

Sarai's face was puffy. She'd been crying, was still crying.

"He's right." Bones leaned on the truck. "Abe started that fight. Best thing we could do was not get involved. Look at Willie. He tried to help, and it just escalated the whole situation."

Joe Kelly spit off the back of the truck. "That was funny as shit."

Sarai didn't laugh. "Abe's in the hospital. His mom said he has to get stitches. At least Willie tried."

"I did more than try. I made him bleed," I corrected her.

"It was a baby punch," Bones said.

"Nobody had to fight anybody!" Joe Kelly protested. "I'm not gonna start a fucking brawl, just for . . ."

"For me?" Sarai asked.

It caught him off guard. He didn't respond right away. I watched him carefully, trying to decide if he was lying or if he actually felt he'd done the right thing.

"I realize you don't wanna hear this," Joe Kelly said slowly, making every word count. "But if we'd jumped in, and the fight got worse . . ."

"He'd be dead," Bones said, and he meant it.

Sarai thought about it for a long second, before she shook her head, slipped off the back of the truck, and started walking back toward the fair. Joe hopped down after.

"You wanna go see him at the hospital?" he asked. "I'd say all of this to his face, too. He probably understands it more than you do."

She didn't turn around, and his voice got desperate.

"I have been on your side!" he shouted. "I have defended you, over and over and over again. I've gotten you out of trouble, I've taken you seriously—please, just trust me that I did the right thing! You don't get how it works around here."

Sarai stopped. She turned back to glare at him, then at Bones for a second.

"No," she said, taking a deep breath. "You don't get how it works around here. They picked me. And they picked Abe, not because he started a fight . . . because they're fucking racist. Because they hate us, and they wanted an excuse to hurt us, and whether it was tonight, or some other night, they were going to find it."

She sniveled hard, wiped a tear from her eye. "And you didn't try to stop that, at all. You told them I was drunk, then you just . . . stepped out of the way."

I held my breath. Joe Kelly stood stunned in front of her.

"And you haven't taken me seriously, by the way," she added. "I've been telling you this was gonna happen—why this was happening—and you never took it seriously. Because that would involve looking at your own fucking house."

Joe swallowed and glared back at her. I saw his fists clench at his side. His whole body rattled with long, slow breaths. When he spoke, it was barely audible over the far-off music of the fair. "You realize what you just said to me, right?"

Sarai was quiet for a long moment.

"You actually think someone we know killed your step-dad?" he asked. "Someone in our town? Someone in my family? Because we're *racist*?"

She didn't flinch, and he took a dangerous step toward her. "I've been patient because I know it sucks. I wouldn't want to accept the truth, either. But if you're gonna accuse people in my family of murder . . . then you need to give me some actual evidence . . . or give it the fuck up."

I felt Bones shift his gaze from Joe Kelly to me, his eyes the same ultimatum. We'd reached the same breaking point.

Sarai's head fell forward and hung there, shaking. Joe looked expectantly for her, but she avoided his eyes. If he wanted evidence . . .

I took a deep breath.

"You picked the mill," I said.

"What?"

"You were the only one who saw the phone that night. You kept it away from the rest of us. You were the one who picked the mill."

No one said a thing. Joe took a few steps toward me. "What's your point?"

"I'm saying, that's what happened, so if you're looking for evidence—"

"Of what?" He was still moving toward me, his shoulders high.

I swallowed. "You knew the body was going to be there."

It was quiet again. I glanced at Sarai behind him, she looked more confused than anything.

Joe Kelly took another step, standing tall over me. "I play on the fucking baseball team. I begged you not to go into the mill. This thing has done nothing but ruin my life. Why the fuck would I have something do with this?"

He screamed the last sentence, rippling across the parking lot.

He looked wild, a dark and ugly expression frozen on his face, as he turned from me back to Sarai. He opened his mouth, ready to deliver a final blow, but instead, he swallowed it and stormed off, back toward the noise of the fair and the rest of Calico Springs.

Bones and I drove home after that.

I knew he wouldn't have much to say to me, so I put the radio on as soon as we got in the car, the country station. Halfway through the first song, he turned it off, swiping violently at the dial, and we drove in silence.

It occurred to me in drips, just how much of the last month I'd thrown away in a night, like the rain starting against the roof of the truck.

We'd probably never play the Game as a group. Drip.

I'd made an enemy out of half of Calico Springs. Drip.

My brother might never speak to me again. Drip, drip, drip.

By the time we were home, it was pouring. The river was already at its highest, and now we were being punished with a biblical rain, too much for the existing structures to bear. It had all become too much.

Bones parked the truck in the driveway, cut the engine, and sat back into his seat.

"You cost me two friends tonight," he said without looking at me. "She called me racist, and you didn't say anything about it. I don't feel like I can trust you."

Finally, he looked at me, and it hit me like a train. I expected rage or disappointment, but it wasn't that. All I could feel was his worry. Like that was the reason he'd gotten in the way so much. Not to hurt me, but to protect me.

"Please," he said quietly. "I don't wanna ever hear about this shit again."

It hurt to say it, but I nodded. "You won't."

He got out of the car and went inside without looking back. I sat for a while, watching rain punish the roof of the house.

It was a hurt I'd never felt before. I was nervous and confused, like half the bones in my body had been removed and the rest were trying to figure out how to function without them. I'd thrown myself into deep water without learning to swim, and now my lungs were full of it. What protections existed, whatever goodwill I'd built, whatever safety I had, it was all gone now. This was the moment Bones had tried to protect me from.

But it wasn't protection, that's what Rodney said. It was control. It was programming. It was trying to suck me into his world.

And he was wrong. He'd been wrong the entire time.

Sarai had been saying it, I just hadn't really heard it until I saw it for myself. There was an evil here, and it wasn't any one person. It wasn't even just the town.

It was an idea, a darkness underneath all of it, an evil that motivated every decision and put the bullet in Winston Lewis's brain.

It was a horror so human no one ever bothered to call my attention to it, and no one dared to speak its name out loud. Calico Springs was a racist town.

Tonight had been a racist attack. The opposition to the merger was a racist attack. Winston Lewis's blood was on the hands of racists.

And whether I wanted to admit it or not—my brother was a part of it. Which meant I might be a part of it, too.

PART FIVE
THE BARN

WHAT WE KNOW . . .

> **HotRod:** Here's the facts as i see them.

> **HotRod:** The Creator has chosen to keep their identity a secret.

> **HotRod:** The Creator can access the locations of anyone with the Game on their phone, at any time.

> **HotRod:** The Creator is in Calico Springs.

> **HotRod:** So I ask, at this point . . .

> **HotRod:** How could anyone other than the Creator be responsible for this?

STATEMENT FROM THE

CALICO SPRINGS POLICE DEPARTMENT

For immediate release—

The use of the game Manifest Atlas has been banned, in all forms, on all property belonging to the city of Calico Springs or Ripley County.

Fines up to $1,500.

CHAPTER 25

BONES AND I stopped hanging out after that.

It wasn't cold, we weren't silent to each other, we still talked about the things that interested us both at home. Mom was home less and less, spending almost all her free time on the pro-merger effort, so she gave us cash and we bought groceries together. But he didn't want to talk about the Game, so we didn't have much to talk about.

After the fair, an anti-merger effort exploded. They bought half the billboards in town, pastors were preaching about it, I even saw a TV commercial warning about the merger letting the government get involved in the business of the town. They'd scheduled the vote for three weeks out, and announced they'd host a town hall the day before, so everybody could say their piece—and people had a lot to say.

Mom said that was the worst part. The mayor's speech made everybody feel like they didn't have to be polite about it anymore. Her Unity committee was sending volunteers door-to-door to talk to people and half the people screamed at them.

Mom started showing up just in time for dinner every day, exhausted and sad.

"I'm still hopeful," she told us. "There's still more people who know how good this would be. We're gonna win."

At first, Bones pushed back, dinners devolving into screaming matches over Bill Kelly's talking points, but eventually, he gave up the fight and would glaze over when the subject got approached.

With the Game getting banned in Calico Springs, there was no safe way to play. I'd tried a few times, setting intentions early in the morning or on the way home from work, but it felt like every time I tried, a squad car would roll by, and I'd have to quickly delete it to be safe. I didn't know if it was because of the Game, but I'd never seen this many police cars out before in my life.

It took less than a couple days for everybody who'd come to town to play the Game to go back where they came from. It took a single police citation for word to spread among the outsiders, and any other news vans quickly followed suit. Even Mitchell Ballis went back to Springfield, leaving the corner booth at the Cherry Street Grille empty, publishing one final blog on his way outta town—"Manifest Destiny on a Forgotten Map" it was called.

"Ultimately, the most amazing thing," the article read, "was how little it took for a whole community to be amazed. . . . For a town with nothing, with a sub-50% graduation rate and a drug problem to rival New York in the '90s, with little prospect of prosperity, save for those in the ownership class, to believe every-thing they wanted was only an app away. All it took was an 8-bit design, some flowery language, and a bit of coincidence, and for one, shining month, the whole river valley believed anything was possible. Even if the truth is, in Calico Springs, it's not."

With nothing else to do, I turned to the Facebook group. The page had grown stale, only the occasional local business dropping an advertisement to capitalize on the traffic, but it still constituted a month of pure data. I cataloged it, sorting by user, adding notes about intentions, and placing small, colorful circles on the target. I bought an even bigger pack of markers with sixty-four different colors and gave each person their own. After filling in every target, the entire history of the Game in Calico Springs was rainbowed across the wall of the garage. Two colors dominated the board.

Royal blue was me. Saffron orange was Sarai.

Nobody was hanging out, really.

Joe Kelly and Sarai had officially broken up, and while club season kept him and Bones in the same place, he hadn't come over once since. I'd heard he took a job at the developments from his dad and was already bossing people around the job site. I saw him at the baseball games, and a few times, I'd felt him looking at me, whispering to somebody, I was sure about me. Other than that, he ignored me.

Rodney was too busy to come over, at least that's how it felt. Bones complained about it a lot, but every time I asked if he'd texted her, he told me he wasn't about to beg for her attention.

We'd see her some mornings, leaving to jump in the blue Subaru. She told us her and Connor were working on a summary of what they'd found, sorta like a research paper, and that they weren't dating, but everybody else had left town, so we figured Connor had a good reason to stay, and it wasn't a research paper. We texted sometimes, but Bones made seeing her almost impossible, skipping baseball constantly, and rarely leaving the house.

Sarai, for all I could tell, had disappeared back into her old life. I went the day after the fair to see Abe at the hospital, and he told me Sarai had been there with him all night, making half-baked plans to try to move back to Lawton and live on her friends' couches. He'd kept me updated every time I went into work, that she was in Lawton every day. I figured after the county fair, she'd be more motivated than ever to prove she was right about her stepdad, but it seemed like it had the opposite effect. She stopped posting online, and far as I could tell, she stopped playing the Game. I'd tried texting, but the responses were always short, and eventually stopped entirely. It had been a week since her last text, so it just sat there in my inbox, a weight dragging everything down—

Just don't see the point

I couldn't blame her. Word of the fight at the county fair— and what she said—had spread to every corner of Calico. The fight had shut down the first night of the fair—police made them stop selling alcohol after the gun was drawn—and nobody seemed to blame Tyler or Rory for that. For the people opposing the merger, Sarai had become a sort of boogeyman, an example of how people from Lawton viewed Calico Springs and the kind of hell they would raise if they were allowed in. "Are you sure this is the kind of girl you wanna be supporting with your tax dollars?" was the implication.

Somehow, it also seemed like everybody knew I was the one backing her up. Nobody said any outright filth to me, but I could feel people staring with shame and curiosity, the miracle boy turned ignorant traitor. Mom and I ran into Mr. Burns at Hy-Vee one day, and he pulled me aside to the quiet part of the bakery section. "You're raising all this hell," he spat at me. "For what?"

I knew for what, but Mr. Burns didn't wanna hear it. Nobody did. To them, I was the problem. She was the problem. As far as they were concerned, everything had been fine until the "Lawton girl" started throwing accusations around.

After dinner one night, I sat alone in the garage, staring at my map.

One thing had become obvious quickly—the Game was sending people to the same places, over and over again. The colored dots were bunched around them, creating a rainbow stain on the map, so I circled them in red.

The mill, a dark stain that had dried as the Game gave it up after a few weeks. The Basin had seen a few dozen visitors, always consistent, not in one spot but spread out across its width. And the only red circle on the Lawton side, Pastor Baker's church, one of the heaviest vortexes, with six different Facebook posts in the last month.

I'd come to two ways to interpret the information.

According to Connor's theories and the forums online, the heavily concentrated spots were vortexes—rips between dimensions or breaks in the simulation, where our reality met a different reality, and the stuff from the other reality spilled out. It seemed wild, but it did tell a story of the last month that made sense. Wherever there were vortexes, crazy shit happened.

The Basin—graves.

The mill—dead body.

The church—where I'd seen the devil.

The other way to look at it was that whoever created the Game was sending people to these places for a reason. Maybe they knew there was something there, like a body or a devil. Maybe they were creating chaos, like Dad had said. Maybe they were pushing random buttons.

But the logic held. Targets were given exponentially, each new person increasing the odds of the target being used again. It was a kind of algorithmic horror, the terror of the Game knowing too much, optimizing too well. And whether it was intentional or not, it had gotten a hold of the darkness in Calico Springs and multiplied.

I fell asleep in Dad's recliner, staring at the map.

It was so familiar; the streets I'd spent my life biking up and down, made completely unfamiliar by slashes and circles.

Calico Springs, infected with a rare and invisible disease.

CHAPTER 26

BONES WOKE ME up one morning like nothing was wrong.

"Willie, come on," he said, shaking me. "We've got work to do."

"Why?"

"'Cause it's Friday and nothing else is going on. . . . We're throwing the fucking bonfire."

It took me a minute to shake the morning fog and remember the state of things between us. And I'd forgotten about the bonfire entirely. After the fair, I figured it was a lost cause. We'd hardly spoken to anyone, even our friends.

But Bones woke up determined. "It's gotta be huge. Like, so big that people just gravitate toward it. . . . One of those classic town parties. I'll get Sam and all them, just invite anybody. Joe'll wanna come. Rodney, she can bring all her weird friends—"

"They're gone," I told him. "It's just Connor now."

He nodded, put on a smile. "Great. Connor then. Come on, get up." He looked at me earnest, like he'd really thought about this, and tossed a shirt at me.

A classic town party felt like the last thing anybody needed, and I couldn't imagine Joe would wanna get anywhere near me, but at least it would be a chance to see Rodney without Bones hovering. And maybe an invitation like this was the thing Sarai was waiting for.

I went with him to the Basin to collect firewood, difficult after such a wet summer. As we drove back into town, I noticed how quiet the streets were, how empty everything felt with the news vans and unfamiliar faces no longer scavenging around, their heads in their phones. Instead of turning toward our house, Bones pulled into the DQ and up to the drive-through.

"Welcome to Dairy Queen," the voice crackled in the box. "If you're going to use our parking lot to jerk off, we ask that you do so quickly; there are children here."

"Two Oreo Blizzards," Bones shouted back. "And they're on you, because we're having the bonfire tonight and I'm buying booze."

Rodney had the ice cream ready by the time we got to the first window.

"Text Lindsay," he instructed her. "Invite anyone. It's gonna be massive."

Rodney winced as she leaned into the car to pass us the ice cream. "Tonight?"

"Yeah, tonight. What?"

"I work 'til six, and then . . ." She looked back into the restaurant. "A bunch of us were gonna get together."

"Us?" He looked past her, through the window. "You mean Connor?"

Rodney shrugged. It was exactly what she meant.

"Rodney, what the fuck? This is a summer tradition. We've literally had a bonfire every summer since—since I don't even know when!"

"Yeah, but you just decided!" she protested. "Can it be any other day?"

"I've already told like twenty people!"

"Well . . ."

Rodney leaned back against the frame of the drive-through window. I could see her coworkers glancing over, impatient, and her resolve crumbling inch by inch—but it didn't give.

"I'm sorry," she said. "I can't today. Let me know if you change your mind."

"So this is just who you are now?" Bones spat back. "Some fucking . . . college loser?"

I could see him struggling to make it as painful as possible. He wanted her to hurt.

"You can't just randomly decide when you wanna be my friend—" she started, but it only set him off more.

"Me? Are you fucking kidding me? I guess twelve years means basically nothing to you, 'cause ever since you started hanging out with that guy, it's like you don't wanna be around me anymore—"

"It started long before that," Rodney said, and punched a button on the screen in front of her. "Welcome to Dairy Queen."

Her voice was artificially cheery. "How can I help you today?"

"Yep, got it," Bones said. "Okay, have a good day, fuck off."

He slammed his foot on the gas, the tires screaming against the cement, and whipped out of the parking lot, nearly colliding with another truck as we swung out on Cherry Street.

I gripped the oh-shit handle and glared at Bones with a new certainty building in my chest.

I'd never doubted him before. Even when I knew he was lying, even when it was to me, I always figured there was a good reason. I'd lived in his shadow. I'd seen him as impenetrable. I was lucky to have him. I needed him.

But as we sped down Cherry Street, the truck rocking up and down with every break in the concrete, and I watched him fume behind the wheel, humiliated and smiling through it, I realized that none of that was true, it was just the way he'd made me think. Bones was a liar. Bones manipulated me. Bones was the one who needed me, and not the other way around.

I sat up a little taller in the passenger seat, and, for the first time, gave back a look I was used to getting from him—pity.

He drove for a minute in silence, before suddenly yanking the steering wheel hard to the left, a U-turn in the middle of Cherry.

"Where are we going?" I asked, but he didn't answer.

Bones drove straight to the empty parking lot behind the old fast-food spot. We called it that because, in our lifetimes, it had housed four different restaurants, each one meeting a spectacular death. Burger King burnt down. China Express got robbed.

Steak Express lost its first shipment in a semi accident. And the Happy Joe's franchise folded before they could even have their grand opening. Now it was empty, and people parked their beater cars for sale in the parking lot.

"What's going on?" I asked.

He jerked the car into park and reached into the back seat, where he found five empty pop cans. He dumped them in my lap. "Line 'em up on those stumps, okay?"

He reached across me and snapped the handle to the glove compartment. It fell open, revealing the 42 inside.

I stared at it, a seizing in my chest. "You've been driving around with that this whole time?

"It's legal, Willie," he said as he reached over me to grab it. "It's registered."

I watched it the whole way across the cabin. "I don't like guns," I said, trying to measure my voice to sound controlled.

"I know," he said. "But you're gonna have to get used to them eventually."

I watched him feed the ammunition with a confident slap, like he knew what he was doing. It felt vindictive and intentional. Like he wanted me to feel how I'd felt around Joe Kelly, around all those people he used to protect me from. Almost like it was a threat.

"Please put it away," I said. "Please."

But he shook his head. "It's time, Willie. You can't keeping living in the past." He kicked his door open. "Line 'em up straight!"

I controlled my breathing and did as he asked. I cradled the cans to walk them to the stump and set them up one by one, two feet between them, constantly checking on where Bones was examining the gun across the lot. At one point, he raised it to check his aim and I nearly collapsed, knocking all the cans over.

He rolled his eyes. "Jesus, Willie. I've got it."

As soon as the cans found their balance, I walked straight back around the truck and cowered on the opposite side, as far from where he was aiming as possible. I saw him check on where I was, but he decided not to say anything and returned his aim to the cans.

Patiently, he raised the gun and narrowed his focus. Once the shot was lined up, he glanced at the street, nervous even if he swore he wasn't, and then back to the cans. He mumbled something I couldn't hear. And then—

CRACK.

The sound exploded through the still air, breaking the summer in half.

"He's bleeding! Jenny, he's bleeding!" Dad had been the one to find us in the garage. *"It's his head! Oh my God, what did you do?!"*

I pushed myself into the truck as vibrations rattled the siding, covered my ears and squeezed my eyes tight.

The trees rustled as birds took flight, a nearby dog started howling. Bones had nearly fallen backward. He was holding his arm and trying to steady himself. But the cans stared back, completely undisturbed.

CRACK. CRACK. CRACK.

"I can't find his heartbeat, Jenny! There's no heartbeat!" Blood flowed like I was swimming in it, I could hear it more than I could see it—

He fired off three more, each echo drowned by the next.

"Fuck! What did you do?! You shot him! You killed your brother! You murdered your brother—"

"FUCK!" Bones screamed at the cans.

It was silent for a long moment. When I opened my eye, all I could see was sky, birds escaping upward in perfect, algorithmic design, a funnel, swarming up over the river.

Bones let out his frustration with one more giant, violent kick at the concrete below him.

I turned and watched him come steady. He had one shot left. He lined it up. Anger piercing through his body.

I turned back to the birds, still circling, swarming—

Behind them, the sky started to blacken, dark clouds trickling upward, dancing like—

Smoke. It was smoke, floating from a single spot, over the top of the river. I stared at it. It was a perfect portrait, the blackness of the smoke, a backdrop for the whiteness of the birds—

They weren't just birds—

They were doves.

The piercing whine of sirens came hurtling toward us from a distance.

"Shit!" Bones stuffed the gun in his pocket. "Knock those cans over. Come on, we gotta hide!"

He ignored the car and ran to the park across the street, a

hand down his pants to stabilize the weapon. I took off after him, the sirens whirling toward us. As I crossed the street, I saw them. Four cars—half of the Calico Springs fleet—speeding down Cherry, straight at us.

"Fuck me!" Bones's animal instinct kicked in, and he leapt into a tree. I followed without question, trying to swing a leg up, but I wasn't strong enough. I was hanging there, suspended in midair when the cars got to us—and continued speeding past.

We watched in awe. I'd never seen this many cops dispatched at once, not for anything. From another direction, a different siren began—a fire truck, pulling away from the station two blocks down on Main.

The overlapping screams of sirens rang in my ears. Whatever this was, it was bad.

The last police car in the line saw us and pulled off. Bones started to cower, but they'd clearly seen us. The window rolled down. . . .

It was Deputy Schnack and a junior officer riding shotgun.

"Boys!" he shouted. "Go home, now. If you're on your bikes, call somebody to pick you up."

"What the hell, why?" I asked.

"There's gonna be an early curfew. Just go home now."

He started to roll the window back up, but adrenaline sent me hurtling toward the car, and I ran up on his window. "Why? You can't just make curfews and not say anything. What happened?"

"I can't say anything!" he said from behind the glass.

"Tell us!" I slapped the window. "If you don't tell me, I'm not going anywhere."

"Willie, what are you doing?" Bones shouted.

But I kept slapping the window, stopping them from driving off.

Schnack let it down a crack. "Okay! Okay!" He checked the officer next to him. "There was a fire. We don't know anything about it, but just in case things are dangerous we don't want anyone . . ."

My heart stopped. "Where was the fire?"

"Church in Lawton. Just get home, all right? Until we get this thing cleared?"

I stumbled back and the vehicle sped off. My head pulsed.

I looked back to the doves in the sky and realized the sign had been obvious the entire time. They were a warning. And what they were warning us against, it was here.

CHAPTER 27

MOM WAS SITTING in the driveway when we got home. She hugged both of us as we walked up.

"Are you okay? Neither of you were texting me back—"

"We're fine," Bones said. "We heard about the fire. What's going on?"

"He was in the church." Her hands were shaking. "The pastor, he was in the building. . . . People saw him getting put in the ambulance."

My stomach lurched. "Is he okay?"

"They said he gave someone a thumbs-up when they were loading him in, but . . . I don't know." Mom shook her head. She was struggling. "Evidently, there's gonna be another curfew."

"Just 'cause of a fire?" Bones asked.

"They don't know what caused it yet."

"They think someone did it on purpose?" I asked.

She shook her head. She didn't know.

Bones looked between us, more annoyed than worried. "Didn't you say he was living at the church? Maybe he left the stove on or something."

I swallowed a response. It wasn't a stove, I knew that. It was whoever found me in the woods that night. It was the devil.

"Well." Bones shrugged it off. "Hopefully they get it cleaned up in time for the bonfire."

"Wait—we're still having the bonfire?"

"Of course." His voice rose. "Why wouldn't we?"

Before I could respond, Mom looked up over his shoulder, watching as a blue Ford Aerostar pulled up on the street.

Sarai came around the front, and to my surprise, Abe let himself out of the passenger side.

"Oh, but Willie can have friends over. Great," Bones said, and stomped off to the backyard. Mom gave me a warning glance as well but didn't protest. She waved to Sarai and followed Bones inside.

"You heard Baker's in the hospital?" Sarai asked as she approached.

I nodded.

"It was another attack. He was in the church when it went up." Her voice got quieter. "He said people had been in the woods, watching him. We found those cigarettes. . . ."

I nodded again, and she trailed off. For a minute, she looked haunted, so I whispered back, "There's no way we could have known."

"The police know it was an attack," she added. "They wouldn't have a curfew otherwise, just for a fire. This is it. What our parents always warned us about."

"Warned you about what?"

"War," Abe said, completely serious.

He was standing in the middle of the garage, transfixed by the map on the wall. "This is . . . results of the Game?" he asked.

Sarai joined him in front of it and her eyes lit up.

"The different colors . . ." Abe pointed. "Those are all different people?"

I nodded.

"How'd you find out about all this?"

Sarai answered for me. "You went through the Facebook posts."

"And these red circles." Abe got closer. "Those are . . ."

"Places the Game has been sending people over and over and over," I said. "Vortexes. That's what people online call them, anyway."

Abe pointed to the red circle in Lawton. "That's the church."

I nodded.

"And this over here . . . This is the mill?"

I nodded again.

"Jesus," Abe breathed. "So . . . this is proof, right? The Game knows what's gonna happen?"

I watched his finger trace between the targets on the board, trying to draw a pattern between them, until it froze on the third.

"The Basin," I said. "Where I found the graves."

Sarai stared at it for a long moment. "Willie . . . didn't you say there was a barn?"

"Yeah?"

"What if that's the vortex?" She winced as she used the

word. "Instead of the graves. Do you think you could you find it again?"

I thought about it, picturing the Basin, and shook my head. "The water's gonna be too high at this point. Most of the Basin is underwater."

"Take a boat," Abe suggested. "Or waders."

"I can try," I said. "But there's not gonna be any physical markers on the ground, so it would be hard to navigate. Almost impossible."

"There's gotta be a way. . . ." Sarai said.

I let out a heavy sigh. I did know one person, the only I was aware of who knew the Basin well enough to navigate, even in high water—and he was building a giant pile of wood in the backyard.

Bones was on his hands and knees when I approached, turning over soil with his gloves and a hand shovel to make a burn pit.

"Good," he said when he saw me. "Can you set up some chairs around this? We might have to borrow some of the O'Neils'."

I ignored the question. "I need your help," I said.

"Help with what?"

I took a deep breath. "The Game has been sending people to the same couple of places, over and over again. One of those places is the mill. One is Pastor Baker's church, which just burnt down . . . and one is the Basin. Where I saw the barn."

His face hadn't moved. I figured he was ready for this, sooner or later, and he'd made a clear decision . . . just ignore me.

"Even you have to admit. That's a pretty crazy coincidence."

"It just sounds like the Game is broken," he said without looking up. "Whoever made the app probably made it cheap."

"But the fact that something has happened at basically every vortex . . ."

"Vortex?"

"That's what people call them."

He shook his head and returned to the pit.

"It tells me there's something bigger going on here. And if something else is going to happen . . . it's going to happen in the Basin."

He was quiet, so I kept going.

"I have to find that barn, and I figured, nobody knows the Basin like you, so I told Sarai and Abe that maybe we could take the runabout out later and try to find it—"

His hands slowed to a stop. "Willie . . . are you fucking kidding me?"

"What?"

"The bonfire. For fuck's sake. I need your help setting up. Have you even invited anybody yet?"

"I mean . . . can I just take the boat out then? Do you think Joe Kelly would let me?"

He dropped the shovel. "Are you serious, Willie?"

"I'll take good care of it—"

"You have to come to the bonfire!" He sounded like he was whining. "It's at our house, it's our fucking party!"

"It's your friends—"

"Just 'cause you don't have any!"

I stood my ground and glared back at him. I'd never found myself on this side of Bones, not seriously, anyway. I felt completely on an island. But I was already here, so I kept pushing.

"If you're not gonna help me, then I'm going by myself," I said. "And if I don't have the boat, then I'm doing it on foot."

Bones shook his head. "I can ask about it tomorrow, but who knows if Joe Kelly will wanna let us use the boat for something this dumb."

"Bones, this is urgent," I said. "Lives are at stake—"

"Lives are at stake? Listen to yourself! Whose life is at stake if you don't go boat around the Basin, looking for a tool shack in the woods. Just so you can prove some shit to me, win a bet you lost a month ago?"

I glanced back at the garage, and his eyes followed.

"You gotta be kidding me," he said, hanging his head.

I didn't say anything.

"Whatever." He chucked a clump of dirt at my feet. "Suit yourself. Have a good night with your new friends. Don't come to the bonfire. And no, you can't take the boat, you're fifteen."

He turned back to the pit and started churning dirt like I could feel it. The message he was sending was clear—if I skipped the bonfire, it would do the kind of damage to me and Bones that couldn't be undone. On his hands and knees, I could see this was the Bones from the car after the playoff game, from the DQ drive-through, the Bones who had lied about his future. The Bones who had been abandoned by everybody else in his life.

When I got back to the front, Abe and Sarai had made a plan to check out the site of the church fire for clues, then on to the hospital to try to talk to Pastor Baker. They were sitting in the van, waiting for me to join.

I hung my head and told them I couldn't go.

I took every chair from inside the house, and the couch from the living room, and dragged them to the backyard. I didn't text anyone—inviting people felt like supporting Bones, and I had no interest in that. Bones took the leftover liquor from the workbench cabinet and paid Bobby from the trailer park forty bucks to grab us two cases of beer. He emptied them into a cooler and hid them in the garage, in case Mom came out and complained about underage drinking, which she wasn't going to do. He complained about Rodney the entire time.

"It's a fucking priorities thing. I get it, you get all excited because he's new and older and into the same nerdy shit as you, but . . . for Christ's sake. It's the bonfire. Some people"—he looked right at me—"are pretty quick to forget who their real friends are."

At seven thirty, when the sun was finally down and the party was scheduled to start, Bones circled the fire with an old can of lighter fluid and lit the blaze. It shot upward, sending up a thin spiral of smoke. Bones admired his handiwork and we both took a seat, in opposite folding chairs and facing the fire, saying nothing.

At eight, our neighbors in the back, the Halstons, came over and asked us to keep it down because their daughter just had a new baby and she was a crier. Bones said he would do his best, but it was only one night in the summer so they couldn't really complain, and after they left, he turned the speaker up a few notches.

At eight thirty, Bones texted Rodney again, asking if she for sure wasn't coming, then proceeded to check his phone three or four times a minute. She never texted back.

At nine, Bones apologized for calling me an asshole and asked if Abe and Sarai might wanna come, then reassured me for the fourth time that people loved showing up late to parties, because everybody knew it was lame to show up on time.

At nine thirty, Mom came outside and asked if we'd canceled. Bones yelled at her to go back inside.

At ten, Bones polished off his fourth beer and chucked the can as hard as he could at the fire. The wood in the center tumbled over and threw fire in all directions, but he let it burn.

I felt myself slipping, from protesting the way he was treating me to trying to comfort him. I agreed with him every time he said anything, yes, people usually come late, and, yes, anybody who didn't come was probably just being a bitch about the curfew.

But as the hours wore on, his resentment ran out. I barely recognized the look on him. He was so unshakeable, unwilling to admit defeat even in the very face of it, incapable of shame even when he was silently drowning in it. But here it was, rising like a tide.

At ten thirty, he stood up, twitching away tears. "Fine. Fuck it. Let's go dig your grave."

CHAPTER 28

JOE KELLY'S FAMILY had two boats they talked about and one they didn't, a dinged-up runabout with a new motor and an oar for shallow water paddling, chained up on a fence at the edge of their property.

Bones had used it a few times before and led me to it, leaping the fence and stepping onto the hull in one motion, not even looking back to see me stumble. He pulled the boat in by the chain and dug out a rock at the base of the fence. The key was inside. He fought the lock, impatient and clearly drunk. I'd insisted on driving, and he hadn't put up a fight, as clear a sign as any that something was really wrong with him.

He kicked us off the shore, then idled out of the bend and turned on the motor once we hit the open water.

It was misty on the river, not raining but still wet, and the gurgle of the water masked the sound of the gas engine. I navigated us toward the Basin by the light of my phone, and Bones made a show of making almost no effort, but still kept us perfectly on course.

Two miles upriver, we took an inlet that opened into a marsh, too shallow for the blade. I cut the engine and we idled in, using the oar to direct our momentum.

We started at a bend that looked like where I'd seen the barn, best as I could remember, assessing the spot from the water side. Bones used the Tupelo trees sticking out of the marsh to track our location and steered us in spirals around them until we felt we'd checked every crevice and could move on to the next patch of trees. Every time we got too close to shore, the boat would catch on mud below, and we'd use the oar to kick us back out.

"It was in a clearing," I told him. "Just like this one."

"And when you saw it, what color was it?" Bones asked. His voice sounded unfamiliar, too soft to be my brother.

"Dark white, chipped paint. You know, like an old barn."

"Stable doors? Or smaller?"

"Um, I think stable doors—"

"Was it two levels or just one?"

The mist had started to materialize into an actual rain. I could hear drops tapping along the tree cover. The image in my head got fuzzier with every question. I could tell what he was doing. "I don't know," I snapped. "Just look."

Bones stopped rowing behind me.

"What?"

He gently set his oar across his lap and looked not at me, but past me, up into the trees. I followed his eyeline, but there was nothing there.

"What?" I asked.

"There's a lot of shit I've been keeping to myself lately," he said quietly. "But you need to hear it now."

"If this is gonna be some lecture, save it."

"You have a wild imagination," Bones started. "I think it's cool. You create scenarios in your head for yourself, and you believe them so much, you act on them. Which is fine when we're just talking you and me . . . but you're too old for this shit with other people, Willie."

"I said save it—"

"I've been saving it."

I gritted my teeth and asserted, for what felt like the thousandth time, "I'm not making anything up. I've been right about everything so far—"

"I know you think that, but you have to see it. When you exaggerate things, or escalate things, or accuse people of things—it's us, the people around you, who pay the price."

"I exaggerate things? You're the biggest liar I know."

It bounced right off him. "You never have to answer for any of it because everybody treats you with kid gloves. Poor, precious little miracle boy. But Mom, Dad, and me, we have to deal with it. Do you not see that?" As my flashlight fell back over for a second, I swore I saw his lip tremble. "Do you not see how hard this has been for us?"

"It's not about you—" I started, and it set him off like a rocket.

"It was supposed to be about me!" he nearly screamed. "This

was the most important summer of my fucking life! I worked for so long to get to this summer, to get to celebrate all that I've done here, and then . . . I needed this summer. Did you even think about that?"

I didn't say anything, trying to avoid feeling bad for him.

"Of course you didn't. 'Cause you're fifteen, and you've still got time to figure out your life. I don't, Willie. In a month, every friend I've ever had is gonna leave, and you know where I'm gonna be? Right here, by myself, probably working for Dad like a fucking loser. Except evidently I can't even do that!"

I avoided looking at him. Even the idea of building his empire was a lie. Just like the scholarship was a lie. He swore his life was going to be better than it was—but even he knew it was a lie.

"Maybe if instead of making up a scholarship, you'd have actually tried to get one, you wouldn't be so pissed off—"

"You have no fucking idea. You have no idea." I could feel Bones shake as he said it. "You know, I was actually excited to stay? I used to love it here."

He wiped his face, breathing himself calm, shaking as he exhaled. I'd never seen him this wounded before. He seemed human, not just vulnerable but weak.

"But now, the whole town thinks I'm crazy, my friends don't wanna talk to me, I fucked things up with my best friend beyond repair. . . ."

Finally, he looked down at me. "And all of that is your fault."

A rush of wind brought a cold I wasn't ready for. The

sweeping rain picked up. Behind us, a far-off droning started, a low, electric buzz that I could feel in my stomach, getting louder as it turned in our direction. It was the thunderstorm warning alarm, telling all the vessels on the water to get to safety immediately. Along with it, a faint yellow light passed over the Basin, washing over us every few seconds from down the waterline. Growing up with it, you knew—when the yellow light started turning, things were about to get gnarly.

I was quiet for a while, not allowing myself to be manipulated by him again.

"I didn't do any of that," I said, measuring each sentence as it came out. "It's not my fault nobody came to your shitty party."

He took his last unsteady breath, cracked his neck, and was right back to being Bones. "I'm done sticking up for you," he said.

"Can we just stick to the route?"

"And I'm done protecting you."

"Turn around here—"

"Because the real person you need protecting from is yourself."

"Turn!" I screamed.

Quietly, he put his oar in the water and did as I asked.

Neither of us said anything for a long time, only a brief passing of yellow light to interrupt the darkness.

Maybe every little brother comes to this point, where they realize brotherhood is a scam. That you can only so many times be stepped on to make someone else taller before realizing that you're the entire foundation.

I'd never hated Bones more than I hated him in that moment. As the boat cut through the water, I made a plan to get away from him completely. I'd tell Mom he wanted to go live with Dad. I'd tell Rodney that Bones still had feelings for her and everything he ever did was a scam to get back with her. I'd tell Joe Kelly that Bones changed his whole personality just to impress him. And we'd never talk again.

I felt the storm pick up, wind pushing raindrops sideways into our faces, under our hats. Rain pelted the water around us, impacting like rounds of unending machine-gun fire in all directions. We'd been coasting in silence for a few minutes when I heard him starting to tinker with the engine.

"Not yet," I ordered, but he didn't listen. "We're not done yet," I repeated.

"We're not even in the Basin anymore," he said. "This part's year-round. We're just in the river."

"Then turn around."

Out of nowhere, the entire Basin lit up with a flash of lightning, and only a second behind it, thunder shook the river valley.

"I saw something," I told him. "That way."

"We're going home, Willie."

"I'm not done yet."

He pulled the string again, and the engine rumbled to life.

In that moment, I decided I'd had enough.

I leapt toward him and grabbed the steering rod, jerking the boat to the left. I lost my footing as I flew, and inertia carried me over the motor, over the side wall of the boat. Without hesitation, Bones let go of the rod and grabbed for my shirt, catching me just in time to keep me from falling into the motor, but our momentum swung the handle and sent the boat spinning. Bones yanked the tiller, overcorrecting to shoot us forward into the low water of the Basin.

We both screamed, ready for the shallow ground ahead. The motor would catch on the riverbed at full speed, and the boat would be ruined and there was nothing we could do to stop it. We'd go flying, hopefully not landing on rock, almost certainly breaking bones.

But it didn't happen. Something underneath the boat caught and shot the front end upward, completely stopping our momentum. We both fell into each other at the base of the motor and Bones cut it, the boat stabilizing with its front end slightly elevated.

"Where the fuck are we?" Bones asked, trying to judge from the trees.

As the warning light turned toward us, I took in the dense tree cover, thicker than anywhere I'd seen in the Basin. I looked to Bones. He was frozen, staring ahead.

I followed his eyes forward, waiting. As the river light circled overhead, it caught on a reflective surface, ten feet off the ground, inside a small cover. Chipped paint. There was something there.

Bones took the oar and pulled us toward the shore. Every few seconds, the light came back and revealed more to us, a structure growing out of the blackness of the woods. When we were twenty feet away, the trees ended—someone had cut a clearing in the Basin.

"Holy shit . . ." Bones whispered behind me.

A flash of lightning ripped down from the sky for a single second revealing to us the full picture.

It wasn't a shack or my imagination, but tucked into a crevice, left like it was stranded in time, there was a structure. It looked big enough to hold a dozen people but had been covered with enough foliage to hide in the forest around it. The only easily visible parts were a padlock on the front and a small window in the middle, where I'd seen the yellow light.

I held my breath. The barn was real.

PART SIX

THE CODE OF THE HILLS

CHAPTER 29

ABE AND SARAI met us at the garage, and we passed the photos of the barn around on my phone. I texted Rodney, too, and she showed up less than a minute later in pajama pants and an old track T-shirt.

"It looks like an insane asylum," Abe pointed out. "With the padlocks."

"You're not supposed to build down there," Bones reiterated for the hundredth time. "The river should have leveled it by now. It must be built into the cove with an elevated foundation. I don't know why anybody would do that. . . ."

"Unless they really, really didn't want to be discovered," I pointed out.

Sarai stared at the photos the longest. Her stare was intense, unusually emotional for how practically she'd addressed everything else today. She looked like she was staring down an enemy.

"Whatever it is," she said, "it has the answers we need."

Sarai and Abe had updated us on the scene of the fire in Lawton. "Everything we saw that night, it's gone," she told us.

"The cigarettes, the symbol—like they never even happened. I thought I was losing my mind, because even that fallen log, I couldn't find it . . . and they wouldn't let us see Baker."

I was trying to be keenly aware of my imagination. It sounded too much like fantasy to be real. Like with the graves, it was as if the forest was moving, fixing itself every time we looked away, covering its tracks. Like the thing we were at war with was Calico Springs itself.

"We can't just go charging in there without knowing what it is," Abe said. "There's gotta be some way of figuring out what it's there for, or at least who owns it—"

"It's the city," Bones said. "The Basin is part of the river, technically."

"How do you find out who owns land?" I asked. "It's gotta be written down somewhere, right? Like, deeds and shit."

"Land records," Rodney said. "That's what we had to do to find the Creator. Physical land records."

"It's the County Clerk's office," I said, remembering when Dad had taken me with him to register the truck. "There's a room at City Hall."

Sarai shrugged. "So we go ask?"

Bones snorted. "Yeah, that's not gonna happen."

"Why not?" I asked.

"Everybody knows what y'all are doing." I wasn't the only one who noticed how aggressively he separated himself from us. "They're not just gonna answer your questions. No one's gonna give you shit at City Hall."

We were quiet for a minute. It was Sarai who made the

decision. "Then I guess we just go check it out ourselves."

Bones rolled his eyes, but his face hardened as he clocked how serious we were.

"You're not gonna break into City Hall," Bones said. "That's fucking stupid. Just to figure out who owns some land?"

Sarai shrugged. "It's either that or break that window of the barn—"

"Not for nothing," Bones said, looking wildly around the garage, "but City Hall is also the police station."

That shut everybody up. The police definitely knew who we were, Sarai especially.

"Maybe they're online," Bones suggested, looking to Rodney. "Maybe Connor could hack it for us."

Rodney flinched, her face dropping. "I can ask him, but, uh, he actually didn't text me back tonight."

I saw Bones's eyebrows go up, but even he could recognize she wasn't taking questions.

"They're probably not even digital," I said. "We had to do the truck title by hand."

Sarai looked like she got struck by a bolt of lightning.

"What?" I asked. "What's that matter?"

"It means they're fragile," she said. "It means if they disappear . . . they're gone."

Bones shook his head, definitively. "Nope. Not doing it. Not even listening to this. Willie." He looked between me and Rodney. "If you do this, you will get caught. And I won't be there to bail you out."

We were all silent.

"We could break a window," I said, and Bones threw his hands up, marching out of the room.

"Then they'll know something happened." Abe discarded the suggestion. "We gotta get in and out undetected, so they don't even know something's missing. If they know we've been there at all, we're fucked. They'll file charges, they'll get it back."

"When does the building lock at night?" Sarai asked. "Maybe we could stay around, try a twenty-four-hour thing."

"Cameras," Abe said. "Plus, we don't know what security looks like at night."

"Joe Kelly would," I pointed out.

"And he could probably get a key," Rodney added.

Sarai rolled her eyes. "Yeah, cool. You guys can text him, then." She started to pace. "What about when the building's open? It's a public building, we're allowed to be in there, right? We're not breaking any rules—right up until the moment that we take something."

I nodded. "We would just need a distraction. Something big, something that gets people out of the room. . . ."

The door to the house clicked open softly, and Mom leaned her head in. "Willie, what are you doing—oh." She froze when she saw Sarai, Rodney, and Abe. I saw her check for Bones, and noticed he wasn't there. "Sorry, I didn't realize we had company."

Sarai turned to Mom and gave her a smile that felt familiar and warm. I hadn't considered it, but all this time Mom had been spending on the merger, she'd likely run into Sarai. "We were just leaving, Ms. Olson," she said innocently.

I felt my body recoil. Ms. Olson. I hadn't heard anyone refer to Mom by her maiden name, ever. If that's what she was telling people, then that meant it was final. We weren't the Eckleses anymore.

"It's all right," Mom said cautiously. "Just be careful driving home with the curfew."

They both nodded, and she turned to me.

"Willie, you'll be up in the morning for the merger hearing? I wanna leave early to get a good seat."

"Of course, Mom." I nodded. "Good night."

When I turned back to the other three, all their eyes were wide.

"What?"

It struck me before they could say it.

The merger hearing was being held at City Hall.

CHAPTER 30

IT WAS STILL raining the next morning.

The news said it wasn't going to stop for a full twenty-four hours, dangerous with the river already at its season peak. Some people in town had taken the day off to lay sandbags, which was pointless this late in the storm, but it was something to do, and what else was life, if not a meaningless revolt against nature.

Everyone knew City Hall was gonna be packed. It was the last chance to say something before the vote, and both sides seemed to think this debate would swing the balance. I wasn't sure who anybody thought they were gonna convince— everybody I talked to seemed like they'd made up their mind, but I guess what's another meaningless revolt?

I was sitting by myself in the garage, waiting for Bones and Mom to finish getting ready, when I heard a truck pull up outside. I had my head in my phone, but when I looked up, Joe Kelly was standing in the driveway, no umbrella, being pelted by the rain.

"Can I come in?" he shouted.

I shrugged and he took a step inside. I waited for him to pass to the house, to go find Bones, but he didn't move.

"I came by 'cause . . ." He shifted. "I have something to say to you."

"Uh . . ." I sat up, double-checking to be sure it was me he was talking to. "Okay?"

"I've been thinking about it," he said. "And I don't like how I responded to you at the fair. I don't like how I did anything that day, but . . . getting pissed, storming off. That's what a guilty person would do. And I'm not guilty." He cleared his throat, thought about it for a second. "At least not guilty of what you're accusing me of."

His face looked like it always did, a little haunted, a little like he knew something you didn't. I remembered what Sarai had told me, about how Joe Kelly was trying to rewrite his programming.

I stood up, and as I moved, the garage fluorescent washed over the top of his face, revealing him in a new light. From this close, from level ground, I could see he was scared.

"I really didn't see it," he said. "I swear. Not just that I didn't want to, I actually made myself not see it."

"See what?" I asked.

He swallowed and looked around. He was nervous.

I'd never thought about Joe Kelly like a regular person before. He always seemed so sure of himself, so certain of his place in the world, that I'd never considered how difficult that place might be. How much pressure he had to stomach just waking up. It's easier if you just do what he says. That's what he told me about his dad. It wasn't a threat, or a claiming of high ground . . . it was a survival strategy.

"I don't think my dad did this—or did anything," he said quickly, like it was an obvious caveat. "But . . . there's meetings. They talk to each other, all of them . . . Arrington, especially." Joe swallowed. "I'm not saying they killed anybody, but . . . Arrington definitely wanted him gone."

It looked like it took everything for Joe to say it without passing out. As soon as he was done, he distracted himself with the map on the wall for a moment, then turned back to me earnestly.

"I was honest when I said I didn't know anything about that body, Willie. Just like I was honest when I told you I thought the Game was bullshit. . . ."

"And now?"

"And now," he said, "I'm willing to be convinced."

I sized him up. A month ago, it would have felt impossible, but at my full height, I felt like we were seeing each other eye to eye.

"I know who I wanna be now," he said. "So, is there anything I can do?"

"Actually," I said, offering a hand to him, "you're just in time."

We were a half hour early, and we still had to park in the back row of the lot at City Hall.

Mom had been to town halls before, and she said almost

always, they were like shitty theater—a couple folks giving the most dramatic performance of their lifetime with nobody there to see it. But that wasn't the case today.

It was the only town hall before the vote, so Mom expected people would be coming out of the woodwork. She told us her job was to make sure people were hearing from the good guys, too, but she looked nervous as hell.

Inside the council chambers, they'd set up every folding chair in the building, even opening the three double doors at the back to spill out into the hallway. There was already at least a hundred people milling about, a couple news cameras, and a few politicians at the front.

Around the room, contingencies were starting to form, Bill Kelly and a few other city government folks in the front left, John Arrington and the businessmen behind him, a sizable group from Lawton occupying the back right.

Mom marched us down the center to the fifth row, claiming unincorporated territory between them, her black Unity shirt making it clear which side she was on.

"Please tell me you guys decided not to break into anything?" Bones whispered to me as he scanned the room.

I ignored him.

The room continued to fill. There were policemen in uniform, most migrating to the Bill Kelly side, while some of my teachers joined Mom to help form a wall around the Unity crowd.

By 9:59 a.m., the room was full, the arrival of people too

random to sort by preference, so they filled in everywhere. The energy in the room crackled, low conversation burning like a live jumper cable that shoots sparks when you touch it. At ten exactly, Bill Kelly rose to the podium at the front and asked everyone to be seated.

Behind him, the city council filed in, all four of them as stoic as Greek gods. When they sat, there was one chair on the far left that was glaringly empty. They'd left the placard up in front of it—

Winston Lewis, City Council

Bill Kelly turned it over to the parliamentarian, who said we were going to now hear open comment.

CITY HALL OPEN COMMENT
Michelle Fischer (*Rodney's mom*)

Many of you know my daughter, Rodney. She's a brilliant student. In fact, she's a straight A student. Yes, thank you. Her father and I are extremely proud of her. Since preschool, she knew she wanted to be valedictorian. She never let up on that dream. In sixth grade, she went to church camp, and she was upset that they wouldn't grade her art project. She just graduated Calico High with a four point oh grade point average, and, God willing, she'll keep that at Mizzou next year. She's living her life's dream.

At Calico High, the average student grade point average is two point eight.

At Lawton, it's two point four.

At Calico High, the average SAT score for graduating seniors is nine hundred fifty.

At Lawton, it's eight ninety-two.

My sister, Rodney's aunt, works in admissions for Missouri State. Are you familiar with aggregate school score? I wasn't, either. But it's a measure given to a school based on cumulative school performance, which colleges use to determine the quality of a school, and then apply to an applicant's grades. A four point oh from a rigorous academic school does not mean the same as from a rinky-dink charter school. And that is measured by the quality of your classmates.

The Calico High aggregate school score is about to go down.

Way down. And it's time that we talk about this like exactly what it is. A punishment to our students.

It's more than just that. Students learn at the pace of their classmates. The average student in Lawton is reading two years behind their grade level. And our students are just supposed to wait for them to catch up?

All of this to say nothing of behavioral problems, violence problems, family problems, all shoved in the face of our students, and for what? So City Hall can save a few bucks on its taxes.

I want everybody to get a good education, just like you. But I also want what's fair for the people who have worked so hard to make Calico what it is.

CITY HALL COMMENT. TESTIMONY.
Sarah Malone (*Mom's friend Sarah*)

Those who do not remember history are doomed to repeat it. It's been quoted too many times for anyone to remember where it comes from, so I'll just pretend it's Abraham Lincoln.

So here's an important history. My great-grandparents lived in this area. They worked on the mills. They built a life here. And they lived in a small cottage home . . . in Calico Springs.

This is the true soul of the area. When we settled this river, we did it together. When we found prosperity, it was not mine or theirs but ours.

The splitting of that soul has been a hundred-year process. The relegation to Lawton. The building of economic barriers in Calico Springs. The choking out of public resources. The economic prosperity my great-grandparents started, it built a beautiful school in Calico Springs. It built roads to get there. And now, their great-great-granddaughter can't attend it.

Miss Fischer, do you want to know why those test scores are lower in Lawton? Do you want to know why the average Lawton student is reading two years behind their grade level? Because we don't have enough teachers. We don't have the resources to offer after-school reading programs. Ninety percent of the river valley's economic activity is housed in Calico Springs, despite the fact that half of its consumer base is in Lawton.

I don't know where this idea comes from, that these two towns were founded and grown separate from one another, walled off by the river. That's not how it happened. Calico Springs kept what it wanted and sent the rest to Lawton. The people it didn't want, it sent to Lawton. When I teach my children, I call that theft. That's the only behavioral problem I see. The violence done unto us is the only violence you should be worried about.

But this merger gives us a chance to reset that. To fix our past mistakes and share in the area's bounties. To stand together, not apart, to fight the many problems that plague us both. To restore the true soul of the river valley.

CHAPTER 31

RODNEY'S MOM'S SPEECH had elicited some boos from the back of the crowd, which caused a few at the front to turn around and look for their source. I could tell they were annoyed, whispering, something about decorum. Mom's friend Sarah's speech got even more of a reaction, some intentional groans from the decorum crowd.

I turned at one moment to sneak a glance at Sarai, and saw that she was holding her head high, as if shining a light at Rodney's mom, but I could see the reflection of tears on her face.

Joe Kelly arrived late.

He snuck in a door by the front, claiming a seat saved for him in his dad's section. He was wearing the Kelly family uniform, khaki pants, neutral-colored polo tucked in. His dad put his arm around him as soon as he walked in, and Joe beamed back, his eyes eager for approval.

I watched him intently. The speech ended and Joe stood to shake all the hands around him. At the very end of the line, he lingered on John Arrington, disappearing behind Arrington's wide shoulders as he leaned in to whisper something in Joe's ear.

When he stood back up, Joe was smiling. He took a step back, allowing Arrington to slide past him, past Bill Kelly, and walk up to the front podium.

CITY HALL COMMENT. TESTIMONY.
John Arrington

I know there's a lot of emotions today, a lot of people who feel very strongly, so I wanna step back for a minute. Take a second to talk about what actually changes in the event of a merger.

Two governments become one. Sounds simple, right? Problem is, we pay for our governments. In the event of a merger, the responsibilities placed on the single, unified government become undue, the burden spread out. People with the lower burden take on a higher one as the equilibrium shifts to accommodate. Not all bad, so long as the balance between the two is correct. Problem is, there's no balance here.

I know we're all enjoying the economic lift that the Calico Heights development has brought to this town. I heard somebody at the store the other day call it a revival. Sure feels like it, don't it? You're working, you're working, I know he's working. Hell, I'm working more than I have in years, and it feels amazing.

If you take this pie we've got now and try to spread it out across twice as many people, you know what that means, don't you? Smaller pieces. Smaller pieces for everyone involved. Either that or you need more pie. And you know where the government goes to get that pie? The people who can afford to pay for it. The businesses. The people who are working. Those of us who have worked hard to earn what we have and pass it on to our children. I know my friends in Lawton feel the same.

And that's the point. Some of my very best friends live in Lawton. They're a good, strong, proud community. But they are not Calico Springs. And we are not them. And this whole thing, dreamed up by a man, God rest his soul, who was more interested in a political victory than in the well-being of his own community, is a deliberate ploy to force together what does not want to be joined. To take that economic revival and stretch it until it snaps.

And I'm going to be frank. Unemotional. I am a businessman. I make decisions in the best interest of my business. And if my business is required to pay the undue tax burden of this merger. If we are required to prop up an entire town with our own economic success. Then I'm not sure we'll continue. In fact, I can say quite confidently, if the merger passes, we will pull our business from Calico Springs . . .

CHAPTER 32

THE ROOM EXPLODED.

"He can't do that!" The shouts came loudest from the group in the back, but there was anger spread all over the room.

"This is a business decision," Arrington tried to assert, but the tide overwhelmed whatever argument he was going to make, and Bill Kelly had to rush back to retake the room.

"That's illegal," Mom screamed loudly. "It's extortion!"

"It's not extortion," someone spat back at her, and it was impossible to tell who.

"Please, sit down," Bill Kelly was screaming. "Sit down!" He stood back from the mic and waited.

I scanned the crowd for Joe, and when I finally found him, I saw he was buried in his chair, looking toward the far wall, ignoring the commotion.

"Just as a note," Bill Kelly spoke loudly over everyone else. "And I'm not going to address every militant remark that gets shouted—but no law has been broken by speaking about the realities of decisions people will have to make in light of this merger—"

"That's bullshit."

"And we will not tolerate shouted remarks. They won't be entered, they won't be heard, but we will ask that you be removed from the room."

Bill started scanning the room for the next speaker, someone friendly. I sat up, waiting for Joe to volunteer, but he'd fully turned around in his seat, avoiding his dad's gaze, pretending to talk to someone behind him.

I stared at him. Back in his natural habitat, he looked nothing like the shivering, remorseful lump that had showed up in our garage this morning. He looked like his truest self. This was where he belonged, not with us, not with Sarai. It was obvious in the way he was sitting, the comfort on his face. I started to wonder if maybe his apology had been too sincere. If it was a performance to gain my trust, and I'd believed him, hook, line, and sinker. Why else would he choose this morning, of all mornings? Why else would he be ignoring his dad like this? This wasn't the plan. Joe Kelly was ignoring the plan.

But then I noticed a few others turn around, too. They were actually looking at something. One of them gasped, and it started a rumble. More gasps, more excitement, enough noise that even Bill Kelly looked up from his podium. I followed their gaze.

A wheelchair was being pushed into the room by a woman I didn't recognize. A few people erupted in cheers. They were headed for the front of the room.

Bill Kelly noticed as well. "Yes," he said tentatively. "Of course."

He backed off the microphone, and the whole room held its breath as Pastor Ronald Baker—bandages on his arms, a blanket over his legs, a steely look on his face—was wheeled to the front of the stage.

CITY HALL COMMENT. TESTIMONY.
Pastor Ronald Baker

I'm not here to talk about a merger.

When I was a kid, I used to ask my mother about that town on the hill. We could see you, up on the ridge. Your lights, your boats, your bridge. I'd see you, but we never visited. We never even talked about it. And when I asked, you know what she'd tell me? She said they're not your friends. Don't go over there, Ronny, you are not welcome in their kingdom.

I didn't listen. Good way to get a kid to do something, tell them they can't, right? Forty years, I've been breaking her rule. I've worked in your streets. I've taught in your school. I've prayed in your churches. I've prayed over your family members.

It took some growing up and some ugliness for me to finally learn what she meant. When she said they're not your friends, she didn't mean Calico Springs. She meant you. The you I'm talking to today. You know who you are.

I've learned I love Calico Springs. But I hate you. And I'm not scared of you anymore.

In fact, I'm coming for your castle.

I wish my friend Winston could have been here today to see this. That's his seat right there. You know what he would have said. How convincing he would have been. He'd already won. . . .

But of course, you knew you couldn't have that, could you?

You knew! You knew. You knew that if you let him live, he'd end you . . .

CHAPTER 33

"... FOR GENERATIONS—"

The mic died. The room hung in desperate silence. Baker tried to keep talking, but his voice was strained, and the reaction from the crowd was too much for him to speak over.

Bill Kelly scrambled to the front. "That's enough—we won't have—the forum for"—the mic popped back on—"accusations!" The word screeched with feedback.

It was clear Baker wasn't finished, and half the crowd was shouting for him to stay, but Bill Kelly gestured wildly for the woman wheeling him to lead him off the stage, and in the confusion, she did as he asked.

"I'll repeat," Bill Kelly said, fire in his voice now. "Even for respected leaders in our communities. This is a forum for reasoned debate. Not wild stories and emotions. Is there anyone here who can do that for us?" His head jerked back and forth around the room. "How about someone who can speak to the actual realities of a merger?"

The room wasn't satisfied, but he had control now. Whatever threat existed of the lid coming off the meeting, it had subsided back into a dull roar of whispers and accusations.

"How about"—Bill Kelly landed on his side—"an all-state athlete, a straight-A student . . . and he just so happens to be my son. Joe, come on up."

Joe sank into his seat. I held my breath.

It was clear his dad wasn't backing down, and the people around him were tapping him, propping him up. So Joe stood slowly. As he made his way to the stage, he twisted his spine to stretch, making a show of his preparation, and as he turned . . . his eyes landed on me.

He gave me a small nod.

I took a deep breath, praying I could trust him, and stood to slip into the aisle. But before I got there, I felt a hand on my arm, rough and violent.

"Where are you going?" Bones asked, his face pale.

"The bathroom."

He stared me down. His face was twisted. He didn't believe me, but I didn't break. I brushed his hand off me and nearly ran back up the aisle.

On the stage, Joe swaggered to the front. I could see satisfied smirks on the faces of the merger opponents. Joe would be difficult for people to not take seriously. He was the epitome of Calico Springs excellence and too likable to be treated as anything other than reasonable. He might actually make the case against the merger sound decent and empathetic. For the children.

I reached the back of the room, passing into the hallway.

Even that was full, every chair, every employee in the building, even the janitors glued to the stage.

Even the woman who was usually in charge of the Records Room.

I turned to watch as Joe cleared his throat at the mic, gripped the sides of the podium. "Thank you for allowing me to speak here today."

I saw a few folks on the Lawton side shaking their heads.

"If the schools merge next year, the prospects for the lives of students at Calico High would change dramatically."

I held my breath.

Joe turned. He looked directly at his father, his face tight and determined.

"For one . . . Calico Springs might actually win a football game."

The room erupted. In the chaos, I disappeared down the hallway.

CHAPTER 34

I WENT TO the men's bathroom and waited just inside, the door propped open, listening.

Joe was still talking. His dad knew he couldn't cut him off, and I could tell it was doing exactly what we needed, exactly as we had planned it that morning. Half the audience was cheering him on, the other side was stunned into silence. As I walked out, I saw people throughout the building rushing down the hallway toward the meeting room. He had grabbed everyone's attention in a way that only Joe Kelly could.

And the rest of the building was empty as a result.

I listened to the echoes of his speech with a smile on my face, feeling bad for ever having doubted Joe Kelly. The whole of Calico Springs now knew which side he was on.

It was still quiet just outside the door, until I heard the slow fade in of footsteps. This was it, Sarai and Abe. I lined myself up, timed it with the arrival of the steps, waited for the first glimpse of them, and spun out the door . . .

Directly into the chest of John Arrington.

"Whoa there!" He smiled. "Willie Eckles. Where are you headed so quick?"

My knees locked out, but I smiled up into his face. "Just using the bathroom."

He stared down at me, his face hardened. I could feel him looking through me, like I knew too much, and he knew that. For a second, I wondered if he'd seen me leaving and followed me out, as if he knew what we were up to. He stretched and cracked his fingers, just below my eye level, an absent-minded habit that I felt in my bones as a threat.

"Not causing any trouble, I hope?" he asked.

"No, sir," I said, and with a sweeping gesture, let him pass me, into the bathroom. "Have a great shit."

Sarai and Abe watched the whole thing, and as soon as he was gone, they came marching down the hallway, Abe's giant "Unity" sign held high, up over his head.

I waited, eyes flickering behind me, until they passed the bathroom door, and fell in directly behind the sign. Neither of them acknowledged me. They made a show of pretending I wasn't there. We marched in lockstep until we reached the door to the Records Room.

"You know what?" Sarai stopped on a dime, Abe and his sign stopping with her. "Maybe we should go back in instead."

Behind the sign, perfectly hidden from the hallway's only camera, my hands shook as I fumbled with the handle.

"You think?" Abe said. "I mean, it's so hot in there."

"Yeah, but I like the heat."

I felt the door click open, unlocked, and I inched it forward.

"Yeah, you know what? Let's do it. It's an important day for the town."

I slipped into the room, clicked the door shut, and watched through the stained glass window as they turned and walked the other way.

The timing was perfect. Now, even if they noticed something was missing and went to watch the cameras, they wouldn't be able to find footage of me sneaking into the room. It would be like I was never here.

The physical land ownership records—and every other type of record in Calico Springs—had yet to be digitized, so instead, the back room behind the desk was full to the brim with file cabinets, two rows with ten on each side, containing the entirety of the town's history.

I started on the far end of the room, unable to read the labels scratched and fading on the front, instead forced to check the contents. Vehicle records, marriage filings, incorporation documents, petitions—it was all so temporary. Like I could burn it and history would cease to exist.

Above the cabinets were photos from the town's history, all in plastic frames and lined up next to one another with no space above, below, or to either side. They were chronological, black-and-white photos of the late-1800s settlements, growing more and more current as you spun around the room.

It took me three minutes to find the cabinet labeled "Land Records."

They were organized alphanumerically by street name then street number. Because the lots in the Basin were frequently underwater, there weren't physical addresses to locate them by, so we had drawn extensions of the surrounding streets and used what few structures did exist nearby to estimate what the numbers would be. It was an inexact science, but it produced thirty-nine potential addresses for the land in the Basin.

I couldn't find any for the addresses on Cherry Street. Madrid Avenue only went as high as the 1300s. Poplar had a lot listed at 2400.

I checked it against my list. The last house on Poplar was 2132. I pulled the folder and opened it, a single sheet inside. The paper was worn and yellowed, its text fading, with small scribbles in the margins. Before I could read it, I got a text from Sarai:

Clear but hurry, Joe speech ending

I stuffed the folder in my bag. There was another lot on Sierra Street, even farther down, and I noticed its folder was worked over, same as the one from Poplar. Most in the cabinet were pristine, like they'd never been touched, but these seemed to have been handled time and time again. I thumbed forward—there were six more folders in similar conditions. Four of the six were matches. I grabbed them all, anyway.

A few voices fluttered down the hallway. I could hear the microphone still buzzing in the other room, so I chanced removing one of the pages and pausing to read it.

A deed of ownership, filled out with three different

handwritings, crossed out in several places. It dated back to the early 1800s and had passed through surprisingly few hands. At the bottom, the final name was clear, bolded, and obvious:

John Arrington.

A wave of sound rolled toward me from outside. I dropped the folder in my bag and kicked the cabinet shut with my knee. People were leaving. I didn't know how many of them. It was my chance to get out. Sarai confirmed it:

Leave now

I rushed toward the door, clicking the light off as I went, and felt myself freeze.

My eye had caught on a photograph by the switch. An old one, black-and-white, of six white men congregated on a familiar hillside, shaking hands with two men in overalls. The caption read, "Mayor Joe Steely and Two Contractors Celebrate Breaking Ground on New Fair Grounds, 1923."

My gaze drifted to the center, bile rising in my throat.

"What the fuck . . ."

I stared at the thick overcoat draped over the shoulders of the man in the center. It was the symbol. The dove crashing into the earth. The warning. But it wasn't left behind on accident. It wasn't etched into a tree or graffitied on a wall. It was a pin, worn proudly, just over the heart of the former mayor of Calico Springs.

My phone buzzed with a text:

SOS!!

I turned to sprint for the door, but from the hallway light,

I could see the silhouette of someone going for the handle. I dropped straight behind the desk, and a second later, the door creaked open. I heard the shuffling of feet inside. Feminine shoes, old lady shoes. It was the woman from the Records Room.

I clung to the ground, making myself as small as possible. Her steps weren't hurried, but they were deliberate. She lifted the partition and slid behind the desk.

This was it. What I'd stolen was a felony, but it was much, much worse than that. If I was caught stealing records, these records, then whoever these people were would know what we were doing. And we already knew what they were capable of.

My phone buzzed with light. A text:

Arrington is hovering

The woman noticed.

"Ahh!" She lurched backward. "Oh my God."

"I'm sorry," I said, scrambling to my feet.

"What—what are you doing? What were you going to do to me?"

She was terrified. I tried to shush her, but that just scared her more.

"Why are you here?"

I panicked. I had no answer. I tried to find a lie but accidentally glanced to the door and her eyes followed.

"Security!" she shouted. "Excuse me, is there security out there—"

"No!" I tried to get past her, but she blocked the path to the door. "Please, please—"

"Security!" she shouted, leaning back to shout out the door, trying to get someone's attention. "Security, please—"

"I GOTCHU MOTHERFUCKER!"

Bones burst through the door, nearly knocking her backward, shutting her up.

She looked to him wildly, and his arms dropped in frustration.

"I told you, Willie," he said. "You can't hide in offices. I can't search all those, you know the rules."

"You're playing hide-and-seek?" she asked.

"Obviously," Bones said. "You expect us to actually listen to those speeches? How'd you even get in here, Willie?"

"The door was open," I said. "You said any open doors were fair game."

She stared between us. "I'm sorry. I have to get the police, just to be safe—"

"The police?" Bones said. "For hide-and-seek?"

She leaned her head out the door and waved someone over.

Bones threw a secret glance at me. It wasn't angry or accusing. It was wild and excited, it said, "Well hey, at least it was fun."

I turned to the door to face my fate, and Deputy Schnack poked his head in.

"This boy was in my room," the records woman told him.

Schnack's eyes got wide, staring at me.

"We were playing hide-and-seek," Bones groaned. "It's not a felony, we're just bored."

Deputy Schnack didn't know what to say. I watched his eyes fall from my face to my bag.

"Can you detain them?" the woman asked. "What if he stole something?"

Schnack cleared his throat. "They're just kids being idiots," he said. "No more of this shit, okay? Leave this poor woman alone."

He held the door open and let us pass into the hallway. We marched in silence with our heads down and were halfway back to the hearing when I realized Schnack had kept with us, walking behind in silence. None of us said anything or even looked at each other. Just before we reached the chambers, he took two quick steps to cut me off, casually scanning the room without turning around.

My hands naturally drifted to protect the contents of my bag as I waited. If Schnack was in on it, that's what he'd be going for. When he finally turned, he didn't look at me but over my head.

"I don't know what you're doing," he whispered, barely moving his mouth. "But do it quick." With a small nod, he brushed past us and strolled the other way around the outside of the room.

CHAPTER 35

WE LOOKED OVER the deeds together in the garage.

I took notes on my Notes app, marking the details as best Sarai could interpret them. For the first deed we pulled, there were four previous owners—Laurie Snell, purchased 1890. Jonathan Mehon, purchased 1905. Robert Arrington, purchased 1915. John Arrington, inherited 1970. There was no information about purchase price. The seller information and signature lines were left blank.

"Here he is again." I removed a particularly messy deed and studied it. "It's not even a property, it's just a lot. 100–250 Peachnell."

Abe plugged the address into his phone. "That's not the Basin. That's way south."

"How far south?"

He turned the map toward her. The arrow was nestled into a familiar cut of the ridge, a winding road that disappeared into the mountain. It was at least two miles south of Calico Springs, but squarely inside the county line.

It was Joe Kelly who recognized it. "That's the road I take to work," he said. "That's the developments."

I recorded it.

They were covered with scribbles, all of them, most of the time a name or address correction, signed and initialed by the buyer. A few times, there were notes scribbled in the margins by the county clerk, commenting on the nature of the sale or even the physical appearance of the purchaser. She noted in one that she was grateful, for the purchaser's sake, the home had a bath.

But the penmanship on the Arrington lots was always the same, presumably the same clerk. By the fourth lot, we confirmed the pattern.

"Purchased by Robert Arrington . . . January 1916."

"October 1915. November 1915. March 1916," I read. "Arrington's dad bought the whole Basin in the same winter."

"And Peachnell?"

I nodded. "December 1915. And not a single one has purchaser information."

Sarai pulled a folder we'd set aside, the ones I'd taken on accident, land records that didn't belong to Arrington. "Look," she said. "All of these have purchase information listed. The price, the address, everything. It's not like the clerk forgets or they only started recording the information recently. It's protocol. This one has purchase info from the 1800s."

I understood her suggestion. "So either Robert Arrington is really lazy about his paperwork . . ."

"Or he didn't buy the land at all," she said. "He stole it."

Something about the dates clawed at me, eerie and familiar. Quietly, I searched them on my phone, alongside Calico Springs.

"So in 1915, the Arringtons claim a bunch of land along the river," Abe said. "They wait until it's got maximum value and finally start developing it a hundred years later. . . ."

"But my stepdad gets in the way," Sarai finished for him. "Tries to merge the towns, split the bounty. Sounds like motive to me."

"Then what's the barn?" I asked.

The theory stalled out.

Rodney had barely participated, instead sitting on the edge of the couch with her head hung over her phone. She wasn't typing, just scrolling endlessly . . . but whatever she was looking for, it was clear she wasn't finding it.

Bones noticed, too. "Is everything okay?" he asked.

She nodded. "Yeah, just . . . still haven't heard from Connor."

I remembered the empty seat next to her at the town hall. She was waiting for him, but he didn't show. Just like he didn't show yesterday.

It was quiet, even the rain slowing up against the roof.

"Did something happen?" Bones asked innocently. "Between you two?"

Rodney shook her head. "No. Everything was normal. I've been going back through the forums, just to see if there's anything I missed, something he might have said . . ."

She was trying to hide it and process it in her logical, Rodney way, but I could see she was hurt. Bones sat next to her on the couch instead of saying anything, just reading over her shoulder.

"He comments on basically everything," she said. "He's so excited about the Game, trying to get people to play it. . . . It makes no sense why he would all of a sudden bail, before we even figured out how it works—"

"Not that one," Bones said, tapping the screen to stop her scrolling. "Look, he literally says, 'don't wanna throw cold water.'"

Rodney's finger hovered. "Yeah, but that's not really about the Game. He's just trying to caution people about getting too excited about the Creator's address."

Bones stared at it, his face turning intense. He scrolled up, then back . . . his eyes exploding out of his face. "That fucker," he said quietly.

"What?"

"Look." He pointed to the top of the screen. "There."

"What? The address on the business filing? That's just a fake address. They could have picked anything."

"It's an auto parts warehouse." Bones gritted his teeth. "He wouldn't shut up about my fucking truck. He kept saying he could get me a deal . . . 'cause his dad sells parts."

Rodney's face flushed. It was like she was being introduced to something she already knew, the truth unspooling in front of herself as she laid it out.

"He was obsessed with getting other people to play the Game—but then undermined us when we went to find it. He kept trying to prove it worked, advocated for it like he's selling something . . . but was totally uninterested in trying to understand how it worked. None of that makes sense, unless . . ."

It was Sarai who said it for her. "He made the Game."

"What about the apartment?" Joe Kelly asked. "Didn't you say it was torn apart—"

"It was staged," I answered. "I remember thinking how weird it was, like somebody had destroyed the room looking for something . . . but the paper spread everywhere was blank. There wasn't actually anything there. It was like the Creator knew we were coming, and wanted to make it look like somebody got there before us . . ." Another detail clicked into place. "And that's why it opened. He must have had his key fob, and accidentally hit the sensor when he grabbed Sarai."

My heart started to pound. It was too much to process in one moment, but too simple at the same time, the kind of answer that only prompted more questions. The great, reality-defining explanation I'd been waiting for . . . was nothing.

I could see Sarai was having the same reaction, her eyes glazing over. "But why?" she asked. "Why would Connor want to send us to the mill or the graves or . . ."

The sentence died before she got all the way to Winston's name. She didn't have to.

"I don't see why we couldn't just go ask him," Bones said. "You've still got the address to his Airbnb?"

CHAPTER 36

WE SPED OVER in a convoy.

Rodney wanted to confront him alone, but Bones said he was afraid he might react poorly and wanted to be within arm's reach. The compromise was that she would approach him alone, while we sat in two cars, parked at the front and back of the Airbnb, listening to the conversation through her phone, which she'd keep in her chest pocket.

Rodney was quiet on the ride over, meditatively so. We all were. We'd obsessed over the question of where the Game came from, so to learn we'd been sitting next to the answer the entire time and not seeing it made reality seem dangerously fragile. Bones knew better than to say he told us so, but I could see that he was satisfied with himself, realizing he was right all along.

"Don't use words like *might* or *I think*." He offered Rodney a quick coaching, his skill in bullshitting finally paying real dividends. "Tell him you know. If he tries to go back to it, tell him you're past that part of the conversation. He's gonna try to wriggle out."

We rolled up slowly and let Rodney out down the street, so there was no chance he'd see the rest of us with her. In the other car, Abe rolled slowly around to the back, where there was a giant glass window, and Sarai texted us—

kitchen table

With the cars in position, Rodney held her breath and threw the door open without knocking.

"There's no way he gets violent," Bones said, reassuring himself more than me. "It's not that serious."

I plugged Bones's phone into the car's speaker system and turned it all the way up. Music faded into the crackling of her phone, and we both jumped as we felt her adjust it in her pocket, the interference powerful through the car speaker.

"What are— Did you— I'm not—" Connor's voice was muffled, cut out intermittently by the crackling of Rodney's pocket against the mic. We heard her sit, and he stopped talking abruptly.

Bones looked wildly around the truck. "Did something happen?"

The next voice through the phone was Rodney's, much clearer. "I know why you're here and who you are. I know that it's your game and that you've been lying to me."

"What do you mean—"

"I don't wanna hear it." Her voice was resolute. "I know how good you are at lying now, so I'm not interested in that. I only want you to answer one question for me, and then I'll leave you alone forever."

The phone crackled, plates clanging in the background. We could hear footsteps; he'd stood up and was walking away. We waited, everything tensed. Bones had his hand on the door handle.

Finally, Connor answered, his voice cracked and distant. "What's the question?"

It was as good as an admission. Bones slapped the dash, triumphant for her.

Rodney's voice didn't waver. "Why didn't you tell me?"

It was quiet for a long minute.

"You let me spend hours on company reports, forums . . ." she said. "We drove all the way to Redding and broke into a house, your house—why? Why didn't you just tell me?"

It took him a long time to answer, long enough that Bones shouted, "Come the fuck on!"

When he finally did, it was so quiet we had to crank the speaker to its limit. "It would ruin the whole thing," he said. "If people knew I made the Game, they wouldn't have believed it. This is the first and only place where it actually caught on. I couldn't poison that data."

Data. The world hit me in the stomach, months of my life reduced to the most inhuman word in the English language.

"Data for what?" Rodney asked, her voice quieter.

"You said one question—"

"I'm gonna ask whatever questions I want."

Bones smirked in the front seat. "Fuck yeah, Rod," he whispered.

"Data for what?"

"To see if it works," Connor said, like it was obvious. "To see if people believe it. I guess sort of like . . . a social experiment."

I had to steady my breath to keep from toppling over. I felt like I was in free fall. That was it. For all my believing, as certain as I was that the Game constituted something intentional, something mystical and universal, at least something that would make sense, it was nothing. I felt my body clench, angry at him for cheating me. I felt like a part of me had died.

Bones must have heard me, because without looking, he reached out and put a hand on my shoulder.

"So it was just fucking coincidence?" Rodney asked, her voice shaking with the same anger I was feeling. "The vortexes, the strangers . . . the fucking body. All of it was just random?"

"Yeah." He was quiet for a long minute then added, "I'm sorry."

We heard the silverware on the table rattle as she steadied herself to stand.

The conversation was over. The explanation we'd devoted our summer to was nothing. The cold, meaningless results of some college science experiment.

From the quiet, we barely heard Rodney's voice ask, "Why Calico Springs?"

"It just happened here."

"Did you choose us?" she asked. "Did you set us up—"

"No, no, I made the Game, like, a year ago. The only thing I ever did to get it out there was put it on a few message boards—Reddit, 4chan, a few alt-right, white supremacist sites . . . you know. Trying to find people who like conspiracy theories, who might buy into it."

My lip quivered. He was talking about me. Bones squeezed my shoulder again, harder this time. I didn't want to look at him, even if I knew he was past the point of gloating.

The line went quiet. Rodney was thinking.

"Why take people's locations?" she finally asked.

"What?"

"Why are you stealing everyone's locations?"

"I'm not—"

"Stop lying to me. I already know it! The Game keeps user locations even when they're not playing. What's the point of that?"

"I don't know what you're—"

"I can show you!" Rodney almost screamed it, loud enough to screech feedback in the car, both Bones and I ducking away. "Stop lying to me. That's why you didn't tell me."

Connor was quiet. I couldn't see him, so I didn't know if it was confusion or if Rodney had struck something. I held my breath, urging her forward.

"It's not 'cause you didn't wanna poison the data or whatever," she said definitively. "It's because what you're doing is illegal."

"It's not technically illegal," he protested.

"It is illegal—"

"It's in the Terms of Service."

"Why?"

We waited. Bones edged the volume on the speaker up again, and when Connor spoke, it was reluctant and jittery . . . the actual no-bullshit secret of Manifest Atlas.

"Because that's what makes the Game work," he said.

Bones and I exchanged a look.

"The Game uses locations of other users to create targets," he said. "Not just places where they go while playing, but anywhere they spend time. The more time they spend there, the more the Game registers it, like a heat map.

"Then, you take out all the residential addresses and business addresses . . . and you end up with a collection of the most popular places in any given area. Favorite spots, secret hideaways . . . and the Game sends other players to those spots.

"I figured, if people were going places that other people had been, they'd be more likely to think they'd been sent there for a reason. They'd start to make connections to the things they'd asked for, and from that, they'd start to believe that the Game actually worked.

"The whole goal was to prove that manifestation technology is real, if people only believe in it enough. And once it started happening here . . . I mean, did you see how much news coverage this got? It was the top post on Reddit, for God's sake. There are probably labs all over the world that started studying this. Trying to move us forward. We might actually make some real breakthroughs in quantum technology—"

"Except it was a lie," Rodney said. "You tricked them. You tricked me."

My heart raced.

It was like I could hear Rodney's, too, because she stood up, her legs banging against the bottom of the table, the phone scratching in her pocket, obscuring her final words to Connor.

"Don't come back here. Ever."

Bones revved the engine as she rushed out the front door and jumped in the car. Abe pulled his car back around to the front, peeling in to line up front windows.

"That's it!" I shouted into their car. "That's the solution!"

Rodney slammed the door behind her, a wild look on her face, her hands shaking. There was a logic to it. There was a puzzle that could be solved. And we had the answer key in the garage.

"I'm confused." Bones looked around at all of us. "What does that solve?"

"It means if someone has the Game on their phone," I explained, "then it'll send other people to places they've been."

Bones thought about it. "So, for the body . . ."

I sat up, a chill running down my spine as I said it. "It means whoever was playing the Game before us had been to the drop site."

CHAPTER 37

THE FIRST MORNING, when I heard Tyler and Rory talking about the Game, I remembered them referring to it as new, something they were introducing, something no one else had discovered yet. They said it bold and bragging. There was no mistake, from the way they showed it around the shop, they were the ones who found the Game, who played it before us. Which made it as good as fact—

Rory and Tyler had been to the mill.

Joe Kelly struggled to process the information. "There's no way," he said for the fourth time, once we were back in the garage. "They're assholes, but they're not murderers."

"And not for nothing," Bones added, "they were at the baseball game, too. So how could they have killed him?"

"Maybe they just dumped the body," Rodney answered.

"But then why wouldn't they tell the police that?" Joe Kelly argued. "Why would they lie about the murder, if they didn't do it?"

"Willie," Abe said, turning to me. "Do you remember, that

first day in the shop . . . did they say where they heard about it? Was someone else playing?"

I shook my head. I'd been running the conversation over and over, trying to find any missing details.

"Probably from one of those alt-right sites Connor said he put it on," Rodney answered, disgust still pouring out every time she said his name. "You know Tyler and Rory are into that shit."

Sarai had been sitting in the corner, processing without saying a word, but she finally sat up and asked, "Does any of this matter?"

It sucked the air from the room.

"What do you mean?" Joe Kelly asked.

"We accuse John Arrington's son of murder with no proof, a motive that's all based around some hundred-year-old land records, and a vague theory about a game that no one will understand? What's that supposed to do? The police already don't take this shit seriously. . . . What are we expecting to change?"

I hadn't been in the car with her, so I hadn't realized she was taking the news about the Game much harder than me or Rodney. She'd lived the worst month of her life and kept moving straight through it, eyes forward. She'd used the Game for much more than fun—it was her one source of hope. It was the thing she could turn to to avoid the guilt she felt about Winston's death. I don't think I'd understood how bad things must have been, and how devastating it must have felt to have that final strand of hope taken away.

"We could at least try to tell somebody . . ." Joe Kelly offered with optimism I knew was blind, and Sarai knew it, too.

She shook her head and swallowed. "We got fooled into thinking we could actually do something about this . . . by some fucking college computer project."

"We know he got killed," Rodney tried to assure her. "We know why—"

"It doesn't matter what we know." Her lips twitched. "Because we don't have anything real to show for it."

The rest of the group gave up on trying to reassure her of anything. Abe crossed the circle and put an arm around her, squeezing her shoulders in a hug.

But as I stared past her in the garage, studying the map of our last month for the millionth time, I realized we weren't out of hope just yet.

"There's something else," I said, going to the map. "We were following their footsteps when the Game sent us to the mill," I said, pointing to it. "So wherever the Game sent us before that night, it's basically a map of all the places Rory and Tyler had been." I looked to Sarai. "Remember your first theory? That the mill was just their backup plan? Maybe that's where they dumped the body, but they picked it up"—I moved my finger to the Basin—"where it was supposed to go. In the graves."

The garage got suddenly chilly. The rain hadn't let up

outside the garage, and the sky was turning dark with clouds, night stretching into the day.

"He got dumped in the mill," I said. "But he got killed in that barn."

"We have to check it out," Abe said, sitting up. "There might be something in there that can prove what happened—"

"No."

Joe Kelly looked like he'd seen a ghost, staring at the map. His eyes were wide, his lip quivering. Something had unlocked inside of him, we could all see it, and it was choking him as it washed over his face.

"Look," Abe said. "If you don't believe us—"

"It's not that." Joe Kelly shook his head. "I believe you. I believe all of you. So much that I know . . . we can't go to that barn."

"Why not?" Bones pressed him.

He let the air out of his lungs slowly. "He's talked about it before," he started, struggling to get out what he had to say. "My dad."

"Talked about what?" Abe glared at him.

Joe Kelly looked up, directly at Sarai. "The barn. I thought it was just an expression, 'Bring him to the barn. Show him the barn.' I didn't get it until now, but it's a threat. . . ." He looked at Sarai. "I can't let you go. Especially not someone from Lawton. That's . . . They'll . . ."

I watched Sarai look back at him, and for a second, I thought she might lose it, blame him for denying the truth so long he missed obvious signs . . . but she didn't. She nodded, accepting it.

"We could try the cops . . ." Rodney said, but Abe and Sarai cut her off in unison.

"It won't help," Abe clarified. "They're already ignoring it. Whatever's going on, they're probably a part of it. . . ."

Again, the conversation stalled. Out of the cold silence, it was Bones who sat up.

"Then me and Willie should go."

I felt my chest swell as I met his eyes. Bones was smiling at me, sheepishly, either unaware of the danger or choosing to ignore it, and suddenly, I recognized him again. The Bones I'd known my entire life, sitting across the garage.

"What'd you say, Willie?" he asked.

I nodded back.

The rest of the group looked terrified. "I don't think it's safe for anybody—" Rodney started.

"Look," Bones stopped her. "We're Calico to the core. We know that Basin better than anybody in the world. If not this . . . then what are we for?"

He looked sideways to me, and everyone else's eyes followed. I felt it in my chest before I put it together in my head—this was the moment. The miracle boy, saved by God for a reason. If not this, then what was I for?

I stood up and walked to the back of the garage. The toolbox was hidden in its usual spot. I opened it with a deep breath and took out our father's 42. For the first time in my life, I gripped it by the handle, feeling its weight, turning it over to examine it in the dim light. I could feel Bones holding his breath as he watched me.

"Well," I said to the group. "What the hell are we waiting for?"

CHAPTER 38

BONES TOLD ME that sometimes when he closed his eyes, he could see the Basin, the labyrinth of branches and fallen logs laid out in front of him. With how quickly and fearlessly he walked across the sunken, soaking ground, it felt like that was exactly what he was doing.

We didn't say anything as we pushed through the forest. It was softly drizzling, just like the first night in the Basin, but the mud had already absorbed so much water, I could feel it soaking through the soft cloth of my Vans. I was quickly losing feeling in my feet.

On our last trip, I'd dropped a pin, so we charted a course that would allow us to walk to it, approaching the barn from the inland side. As we approached, I compared the location on my phone to what I was seeing in front of me. The barn was completely covered by foliage, tucked away out of view, an optical illusion guarded by the bend of the river. Without the light on inside, I'd never have noticed it. It wasn't until we were within twenty feet that the edges of the building finally became apparent.

"Willie," Bones whispered, nodding to where he was standing. Below him, water was pooling up in two parallel indents in the mud. Tire tracks from a truck with a high liftgate.

The padlock was still secure on the front door. Bones had taken the bolt cutters from our truck, but the lock was curved to prevent anyone from lining up a clean cut, which was exactly what we were trying to do. After a few failed attempts, we gave up and roamed the exterior of the barn. There was only one window, a small one, blacked out from the inside.

I went to it immediately, but Bones held me back. "We're sure we wanna break a window?"

With his hand on my shoulder, I felt the sting of the last month catching up, his unending wave of caution and control. "I'm going in, Bones," I said. "I don't need you to look after me."

Bones didn't respond. He pretended he hadn't heard me, and maybe he hadn't. Or maybe he'd spent so many years training himself to listen selectively and filter out the bad stuff, that the words actually didn't register. I waited for him to try to give up and turn back, but he didn't.

"I'm sorry, Willie," he said. "I ignored you because I was being fucking selfish. Because every time you said bad shit about Calico, I felt like you were saying it about me. Because I'm stuck here, and Rodney's leaving . . . and you're gonna leave, too. And you're gonna do so much more than me."

Raindrops slammed against his cheeks, but he ignored them, forcing eye contact with me. "And I still feel so guilty. Every time I look at you . . . I remember that I broke you. I made life impossible for you. And once—just once—I wish you'd get pissed at me. Tell me 'Yes, it's your fucking fault.' I wish you'd have tried to take my eye, like in the Bible."

I stared at him, frozen. "You didn't break me," I said. "You didn't break shit."

Bones nodded. Without another word, he scooped a large rock from the ground at my feet. It was smooth, a few inches across. He tossed it, one hand to the other, to judge its weight.

"Well," he said. "Then, please. Allow me."

He turned back to the barn and stared down the window. With full effort, he rocked backward. His leg swung up, his full rocking motion, and he whipped a fastball at the glass.

It struck perfectly, inside corner, shattering the bottom pane clean. The noise sliced throughout the Basin, then subsided into soft rainfall.

"Tough pitch," I told him, and he smiled, like it really meant something.

Bones used the butt of the gun to clear as much glass as he could, then steadied himself against the frame, slowly leaning in. I saw a sharp edge of remaining glass catch his skin, drawing blood, but Bones pushed through it without complaint. Once he was inside, he returned to the window and help pulled me through. I landed with a thud against the wood and turned to face the pitch-black barn in front of us.

By the light of our phone flashlights, it seemed abandoned. On the floor, a blue tarp gathered rainwater from the roof overhead, leaking in several places. We circled like detectives, defining the edges of the space, but there was nothing to find. The only thing I noticed in the corner were chairs, twelve of them, stacked carefully and placed out of view. So it wasn't totally abandoned.

Behind them there was another tarp, hanging from the ceiling. "Bones," I said, nodding to it.

He nodded back agreement.

I took a deep breath, gripped it, and yanked as hard as I could. Immediately, I realized—the barn wasn't abandoned. Not even close. There were more chairs, a stereo, some tall candles, an ironing board—it looked almost lived in.

We both made our way to it and started to examine the items. There were a few milk cartons that stood out—one full of canisters of spray paint, another filled with old, recycled guns. Behind them, a stack of Bibles leaned against the wall. This wasn't any church to me. I thought about the stumps outside. Maybe for rituals or a cult?

I tried to the dam the flood of ideas in my brain, each more twisted than the last.

In the back corner, the light caught a row of reflective bars, a few feet off the ground. It was a small enclosure, a cage. As I studied it, I saw white droppings inside, from animals. Birds. Doves. My heart dropped. Maybe the doves weren't a coincidence after all.

I noticed something else, in the other corner. A rope hung from above, disappearing into the rafters at the ceiling. It looked like the rope at my church that rung the bell on the top, but there was nothing like that on top of this barn. I walked to it and stood underneath—it was clinging to a thick cloth, bundled over our heads.

As I made my way to it, headlights flooded the barn door, spilling in through the cracks. We hadn't noticed the truck approaching behind us.

"Shit," Bones whispered. "We gotta get the fuck outta here."

But I was mesmerized. I gave the rope a tug, and that was all it needed. The cloth came tearing down, falling from the ceiling above me. I ducked for cover, but it missed me, falling to the barn floor. It was a banner, a giant one, now unfurled.

Bones and I both stared in awe, our phone flashlights illuminating the wall.

It was the dove.

I knew it then. This barn was the source. The only true vortex in Calico Springs.

The headlights washed over again and came to a stop, the vehicle parking outside the barn. We ran to the window, but it was too late. I could already hear movement outside, the shaking of a lock.

Bones let me go first, angling to a position to lift me up, but as I placed my hand, my palm caught glass on the edge. The skin broke immediately, and reflexively I pulled my hand back.

The door began to shake. Before Bones could get in position again, we heard the lock fall, and the wheels start to squeal against the track.

"Go, go, go!" he whispered, but it was too late. There was no time to move or run or hide. Our only choice was to answer for our sins.

Inch by inch, the door shrieked as it was pulled back. I held my breath, and Bones took the 42 from his pocket, raising it toward the door.

I knew this was it. John Arrington, Tyler, Rory—whoever was behind this building, behind the dove, surely they'd punish us. They'd killed Winston, they'd burnt down Baker's church. I could only imagine what they'd do to us.

The crack in the door let the outside world in. There was a sliver of headlight, the slow passing of the river's alarm light, leaking in and over our faces. Bones felt for my hand below and grabbed hold.

"I love you, Willie, I really do," he whispered.

The door leapt back another inch, enough for people to pass through. It was just one person, ducking his shaved head for cover from the rain, lifting his eyes to us as soon as he was inside.

He saw us and froze. He saw the banner behind us, the terror on our faces, the phone in Bones's hand.

"Boys . . ."

It was Dad.

I was too scared to cry.

PART SEVEN

THE DOVES

CHAPTER 39

WHEN I WAS five years old, I died for five minutes.

It meant I was special, that I was chosen by God. At least that's the story Dad told me.

Turns out, it was actually the start of a much longer story, a story my dad would keep telling me for my entire life. The Legend of Dad the Protector and Willie the Needer of Protection. I was special but fragile. When someone insulted me, they needed to be dealt with, otherwise the pain might break me. I couldn't be trusted to think for myself, being so young and so childish, so best to make decisions for me, best to keep me on the path, best to keep me from ever looking off it. And up until that moment, I thought he was doing that because he loved me.

Turns out, it wasn't love. It was control. Turns out, the things he didn't want me looking at were the real parts of him, who he actually was. Turns out, his whole story was just a cover.

And the real story was much, much worse.

* * *

Bones dropped the gun and rushed to him immediately. "Dad! Holy shit!" He grabbed Dad by the shoulders. "What is this?"

Dad had the look of a bewildered animal, unable to speak. He stared past Bones, talking to me. "Who told you to come here?"

"We were just exploring," I said.

He saw the smashed window behind us. "You broke in?"

Neither of us said anything.

On a dime, he started to rage. "Why the fuck would you break into a toolshed?" he screamed and turned to Bones. "Why'd you come out here in all this? It's fucking pouring! Who the hell is raising you boys? You should be home taking care of your mom!"

Bones took a few steps back but kept his shoulders squared.

"Seriously, I'm taking you home now, and we're gonna have a serious fucking conversation about this—"

"It's not a toolshed, Dad," I said.

He looked me over, wiping the rain from his eyes. "Willie, we don't have time for this. You boys are in big shit with me, and I'm not gonna listen to your bullshit. . . ."

He started to move toward Bones, but Bones ducked him. Dad went at him harder, grabbing his jacket to corral him to the door, but Bones held steady, not allowing himself to be moved. Dad had underestimated Bones's frame, too sturdy now for Dad to control him. Bones shook wildly, out of his grasp.

"What is this place, Dad?" he asked.

"Oh, you're both so smart now." He swung at Bones's neck,

throwing an elbow out to put him in a headlock, hard. Bones yelped in pain.

"It's not a toolshed," I said over the sound of the struggle. "And we're not gonna leave until you tell us what it is."

He yanked Bones forward in total submission. "Willie, I'm not fucking around, okay? We have to get out of here—"

"Before what?"

"Before some friends of mine show up and are very fucking angry that you broke into their toolshed—"

"It's not a toolshed," Bones shouted, jerking his head back to break the grip and scrambling across the barn. Dad took a couple of quick steps toward him then stopped short, as a faint headlight passed over the barn.

Someone else was here.

Dad took a deep breath, his anger turning to desperation. "Don't talk, just listen, okay? Leave out the front, go south and make a wide loop and get the fuck out of here. We'll talk about this later." He looked directly at me. "We will talk about it later, Willie, I swear, and I will explain everything."

It was quiet for a long moment, as the wind and rain shook the foundation. The headlight washed over us again and Dad screamed, "Fucking go!"

For the first time in our lives, Bones looked to me.

"You left the baseball game early," I said.

Dad looked wildly between the two of us. "What the hell do you mean, Willie? What baseball game?"

I'd been watching him since he walked in. This was an act.

He knew exactly what I meant. So instead of talking to him, I said it straight to Bones. "He left the game early," I repeated.

"What fucking game, Willie?!"

The pieces fell into place for Bones. "My game," he said. "You said I did great. I was so confused . . . but it's 'cause you left early. You didn't see the ending. You tried so hard to convince me you were there, but you left. You were here."

"What does that have to do with anything—"

"You chased Willie that night," Bones said over him. "You were the man in the Basin. Libby was the dog—"

"What man? What are you talking about—"

"You fucking killed him."

Bones lurched forward. Dad cowered back, but Bones wasn't aimed at his body. Instead, he dove to the ground between us, coming back up with the 42 and pointing it at Dad.

We all froze. I heard the slow groan of tires.

"I don't know who the fuck is putting these crazy ideas in your heads, but your lives are in danger if you don't listen to me."

"Bones, let's go," I whispered. "We have to get outta here."

"You're a fucking liar." Bones held the gun steady at his chest.

Dad looked calm, locked in on Bones. "You have to either turn and run right now," he said squarely. "Or give me that gun, so I can shoot whoever walks in here. Because if not, they will kill you."

"Bones, let's go!" I tried to yank him toward the door, but it was too late. We heard a car door slam. The headlights went out.

As soon as it was dark, Dad leapt at Bones, smacking the gun to the floor. He came up with it and scrambled away from both of us. "Get in the corner," he hissed. There was nowhere to hide, the entire room was exposed, so we huddled behind the ladder. Dad rushed to the broken window and moved a piece of plywood over it, blocking the view from the door, then returned to the center of the room, taking aim at the open doorway.

He took a deep breath, steadying himself to fire.

We heard footsteps outside. No one was talking, so I assumed it was one person. Bones watched the door. I watched Dad.

Slowly, he backed off his stance, standing taller. He dropped the gun to his side, then casually tucked it into his waistband and turned to us. He took a few steps toward us and started talking.

"It's about tradition and protection. And I know you boys are ready, so you're just going to have to show everyone else—"

"Markie."

John Arrington stood in the doorway, both shoulders nearly touching the edges of the frame.

Dad launched in. "John! Got a little surprise for you. I know this is crazy, but my boys have been curious, and that has convinced me more than ever—it's time. They're ready."

Arrington pulled his gun, a sleek silver piece. "Give it to me right now. Any weapons."

Dad flinched, but his hands didn't move. Arrington stared at his waistband. "Now."

Slowly, Dad removed the 42 and tossed it at Arrington's feet.

"Phones, too."

I reached for my phone in my chest pocket, careful to keep the screen angled away from him. He stared at me the whole time. Bones casually tossed his phone on top of the weapon at his feet. I held mine for a moment, waiting for Arrington to look away.

"Just a precaution, boys, like I told you," Dad said, and Arrington looked back to him. I threw it quickly, the phone tumbling to his feet, landing in the grass with the screen upward, lit up, a phone call to Sarai in progress.

"Hey!" I barked. It caught Arrington off guard, grabbing his attention just before he looked down. "We don't want any trouble," I said.

At his feet, the screen went dark.

"Yep," Dad said. "No trouble here."

I held up my hands, heart in my throat, as Arrington scanned the room. For the second time in my life, I thought about what it would be like to die.

The following is an excerpt from the Springfield Journal
November 15, 1915
(This passage has been edited
for clarity and to remove traumatic language)

THE ABANDONING OF "OLD TOWN"
The Black Community Took Seriously an Announcement That They Would Be Killed and Left Their Possessions Behind in Their Hasty Departure From Their Homes.

Birds chirp in the grave-like stillness where formerly laughter and song echoed. But few of the 150 Black families who once resided here remain, and these are hourly expecting the visit of an avenging nemesis.

ONE violent act depopulated "Old Town" at Calico Springs, Mo. Where lately was a village of a hundred and fifty families, birds and bats are the only occupants of the houses.

It began the evening of Nov 11, when a small building in the neighborhood was raided by Night Riders, a mob from the local community. Three Black folks who lived in the building were shot and killed. They were said to be buried in the nearby basin of the Current River.

That evening, the anonymous letters were sent through the mails to two Black folks of the town. They threatened that unless all the Black folks left the town the adults would be killed.

Although it is not certain whether they emanated from an organized body of whites bent upon driving the Black people out of the community, they took the warnings seriously and by every means at their command they left the place as fast as they could, abandoning real and personal property. Panic-stricken, their only thought was to get out of Old Town. To them, the fire was as a doom spoken against the town and all that remained in it, and no sacrifice was too great to get out of it.

They left their occupations, the school was closed and they left across the county line to Summit County, where they hoped to find an asylum free from the menace of vigilantism.

As soon as they were made aware of the contents of the letter they had received, they made their preparations without delay to get out of "Old Town" and leave Calico Springs forever.

CHAPTER 40

"HOW MUCH DO they know?"

"Not enough to cause any trouble. Not hardly anything at all."

Dad was trying hard to recapture his casual nature. He kicked at a spot on the ground, put his hands back down into his pockets. It was clear Arrington didn't believe him.

"Matter fact, I was just telling them about this supply shed we keep out here, just in case we need to do any maintenance, anything like that. Protecting the town and all."

Arrington took a few steps into the barn. "I told you there was no sense in lying to me. You think I forgot that?"

Dad looked confused, until he realized Arrington was talking to me.

"I see you around town with that girl. The fucking messes I've had to clean up. Making wild claims, accusations—people don't like that. They don't feel comfortable living in a town with somebody who keeps accusing people of shit."

"No, no, no," Dad jumped in. "You got this all backward.

They barely even know that girl. In fact, Willie said he had to stop hanging out with her because of all the accusations, right?"

Off Arrington's shoulder, I could see Bones staring bullets into me. "Yeah," I lied. "I barely know her. I was just trying to . . . smash."

It felt gross coming out of my mouth, but Arrington snorted a laugh.

"That's what I was trying to tell you, John," Dad said. "These boys, they were born here, Calico Springs is in their blood. Bones didn't even want to go off to school, he wanted to stay here, because they know how important this town is, how hard we've worked for it . . . they're ready."

"Yessir, Mr. Arrington," Bones added. "We're ready."

Arrington pointed at me. "That boy's twelve years old."

"I'm fifteen," I corrected him.

"And smart for his age," Dad added. "Got straight As this year. History teacher said he's as good as he's ever seen here. He knows what matters around here—"

Outside, we heard another truck pulling down the long driveway. Arrington said nothing, letting it approach. The car door slammed, and two voices, shouting and laughing, came floating through the crack in the door.

"John, it's me." Dad looked like he was about ready to fall to his knees and beg. "You seriously think I'd bring trouble against you?"

The door opened again, and Rory and Tyler came through, freezing when they saw us.

"What the fuck are those rats doing here?" Tyler asked his dad.

"That's my sons you're talking about—"

"I would be very quiet, if I were you, Markie," Arrington said. He looked back to Tyler.

"They hang out with the girl," Tyler said. "They've been following us around, trying to stir shit up. The little one followed me into the woods one night out at Baker's church—"

I swallowed. Tyler was the devil in the woods.

Arrington held up a hand. "You two," he said, pointing to us. "Faces on the ground, over in that corner. If I hear a single word, see a single fucking movement, I'll shoot you. And it'll be legal, seeing as this's my property and you're trespassing."

We did as we were told, moving with no wasted motion. As we lowered ourselves to our hands and knees, I could feel Bones shaking. We set our faces inward and whispered apologies to each other with our eyes.

I tried to calm myself by focusing on what I did know. Rory and Tyler had dumped the body, the Game told us that. And if my dad was the one person not at the baseball game, that meant he must have been the one to pull the trigger. Arrington seemed to be in charge of all of it—but I didn't know what it was yet.

We could hear pieces of the argument as they hissed at each other across the room.

"They're here because they wanna fuck us over, Dad. They've been at this for a month—"

"You don't know what the hell you're talking about. The only reason you've seen them around is because they're ready to make the covenant—"

"They're dangerous! They're gonna tell people we're murderers, and now they've seen too much—"

"They wouldn't say that! And they're kids, anyway! Who gives a shit what they say—"

"Twelve hours before the merger vote? You want them running around, showing people pictures, telling everybody we killed Winston—"

"You know the fucking rules. If Bill was here he'd shoot you himself—"

I felt the name in my stomach. Bill Kelly. He was a part of this, too. They were in it together. I pictured them huddled at the funeral, remembered Joe Kelly telling us Arrington would give his dad anything he wanted, how they had secret meetings, shared interest. This was the plan all along. Every part of it was intentional.

It wasn't just Dad or Arrington or Bill Kelly. It was everyone. The rot was all the way to the core.

I noticed the barn was quiet. They'd stopped talking.

My whole body tensed as I heard footsteps, Arrington's, moving across the room . . . toward the broken window.

"Oh," Dad tried to cover. "We accidentally bumped it when we came in."

The plywood shifted, and I shivered as the cold, wet air from outside swept over us. I could feel whatever survival instincts I had giving way to regret; regret that we'd volunteered to visit the barn, regret that I'd gotten involved with the Game in the first place.

"I fucking told you," Tyler hissed. "They broke in. They're trying to blow this up!"

"They're not a threat," Dad yelped. "And who gives a fuck what they say, no one can prove shit, they're just kids!"

"You lied," Arrington said flatly, and again, the barn got quiet. I heard his footsteps, slow across the barn floor, louder as he got closer.

"I didn't lie," Dad urged. "I said I found them poking around."

I felt the shadow of Arrington's frame passing over me. I squeezed my eyes and said a silent prayer.

Dear God.

We are your servants, loyal and true. Please protect your children. Please protect my brother. Please protect me.

"But the reason they're here is because they want to join, just like their old man—"

THUD. Arrington swung his boot into Bones's chest, collapsing him to the floor with a whimper. Arrington made a show of walking slowly around toward me.

Watch over and deliver us from evil. Forgive us our sins. Reveal our true intentions.

"For fuck's sake, I've done everything you asked!" Dad was crying now. "Let me take them far, far away. I'll send 'em to live with my sister, I'll get them committed, I'll do anything!"

And if this is to be our time, then please, welcome us into your kingdom.

Amen.

Arrington spat at the ground next to my head. "It's too late for that."

CRACK. I felt my ribs collapse as the toe of Arrington's boot flew upward into my chest. My breath disappeared, and I rolled over, unable to breathe. The world danced in front of me as my vision faded and returned.

It was still quiet, just the steady assault of rain against the siding.

I was in too much pain to do anything but make peace with it. Whatever this was, to him, it was worth killing for. I was going to die.

"You can't," Dad said finally. He'd gathered himself and was trying to speak with authority. "You can't kill them—"

"I'll fucking do it," Tyler said with an ugly snort.

"I can get rid of them," Dad reasoned. "And make sure you never hear a word from them again. But you can't kill them and you know it."

For the first time, I heard Arrington's voice rise. "If you weren't willing to lose a child, you should have been a better parent. Being sentimental isn't going to—"

"For fuck's sake, John, I'm being pragmatic. You think Covenant can exist if every last person in town knows who we are, what we do, and what we're capable of?"

"Is that a threat?" Tyler's voice ripped out of his throat.

"Of course not. But that's what's going to happen if all of a sudden two more people—kids—are murdered. The FBI would open an office here for good. Be fucking pragmatic."

My chest seized. I didn't know if Dad was telling the truth or if it was just another bluff, but the logic held to me.

Finally, Arrington sighed. "He's right. We can't invite that kind of reputation. But . . ." Arrington continued, "with the vote tomorrow, I'm not taking chances they'll say something and people will believe them."

He walked over and lowered himself, inch by inch, to where I was still splayed on the floor. I tried to steady my breath, let him know I wasn't scared. He grabbed me, fingers clenched down against my arm, and looked directly into my eyes.

"So what we can do, is make sure they understand how serious we are."

He released my arm and stood, spitting toward his sons.

"Tie 'em up."

Tyler and Rory zip-tied our hands and yanked bandanas tight over our mouths, while Arrington pulled Dad aside. I couldn't hear what he was saying, but from his tone, it sounded like Dad was still begging for our lives. As I watched him, though, I realized I didn't even know if I could believe that. I couldn't believe anything he said.

It was all a lie. This was why Mom kicked him out of the house, and why she couldn't explain it to us. His new job, his place in town, on the developments, it all flowed from this. "There has to be another way." That's what Mom told him. It was why she didn't want Bones to get a job at the developments. She knew what it would open him up to. All those moments he'd tried to earn his way back, all the times he'd told us she'd come around—she was protecting us, from this. And Dad had let us believe it was her fault.

I turned my head slowly and saw Bones watching Dad on the other side of the barn, but with hope in his eyes. Like he was waiting for the moment when Dad would pull something crazy, flip the situation, get us the hell out of there.

I wanted to cry for him. I knew it wasn't coming. I wanted to slap Bones and shake him. I wanted him to feel the anger that I felt, to understand how much we'd been betrayed.

They yanked a blindfold over his eyes, then laughed to one another as they tried to figure out how to tie mine. Tyler took me by the arm, Rory took Bones, and they led us outside, intentionally throwing us into the wall of the barn, the side of the truck, as we walked. They shoved us into the back seat together, and for a second, we were alone in the car.

"Don't worry, Willie," Bones whispered. "I'm gonna get us out of this."

I wished I was still young and dumb enough to believe him.

EXCERPT FROM "DEVILS OF THE HILLS"
by LINDA DONAHUE

Residents of Calico Springs were quick to forget the incident. The mayor, Robert Arrington, for his part, told the Springfield Journal *at the time, "Print what happened, but please don't make this bigger than it was. I do not believe that the people of Calico Springs hold any animosity toward Black people as a race, but rather just wish for safety for their community. It's my understanding they've already settled into their own community, south of the river. Separate but equal."*

Quickly followed the formation of a Calico Springs Honor Committee to protect the town from what they described as "undue criticism." While the group was willing to admit it was townsfolk responsible for the lynchings, they also criticized Black residents, for whom they felt every chance had been offered to live peacefully.

Arrington was unwilling to comment on the involvement of any local vigilante groups in the expulsion. . . .

The Ozarks, long known for physical isolation and lack of government interference, has always been home to vigilante activity. It began with the end of the Civil War, in which local townsfolk with Confederate sympathies had been taught techniques of guerrilla warfare, using the natural landscape to launch attacks. The militias disappeared, but the tactics never did.

While the stated purpose of the vigilante groups, such as the famous Bald Knobbers, was to support sparse law enforcement and fight the encroachment of the federal government, many of the small-town militias had the effect of keeping recently emancipated African American settlers out of small towns. Where African American settlements did form, such as Calico Springs, they didn't last. Lynchings became common, and by 1916, white people in five cities in the Ozarks had driven Black people out. It was dubbed "White Man's Heaven."

In some places, the vigilantes gained political power, winning local elections and even forming their own parties in local politics. Once they gained control, they kept their enemies out of power using violent, sometimes fatal, means.

By the early 1900s, most of the groups had ceased public activity, and more traditional methods of law and order had replaced them. However, the Ozarks remains a hotbed of white supremacist organizations. Many of those organizations can trace their lineage to the vigilante groups of old. . . .

CHAPTER 41

BONES AND I were shoved into the back seat of the truck, Dad driving and Arrington riding shotgun.

"We're not your enemy, you know?" Bones said.

"Shut up, Bones," Dad said from the front seat.

"We're not even a problem. God put us on this Earth in units for our own survival, to tell us what's important, right? Well, I was born into this unit, this town. I was raised by it, and I'm protected by it every day. And I'd die for anyone in this town and nowhere else. I would die for Calico Springs."

Arrington snorted. "You lie like a goddamn politician."

"I'm serious," Bones said. "Ask anybody. Ask our mom."

I knew Bones was trying to play the part they wanted him to play, give them what they were looking for in hopes they would reconsider whatever they were going to do to us. But it was a moment too late, and it was clear Arrington was done with his—and Dad's—bullshit.

I sat in silence next to him, trying to trace the familiar roads by feeling. Hard turn left, going north. A stop, meaning we'd left the Basin. Slight left toward gravel river roads.

Behind my blindfold, I couldn't stop seeing the bloody mess of a body, splayed across the floor, except now I could see my own face, mixed up in the mush. My arms shook in fear. My breath fought back, shallow in my throat, and for a second, I thought I might suffocate before Arrington had a chance to do it for me.

"I'm not a politician," Bones said proudly. "I'm a soldier. I'd go to war for this town, to protect what's ours. Against the fucking Lawton coalition, trying to take what's rightfully ours. To protect the land we claimed in the Basin, to keep them from trying to use the merger to . . ."

Bones heard the springs in the front seat groan as Arrington turned around, and he tailed off into silence.

"What the fuck did you just say?" he asked.

"I said . . . I'd die to protect what's ours?"

Arrington sucked in air through his nose. "What land are you talking about?"

Bones was silent.

"Speak now," Arrington said. For the first time, he sounded vulnerable.

Bones had found a weakness. I raced to put it together. The land was stolen, and people must not have known—that's why the merger made him so vulnerable. If he lost control of the town, he might lose control of the land. His entire empire could be taken away.

Bones felt it, too, saw our advantage. He shifted in his seat, his energy changing completely. "Oh, you mean the land your grandfather stole?"

It didn't seem like a good idea to make him angry, but Bones was in survival mode. He was going to say anything, tell any lie, to try to change the circumstances. But if he knew what we knew, he was giving away our only advantage. Even worse, it would put everyone else in danger.

"We know all about that," Bones bragged. "Forcing everyone out of Calico Springs, stealing their land?"

Arrington laughed. "You don't know anything. Nothing about that was illegal—"

"I'm sure that's why you've decided to hide it for so long," Bones snarled. I tried to find his foot on the ground to step on it, but it was too late. He'd decided this was our hand, and he was going to play it.

"In fact, our friends are going to the press right now."

The springs squeaked again as Arrington turned around once more.

"By the time people are voting on the merger tomorrow, everyone's gonna know about your blood money. Who cares if it's legal. No one's going to vote against the merger knowing that's what you want, you lying piece of shit—"

"You don't have proof—"

"He's lying," I tried to say, but I was too late.

"We've got the land records."

That was it. Arrington had been hit.

He was quiet in the front seat for a long moment before I

heard him fumbling through something, clattering like aluminum. Out of nowhere, his fingers appeared on my head, threading through my hair, then squeezing, taking control of my head.

"Phone password," he said quietly.

"Don't give it to him, Willie—"

WHACK. He slammed my head against the window, the blood exploding from my forehead.

"Phone password, now."

"Stay strong, Willie!" Bones shouted.

WHACK! He swung it again, harder this time, and the blood started to rush.

"For fuck's sake, it's his birthday!" Dad shouted. "Zero one zero four."

The car went silent again, other than the tiny thud of Arrington's fingers against the screen. I heard his breathing get heavier, angrier.

"A phone call, huh?" he said after a moment. "How long?"

I swallowed. "Probably a butt dial."

The tapping got faster, more frantic. If he was looking through my texts, he'd know everything.

"Huh," he said. "Maybe you're not bluffing."

"I was." Bones changed course, yet again. "I was bluffing. We don't have them. We've just seen them. . . ."

"Well," Arrington said, "probably best to congratulate her in person though, right?"

I heard the *swoosh* of a message being sent.

I felt the truck make a hard right turn onto gravel, rocking violently as we drove forward. I could hear rushing water ahead, slapping against the rock. I didn't even need to know the directions; I knew it just from the feeling. We were back at the Calico Mill.

THE FIRST MESSAGE OF COVENANT

the original protectors of the Ozarks,
first sons of Calico Springs,
the devils of the Missouri woods.

Beware!
These are the first victims of the
wrath of outraged citizens.
More will follow.

CHAPTER 42

RORY AND TYLER yanked us from the truck and marched us forward past the mill, downhill toward the water. I tripped a few times as we stumbled down the rocky coastline and Rory let me fall, kicking me in the back to push me along. With every step, I tried to picture my surroundings, imagining a way out, but I knew we were outmatched. The sound of the river swarming started to get louder and louder as we approached the dock.

"What're you gonna do to them?" Dad asked as they marched us forward.

"Step," Rory's voice said behind me, and I extended my foot forward, bumping the edge of a railing. A hand guided my foot over, into the aluminum basin of a small speedboat.

"Where are you taking us?" Bones asked to no answer.

There, we waited.

It might have been a full hour we sat in the boat. I knew it was just Bones and me inside, I could hear Arrington moving around on the deck. I kept my ears attentive, waiting for some sign of life from my phone, but nothing came.

With every ounce of energy I had, that wasn't escaping my body in blood from my forehead, I prayed that they wouldn't come. Maybe she was already asleep—unlikely, Sarai usually didn't go to bed until the early morning. Maybe they'd see through his suggestion that we meet at the mill—although if I was being honest, it did seem like something I might do.

I could feel myself slowly getting weaker. I'd stopped trying to invent plans of escape and instead just continued praying that Arrington would keep his word, that he'd let us live.

After what felt like a lifetime, Bones decided to try Arrington's patience again.

"Looks like they're not coming," he said. "Which means everybody's gonna know you stole that land."

Out of nowhere, I felt cold water splash against my face, shooting up my nose, almost like drowning. Arrington laughed.

"It's not stolen," Arrington said, a kind of violent pride stamping every word. "It was claimed rightfully. My family built this town."

"I'm pretty sure Black people built this town," I said.

"You're wrong," Arrington said. "My great-grandfather showed up two hundred years ago and put his shovel in the dirt. There was never a single slave in Calico Springs. We never had problems like that here."

"Until now?" I asked.

I felt the wood under Arrington creak as he rocked. "Now is a question of survival. We built a town where our people could thrive, and every time it started to prosper, people tried to take it from us."

"That's not how prosperity works—"

"Don't tell me what prosperity is." Arrington spat off the dock. "We built the fucking mills. We're building the developments. And every time, every time you succeed in America, you get a whole new crowd of beggars and thieves. That's the real American story. That's what fucking ruined the cities. And I'll be damned if I'm gonna let it happen here."

He stood up from the dock and walked back over to where I assumed Tyler and Rory were standing. As soon as I heard he was gone, I used my shoulder to remove my blindfold. Bones had done the same.

As with every other time in my life, I looked to Bones.

He was staring at me intensely. He winked, then jerked his head behind us. In the next boat over, Dad was standing at the motor and staring back, steely-eyed. I followed his gaze back to Bones, and Bones nodded. It was as much of a plan as we needed.

"They're not coming," Arrington said, shaking his head as he came back down the dock. "So I'll give you this option. Call your friends now. Tell them to bring the records here, just to you, and we'll see how much goodwill that earns you."

Bones looked to me, desperate. He swallowed but didn't say a word.

"Eat shit," I told Arrington.

He sighed. "You're fighting a war you don't even understand." He looked back to Rory and Tyler. "Go back into town, check their house, check the girl's house, anywhere they might be hiding." He turned to Dad. "You and me, Markie, are gonna give your boys a history lesson. Follow close."

Our boat shook as he stepped in and revved the engine.

It was too loud to speak as we glided toward the middle of the river. I turned my body away from the engine and watched the second boat behind us, Dad steering it, following our lead. I couldn't read his face or catch his eyes.

"When we first settled this town," Arrington started, "we swore a vow to protect it. It was a covenant made by men a hundred fifty years ago. A covenant"—he leaned into the word—"made by my grandfather, to do whatever it takes to protect what is ours. And we've done what it takes. We've disposed of enemies—"

That was it, in plain English. The truth we already knew— this group was responsible for killing Winston Lewis and trying to kill Ronald Baker. It was the same group that had set fire to the mill and destroyed Old Town in its wake, running Calico Springs' original residents into Lawton. The Night Riders. The devils. The rot at the core.

"We offer that protection to our sons, but only if they, too, are willing to make that covenant."

I felt sick to my stomach. How many times had I brushed shoulders with this group, broken bread with its members, treated their word like God. I loved Calico Springs. I argued for its virtues, for how everyone felt like family, how everyone felt safe. I'd lived under their protection.

"Protection?" I spat back at him. "You're killing people—"

"Cleansing. We're fixing ourselves. It's what my grandfather did, clearing out that rancid part of town, and why we leave it there in the city, for everybody to see. A warning you should have heeded."

The boat banked hard to the right, circling back around so we could see the mill in the distance, towering over the river. He cut the engine, and the boat started to rock back and forth, the current tugging below us.

We were at Dead Man's Bend. Where eight men building the mill had died. Where boats went to sink.

"And now I'm in charge of that legacy. So congratulations. You're about to become a part of a long and storied history, about a town that persisted and succeeded, no matter how many times its walls were stormed. Who knows. Maybe you'll get a fucking plaque."

My heart sank. Arrington had lied. He wasn't just going to scare us—he was going to put us on a boat and sink it, making it look like it was another harmless accident.

Bones realized it, too. "I'll do anything," he said, his voice desperate. "I'll do whatever you say."

The wind picked up around us, and I watched as the other boat drifted toward us. Dad threw Arrington a rope. He tied off and stepped over the ledge, so he had a foot in both boats.

"What are we doing here, John?" Dad said. "You said no harm—"

"Easy," Arrington said. "All of you." He inched his way carefully toward the other boat. "Up here," he said to Dad. "Help me move 'em to this one."

Bones and I cowered as far from him as possible. Dad ignored him, sitting in his own boat, unwilling to move.

"Don't do this, Markie," Arrington said. "You're just gonna make it harder."

But Dad ignored him. Arrington sighed and stood himself, stepping back into the other boat. The whole apparatus began to spin as Arrington reached back toward Bones. I felt his pulse rising. This was it.

Arrington leaned over into the boat as far as he could, grabbing for Bones's collar when Bones screamed, "DAD! NOW!"

I hit the floor, ducking into the corner of the boat, waiting for us to go crashing over. Arrington let go of Bones immediately, shooting upward—

But nothing happened. The boats continued to drift harmlessly. Behind Arrington, I saw Dad standing with the rope in his hand, a blank expression on his face. He hadn't moved.

"Dad," Bones cried. He was making a face I'd never seen before. Terrified, apologetic, angry, scared, but more than anything, lost. He'd truly believed Dad was going to save us. But he wasn't. He'd chosen his side. He'd let go of his family.

"I'm sorry," Dad muttered under his breath. "I'm so sorry."

Arrington let out a howling laugh. With almost no effort, he reached down and grabbed Bones by the shirt, yanking him upward, then stepping into the other boat to pass him off. Dad held Bones by his shoulders, what looked like a support, but we knew was actually a cage.

His face had collapsed. He was out of tears. He didn't know what to do.

But I did. I held my face determined, caught his eyes with a quick look, and nodded. It wasn't much, but it was a plan.

Bones's face collapsed as he processed the weight of what I was suggesting. We'd come to this moment before. It existed in everything we did together. His moment to lead, my moment to follow.

But instead, barely visible, but with a certainty that stayed with me forever, he gave me a tiny nod in return.

I took a deep breath and stood up.

Arrington grabbed me by the shoulder. "One foot up—"

I did as I was asked, letting my foot clumsily move over the siding, inching like I couldn't see it, even though I knew exactly where it was.

"You can't see shit, can you? Well, maybe you'll get your eye back in heaven. Here, take this fucking . . ."

He reached his arm around me, giving slack to the rope behind him, now using me to steady himself between the boats. I brought my second foot quickly forward, catching on the lip of the other boat, spreading them ever so slightly, creating an inch of instability. Arrington gripped onto me tighter.

"HEY!"

The sound came from the shore. Screaming. Not just one voice but multiple.

"WE SEE YOU! WE CAN SEE YOU!"

Standing on the Lawton side of the shore, as close to the water as you can get, Sarai, Joe Kelly, Abe, and Rodney held each of their phones in the air, videos recording.

It had worked. The phone call had given them enough, enough

to know that we were in danger and that the text wasn't me.

Arrington froze for a single second, staring at them.

I planted my right foot on the ledge and kicked backward, my full weight driving into Arrington's rib cage. With no rope to hold them, the boats spread and continued to shake as Bones began to rock violently. Arrington grasped for the boat for balance, but all he could get ahold of was me, and I was moving with him.

Together, we tumbled backward into the water.

CHAPTER 43

ARRINGTON AND I locked ourselves in a death spiral.

My hands were still zip-tied, but I managed to loop them over one of his arms. As much as he tried to shake me off, he couldn't. I clung to him with the violence of nothing to lose.

Above us, the engine of the other boat rocketed to life, shooting a stream of water in our direction, pushing us farther downward, deeper into the water.

I felt the current pulling us downstream, just as it had so many others.

Arrington tried to push his way back to the surface, but I wouldn't let go. With his other arm, he grabbed for my neck, eventually getting ahold with one hand and trying to force the air out of my throat.

I lost my grip, and he shook away from me. Arrington glided back up to the surface.

But I wasn't done with him yet.

I latched his foot as it passed, shooting upward with him. He tried to shake me off, but instead, we both crested the surface, gasping for air. Far behind us in the distance, I saw the boat whip around and start toward us.

Bones had control and was driving the boat. Dad was standing behind him.

I pulled myself up onto Arrington's face and forced him back into the water.

Again, we tumbled downward. I forced my eye closed, summoning all the strength I could, and when I opened it again, the river around me was full of ghosts.

They danced and cheered around us. I knew them, and they knew me. Men who'd died in the mills, families who'd died crossing the river, families who'd been murdered by the violence that defined the area were watching me, alive and pushing me forward.

"Go on, Willie!" they shouted. "Fight like hell!" they urged me. Arrington had tortured them, too.

When my face crested the surface again, I could see the shore. Sarai and the rest were trying to keep up, but they couldn't run fast enough to keep up with our momentum downstream, so they were watching from far behind. I could feel Arrington trying to get away from me, so I gripped him even tighter. If I was going to die, he was going down with me.

CRACK!

A bullet ripped through the still air as it released, wavy and distant as it pierced the water next to me.

I fought to the surface. The shot had come from the boat that was following behind us.

It was Dad. He had Arrington's gun.

The current had pulled us a hundred yards downstream, away from shore, but the boat roared in our direction. Bones drove it like a madman, trying to catch us from behind, while Dad stood on the hull, his gun trained in front of me, lining up his shot—

Not at me, but at Arrington.

"WILLIE!" he screamed. "WILLIE, let go! Let go!"

With one last look to my dad, I let go of Arrington's leg and let myself drift.

The loud crack of a gunshot exploded from the shore. I held my breath.

That was the only way to kill a ghost, I realized. Somebody's gotta be willing to die with it.

EPILOGUE

WHEN MY EYE opened again, the world was light orange and soft knit, slow beeps and steady breathing.

The Calico Springs Hospital had only two rooms for patients. They gave me the nice one.

"Aw, shit." I heard the most familiar voice in my life. "Mom's gonna be pissed she wasn't here when you woke up."

I managed to lift my head, just barely, enough to see that the room was empty, other than a small army's worth of tech strapped to my chest and Bones in a rocking chair at my side.

I didn't bother to ask how long I died for this time.

"You want the good news or the bad news?" Bones asked.

I just grunted. It was all I could handle.

"Bad news is, you got shot," he said as though I hadn't figured it out yet. "Which made you take in water, and you started to sink pretty bad. Almost drowned. They said they're gonna have to see if you got any brain damage from that. But don't worry, I told them your brain's already pretty damaged, so they should be careful not to assume."

My voice was too strained to laugh. "How'd I get out?" I asked, raspy and harsh.

Bones didn't respond. I peeked my eyelid open wide enough to see that he was leaning over me, stupid-grinning.

"Well," he said. "I was always a better swimmer."

I let go of my first pure breath. I could still breathe. It was a good sign.

"The bullet pierced your stomach," he explained. "Which means it's gonna suck to eat for a little while, and your liver's probably fucked for a few years, but . . . good news is . . . it coulda been worse."

"That's what they always say," I whispered.

"I know." Bones took me by the shoulder and squeezed. "But don't worry. This is nothing compared to last time."

Bones moved our hands to my chest, and our pulses fell into rhythm. He cleared his throat.

"If it makes you feel better," he said, "Dad wasn't trying to hit you. He only fired when he thought he had a clean shot at Arrington. . . ."

I heard the beep of an extra-loud heartbeat. "Where's Arrington?" I asked.

Bones smirked, glancing to the door to make sure no one could hear him. "Turns out . . . Dad's a pretty good shot . . ." He looked down at my stomach. "Well, sometimes."

My chest melted. God had been watching. Arrington was gone. Another thought struck me, and I tried to sit up, but Bones held me in place.

"What about Dad?"

I heard Bones grit his teeth, stutter in his answer. "They're holding him at County, but . . . not for long." He squeezed my hand even harder. I saw him fight whatever was welling up in his chest. "Looks like we're gonna have to take care of each other from here on out."

Bones walked me through what had happened in the forty-eight hours since he'd pulled me out of the river.

Instead of going back to the mill, Bones took the boat straight to the Lawton side, where Joe's truck was ready to take me to the hospital. He said Sarai and Rodney had been checking in every hour since, standing outside the room as the doctors operated on my stomach, leaving only when the sun came up on a different mission.

They had the land records. They had a recording of my call from inside the barn. They had a video of Arrington trying to dump us in the river. They took to the streets, and by the time people were lining up outside the community center to vote, every resident of Calico Springs and Lawton knew Winston Lewis had been murdered to protect John Arrington's empire. If there was one thing people in Missouri hated, it was being manipulated. The merger passed, and the sign outside town had already been changed.

Of course, in Calico Springs, it couldn't be that simple. There was no physical evidence for anyone else, only the hearsay of children, so Rory, Tyler, and the rest of Covenant hadn't even received a visit from police, no matter how many times Rodney and Sarai tried to hammer them with the evidence from the Game. Bill Kelly went to work in the morning. Whatever proof existed of Covenant, it seemed like it had once again been drowned in the river, a secret that would live forever with the men who knew.

Except, of course, for the one man who couldn't live with it. Dad brought himself into the station and confessed to the whole thing. Turns out he'd kept videos, in case things ever went south with Arrington. There were no charges yet, other than Dad himself, but rumor had it the police were building a case.

Later that day, everybody would come by. Mom cried for almost a full hour at my bedside, telling me all the things she said she wished she could but was afraid we loved our dad too much to hear. Sarai told me her family had been doing nothing but praying for me for two days, and her mom couldn't wait to meet me when we got the chance.

But while it was just me and Bones, he had one more truth to get off his chest—and one more mystery.

"I should have believed you," he said. "Everything I told you was crazy, every stupid discovery, that fucking game . . . I keep thinking about how all this shit, that entire night . . . none of it woulda happened if I'd just listened to you." He shook his head. "You were right about the whole goddamn thing, except . . ."

His voice caught in his throat.

"Except what?"

"Doesn't matter," he mumbled, looking at his hands, then the door, like he suddenly wanted Mom to come back.

"Tell me."

Bones rocked slowly in the chair, looking out the window. "Except nobody dug any graves," he said. "They never dug anything. Not Dad, not Rory and Tyler . . . nobody ever said anything about graves."

I felt a pang in my chest, in the places I could still feel. It seemed impossible that I'd started all of this on a lie of my imagination, but I guess it didn't matter now.

"But"—Bones sat up in the chair—"here's the bitch of it all. You know when Arrington was talking about how his grandfather had done this before, cleansed the town or whatever?"

"Yeah."

"We already knew about that," he said. "It was the fire in the mill. A mob of people set fire to the jail while they had three Black guys locked up in there. It wasn't everybody in the town rushing to save them . . . it was everybody in the town burning them."

I shifted over in the bed.

"It was a warning, like Arrington said. So the guys in Covenant . . . they made a whole big show outta burying their bodies . . . in the Basin."

I felt my breath rise and fall a few times. "So you mean . . ."

"Yep." Bones nodded. "It was a hundred years ago. But it was three graves."

The investigation was reopened four times. Dad testified in four different criminal trials. Tyler Arrington was serving life at a federal facility somewhere in Kansas. Our dad was in the early years of a twenty-five-year sentence for kidnapping and first-degree murder.

Rodney went to Mizzou, just as planned, and started making her computer shit. She said once she got to school, Connor was nothing more than competition, and soon he wasn't even that.

Joe Kelly stayed in Calico Springs but moved out of his parents' house and stopped speaking to them. His dad was removed in disgrace and replaced with the kind of poetic justice the universe rarely makes good on—Ronald Baker was elected mayor of the Calico Springs–Lawton Municipal Area.

Sarai stayed in Lawton with her family, through the circus of press and lawsuits against the town and countersuits, always next to her mom in the photos.

And me, I made my own way. I made some friends my own age, got my license, and buried the 42 in our backyard. It wasn't until my senior year that I took a creative writing class, and turns out, I had a knack. Only problem was, every story I wrote went nowhere. I'd write about the same two characters—Bones and Willie, Willie and Bones—on a series of aimless misadventures, learning nothing but staying forever etched in marble, where the reality of the world couldn't hurt them. One day after class, Mrs. Felton pulled me aside and told me that these stories were a lesson to myself, and I had two options—learn it or bury it forever and live with the consequences.

Bones still lives in Calico Springs with me and mom. He's got plans to build an empire, but hasn't found it yet, or anything steady, really. He took over caring for Libby when Dad went to prison, and now he's got four dogs that live in our backyard. He still visits Dad once a week.

That's where all this left us, impossibly far from yet dangerously close to exactly where we started. As it turns out, the past never really goes anywhere. Best we can do is stand up and look it in its face, and hope that when the generations turn, we do just a little bit better.

AUTHOR'S NOTE

In 1999, historian James Loewen began research on a string of small towns in southern Illinois that had, whether by legal statute or public intimidation, kept their towns white by expelling and preventing the settlement of African Americans. Calling them "Sundown Towns" (as in, *don't let the sun go down on you in Calico Springs*), he set out to search for them across America, expecting there would be one or two dozen.

He found nearly a thousand.

The violent, racist history of many small towns in America is one that has been left out of the record by its powerful perpetrators, swept under the rug by the guilty generations while the effects are passed on to today. While spending several months in southern Missouri writing this book, I would ask current white residents of Sundown Towns about their histories. It was rare to find someone who'd heard of them; even more rare to find anyone who wanted to talk about it.

But the story of Calico Springs and Lawton is not sensationalized, and not without precedent.

That's why I chose to include actual documents in Part 7—either directly sourced from newspapers of the time, or heavily inspired by firsthand accounts of actual events. "The Abandoning of 'Old Town'" is a 1903 article from the *St. Louis Post-Dispatch*, describing the expulsion of African Americans from West Plains, Missouri. The only language altered was the names of the towns and the removal of traumatic rac-ist language. "Devils of the Hills" draws on academic articles describing the 1901 lynchings of French Godley, William Godley, and Peter Hampton, and the subsequent white mob, in Pierce City, Missouri, and contains several direct quotes from city officials in the aftermath.

The stories of West Plains and Pierce City, Doniphan and Monett are not aberrations; they represent a shameful era of American small-town life, and unless reckoned with, we doom ourselves to repeat them.

For those interested in learning more, I'll recommend a few books I found inspiring on the subject:

•   *White Man's Heaven* by Kimberly Harper: a complete history of the Ozarks and the lengths many towns went to to keep the region white

•   *Blood at the Root* by Patrick Phillips: a poetic reckoning from a resident of an all-white county with the bloody history of his home

•   *Between the World and Me* by Ta-Nehisi Coates, which should be required reading

ACKNOWLEDGMENTS

THANK YOU FOR reading.

Dark Parts of the Universe was a lengthy, heavy, sometimes-disorienting climb, and it wouldn't have been possible without the relentless energy that surrounds me always.

My wife, Kimberly Dawn; our son, Elijah Sol; and his brother/grandfather, Addison. The whole world spins around you.

My family, near and far, but especially the immediate—Mom, Dad, Leah, Caleb, Seth, Joe. You're the source of every opinion I have.

My incredible literary team, Ben and HarperCollins; Joanna and New Leaf. You make me wanna write.

My writing partner, Nick Brooks. You're a fucking genius.

The folks I met along the way, too many to name, but specifically Nanda Nunnery, Gary Kremer, and Nancy Allen; the teachers, librarians, activists, and bartenders of southern Missouri.

And finally, you, of course, for making it this far. See you on the next one.